M. A. LOBBAN

Suvla John

Suvla John

By

Warwick Deeping

Author of "Sorrell and Son"

CASSELL AND COMPANY, LTD
London, Toronto, Melbourne and Sydney

First published   *October* 1924
Popular Edition   *April*   1926
Second Impression *August* 1927

Printed in Great Britain

To

MY FRIEND MARY VINCENT

SUVLA JOHN

HE came up the hill, walking with a slight swing of the shoulders, loins hollowed, head in the air. The brim of his old green felt hat was turned down to keep the June sunlight out of his eyes. He wore a short black beard cut to a point, a beard such as some Spanish captain might have worn in those fierce days when Spanish swords and halberds made Antwerp a place of weeping and of blood. An ash stick, sloped over his left shoulder, carried a canvas bag.

He was tall and lean and tanned, and though his clothes were the clothes of a tramp, he carried them like a soldier. They did not matter. It was his air of ironical audacity that mattered, his scorn of the world's scorn. Lymington, with its broad stretch of sunlit street between the red and white of its Georgian houses, lay under his shabby marching boots like a tame town at the feet of a conqueror. He smiled as he swung through it, and his mouth was both laughing and cruel.

The Hampshire town was busy with a pleasant and peaceful self-sufficiency. Motor-cars waited outside the shops, or cruised to and fro. White clouds floated overhead in the blue sky above the houses. This most English town went about its affairs with an air of serenity. People came to it out of the Forest and chattered in its shops, and went away with a bundle of garden brooms or a roll of wire netting or a box of groceries in the back seat of a Ford car or in the tail of a cart. There was red meat in the butchers' shops. All the English country smells were there for the smelling, drifting through the doorways of the seed-merchant, the baker, the fishmonger, and hang-

Suvla John

ing in the musty throats of the ale-houses. Here, too, were the usual loafers, heavy, stupid men, vacuously staring, inarticulate, more lavish with their spittle than with their words.

The tramp went through one such group as though they were cattle. The idlers stared at him as he approached, and stared after him when he had passed them. An indifferent and swinging shoulder had brushed against one of them, and had persuaded him to move a little nearer to the gutter. Dull cattle though they were, they had felt his scorn of them, and they resented it. Glances of slow malevolence passed between three of them who remembered the war. A jerk of the head, a splodge of saliva striking the pavement, a laugh that was like a snarl. "Might be a blinkin' sergeant-major."

The tramp paused and turned suddenly to the right. He stood there with his head up, black beard cocked, his eyes looking through a dark entry. He remembered that entry; it led him back to the memory of an idle half-hour on some such day as this. His brown eyes, ironical and defiant, seemed to gather a sudden fierceness; his mouth looked twisted, his nostrils shadowed with scorn. He passed through the entry towards a panel of blue sky with the mass of the church tower cutting it.

He stood and gazed.

It was very quiet here, quiet with the broad silence of an England that was passing. A church, gravestones, green grass with the sunlight sheeted upon it, old houses, a sense of slumber. The man's eyes took it all in as though it were part of a picture that he had not seen for many years. His fierce lips softened. Something had surprised him, touched a part of him that had lain forgotten under the hard tan of his vagabondage.

"Yes, it's English," he thought. "Queer! You get it nowhere else."

He stood back against a wall, one leg crossed over the other, his hat pressed against the brickwork. The brown of his strong throat showed above his collarless shirt. His glance wandered, and then came to rest on the tower of the church. It was as though someone had asked him a question, and he had been startled by it, and was casting about for an answer.

Presently he smiled.

"That's it! Atmosphere. The old sentimental touch; grey skies and greenness, and a mystery that is just—

Suvla John

fog. Strange—that it should get me like this! The sentimental Englishman! That's England. The Russian's a beast in his beastly country Down south they chatter and use knives. Climate. This green and sentimental England!"

He straightened, and with a last quick stare at the churchyard, turned back into Lymington High Street with the air of having cut the throat of an illusion. His figure went westwards with its swinging and audacious indifference.

Near the corner where the road to Brockenhurst turns northward a constable paused and scrutinized the figure on the opposite pavement. The blue English eyes were wise yet puzzled, for the constable had worn three stars in the war, and he knew something of the world and of men. A tramp, yes, wearing a soiled green tweed suit long ago discarded from some gentleman's wardrobe; his boots patched, his blue and white check shirt innocent of any collar. His pockets bulged. There was a rent in the coat that had been boggled up with black thread. Yet, they were gentleman's clothes, and the fellow carried them as though they belonged to him. The constable watched him disappear, and drew his own shrewd conclusions. There went a "tough," a fine blackguard, a fellow who had been a soldier and who had known the feel of a Sam Browne belt. Fierce, too, with that indifferent and smiling fierceness that makes a man feared. Not the sort of fellow to be tackled carelessly in a country lane on a dark night.

"Anyway he's struck it proud. Chap with a history."

The constable ran a broad finger down a broad nose.

"Not booze—either. Hard as nails. Something queer there! I don't know—— Oh—well—let him go!"

2

The tramp entered a shop, and at the sight of him a little fussy woman in spectacles slid away along the counter and opened a glass-panelled door.

"John!"

But she kept her two glimmering lenses on the man who had unslung his canvas bag, and had deposited it

3

on the floor. He looked amused, for this little Hampshire hen with her feathers all fluffed up had sensed the wildness of him, though it was not the sort of wildness that she need have feared.

A big man whose yellow moustache, chin and paunch made three separate convex curves, came in looking hot and truculent. He was in his shirt sleeves, and wearing a white apron over his lowermost bulge, a fat man, flabbily secure behind his irreproachable counter. The tramp smiled at him. How swiftly would that white apron have been bloodied by some fierce devil of a tribesman digging upwards with a long knife.

"Half a Dutch cheese."

His voice was casual and rather quiet, while the shopman, with two red hands spread upon the counter, eyed him mistrustfully.

"A quarter of tea, a pound of bacon; matches six boxes."

A brown hand came out of a pocket and showed silver, and the heavy eyes behind the counter took in the colour of it. He stood to serve.

"What price? Half a crown or three shillings? Half a crown. And the bacon, streaky? Not too much fat?"

"Just as it comes."

"Thank you. Anything else, sir?"

"A couple of tins of milk."

"Ideal? Makes you think of the war."

"It does."

The tramp was abrupt and laconic. He handed over the money, and stowed the things away in his canvas bag, swarthily indifferent yet slightly smiling. The man behind the counter watched him with curiosity. He had become bland and obliging, the utilitarian huckster.

"Very hot for the time of year."

"I have known hotter places. Good day to you."

He ran the ash stick through the handles of the canvas bag, and, swinging it over his shoulder, walked out of the shop, leaving the double-chinned man in an attitude of rebuffed loquacity. The long shadow of him disappeared, and the grocer drew a breath, wiped his mouth with the back of his hand, and glanced casually at the contents of the till.

"Well—he wouldn't have got much. Lucky you were in the shop."

His wife's spectacles glimmered.

Suvla John

"That's what I thought. Nasty looking fellow."
"One of the down and outs. One ain't surprised at anything—after the war."

3

It was evening in the Forest, and though the cynic behind the counter had acclaimed the death of all wonder, the man with the canvas bag had found that the Forest could surprise him.

Wonder at it had come upon him suddenly. He had left the high road where there was too much dust and machinery, and, wandering across a sweep of heather, he had come through a thicket of old hollies and thorns to the sudden stillness of a beech wood. He had paused with the abruptness of a creature surprised, a wild creature sniffing the air, sensing danger, mystery, the shadows of things unseen. He stood quite still, eyes at gaze, black beard sharply cocked, the muscles showing in his throat. Somewhere a blackbird was singing; a wood-pigeon took to flight with a clapping of the wings.

The man remained motionless. It was as though his consciousness, narrowed to the compass of the road, had suddenly expanded, to spread as a landscape spreads under the abrupt sunlight of an April day. He had been caught unawares. The surface of his indifference had been ripped. He was conscious of hidden, tender, inexorable deeps.

"This England!"

He smiled. He looked into the wood, at the grey smoothness of the beech trunks, at all that motionless yet flowing greenness, at the burrs and streaks of sunlight, the glooms and yellow splashes, the bronze carpet of last year's leaves. His thoughts went both back and forward. "Three weeks ago it was all blue." For he could see the seed-vessels of the bluebells. Five months hence it would be a splendour of bronze and of gold.

Dropping his bag, he pulled out a pipe, filled it, struck a match and held to the bowl. His face had softened, but his alert eyes continued to thrust their glances deep into the heart of the woodland. The utter silence of it, its supreme and green tranquillity challenged him. He was comparing it with other green silences that he had known, black Russian forests, palm groves on the edge

Suvla John

of some mud-coloured African town, the high and shade-less flicker of eucalyptus woods. Yet this English beech wood seemed to have some quality that these others lacked, depth of atmosphere, a blurred and beautiful strangeness.

"England again!" he thought, "and all that wet-green sadness that makes men drink beer and feel senti-mental."

An ironical and scoffing expression appeared on his hard, tanned face. He rallied himself, and with a characteristic swing of the shoulders seemed to shake off some foolish illusion. All this was a mere trick of the senses, poetic tosh. He had seen too much, and experienced too many flagrant adventures, to be fooled by a collection of trees.

He bit hard on his pipe stem, and, picking up his bag, went forward with that swing of the shoulders that was the counterpart of a mental swagger. The fierce and smiling animal in him protested. He had not come to England after all these years to be senti-mental, to think dreamy nonsense about eglantine, moon-light, and meadows. He knew himself to be hard, hard with the ironical indifference of a man who had grown wild with much wandering, and whose life had been a series of violent episodes, a turmoil of adventure. He had come to think of himself as a gallant blackguard, a good comrade and a darned bad enemy, a man who could use a knife with an Italian, play at wrestling tricks with a Jap, and take nothing on credit from an American bully. Life had tamed him, ground him with sand, splashed him with blood, slit the throats of his illusions. He took things as they came, with a cock of the head, a laugh, a stare of his black-brown eyes, a few laconic words, a swift blow.

Yet, as he trailed his long legs through the beech wood some tag of a memory again caught him unawares. The past, like a wood spirit, hiding in these green glooms, waited with elvish finger on elvish lip, and then sent forth a whispering. The words came into the man's head like a twinge of remembered music :

"As when upon a tranced summer night,
    Those green robed senators of mighty woods,
    Tall oaks, branch charmed by the earnest stars,
    Dream, and so dream all night without a stir."

6

Suvla John

A fragment of those days so long before the war when he had carried a Keats in his pocket or sat at night at an Oxford window talking windy, moonlit stuff with other men whose blood was delicate and young! Keats! When his own life for the last six years had been nethermost Kipling! He gave a flick of the head, and, coming out into the sunlight where the landscape fell away into blue distances, and a few old yews made a darkness above the green of the young fern, he threw his bag on the ground and saw the white scuts of two rabbits vanish into the bracken. The place pleased him. It offered him stretches of sweet, short turf, dead wood for a fire, and the shelter of the yew boughs, and solitude. He decided to camp here for the night.

Sitting close to one of the yews, with his bag between his legs, he unpacked his kit, spreading it on the grass beside him. It included a small kettle and a frying-pan with collapsible handles, two enamelled plates, an enamelled mug, a knife and fork, two spoons, a water-bottle, a ground sheet, a small bag that could be stuffed with grass to form a pillow. His washing and shaving kit he kept rolled up in a piece of American cloth tied with a bootlace. A spare shirt, a couple of soft collars together with other trifles remained at the bottom of the bag.

His gear laid out, he rose and collected dead wood for a fire. A forked stake, but with his jack-knife, thrust into the ground, served to hold the kettle. Lying on his belly, he put a match to a couple of screws of paper, and laying the dead wood on it stick by stick, blew softly till the glare of the growing fire gave to his eyes a flickering tawniness. He had thrown aside his hat, and as he lay there with his chin on his crossed wrists his clean-cut bronze-black head had an almost metallic lustre.

The fire attended to, and the kettle slung above it, he sat up and took off his boots, for to a man who has tramped fifteen miles the feel of the cool, sweet turf is pleasant. Lounging, propped upon elbow, he became aware of the stretch of country before him, a shallow valley full of the evening sunlight, with hills rising beyond it to the open splendour of the sky. The valley was very green. He caught the glimmer of water, and heard the tinkling of cow-bells. Three or four forest ponies were grazing on the farther slope, where innumerable rabbits were feeding and playing together. On the

7

Suvla John

brow of the hill a wood of Scotch firs broke with their blackness the sheeted gold of the horizon.

With eyes half closed, he lay absorbing the scene, turning now and again to put more wood on the fire. That this English landscape had a most strange effect upon him was as obvious as were the flames that licked the body of the kettle.

It appeared, too, that for some reason he resented the soft and Arcadian glamour of it, for he sat up and gave his whole attention to the kettle and the fire, and when he had brewed his tea, he cut a thick slice of bread and a wedge of cheese, and, with his plate between his knees, ate slowly and reflectively, his eyes fixed upon the food. Only once or twice did he glance at the valley below him, and his expression was one of vague defiance.

Later, with his pipe between his teeth, he unfastened his waistcoat, and, turning up the left flap of it, disclosed a canvas pocket sewn into the lining and closed by a couple of metal buttons. He opened this pocket and drew out a little leather bag tied with whipcord. It was as though this leather bag had some esoteric meaning for him, and that he held in his hand a little sack of memories and motives.

He opened it, and after giving a quick stare over either shoulder, he emptied the contents on to a clean plate. A bullet, a smaller bag made of washleather, the tarnished case of a clinical thermometer. He picked up the bullet and smiled over it. Next he withdrew the cap of the case and shook out into his palm what appeared to be a cutting from a newspaper. This he read with an air of fierce amusement and of slight self-mocking.

"Blaber—Langdale. On the 15th inst. at the church of St. Joseph—Feldhurst, Robert Blaber, to Elsie Langdale, daughter of the late James Langdale, of Beech Hill —Telford."

He returned the slip of paper to its tube, and opening the washleather bag, emptied the contents into his palm. The things glittered there, lying in a little heap in the brown cup of his hand, a fine rose-diamond, half a dozen brilliants, two superb rubies, an emerald the size of a hazel-nut, three or four sapphires, two jasper cameos, a red jargon, and a carbuncle cut *en cabochon*. He sat and stared at the stones, his eyes smiling at them under his fierce eyebrows. A woman had given him the most precious of them, thrusting a little green silk bag into his

8

Suvla John

hand while her blood had made yellowish-red stains upon the snow. She had called him "Ivan," and he had kissed her mouth. He had kissed her again when she lay dead, before lying down to wait for those two men who had fired at them from the pine woods. He had killed both those men. He remembered digging his heel into the mouth of the man who fired the shot that killed the woman.

He put the stones away, and looked down into the soft valley where the cow-bells tinkled and the ponies cropped the grass.

It was very peaceful.

II

1

THE sandy lane trailed upwards and lost itself in a little wood of oaks and beeches, much like a piece of white ribbon disappearing into the mouth of a green box. In the bottom of the valley another lane crossed it where a smithy, a few red cottages, and an inn lay among fruit trees and hedges. Common land stretched right and left, shaggy with gorse, and stippled with the backs of grazing cattle.

The tramp had stopped at the inn, and after buying a bottle of beer, and persuading the woman to sell him two lettuces and half a loaf of bread, he had taken the track towards the wood. The westering sun shone full in his eyes. He came out of the glare into the shade of the trees, and, pausing to light a pipe, became aware of something yellow shining beyond the outlines of a few scattered hollies.

Twenty yards farther on he found himself at the mouth of a glade, and here the yellowness explained itself. Two caravans stood there side by side, one painted a primrose yellow, the other a sage green. Their doors were towards the road. A girl was sitting on the steps of the green caravan.

She wore a rose-coloured jumper and a black skirt, and a swathe of white stuff lay across her knees. That she was a gipsy was plain enough from her hair and the rich, sun-tanned bloom of her face, but the breed of her was of a cast not often seen upon the roads. She was tall and finely built, with her black hair cut in a fringe above her steady, velvet eyes. They, too, were of an extreme blackness. Her nose was short, and rather blunt at the tip. Her large, well-cut, and expressive mouth suggested a certain abruptness and a hot temper.

The tramp stood still in the middle of the road. The young woman was looking at him and he at her, and her black eyes were as fearless as his. Her hands ceased

Suvla John

from their sewing while she considered him calmly and without boldness, much as one proud animal might look at another.

The tramp smiled. Beyond the caravans he could see an old woman lighting a fire under an iron tripod. There were no men about, and the horses had been turned loose on the common. His roving eyes took in everything, even the name painted in small white letters on the undercarriage of the green van.

His glance came back to the girl.

"The luck of the road," he said.

She regarded him steadily. He had taken off his hat, and she was aware of the crispness of his black hair and of the way his head was set on the strong, defiant throat. He was as dark as she was. He had the seal of the sun and the wind upon him.

"Going far?"

She was thinking that he should have had gold rings in his ears, and a red handkerchief knotted about his forearm.

"As far as a fire and a shake-down in the fern."

"It's a good life."

"In summer."

"Any time. Even when it drizzles."

"Oh, it's all right for you," he said, "with one of those houses on wheels.

She lowered her eyes, put in two or three stitches, and then resumed her study of him. He interested her. She had no use for tame men, and she sensed his wildness.

"A job is not in your line?"

"It might be. Fighting's my job."

She nodded, but her eyes remained serious and obscure.

"What name?"

"Suvla John."

"That's queer."

"Queer, but good. Useful in any country. Turn it the other way round and you can make it Jack Suvla. Not so pleasant—of course—as yours."

"Mine!"

"Richenda Lee."

"Where did you get it?"

"Off your wagon."

"You're quick."

"Oh, passably."

She put in a few more stitches, while he told himself that she had a very comely head and a way of speaking

Suvla John

that surprised him, as though she had been to school, and to a good school. She raised her eyes.

"Care to use our fire? You can. The men will be back presently."

"Thanks. If I might put a piece of meat in your pot?"

"Sure. If you want to wash—there is a bucket under the other van."

John Suvla took her at her word, and being a clean beast, with the prejudices of the English gentleman still strong in him, he threw his canvas bag under the yellow caravan and unhitched the bucket from its hook. He noticed that the yellow van also bore the name of Richenda Lee. The old woman by the fire, addressed by him as "Granny," gave him a look that was half hostile and half curious, and told him plainly that if he wanted water in that bucket he must fetch it for himself. There was a stream at the bottom of the wood, and Suvla went down to the stream.

The young woman continued her sewing. The man had returned, and she could hear him splashing somewhere in the undergrowth, and could picture that black head of his snowed over with soap, and his brown hands hard at work in it. A queer cove this! She considered his queerness, and its costume of audacious indifference. And Suvla, in the midst of his soapsuds, was echoing her curiosity, and calling her "this young Queen of Sheba," for she had sat enthroned on those steps with the dignity of a young woman who had never looked up the word "dignity" in a dictionary.

"Lee——!"

He believed that he had some memories of an old chap named Lee, the proprietor of a travelling show, who had led a nomad life, trailing his swings and his round-about and his shooting-gallery from Exeter to Canter-bury. Once or twice some such caravan had spread itself in a field at Feldhurst. He could remember at the age of ten standing at the shooting-gallery, while a buxom, fat, merry woman with black eyes had handed him the loaded guns and applauded him as he had smashed bottle after bottle. "You have got an eye in your head, young gentleman. I don't mind if you break the lot." Yes, he remembered it all very vividly, and how he had pushed Bob Blaber off the roundabout because they had both desired to ride the same particular white horse.

Suvla John

Old Israel Lee had been dead six years, and his wife —Rebecca—had died two years before him.

They had been aristocrats of the road, "originals," with patriarchal propensities, shrewd, clean-living, careful. They had come and gone about the country-side, and if people had troubled to think of them at all they had thought of them as anonymous vagrants, mere shadows upon the highway. The notion of solidity or permanence had not attached to them, and yet Mr. Israel Lee had been a solid man who could have bought up many of the more solid people who had deigned on occasions to take a playful pot shot at his coco-nuts.

At the age of sixty—when the girl Richenda was twelve years old—the Lees had risen to the dignity of a "deed box." It had stood on a shelf in the office of a firm of Winchester solicitors, with "Israel and Rebecca Lee" painted in white letters upon its blackness. It stood there still, but with the name Richenda Lee upon it. And old Butter, of "Butter, Prance and Medlicott," had behaved to the Lees with great decorousness. Property! Property matters. It had mattered in old Lee's case to the extent of a row of cottages in Winchester, a public-house at Wimborne, two small farms, and some five thousand pounds invested in British funds. The vans, wagons, horses, roundabout and steam tractor had been mere accessories, to be considered as cash in hand.

In their own world the Lees had been people of ideas. They had looked upon Richenda at the age of twelve, a long-legged, narrow-hipped, willowy thing, with a shock of hair coerced into two black plaits, a blunt nose and a pair of fiercely mischievous eyes. A fine girl, rather boyish, and too fond of using her fists. The Lees had seen the potential woman in her, a girl who might inherit the best part of twenty thousand pounds.

It had come to them that Richenda should go to school, to one of the best schools, a gentlewomen's school. Old Butter, co-opted upon the family committee, had looked over the tops of his pince-nez, and given the adventure his blessing. It was good and right that Israel Lee's heiress should be able to hold her own with any woman, though her drawing-room moved in a caravan.

Suvla John

So Richenda had gone to school.

Her first rebelliousness had lasted exactly a month. It had culminated in a hearty cuffing of the school arch-snob's ears, and a night flight to the Lee caravans that had been parked at Dorchester. But Richenda was always persuadable where she loved, though her lovers were few, and after one night in her people's caravan she had gone back to Winchester in a spirit of understanding. Love had wished her there, and she had understood.

After that there had been no more trouble. Fierce she might be, and passionate, but there had been a generous bigness in her that had made her idolized by some, if feared by others. At that time the game-spirit had begun to agitate young petticoats, and Richenda, with her boy's figure and her long legs, had led the school. She was very strong and she had the natural grace of a perfect body. Her hockey-stick had sometimes been a weapon of splendid terror. Indoors, she had learnt French and developed a gift for painting in water-colours. Her favourite books had been books of travel and adventure, and she had made Burton a hero because of his methodical wildness, and his unlikeness to other men. She had read most of Shakespeare's plays, and her favourite poet had been Byron.

At the age of seventeen she had come back to the caravan life, and to a van of her own rigged out with special lovingness. Her father and mother had had moments of trepidation. What would she make of the life and of them? Had the wander spirit been schooled out of her? They had heard her spoken of half-derisively as "the lady." But within a week the girl had made them leave their doubts of her lying behind them like the ashes of old camp-fires. She was of their blood; she asked for nothing better than the life of the open road.

Strangest of all, she brought from the school the spirit of authority. She had learnt to lead, and she had the temper of a leader, and during the last two years of his life old Lee had watched her taking charge of the cara-vans. The authority had passed gently from his hands to hers, and in the passing of it the pride of the old man had exulted. She was a fine, strong girl, with a head on her shoulders, and a curious and steady wisdom in her eyes. She had kept the men in order. She could be fiercer than any one of them, but with a quiet, compelling fierceness.

14

Suvla John

Later, old Lee had died, and Richenda had buried him in a Hampshire churchyard beside her mother. Cottages, farms, securities, vans, horses, engine, roundabout had become hers. For five years she had been the sole mistress of this little travelling world, ruling it like an autocrat, and running it as successfully as her parents had run it before her. She could speak two languages, the language of Shakespeare and the lingo that it was necessary to use to rough men.

She had used the rougher tongue on Suvla, but when he came round from behind the van and sat down on the grass at the foot of her flight of steps she felt that he would understand a language that was more delicate. He had put on a soft linen collar; his upper lip and cheeks were clean, and one glance at his hands set her wondering what his life had been. But for the moment she spoke as she would have spoken to her men.

"Did you wash out the bucket?"

"I did."

"You're used to sleeping rough."

"My back's hard."

"A soldier's back—I guess."

He showed his white teeth.

"You bet. I have been at the cut-throat game long enough."

"You look it."

"Thanks! The real old blackguard!"

He pulled a piece of grass and chewed it, his back half turned to her, while she sat and considered him, her hands idle in her lap. A slight frown showed on her straight forehead. It gave place to an elvish gleam of the dark eyes.

"I don't know whether you care for Leader's tree pictures? I don't. They give you something—and yet just miss the real world atmosphere. Now—that group of firs over there——"

She saw his chin swing round. He gave her a look that was like the grip of a hand.

"Ha—you think you have got me—all pinned out and labelled!"

Her eyes steadied to his.

"Does it matter? I can talk either lingo."

"Can you!" he said. "Can you! I have forgotten the nice drawing-room drawl."

She was serious as night.

Suvla John

"I think not. But as you please. As I said before, does it matter?"

"Not a damn," he said rudely, turning on his side so that he saw nothing but her feet.

She went on sewing, and for a short while there was silence between them, a silence in which they felt and defied each other and yet were drawn more near by the very feeling of defiance. Presently she saw that he was smiling. He raised his head.

"I apologize. But you caught me. How was I to know?"

"There was no need."

"You stood there in the dark and pulled me to pieces. You said to yourself: 'Here is a disreputable devil, one of the failures——'"

"I thought nothing of the kind. What is failure?"

"Most 'white' men fail because they are white; the yellow men succeed because of their yellowness."

"That sounds bitter—if true. And you are not bitter."

"How do you know?"

"I feel it. Failure makes a man bitter. You have done what you have wanted to do."

"Therefore I am not bitter?"

"No, but scornful."

"Oh, yes, scornful. The thing is to scorn other people's scorn."

He turned, and with his long arms about his knees, looked up at her railingly.

"There you are. You have me, while you sit up there talking like a girl graduate at a dinner party. It takes a good deal to surprise a blackguard."

"Does it? My people sent me to school."

"What was the idea?"

"It did me no harm. I can run my show all the better for it."

"So you run the show?"

"We open at Romsey next week. The vans and the engine are there. One does not always want to be with one's show. I have got the men well in hand."

His ironical eyes admired her.

"I think you would. But—I'm wondering——"

He unclasped his hands, and gathering himself—stood up. She waited, her eyes on her work, aware of the conflicting prides and wildnesses of him.

"It's a question of etiquette—you know. I seem to

16

have got out of my depth. Obviously—I have used your bucket, but beyond that——"

"I see. But I think there is no need for that sort of self-consciousness. I dine at half-past seven, Mr. Suvla. You need not trouble to dress."

Now that he was on his feet his eyes were on the same level with hers as she sat on the steps. He looked hard into hers, and then he laughed.

"Thanks; I accept."

3

An old man, a youth, and a girl came up through the wood, and the old woman's voice began to shrill at them while she fussed about her cooking.

"Where you've been? Have you got the coffee? And the lettuces and chives? I want you, Baba."

The girl and the youth fell to helping her, glancing over their shoulders at the strange man talking to Richenda Lee. The old woman kept up a vague grumbling, coming once more round the green van to speak to Richenda, while the old man, who was her husband, sat and smoked a clay pipe.

"Out or in, my dear?"

"Outside, Jenny, for all of us."

Jenny's eyes pulled Suvla to pieces. She was a woman of dark and oblique glances, hook-nosed, with the bushy eyebrows of an old man, and Suvla heard her scolding the others as though a scolding tongue had become her privilege. But she cooked a very passable dinner. It was simple and savoury, and they sat in a circle, all six of them, Richenda on a scarlet cushion, the rest of them on the grass. A low circular table with folding legs had been set out and covered with a clean table-cloth. The spoons and forks were silver. Suvla sat next to Richenda, with a little space between them and the four Beckets, who looked under their eyebrows at the tramp like good Hebrews in the presence of a Gentile. And somehow—the scene was not English, though the trees were the trees of an English wood. It reminded Suvla of desert nights, with a few palms scattered near, and camels gurgling somewhere in the darkness; or of Russians in the Crimea, mistress and servants together in the common tragedy of their exile. But chiefly he was aware of the girl on her red cushion, and of the vague hostility of the four people on the other side of the table. They were jealous of him as a stranger, and the significance of his strangeness kept them inarticulate and watchful.

Richenda talked, a woman seated at the head of her table, grave and unembarrassed; and he talked as a guest to his hostess. The sunset flared. The girl Baba got up and served coffee in little Chinese cups, while Suvla told them how the Arabs prepared coffee over a fire of camel dung. Old Jenny's oblique eyes watched him. He knew that she thought him a liar.

"Guess, cove, you've been a sodger."

He smiled at her.

"That's so, granny."

She seemed to resent his playfulness.

"All sodgers are liars."

"Well—there were about eight million of us at one time and another!"

The old man and the youth laughed, and Richenda, with a quiet stare at Jenny, rose and picked up her cushion. The tops of the trees were full of the after-glow, but the lower foliage was changing from green to black, with the dusk flowing in like water, and turning the grass and the tree trunks grey. Richenda went back to the steps of the caravan, and, placing her cushion on the top step, seated herself there, while John Suvla stood and filled his pipe.

"Jenny is a sceptic," she said.

He struck a match.

"She has her reasons. When people travel about with a little Queen of Sheba——!"

Her eyelids flickered, and she watched the light of the match playing upon his face as he lit his pipe.

"You are not quite bold enough to say what you think."

He puffed for a moment and threw away the match.

"That's daring me——"

"What if it is?"

"Jenny does not like me near you. I don't blame her. But if you choose I will tell them some yarns, good hair-raising adventures. They will enjoy them, even while they think me a liar, which I'm not."

"I might come to hear them."

"And believe them?"

Suvla John

"Yes."

She called to her people, and told them to gather round. Her smile went straight to him: "Sit on the steps, Odysseus." She had brought out a queer little pipe with a mouthpiece of amber, the bowl of it carved in the shape of a flower, and Suvla he came to take his place below her; she held out a hand.

"I'll try yours. What is it?"

"Navy cut."

He passed her the tin box.

"Roll it between your palms."

"I know."

She was lighting her pipe when the others came from the fire and gathered round at the bottom of the steps. The youngsters lay on the grass; Jenny and her man shared an old waterproof sheet. She was fingering a short clay pipe, and Suvla passed her his tobacco box.

"You may not believe my yarns, granny, but you can smoke my plug."

She accepted the tobacco.

"Sodgers see things," she allowed. "Been in Egypt, cove? I had a boy die there."

With the stem of his pipe Suvla made the sign of the cross.

"A soldier, granny?"

"Wounded in Galli-poly, he was. They took him to Egypt. They do say that in those days the wounded were stuck to the decks with blood. Anyway, he died there and was buried."

She nodded her head and brooded as she lit her clay.

"Men have the best of it. Did I grieve? Well, more than my man here. Men don't have to put up with pangs. But I should like to have seen the place where the boy was buried."

"I think I know it, granny. Shall I tell you about it?"

Her queer eyes looked at him less obliquely.

"You can. And that there place where he was shot."

"Cape Helles."

"Anyway, the devil must have made it."

Suvla drew up his knees, and, crossing his arms on them, began. He told of the Greek seas, and of the island of Lemnos, with Mudros harbour and the mountains and the great ships of war, of Helles and its beaches burning under the fierce sun, of old Sed el Bar, grey and stub-

Suvla John

born, of the *River Clyde,* beached where the blood of
heroes had coloured the sea. He told of the yellow cliffs
that turned to gold at sunset, of Imbros flushed with the
dawn, of the healthy plateaux and the gullies and old
Achi Baba, grey with smoking shells. And the hospital
ships with their lights, all red and green, and the moon
rising over Asia and shining on where Troy stood, and
the dust and the heat and the flies, and sickness, the
thirsts and the deaths.

"Jam, yes, where I see jam, granny, I think of flies.
And the smell of the incinerators and the dead mules on
the beach! Oh, ye gods!"

He paused, and they sat and gazed upon him.

"Tell us more," said the girl.

"Yes, what you did next."

He seemed to grow rigid, looking above their heads
into the darkening spaces of the wood, and when he took
up the tale of his adventures his voice had a note of
raillery. He became gaillard, fierce, yet mocking. He
coined quick and stabbing phrases; he painted pictures
with bloody fingers and a burning stake. He spoke of
cities and great plains, forests and rivers, of cruelty and
terror, of dim figures struggling together, of dead-eyed
girls and women paddling with naked feet in the snow,
of dead bodies by the roadside, flames and the crack of
rifles. Presently, he showed them old Stamboul. Next,
he was in a ship. There was a glare upon the sea, coral
islands, palms. He had gone from there to China and
Japan. Then—Mexico. Yes, he had some fighting there,
but dirty fighting, a dago's game.

Above him sat Richenda, her white teeth set on the
amber mouthpiece of her pipe, her eyes watching him as
though she sought the man behind the words. Was it
all true? She had a feeling that it was as true as he
could make it, and that there was more to be told had
he cared to do the telling of it. She sat and wondered.
The most obvious of questions rose to the surface. Why
had he come back to England? Had he grown homesick,
or did England hold some uncompleted episode, some
adventurous sequel?

Suddenly her chin rose sharply, and she took the pipe
from between her lips.

Suvla John

A man was standing there on the grass behind the seated figures. He seemed to have come suddenly out of the dusk, without a word or a sound, so silently that the others had not heard him.

But Suvla had seen him, and had made no sign. He talked on, keeping his eyes upon the figure that stood there listening like some ghost drawn towards the firelight and the sound of a human voice.

Yes, and a very substantial ghost in old army riding breeches, leggings, and a brown coat. The full round chin of him showed, and the protruding coarseness of his lower lip. His eyes and the upper part of his face were hidden under the shadow of his hat, yet there was something hostile in their hidden stare. A big animal, strong, menacing, biding his time while the other man talked.

Suvla finished, and took out his matchbox, for his pipe had gone out. He felt Richenda shift her position on the steps above him, and one of her feet touched his arm, but whether there was any meaning in the touch he could not tell. The man made a movement, pushing back his hat, so that the heavy breadth of his face was visible.

"Seems you have got a dandy sort of ranter on your staircase, Richenda."

Old Jenny turned with a start, and got upon her knees with her two hands up.

"Bless us!" she said.

Her man and the two youngsters sat quite still, peering round over furtive shoulders.

Richenda spoke, and her voice was strangely austere.

"I have. It is my pleasure. And—thank you."

"For nothing! It's no pleasure of mine. You—there—I'll trouble you to shift."

Suvla stood up; he was holding a lighted match to the bowl of his pipe, and he seemed to hear the sound of heavy breathing. He smiled and was aware of the shrinking figures of the Beckets.

"I have got your place, buck. Well, that's all right. I'm keeping it, unless the lady bids me quit."

"You'll quit," said the man.

Suvla felt himself touched. He understood that the

girl behind him had something to say to him. He turned and met her eyes.

"It's his job," she said in an undertone, "fighting."

Suvla nodded.

"So's mine."

He faced about again.

"A rough house—what! All right—I'm with you. Over there on the other side of the road, all on our own and no favour."

"You're a darned fool," said the man savagely.

"That's all right. Don't worry."

They went away together into the darkness, and there was a short silence, while Richenda and her people sat very still. They could not see the two figures, but they heard them, the blows, the scuffling of feet, the heavy breathing. Once, old Jenny got on her feet and would have run forward into the darkness, but Richenda made a sign, and her man caught her by the skirt and pulled her down beside him. None of them spoke. The breathing of one of the men grew moist, and they could hear him spitting, and they knew that his spittle would be blood. More blows, the tense rush as of a clinch, and then an oath, and the sound of bodies falling. The strained silence was full of a poised and savage grapple somewhere on the ground. Then a furious and halt-smothered voice, snarled in defeat: "Blast you, stop twisting. My shoulder's gone."

More silence, and then they heard a match strike, and saw a man standing in the middle of the road, lighting a pipe. He came across to them. It was Suvla.

He had a great smudge of something on his forehead, and his breath still heaved, but above his black beard his teeth showed in a smile.

"Sorry. I suppose I can sit here now."

He passed the figures on the ground and took his place at Richenda's feet.

"Finished?" she asked him.

"Yes, finished. Peace, and a broken shoulder."

5

John Suvla spent the night under the green caravan, lying on some straw and covered by a horse-cloth. Sleep came to him quickly, even while he lay listening to the

Suvla John

faint creaking of the woodwork as Richenda moved to and fro. She was slow that night in undressing, and for quite five minutes she sat on the edge of a bunk, with one stocking on and the other off, and she was awake long after Suvla had fallen asleep.

In the morning she was stirring before the yellow caravan had roused itself to life. The sun was shining on the little window with its old rose damask curtains looped back with green cords. She had forgotten to draw them on the previous night, and, rising on her elbow, she looked round this familiar cabin as though it had suddenly acquired a quality of strangeness. On the table lay the book she had been reading yesterday, Hewlett's "Open Country." One of her black stockings trailed across the Bokhara rug that covered the floor. A red rose had fallen from the old blue Canton vase on her bookshelf, and her black stocking seemed to be crawling towards it like a snake.

A sound of splashing water reached her. She swung her feet out of bed and went softly to the window.

"I wonder," she thought, "I just wonder whether he meant to sneak off? It would be like his wildness."

She had a view of John Suvla, stripped to the waist, and bending over a bucket. The water glistened on his hair and body, and she saw the ripple of the muscles under the white skin. But she saw more than that. A purplish and puckered mark showed below the right shoulder-blade, the scar of an old wound.

She dressed, and leaving her black hair loose upon her shoulders, she opened the door and stood on the steps of the caravan. Suvla was shaving, sitting on the ground, a tin mug full of water beside him, and a little mirror propped up on the upturned bucket. He had a bruise on his forehead, and she noticed that the skin was raw on the knuckles of his right hand.

"You're early," she said.

He held the point of his short beard between left thumb and forefinger, and his eyes remained fixed on the mirror.

"Twenty miles to-day."

"Tramping?"

"Hard."

"You use up a lot of shoe leather."

"Better than using up your heart."

She came down the steps.

"I guess yours is pretty tough."

Suvla John

He gave a short laugh.

"Tough! What else? It is what the world has made it, my dear."

He began to wipe his face with the towel, and she wandered across to the fire, and finding the ashes alive she threw on more wood, and, kneeling, worked up a blaze. She was bending over the fire when Suvla joined her.

"You will find a small kettle and a frying-pan just inside the door of my van."

"Breakfast?"

"I suppose you'll not quarrel with a couple of rashers and a cup of tea?"

He was looking down at her gravely.

"No; not if your goodwill goes with them, in spite of last night."

"My goodwill won't fill a kettle," she said rather sharply. "Get it."

Suvla climbed the steps to her caravan. The kettle and the saucepan were there under a shelf covered by a green curtain, and as he paused for a moment on the steps his quick eyes took in all the details of her cabin. He saw her books, her bed, the red rose lying on the eastern rug, the pieces of china, the pictures, the little washhand-stand backed by a panel of beautiful old Persian tiles. The walls were coloured a soft buff. And even his vagabond spirit felt the charm of it, the rich simplicity, the ingenious compactness of it all. It appeared to him that in her character she had reconciled two opposing instincts; she wandered, but she wandered with a proud niceness, carrying with her an atmosphere of fastidious tranquillity.

"Maybe her practice beats mine," he thought, as he descended the steps; "but then she hasn't seen the human dirt that I have."

They breakfasted together by the fire, the yellow caravan remaining mute and slumberous, nor did either Suvla or the girl find much to say. They watched each other, but without appearing to do so, and when the meal was over Suvla lit a pipe and began to pack his belongings into the canvas bag.

Richenda sat and observed him.

"Twenty miles, is it?"

"Thereabouts."

"Anything at the end of it?"

24

Suvla John

He gave a brush to his wiry hair, and then dropped the brush into the bag.

"I have got a job."

"A working job?"

He looked her full in the eyes.

"That would be telling."

"You are careful. Is it a job you might be lagged for?"

Her eyes held his, and withstood the ironical defiance in them.

"Can't tell. It should be a good job. Yes, and quite clean. I'm not yellow."

He rose, put on his hat, cocked it, slung stick and bag over his shoulder. Richenda rose too. They stood regarding each other.

"My thanks to you, Miss Lee. You have given me the luck of the road."

"Then—keep it."

His eyes showed crystals of light, but hers were very dark and solemn.

"Romsey—you said?"

"Next week."

"And after that?"

He was aware of a fierce pride in her.

"What is worth knowing is worth finding out."

"That's so," he said. "Good-bye to you."

III

I

SYBIL SHERE was sewing on loose covers. The covers had been washed—and they needed it, thanks to the dogs and the children and Dick's gardening clothes; but she forgave Richard Shere his clothes, even while she pricked her fingers and crouched on her knees beside the Chesterfield sofa.

"It is the most tiresome job I know."

Yet she was happy over it, far happier than the other woman who sat in one of the blue and rose arm-chairs with her back to the open french window, and watched Sybil at her work and Sybil's baby sprawling on its stomach over a picture book. Elsie Blaber had no children, and therefore she wanted them. She had wanted Joan sprawling there with healthy, animal selfishness.

"Joan, dear, come and show me the pictures."

"Don't want to."

Her mother turned and took the book away.

"No manners—no book—poppet."

"Oh, please. Not on my account. It's so delicious."

Sybil shook her head.

"Not to live with, Elsie."

And then the dark eyes of Elsie Blaber showed that she was hurt. She could be hurt so easily, and that pathetic mouth of hers would tremble into poignant curves, and her eyes look tragic. She had gazelle's eyes, and when her emotions were stirred, little tremors of the dark lashes made fluttering shadows. Even the outline of her face suggested pathos, wavering tears, a velvet and sentimental surface to be smoothed by a man's kisses.

"Joan, you are a little beast," said the mother, angry with herself and with the child.

A bellow from Joan.

"I'm not a ickle beast."

26

Suvla John

"Little beasts are rude and selfish. Yes, you can yell, my dear, and when you have stopped I shan't kiss you."

Elsie made a little emotional movement in her chair, but Miss Joan Shere did not yell. She got up solemnly on her fat legs, embraced her mother, and, picking up the book, carried it to Elsie Blaber and laid it on her knees.

"You dear!"

Sybil, with a deep, shrewd look at both of them, went on with the tacking of her cretonne frill.

She was a little woman with red-brown hair, and a pair of very dark grey eyes in the serene pallor of her face. She wore her hair drawn back and gathered over the nape of her slim neck, and this most exacting of coiffures became her by reason of the shapeliness of her head. Dick Shere, in his moods of teasing tenderness, would call her "Botticelli."

Her ivory hardness was deceptive. You could judge her better by the colour of her hair. Also, those steady, deep grey eyes, tinted black in certain lights, looked out at life with a curious, wise directness. She was one of those happy persons who do not swerve, and to whom comes an early and intuitive wisdom, making life clean and rich and orderly, like some path in a garden appositely planned. Moreover, she was both practical and sanguine. The north-east wind might blow, but an exquisite day would follow it in season; she waited happily for the day and enjoyed it.

A nurse-girl appeared and carried off Joan. Jack, two years older, was enjoying an exciting morning with his father, watching the men at work at a new power-wheel below one of the fishponds in the park. The two women were left alone, Sybil with her sewing, Elsie with her unhappy thoughts.

Unhappiness breathed from her. She exhaled it like a flower, a soft, sad perfume that diffused itself and spread a sense of helplessness and of languor. Her eyes had a way of falling into long stares. Sometimes she would smile for no apparent reason, the smile of a dreamer. She lived in dreams, in a world of sweetly drugged memories, the refuge of the unhappy sentimentalist.

Sybil, sturdily entrenched behind the sofa, and realizing that nothing was being said, raised her copper head above the top of it.

Suvla John

"Poor Elsie."

She could never succeed in being impatient with Bob Blaber's wife, partly because she hated Elsie Blaber's husband, for she had caught Blaber sneering at her own Dick. Over against the french window Elsie had turned in her chair and was looking out into the Feldhurst Manor garden Beyond the paved walk a broad sweep of turf ran between borders and yew hedges to a classic garden house with white pillars and a leaded dome. A gracious vista, tranquil and stately, backed in the distance by pollarded limes. All about the garden lay the flocculent, soft greenness of old oaks and beeches, rising dome on dome along the gradual uplift of the valley. The pollarded limes hid a terrace walk, and a moat, statues, a grey bridge with gates of Sussex iron, the stone coping of its balustrades set with eight stone balls.

"I wonder," thought Sybil, "what John would have made of you if he hadn't been killed."

She rose to rethread a needle, and Elsie Blaber came out of her dreams. She glanced vaguely round the pleasantly shabby room, so different from the rather gorgeous drawing-room at Wynyats, where the cotton-spinning splendour of the Blabers had sought to impress Manchester upon Surrey. Her husband did not understand these things. Old Blaber had carried a Lancashire accent about with him, and had striven mightily to seem the country squire; his son had no accent, and yet he had had hardly any more success than his father.

"Going to the cricket match this afternoon, Elsie?"

"I don't know."

"Is your man playing?"

"No. Dick asked him."

"I know."

"That's why—oh, you know what I mean. Bob's so horribly jealous."

"That's not Dick's fault."

"I know it isn't. But men are so funny."

Sybil had disappeared behind the sofa. She was sorry for Elsie Blaber, but what could you do to help a woman who could not help herself? Elsie had always been the sentimentalist. She had drowned herself in sentimentalism when John Shere had been killed, and she had emerged only to plunge into yet more dangerous sentimentality when she had married Robert Blaber because Blaber had been with John Shere on the night he had

Suvla John

died. Gossip had it that John's last words to Blaber had been: "Look after Elsie." Sybil had not known her husband's elder brother, but she knew him through Dick and by the picture in the dining-room. A mocking, gaillard man, with light-flecked black eyes and a laughing mouth. "Look after Elsie!" No; it seemed to Sybil most unlikely that that mouth ever had uttered those words.

"Men are kittle-cattle," but she excluded her own man from the generalization.

Elsie had lapsed into another dream. She was thinking that she might have been sitting in this room, waiting for John Shere to come to her through the open window, her gallant John. She was sure that if John had lived and had married her she would have been happy, and the mother of children. She could not have failed to have borne children with John Shere as her lover. Bob was so cold. Or was it that a strange coldness had come upon her on that very first night? And sometimes she had tried to imagine that it was John Shere who held her.

"Sybil?"

"Yes."

"Is Dick really letting the men have Hengest's Farm?"

"It is all settled."

The dark woman sighed, but the sigh was for herself.

"Bob's mad about it. He talks of nothing else. Why wouldn't Dick sell him the farm?"

"The Sheres don't sell land, my dear; at least—not yet."

"Bob says it is your stilted pride."

"No; it's a tradition. Dick is the sort of man who should own land. He knows how to use it."

"And Bob doesn't?"

"I did not say so."

"But—I wish—you see—it makes him so—difficult. He comes down to breakfast every morning and stands at the window and glares——"

"At Hengest's? But you can only see the chimneys."

"I know. But he says: 'I suppose those fellows will be putting out all sorts of tin sheds, and turning that meadow upside down. Cabbages.' It's an obsession, Sybil."

"If he would take the trouble to ask Dick. You can tell him that any new buildings are to be put up on the other side."

Suvla John

"I'll tell him. But it won't make any difference. You see, he's——"

"That sort of man. Poor Elsie."

2

Robert Blaber's wife was not an observant woman, but when she saw Sybil Shere resting her arms on the sofa and looking over the back of it towards the open french window, the particular and happy glimmer in Sybil's eyes was so obvious that it could not be mistaken. And in an old, long mirror Elsie saw the window reflected, the grass walk, the borders and the dark yews, and coming towards the window—Richard Shere.

A tallish man, slight, rather narrow across the shoulders, his legs cased in well-cut box-cloth leggings, he came with his rough green jacket over his arm, his eyes the colour of his faded light blue wool waistcoat. His sleeves were rolled up, showing brown forearms. His sanguine, sensitive face was equally brown under his soft felt hat, a disreputable hat, much loved and cherished. His grey riding breeches had been darned at the knee. He moved quickly, with a certain vital eagerness, a smiling man with white teeth and candid eyes.

"Hallo, Elsie! I say, old thing—I clean forgot about my flannel trousers. Someone said they were a disgrace——"

The eyes of the little woman behind the sofa gave him adoration, but a wise and discriminating adoration.

"I had them cleaned."

"You would. Elsie, Sybil's a great woman. Well, the old wheel looks like being a huge success."

His wife stood up.

"Where's Jonathan?"

"I left him down there. He's quite safe and he wanted to stay. Foster's going to bring him back when he comes up for dinner."

He flung his jacket over the back of a chair, and felt in the pocket for pipe and pouch.

"I came up to change. Lunch is at a quarter to one, Celli?"

"Yes; you said you wanted it early."

Suvla John

He was filling his pipe, and suddenly he swung round upon Elsie Blaber with his air of boyish, sanguine frankness.

"I say, Elsie, why isn't your man playing? We wanted those googlies of his."

Elsie Blaber's dark eyes looked at the carpet.

"Bob does not feel very fit."

"I'm sorry. Not that beastly malaria?"

"I don't know. It may be. He hates fussing."

Dick Shere was searching about for matches, and Sybil, coming round from behind the sofa, produced a hidden box from a china teapot on the mantelpiece, and reminded him that it was a quarter past twelve.

"Is it? By George, I must go and change. Staying to lunch, Elsie?"

"Thanks, Dick, I'm afraid I can't."

"Oh, nonsense!"

"Really. I must be going now. Bob's so punctual."

"Silly ass! Well, come down and see us lick Telford. Pedler the blacksmith's in great form."

"I'll try to."

"Try very hard."

She gave him a kind of wavering smile, and with an appealing glance at Sybil, moved towards the window.

"I'll go by the park; may I?"

"Why—I think so," he said, with a kind look that saw far more than it seemed to see.

When she had gone Shere lit his pipe, and, picking up his coat, stood surveying the garden, for the garden of Feldhurst Manor was made to be looked at lovingly. Five generations of Sheres had given themselves to the making of it, and no one had loved it more understandingly than Richard Shere.

"Celli—what's the matter with Elsie?"

"I think her chief trouble is that she is always seeing ghosts."

"Poor old John's ghost?"

"Yes, and the ghosts of the things she has dreamed of and has never found. Besides—Blaber."

"He's a funny-tempered devil. Clever—too clever. At Oxford he was supposed to be one of the coming men —and yet—somehow—he has always missed things. I suppose he is peeved about Hengest's."

"I think so."

"Well, I had my reasons, and very good reasons. I'm

2*

Suvla John

pretty sure that John, if he had come back, would have done what I am doing."

"You are doing what is right."

There was pride in her eyes, and a little tremor of tenderness.

"Blaber is greedy. His father was greedy before him. They like to swallow things; they can't stand being baulked."

"Sulking? What on earth has the fellow to sulk about? Don't you agree?"

She nodded as she gathered up her scissors, reels and pins.

"I do. I thought I should manage to finish this cover."

He came across, and, putting an arm across her shoulders, he smiled at the sofa.

"You have made a nice job of it, old thing. It must be pretty irritating."

"It is."

"I believe you love tackling problems."

"It depends. I say—Dick, it is half-past twelve."

"Heavens!" and he rushed off to change for the village match against Telford.

His wife wandered to the window, and allowed herself one of those happy and reflective moments when an old garden supplies a pleasant setting for a woman's thoughts. She loved it as Dick loved it, partly for itself, partly because it was his. It seemed to symbolize the rich simple completeness of the life they shared, this clean, active English life with its love of animals and trees and flowers. And Richard Shere belonged to it; it was blood of his blood, mood of his mood.

Smiling, she leaned against the window-frame, and with her glances lifting she could see the massed crimsons and scarlets, whites and purples of rhododendrons in the park, with the dark foliage forming a soft green background. Her thoughts were with her husband. What a boy he was! So unsubtle in some ways, and yet so sensitive. He had no guile. To Richard Shere, gentleman, Mr. Robert Blaber was no more than a "funny-tempered devil," a little too clever to be happy. He did not realize the presence of an intense and grudging jealousy, but Sybil had discovered it long ago and had stood on guard until she had come to appreciate the fact that Blaber's jealousy could not hurt her man.

She understood his jealousy. There were times when

32

Suvla John

she was wickedly glad of it, for its inwardness revealed to her all that her man was, and all that the other man was not. These Blabers! Thinking to turn their cotton into a spider's web and catch all the poor country flies! There had been incidents full of delicious humour. Bob Blaber might give his twenty guineas where Richard Shere gave five, and remain Bob Blaber, machine-made man, an importation subtly out of place. Feldhurst looked at him with its slow and steady eyes and touched a symbolical cap to Richard Shere. Feldhurst Manor was Feldhurst. The centre of gravity remained there, in spite of Wynyats and fifty thousand pounds spent upon imitation Jacobean chimneys and rock gardens, stone pergolas, choice conifers, and a palatial garage. The men came to Richard Shere. He led them at cricket; he was chairman of the village council; his wife gave away the prizes at the August flower show. All these little traditions, prides, courtesies, loyalties! They were Shere's because he was a Shere and the man he was.

Blaber, scowling, clever, loving any little authority, stood aside, fingering an ineffectual cheque-book. His jealousy was understandable. At Feldhurst the Sheres and a tradition had always got in his way.

3

At Wynyats that afternoon a groom waited with a horse, wishing himself down under the elm shade by Feldhurst Green, where the village was playing Telford. Mr. Blaber had ordered the horse to be ready at half-past two, and the clock in the stable turret had struck three, and by way of protest—and because the horse had begun to fidget—the groom was leading him up and down.

Blaber appeared outside the half-timbered porch.

"What the devil do you want to cut up the gravel for, man?"

"Well, sir, you told me half-past two, and 'Solomon' was beginning to fuss."

Blaber ignored the explanation, and, with a critical glance at the saddlery, mounted, and turned Solomon's head towards the gate.

"Be here at half-past four, Sandys."

Suvla John

"Half-past four, sir? There's a match on——"

"Match! What match?"

"Against Telford, sir."

"Plenty of time for that when you have done your work. They won't finish till seven."

"Very good, sir."

Sandys watched Robert Blaber walk Solomon down to the gate. "He's a swine," thought the man. "He knew there was a match on as well as I did." Which was true. But if the master is a man of moods, the man may have to balance them against good wages. Blaber paid well; he could afford it. He paid more than Shere did at Feldhurst Manor, and got no thanks for it.

At lunch he had quarrelled with his wife, or rather —he had snarled at her when she had come in late, a little breathless, and with frightened eyes.

"I'm so sorry! Sybil and I were talking——"

"You would be! The usual Shere nonsense! You seem to live down there."

He had a vicious tongue. The trick of saying clever and venomous things had grown on him without his realizing that he said them. His wife had given him one mute look, hurried through the meal with a nervousness that had annoyed him, and had fled, wounded. She was a fool. He had never believed that a woman could be such a fool, such a hotch-potch of incalculable sentimentality, and yet he could remember the days when he had wanted her most desperately. Yes, but all that was a closed book, and he had ceased to exult over the savage episode that was chronicled in it, perhaps because he had ceased to value the thing he possessed, and because his hatred had transferred itself elsewhere. There were times when he made excuses. "I was mad. We were all mad. Savages. What did it matter whom you shot, provided you shot somebody? One's motives could be fiercely impartial, like the Navy's shelling. Still, it is better forgotten."

But he had not forgotten it. For a year or so he had believed that he had buried the memory, stamped it down beneath the sods of his vital complacency. His complacency was immense. He had inherited all the arrogance of that pursy and successful little man, his father, but he had what his father had lacked, a subtle habit of mind. He was a casuistical egoist. Hence, where the

34

Suvla John

father had plunged through and over things, the son got stuck in a sneering contemplation of them. His complacency was more selfishly sensitive. Opposition hurt him and made him savage, and the egotist who can be hurt is apt to be cruel, especially if he happens to be a physical coward.

Blaber's horse carried him down into the valley. The old park fence under the beeches marked the boundary of Feldhurst Manor, and as he passed the decoy pond he saw the rounded gables and hexagonal chimneys of the house rising amid the trees. He bit his short and rather ragged black moustache, and quickened Solomon to a trot. The road bent to the left between the deep meadows, and ahead of him he saw the elms and Lombardy poplars of Feldhurst Hammer. A Union Jack was flying above the top of a white marquee, and between the trees white figures were spread on the sweep of turf.

"Shere's damned cricket match!"

Blaber rode as far as the crossroads and pulled up under the hedge. Feldhurst was batting. He recognized Shere's old grey felt hat.

"Oh, well hit, sir!"

Shere had lifted a loose ball to the boundary. It struck one of the white rails, shot across the road, and was stopped by the closed doors of the blacksmith's smithy. There was clapping from the marquee. Two enthusiastic small boys raced for the ball, scuffled over it, and were told to chuck it in and stop fooling.

Blaber bit his moustache. He sat there for five minutes, hoping to see Dick Shere bowled, but two more punches to the boundary persuaded him to ride on. The Sheres were exasperating people. They did things well, and with an unaffectedness that took it for granted that they could do things well. John Shere had been the best shot and the finest man after hounds in that part of the country, a good boxer, too, and in his year the Oxford "first string" for the quarter-mile. John Shere was dead, but another Shere stood in his place, a brown-headed, smiling, simple idiot whom the farm labourers addressed as "sir." They did not "sir" Blaber. And there was another Shere growing up, a little beggar with reddish hair, utterly fearless eyes, and with a horrid habit of staring.

Blaber turned his horse and took the main road up past Green Man Inn. There was a stiffish hill here, and

Suvla John

Solomon passed the white inn at a walk. Two or three faces looked at Blaber through the bar window, and one of the faces belonged to Sandys, the groom, who had sneaked off for an hour by way of protest.

"There 'e goes! Couldn't let me off for a couple of hours."

The men discussed Blaber with a frankness that was a part product of the war.

"He always strikes me as a miserable sort of chap."

"Miserable! I'd bally well call it something else," said the groom, spitting.

"He's jealous o' the Sheres. So was his father."

A gruff old gardener made laconic jabs with the stem of his pipe.

"Sure. I see'd it. I used to work up at Wynyats in those days. I mind young Bob comin' in with a bloody mouth, and all blubbery; he and Master John 'ad bin fightin'. Oh, yes, Master John was some lad with his fists. Comes along old Blaber and sees his kid. I can remember his purple face. 'Damn them Sheres!' he said. 'Couldn't you lick him, you young fool?' I always do say that Bob Blaber wasn't broken-hearted when Mr. John was killed."

"Well, anyway, he got the girl," said one of them with a giggle.

"Nice bit of stuff, too."

"Oh, chuck it," said the groom; "let the lady alone. I don't like to see a woman goin' about with scared eyes. Pity she didn't marry the brother."

"What—Mr. Dick? Didn't fancy her, I suppose. Likes 'em red headed. Anyway, he's a good sort."

"He's a great little gen'leman," said the old gardener; "and so was his brother—though he was a bit wild."

Solomon carried Blaber's morose face into the shade of the avenue of great beech trees on the top of the hill. There were people who pretended that they could discover Hebraic qualities in the Blaber face. It was long and narrow, the nose slightly beaked, and the chin prominent, the lip thin under the coarse black moustache. The eyes were of a flat, cold blue. Seen in profile the sweep of the jaw was very long from condyle to chin, the nostrils arched, the lower lip slightly everted. It had very little colour. It suggested an inward sneer, the alert, quick sightedness of a bird, a cold face, yet capable of expressing passion where intense,

Suvla John

ego-centric impulses were involved. Someone had once described him as "That fellow who looks as though he were going to bite," and the description was apposite. The lower part of his face suggested a cold voracity, with its hungry nostrils, and the lips stretched over rather prominent teeth.

Blaber might be a bad horseman, sitting round-shouldered, with his toes turned out, but he had keen sight. Away on the left across a deep valley Feldhurst church sent up its white shingled spire among the green smother of its elms, standing alone on a little hillock, its graveyard surrounded by an old red brick wall. There was not a house within half a mile of the church. Why it had been built there no one knew. From the main road passers-by could gaze down on it from under the foliage of the beeches. It looked like a toy building used by pixies, its gravestones and tombs showing like the backs of sheep against the green turf.

Blaber saw somebody emerge from the shadow-curve of the porch. He pulled up. The figure was a woman's, and in spite of its minuteness he recognized it as his wife's. She came slowly across the graveyard to the swing gate in the brick wall, and took the path running up under the shade of an old thorn edge towards the high road.

Blaber's nostrils expanded, and the creases deepened between nose and mouth.

He knew that Elsie went to Feldhurst Church, though he had never allowed her to know that he knew. These secret and sentimental pilgrimages were no tribute to his happiness or to hers. The silly, dreaming, romantic fool! But her going there humiliated him, woke an old stabbing memory, and bit deep into the flesh of his vanity. She might be unhappy; he had ceased to care about her happiness, but he did care about her method of giving expression to it, for it suggested the irony of what might have been, and what was not.

He waited for her, screened by the beech boughs. She came out by the upper gate. He saw her glance nervously down the road, and the bully in him laughed. Then she turned her head and saw him, and her eyes looked like two dark circles of glass in her tristful face.

Blaber walked Solomon down the hill till he was within three yards of her.

"Do you use tears or metal polish?"

Suvla John

She stood quite still, looking up into his vicious, scoffing face.

"I don't understand you, Robert."

"Brass, you know, brass!"

Her face grew desolate.

"You never helped me to forget."

"Women like you don't want to forget," he said savagely.

IV

I

JOHN SUVLA threw his bag down on the turf of the disused chalk pit, and, pushing his hat back, stood at gaze.

The opening into the road, by which the chalk had been drawn in the old days for liming the land, looked towards the south-east, and through it he could see all the green of the weald stretching away into the distance until it disappeared into the darker blue of the hills. They were very dim, these hills, purple to black in colour where cloud shadows lay upon them, and differing in their moods and texture from the softer valley land below. Suvla knew every line of them. He named them to himself as he stood—"Hacklebury, Heath Hill, Panhurst"—and his face softened.

Hackbury! Hackbury with its sailing pines and the tumbled green sea of its fern. Heath Hill, bleaker and more purple, pushing its lion's head over the cowering plains! Panhurst, gentler, feathery with birches, and clothing itself with a richer green as it fell away towards the oaks and beeches of the Feldhurst valley! What a country! What atmosphere! It had mystery, the smile of a woman after tears.

He held his head like an animal sniffing the air. A sudden thrill had gone down his spine. The bowels yearned in him.

Presently he turned away. It was as though he made himself look elsewhere, and as he moved about among the brambles and old thorns, searching for dead wood, his face had a soft solemnity.

Hidden by brambles and the branches of a white thorn he made his fire in the centre of a little circle of turf, sitting with his knees drawn up, and his head uncovered. He laid the dry sticks one by one upon the freshening flames, but he did it mechanically, as though the inner man of him did not see the blaze. His thoughts had

39

Suvla John

wandered. He was seeing pictures : a girl in a white
dress waving to him on a station platform; blue sea and
brown cliffs; trenches; sleet and liquid mud; a man with
his face all yellow sitting on a box, whimpering; moonlight and a great stillness, and the same man with a face
that was white instead of yellow. Then, himself, casually
turning an old copy of *The Times,* and finding those
pregnant sentences in it.

His eyes hardened. He began to smile as he held the
kettle over the fire on the end of his ash stick, for he
was thinking that he had come half round the earth to
hold a man over the fire much as he was holding this
kettle. It would be unpleasant for the man, but then—
he had deserved it. And the grim humour of the thing !
Had he not kept this supreme jest by him for years,
and grown so fond of its many possibilities that—almost
—he had shirked spending it, for he knew that something
would go out of his life when the jest had been played?

Also, there had been an element of exultation in his
procrastination. Like a hunter, lying hidden, with his
sight on the beast he meant to kill, he had experienced
a certain pleasure in keeping his finger on the trigger.
There would be an added jest in the victim's sense of
tranquillity; the beast would be caught cropping the
peaceful turf, confident that the violent episodes of yesterday were no more than last year's dead leaves.

Suvla made his meal, and when he had finished it he
went and stood in the gap where he could see those soft
blue hills.

He smiled at them, but his smile was ironical.

2

By the group of elms near Feldhurst Hammer Suvla
stood under a hedge in the dusk, and took his choice of
two ways. The lane to the right would carry him straight
to the hills and into the pinewoods, while the main road
would take him through Feldhurst Hammer, and so past
the manor and up through the beechwoods to Panhurst.

He chose the road, and within two minutes he was
among the cottages under the high elms, a dim world
on the edge of sleep, with hardly a light left in the

Suvla John

windows. He walked slowly, carrying his hat in his hand, all his senses strangely alert in the soft June darkness. Old, familiar things seemed to touch him, things half forgotten and remembered with a sudden vividness that made him smile. The gable end of the cobbler's cottage still cocked itself like a listening ear. The village shop had the same white blinds. The grey poop of a wagon showed in the open yard of Pedler, the blacksmith and wheelwright. And then he came to a white slatted fence and paused, held there by a familiar perfume, the scent of clove pinks in a cottage garden. It was old Lavender the postman's garden, and Lavender had grown clove pinks there since Noah and the flood. As a boy Suvla had known the smell of them, associated with a red-brick cottage with a yellow jasmine over the porch, and across the road the green smoothness and the white posts and rails of the cricket field. Old Lavender still grew his pinks, and the white posts and rails were there still, with the row of Lombardy poplars solemnly towering against the starlit sky.

He went on, every curve and dip of the road familiar to him, yet infinitely strange. He was in a ghost world, a world of ghost trees, hedges, fields, woods, though the June smell of it was poignant and real. A heavy dew was falling, and presently there would be a moon. He met neither man, woman, nor child, but at the old toll house where Panhurst lane turned off towards the hills he saw the shadow of some human thing upon the lighted blind of an upper window. Instinctively he took the lane and came round the curve of it to the decoy pond, with its alders and willows and banks of bulrush and wild flag. He heard a water-rat plop into the pond. Ten yards farther on a drift of perfume held him for a moment, head up, drawing deep breaths. He could smell the honeysuckle in the hedgerow.

"England!" he thought, and tried to laugh; "just a smell in a hedgerow! What if it had been some stinking fungus, or a green corpse coming out of the wall of a trench?"

He gave a jerk of the chin, walked on for fifty yards, and pulled up, looking at a light. He saw it over a field gate, slightly above him, a yellow splash that seemed to splinter itself through the foliage of a tree bough.

"Good Lord—the old eye!"

Suvla John

He moved to the gate, and, leaning against it, stared steadily at the light. He had seen it hundreds of times in that very same place, blinking when a wind blew, human almost in its expressiveness. It came from the window above the ridge of the Jacobean porch, and its source was the old brass hanging-lamp at the end of a long gallery. A Shere of two generations ago had been the first to christen it "The House's Eye."

It seemed to look down on Suvla with a stare of recognition, and he looked back at it with a feeling of tenseness over the heart.

"Same as ever—my God!"

Almost he could imagine the spread of the old house about that point of light, the deep red brick of it, the two wings with their curved gables, the main block with its mullions and transoms, and the green cupola and gilded vane in the centre. The light blinked through one of the branches of the Lebanon cedars. Below would lie the lawn, with stone steps going down to it, and nearer still the iron gates with the Shere arms upon them, and the walled bridge over the dry moat. He found himself wondering whether Richard Shere had drained the southern half of the moat, and whether they had ever recovered one of the stone balls that had fallen off the coping of the old south bridge. He could remember trying to recover that ball, but the mud and the weeds had been too much for him.

"That lamp's burning the same as ever," he thought. "I wonder if the heart of the place——? I suppose Dick's there. Kids—too—perhaps. Kids—like we were."

He put his head down, for, suddenly, there had come upon him a fierce yearning for that house, not the mere possession of it, but rather—contact with it. To be inside it, even for half an hour, feeling it, smelling it, touching old familiar doors, the carved posts of the oak stairs. To stand at the one window in front of the little Sheraton mirror, with the broad walk before him, the yews, the white pillars of the garden house, and beyond it the green trough of the deep valley and the rolling beech woods.

He caught at himself savagely.

"Hell—you fool! What game is this for a man whose guts turn to water?"

He broke away from the gate, and without looking again at the light he went on up the lane, swinging his shoulders, and striking the road hard with his heels.

Suvla John

He was laughing, or thought that he was laughing, but his laughter made no sound. His mockery was in the presence of ghosts—ghosts who were more enduring than the wilfulness of man.

Mockery! Well, he had learned to mock at most things. Life was best treated as one long, defiant laugh. Why, there was that advertisement of two days ago on the literary page of *The Times*—"Where Goest Thou?—Mr. Moscrop has written a masterpiece. Second large edition." He remembered Moscrop in the war, a little, fat, solemn, frightened fellow with short legs and a sort of quiver about the chin. So little Moscrop had produced a "masterpiece"! Much wind and yeast! Suvla knew that sort of masterpiece. The world was full of masterpieces, well advertised, with a picture of the author, studiedly impressive, staring at one. Little Moscrop had spectacles. Did anyone believe in Moscrop's masterpieces?

He could laugh at the thought of Moscrop, for Moscrop had always been solemnly ridiculous, not like the light in the house over there.

"Where Goest Thou?" must be obtained and read. He could remember asking a very scared Moscrop that same question during an uncomfortable half-hour in a mine crater. "Hallo, Mossy, where are you going?" And Moscrop had been going where men went when nameless fear was upon them.

Suvla laughed. He swung up the long hill under the beeches, with the park fence on his right, and young fern and the Panhurst woods spreading to the left of him. He was making for Hackbury, and as he cut across the heathland above the neck of the Feldhurst valley he saw the moon coming up huge and yellow.

He waved his hat at it.

"Hallo, Moscrop!"

The moon was just like Moscrop. It wanted only spectacles.

Hackbury loomed up ahead of him, tumultuous with pines. For three miles it made a loneliness of heather, gorse, old hollies and innumerable trees. Badgers had "earths" there, and on a summer day you could lie in the scented deeps of the woods and hear nothing but the cracking of the pine cones. Suvla knew it well. He plunged, and was lost in it, and keeping the moon on his left shoulder he held on until he came to a wood of

43

firs that struck into the sky like some old citadel. His
"earth" lay there, a hollow in the swell of a round
"barrow," hidden by young bracken and a grove of
hollies.

He slid down into the grassy hollow. He had
camped here as a youngster, daring the unkedness of
the place, and the tale that told you not to walk around
the barrow at midnight with your left hand towards it,
or something horrible would happen. He dropped his
bag and stick, and was feeling the grass with his hands
when he heard a clock striking.

He straightened to listen. It was the clock in the
cupola at Feldhurst Manor striking out its rather rapid
but mellow tones. Suvla had counted ten, when he heard
another clock chime in, louder, more metallic, clangingly
pretentious. His head went up.

"Wynyats! The Blaber note! How many years is
it since I heard those clocks?"

3

Suvla woke suddenly, and where the moon had been
he found the sun, though nearer the horizon and hanging
like a great gold shield between the trunks of two firs.
The day was very young, and the hands of his tinpot
American watch showed that the hour was half-past four.

"That ought to give me two clear hours," he thought,
stretching himself and brushing off the dew.

There was a boyishness in his movements, a sense of
adventure. He laced on his boots, took a thick slice of
bread and a piece of cheese, and left the hollow in the
side of the barrow. He had two precious hours when the
world would belong to him and to the birds and the
creatures of fur.

Hackbury had its head in the thin blue of the morning, but the valleys were misty and full of the white
stealth of the dawn. The heather, drenched with dew,
brushed against his ankles as he went through it, eating
his bread and cheese. He was making for the Feldhurst
valley, and it took him some twenty minutes to reach the
field gate close to the group of old Scotch firs.

And here he stood at gaze, leaning upon the gate, and

Suvla John

looking down upon a valley that, of its kind, was the most beautiful in England. It fell away from him into a deepening mystery of greenness, its sloping turf banks rising softly to merge into the foliage of the old oaks and beeches. A film of mist lay over the deeper distances, and nearer still sunlight and vapour were caught in one soft confusion, with the tops of the trees a-glitter, while their feet still rested in the shadows.

John Suvla stood very still. The hush of the place was upon him, and so strong and deep was the spell of it that he seemed unable to move. His face expressed wonder, and a surprise at his own wonder. Something harsh and brittle fell from him, and in its place he was aware of a sudden tenderness. Yet why? Because of the landscape's beauty, its secrecy, because it made him think of the face of a woman wet with tears? Because he belonged to it? Because the very essence of it was in his blood?

He climbed the gate and went down the valley.

It was full of birds, all the birds that he seemed to have known of old. The deep woods were full of their deep notes, plaintive, exultant. He heard the laugh of a yaffle. Dozens of blackbirds and thrushes were busy on the grass. A dove cooed somewhere. Over one of the pools two swallows skimmed, blue-black above the mirroring blackness.

"There is nothing like it," he thought. "Nothing quite like it anywhere else in the world."

Suddenly he saw the house. He had come quite close to the lowest and largest of the stew ponds, the one in which he and Dick used to bathe, breaking up the green reflections of the beeches and the blue and whiteness of the sky. There had been changes here, but he did not notice them, for his eyes were on the house and garden. He saw it just as the sun touched it over the beech tops, warming its red walls and chimneys, though a softness of golden vapour still clung to them. The clock in the grey green cupola chimed the hour. Five. The sunlight reached the moat, turned it to a shimmer of gold, and painted curves of black shadow under the two arches of the stone bridge. The eight stone balls were there, and the grey leaded dome of the garden house.

What a picture! A thickness came into his throat. He was moved, most deeply moved. For a moment he covered his face with his hands, and then he looked

Suvla John

again, a swift brightness in his eyes, his fierce mouth strangely smiling. Someone had planted more roses. The iron gates looked very black, as though they had been repainted. The same green-coloured curtains hung at the window of his old room.

His glances shifted as the sun lit up more and more of the great green hollow, searching out the well-remembered trees in the park. The great sequoia looked taller. Good—they had not touched the old thorns, for he had loved the smother of whiteness they had made. Rabbits, too, innumerable brown dots. How old Foster had used to curse them! And the rhododendrons! Alien plants, and yet—by God—how beautiful, hillocks of rose and white and scarlet, scattering the sunlight from the gloss of their foliage.

He was not aware of it—but he was breathing deeply like a man who had been running.

Other thoughts flashed up.

" Is Dick there?"

From the house his memories came back to the quiet water at his feet.

" I wonder if the lad still bathes here? He might come this very morning."

He threw a quick glance at the beeches on the steep slope of the hill.

" Yes—plenty of cover there. I'll risk it."

4

Richard Shere came across the park with a towel over his shoulders.

Near one of the big chestnut trees he paused to watch some birds, and Suvla, lying flat in the beechwood behind the roots of one of the old trees, saw the master of Feldhurst Manor for the first time for seven years. The figure was as familiar as the house, and almost as changeless. The war might never have happened. The man down yonder wore the same dark blue " First Trinity " blazer, and the same grey flannel trousers. His soft shirt was open at the throat, and he had no hat.

Suvla watched him with eyes of emotion. He saw more than the mere man; he beheld a beloved gentleman,

46

Suvla John

the inheritor of a tradition, Richard Shere, the same yesterday, to-day, and to-morrow.

"It is good and right that he should have the place," was Suvla's thought. "God bless him."

So, Dick Shere came to the pool, and undressed there in the early sunlight, and plunged from the same diving-board and swam, while up in the beech wood a man yearned over him. Those seven years! And here was a thing happening just as it had happened hundreds of times in the happy stillness of a green valley.

Suvla lay with his chin on a grey root. He longed to cry out and to go running down to the water when Richard Shere was swimming, and to shout: "Dick, old man, Dick." But all that was dead. He had realized with fierce suddenness how dead it was. Things that were supposed to be dead had no right to return to life.

V

1

SUVLA lay all day on Hackbury Hill, and it was one of
the longest days of his life.

He heard the two clocks striking in the valley, challenging each other like old rivals, and he knew that the
clock that had been John Shere had ceased to beat six
years ago. He had made his choice then, till now he had
never regretted it, nor, perhaps, had he fully realized
its finality.

He realized it now, for between him and the old life
stood the figure of his brother. Always, in spite of his
wild-headedness, he had carried about with him a love
of this younger man, and it was this very love that had
made it easier for him to efface the old life and to lose
himself in the new. He had said to himself: " What
does it matter? Dick will have Feldhurst. He is more
English than I am; it means more to him than to me."

Yes, all that was true, but there were issues that he
had not foreseen. A man may cut himself adrift, provided that he is ready to renounce all attempts at a
re-knotting of the rope, and to regard all the old appeals
of the heart as dead.

The trouble was that when you thought the old forces
dead, they proved to be only sleeping. They wakened
suddenly with passionate cries and a tumult of emotion;
they clamoured to join themselves to the stock from
which they had been severed.

"You were a fool to come back."

He lay and looked at the pine boughs fringing the
blue of the sky.

" Yes, but you had to come back, my lad. You had
a debt to collect. The manner of your coming back is
the thing that matters."

That was the curse of the whole problem. He had
felt so sure of his own hardihood, of the reckless temper
of his vagabondage, that he had dared this the greatest

Suvla John

of all his adventures with an ironical cock of the head. Tough! Why—he had the hide of an elephant. He could laugh, for laughter was the one and final retort. To laugh at life, make a merry mock of it and all its ironies and contradictions, to scorn scorn, to be beholden to no man. To walk the world like a laughing, generous ruffian whom nothing could abash.

He turned over and stared at the grass.

"You were too sure of yourself. Like the man who said he was through with women. Life gets you. I suppose it goes on getting you till you are under the sods."

This England! It had awakened him; it tore at his vitals. And he had not foreseen it, or forefelt its lure. Half an hour in a green valley, a few old perfumes, the singing of birds, the glimpse of a light in a window, a man coming to swim in a pond. Good lord!

His bowels felt like water.

He was no more than a boy, a silly sensitive, eager boy.

It was then that he realized the finality of the choice he had made back in those wild war years. He could not show himself to flesh of his flesh, or go down and take the hand of his brother.

Resurrections may not be impossible, but they are dishonest.

To overturn the whole scheme of another man's life. To come back after all these years and shake the whole human fabric to its foundations.

Feldhurst was Richard Shere and he—Suvla—had made it so. He could not undo the thing that he had done.

And behind his sense of honour lay a sense of fear. How could a dead man who returned to life be met? Could he count on the eager hand, the quick gladness in the eyes, the generous wonder, the impulsive self-effacement? No; it was too much to ask, too much to expect. And what a damnable thing—to put a man to such a test, and to see him fail as any man might fail, to see in his eyes a sudden grudging realization of his own loss—hatred——

"He would be doubly right to hate me. Even Dick. Why have you come back—now? Anyway, he would suffer. He might want to give the old place back. His sense of security would go. I should be a sort of dispossessed ghost, haunting the place. And that's that."

49

Suvla John

An hour before sunset Suvla lit a fire in the hollow, boiled his kettle and made tea. When the darkness came he was to renew his contact with another part of the old life, and to look through the windows of Wynyats, where Robert and Elsie Blaber lived.

He sat and stared at the fire, letting his thoughts go to and fro between yesterday and to-day. He was conscious of power, of the dramatic happenings that waited upon his pleasure, of the fear he could inspire in the heart of another man. He supposed that he hated Robert Blaber, but as he watched the colours of the fire and of the sunset, and felt the dusk in the tops of the trees, he felt less sure of his hatred. Did one hate a man whom one despised? Was hatred worth while? Weak men gave way to it, and Blaber's hatred of the Sheres had been the source of Blaber's weakness. All that had happened had followed from one snarling and savage impulse, a gust of hatred blowing a man over the edge of his self-control, and landing him—where?

Yes, so much might depend upon what Bob Blaber had become, or whether he was the same Blaber, vain, envious, lusting to possess things, not because he desired them for themselves but because he wished them to be his. A queer temperament. Acquisitive, greedy, yet cowardly, and apt to be basely mean because of its cowardice. How had Bob Blaber settled things with his own conscience? Some men were ingenious at adjusting awkward situations. It was possible that Blaber had viewed the affair as the ordinary cut-throat commercialist regards the bringing off a clever deal. If he had downed the other fellow, well—that was the other fellow's fault. It was possible that the secret soul of Robert Blaber had secretly exulted.

"Yes, Blaber got the goods."

Suvla smiled to himself, and fingered the bristles of two days' growth upon his jaw. He could not convince himself that he hated Robert Blaber, for it seemed less easy to hate a man here in this green country. The English were bad haters. Reaching out a hand he took some of the black ash from the fire, and rubbed it over his face and throat, and reaching for his bag, searched in it for certain things that he needed. He considered another possibility. Blaber might bluff and be insolent, and Suvla knew that if Blaber showed insolence he might kill him. He had killed better men than Blaber, men who had fought cleanly and had died game. Suvla, vagabond knight errant, a fighter wherever fighting was to be had, had learnt to hold life cheap, both his own and the lives of others.

The peaceful people! How they humbugged themselves! How the war must have astonished some of them. Too much fat ease was apt to make men hypocrites. The natural man's impulse was to kill.

He produced a black eye-shade with a loop of elastic attached, and slipped it over his left eye. Then he looked at himself in his shaving mirror. " Yes, a pretty average blackguard."

Getting up, he stamped out the embers of the fire, and, going to one of the old hollies, he hung his bag in it away from the dew. The sun had set, and in the dusk, he began to wander across Hackbury towards the Panhurst road, his thoughts still busy with Blaber of Wynyats. The problem had broadened, and had come to include Blaber's wife; and the intrusion of Elsie surprised him. Hitherto he had been in the habit of leaving her out of the picture; like Mercedes she had married the villain, the good, old fashioned, nineteenth-century villain, and Suvla had lost all interest in her when she had married Blaber. A tainted marriage! How could a woman bring herself to mate with a man like Blaber?

He struck at a furze bush with his stick.

" Is it that I'm a coarse beast, or does being a blackguard make one more honest? She may have children. She may be fond of the chap. Supposing she is—what then ? "

Either the problem was becoming more complex, or he himself was growing more sensitive to subtler influences, just as though this green England had looked at him with her soft, wet eyes. Things that had promised to be easy had become tangled and difficult. His motive even! Had he miscalculated? Or was it that he had been an ironical and cocksure fool, hard on the surface, but with a brittle hardness that failed you when life touched it? The business had seemed so easy, a mere leap out of nowhere to shout "Bo" at a scared man, and to disappear again, leaving the fellow like a quaking aspen for the rest of his natural life.

Suvla John

" Well—why not ? " he asked himself as he broke through into the open road. " It is a mistake to see too much. The people who see too much are left sitting on the wall."

3

Blaber was playing billiards. It was his particular game, and as he moved about the table knocking the balls hither and thither with concentrated precision his face showed a complacent serenity. Blaber played his games without a smile. It was not the game, but the winning of it that mattered.

His opponent, one Gutteridge, who had bought land and built an Italianesque villa on the slopes of Malbury, stood by the scoring-board, politely attentive. He had dined with Blaber, and he was smoking one of Blaber's cigars. He held his cue like an infantryman standing at ease, his mildness flattering Blaber's thin vivacity. Pink and bald, with a drooping honey-coloured moustache, and a chin that receded, his expression was that of a nice person politely suppressing an eructation.

" Good shootin', Blaber. You're in form."

Blaber paused for a moment, slightly frowning.

" Do you mind not talking. It puts me off."

" Sorry; but I never thought you would get in off that shot."

Blaber knocked the ash from his cigar, tucked it into the corner of his mouth, and, leaning over the table, resumed his play. His face was turned towards one of the windows, the blind of which was only partly drawn, leaving a gap of six inches between it and the sill. His attention was concentrated on the game.

But he missed the next shot, an easy shot, and the mild man gave a little chuckle.

" My dear chap, you have let me in—quite nicely."

He came forward to examine the situation, and he did not see the look of scorn that Blaber gave him, but another man saw it and took the significance of it to heart. Gutteridge, in play, hanging heavily and carefully over the table, scored a patient seven, and then broke down over an easy cannon.

" Foozled it ! "

Suvla John

Blaber's look of scorn revived. He returned to the table, and with a break of twenty-three ran out his hundred. He was an ungraceful winner; when he had beaten his man he liked the other fellow to feel beaten.

"Supposing I give you thirty, Gutteridge."

The mild man bore no resentment.

"Just as you like, my dear chap. You are a bit of a pro. at this game. It is wonderfully warm to-night—might be in Italy."

He moved to the near window and pulled up the blind.

"Mind if I open the window a bit more?"

"As you like."

"Wonderful night. I like this loggia of yours. Who did it?"

"Rollo Maunder."

"Oh, Maunder. He was the fashion——"

"In my governor's day. Fine sense of outline, but a little fussy."

"Oh, I don't know. You must have rather a fine view from here. Now—those trees—and the meadow beyond—and the moon."

Blaber's face seemed to grow more narrow

"I have. My neighbour is going to spoil it for me."

"Not really! Shere—you mean? Of course, I had heard——"

"Yes, it's a fact. I wanted to buy the farm. I offered him twice what it's worth. Any reasonable man would have taken it, especially when he is not too flush."

"Obstinacy?"

"Do you know, Shere?"

"Slightly. Rather impulsive——"

Blaber was sneering.

"Heredity. When people have bossed a place for two or three hundred years, Gutteridge, they become little tin gods. I don't doubt that these chaps wanted land, socialist swine."

"But my dear chap, if Shere's an autocrat——"

"There are two ways of keeping the lead, man. Shere's a diplomat. I think his idea was to nobble the scheme, father it, and pose as a public benefactor. There are some men who must run every show. That's the Shere tradition in this corner."

Gutteridge diffused sympathy.

"Sort of co-operative farm?"

Suvla John

"That's the idea. A chap named Merrow is the leading light; was a cowman before the war. Shere's made it easy. I believe he's playing banker."

"Altruistic chap!"

Blaber's teeth showed under his thin black moustache.

"Altruism! Whenever I hear a chap talking altruistic stuff—I know he's a—politician."

Gutteridge laughed.

"I think you are about right there. Well—what about my revenge?"

The click of the billiard balls was heard again, and Suvla, drawing back along the wall, stood leaning against one of the brick pillars of the loggia. The place was a smother of wistaria, vines and roses, a shelf of shadow between the windows and a stretch of moonlit lawn. Suvla was in his socks; he had left his boots in a hedge-bottom; the adventure had some of the stimulating stealth of the war.

He was on the point of slipping away when he saw something, and stood still. A woman was walking on the lawn; he had not heard her, and her figure came suddenly between him and the dark outline of a holly hedge. She was wearing a light-coloured dress, with a scarf of some darker material over her shoulders. Suvla saw her pause, as though to listen, and the click of the billiard balls was the only sound in the stillness of the June night.

Suddenly she turned away, as though she had come to listen for that very sound, and, hearing it, had gone away reassured. Her purpose and its inclination were detached from the two men. Suvla saw her cross the lawn towards a path that went down into a mass of flowering shrubs. He knew the path, and the gate at the end of it opening into the road to the Wynyats' stables. If you turned to the right outside the garden gate you came out into the main road.

Suvla followed her, but not by the way of the path. He took the grass verge beside the main drive, and, standing in the shadow of the gate pillar, waited to see which way she went. He could hear no footsteps, and looking out he saw the dim whiteness of her drifting away from him under the shadow of a hedge. She drew his curiosity after her, out of the main road, into one of the shaggy Feldhurst lanes where the wheel tracks were white grooves between ribbons of turf. She walked slowly; sometimes she paused and seemed to stand as in a dream, making him think that she was afraid of being followed, or that she had been startled by some sound. Later, he realized that these pauses were part of the emotional rhythm of her mood. He had to be very cautious, for the lane curved, and her footsteps made no sound, so that it would have been easy for him to blunder upon her.

He tracked her to one of the Feldhurst gates, a white gate between two panels of white paling, an old thorn growing in the hedge on one side of it, a group of larches on the other. She paused here, full in the moonlight, and it seemed to him that she seemed to hang upon the gate, bending her head low over it till her mouth must have been touching the bar.

She remained thus for fully five minutes, like a woman at some old tragic trysting place. Then he saw her move. She reached up and pulled something out of the hedge, and in doing she touched in Suvla a quick and vivid memory.

For at this white gate, some eight years ago, he had told Elsie Langdale that he loved her. It had been just such a night as this in June, and he had pulled a spray of honeysuckle out of the hedge and had wound it into her hair.

VI

I

THAT this game of hide and seek should have a
cumulative fascination for a man was understandable; this reading of the book of his own life—
backwards—and Suvla remained on Hackbury, un-
discovered and unmolested. He had to go tramping
once or twice in search of stores, travelling well afield
for them, and returning after dusk to the barrow among
the firs. Feldhurst remained utterly unaware of him,
for he was a ghost that walked only at dawn and in
the dusk.

On his second morning he went down by way of
Panhurst, filling his water-bottle at the spring near
Dewlap Farm, and coming out upon the main road
above the valley in which lay Feldhurst church. He
took the steep path under the thorn hedge, while the
level rays of the sun were still entangled in the beeches.
It was a secret world, and its secrecy delighted him, for
he was no great lover of his fellow men. In a crowd he
despised nothing so much as the crowd spirit, but here
there was nothing to despise, and in the beautiful and
calm indifference of the dawn he felt that man did not
matter. Man was an experiment, and in Russia Suvla
had seen him as a greasy, unwashed thing, dirty in
mind and manners. He preferred the trees. He was
sorry that the wildness of the world should pass. Man,
noisy, experimental man, was splurging everywhere.

Feldhurst church made him smile. It was like an
old friend grown more quaint and wizened, a character
by itself, standing apart from the world of concrete and
steel girders. He went in by the kissing gate in the
south wall, and wandered about among the Feldhurst
dead, pausing to read the half-obliterated names on the
lichened gravestones. The Feldhurst yew had spread
an even broader shadow over the brick tomb of the
eccentric Mr. Chandler, a gentleman who—a hundred

56

Suvla John

or so years ago—had insisted on being buried in an ale cask. An elm had cracked another of the tombs. Someone had been scything the grass—old Newdigate, perhaps—and had left swathes of it to be wetted by the dew.

Suvla went round to the north side of the little grey chancel. Here, beside the stokehole, a window with leaded lights between an oak mullion had its sill within a foot of the turf. It was the window of one of his boyish escapades. Armed with a bull's-eye lantern and a jack-knife, he had broken in at half-past eleven one night and shamefully rifled the alms-box, though the plunder had amounted to nothing more splendid than sevenpence three-farthings. It had been the adventure, not the money, that he had desired. He had given the seven pennies to one of old Foster's kids.

As he took out his knife he wondered if old Foster was still alive and cursing the rabbits. "Them black dunged little brutes!" A great old boy, Foster, surly and staunch, the sort of man who had helped to upset the overladen French apple-cart at Agincourt. He could picture old Foster going down on his prayerful knees and then getting up to lick a thumb and send a long arrow heartily into some Frenchman's gizzard. Meanwhile, the act of sacrilege progressed. It was a simple affair, the turning back of the lead with the blade of a knife, and the extracting of one of the glass quarries You put your hand in and manipulated the window catch.

Suvla climbed in. The place returned to him one of the smells of his boyhood, a fragrant and damp mustiness. The sun struck the east window and painted patches of blue and red upon the floor. The unbroken silence of the place had its effect upon him, for he moved about softly, bare-headed, the defiant note subdued. He glanced about him at the oak gallery with the royal arms upon it, the choir stalls, the pulpit, the black-timbered roof. He supposed that Blossom still climbed into the pulpit, smiled at the world through his spectacles, and turned on a voice that was quite different from the voice of the Blossom who played cricket.

The Sheres had a family pew here, panelled off at the chancel end of the south aisle, four yards square, with a table and a fire-place, and blue cushions on the seats. Suvla went towards this pew. He opened the high door, stood a moment, and then sat down in the

Suvla John

corner seat that had been his as a boy. Two letters had been cut into the oak panelling—"J. S.," and beneath them a rude skull and crossbones. His "Treasure Island" days. He could remember cutting those letters one Christmas Day, in despite of Aunt Juliana, during a particularly solemn sermon. He passed his fingers over the letters and seemed to dream, until a lightness on the wall attracted his attention.

"To the memory of John Shere—Captain in the 3rd East Regiment—who was killed at Suvla Bay on the night of the evacuation—December, 1915.

"He lies in a strange land, but he lives in the hearts of those who knew him."

Suvla sat very still. A smile, quick and elusive, passed across his face, and for a moment he bowed his head.

"Do they still remember?" he asked himself. "It seemed to me last night that she remembered. Poor Elsie! Blaber would make most dead men seem heroic."

He thought of Richard sitting here. He was quite sure that Richard Shere came to Feldhurst church, however much the sermons bored him. Their ancestors had believed in the sermons and been bored by them; the belief or the lack of it was the only difference.

Did it matter? If there was anything in the beyond you might catch the shadow of it in an old, simple, solemn building such as this.

A wayward impulse moved him. He looked up at the memorial brass, and taking a pencil out of his pocket and standing on the seat, he drew on the white wall above the plate a cross. Over the cross he put a question mark, and below it in rough black capitals: "Birdcage Walk—midnight. For what?"

He left the church by the window, replacing the glass lozenge, and, walking round to the Feldhurst yew, he seated himself on Mr. Chandler's tomb. Mr. Chandler was a memory, though down below there his skeleton sat crouching in an ale cask. Queer egotists—men! To be remembered somehow—and for something. All these slabs of stone, names, ages, epitaphs! And to think of the innumerable unnamed dead, rotted and forgotten, men who had chipped flints, men who had stabbed with short bronze swords or hacked with iron ones. This yew on the blessed south lawn, no graves on the black north. Life's door and death's. What

58

Suvla John

did it all mean? Did anything matter? Had it mattered because Mr. Chandler had been buried in a beer barrel? Some day another ice-age would arrive, and Feldhurst church and its graves might be buried under mountains of ice, and all this green world would be dead with it.

Suvla got off the tomb.

"That's the moral of it all," he thought. "Make the most of your red blood. Nobody knows anything. We just watch a great wheel turning. But I'm in favour of clean blood, and what your father and your grandfather put in it. No thin, rusty stuff——"

He lifted himself over the brick wall, and went on down the valley. He felt more able to accept life at half-past five on a June morning. If Dick was happy in the old house, well, that was the main thing that mattered.

And Blaber's wife? Poor, dark-eyed Elsie, winding the memory of a slip of honeysuckle into her hair!

What could he do? Unalterable things had happened. Elsie was almost nothing to him now, and had she mattered supremely—he—John Shere—was dead.

2

As he went down the valley the silence of it seemed to challenge him.

"Sing, Suvla, sing."

He threw his hat in the air, caught it on the point of his stick, and burst out with the first old song that rose from his heart to his head:

> "There was a youth and a well-beloved youth,
>   And he was a squire's son,
>   And he loved the bailiff's daw-aw-ter,
>   Who lived at Islington."

He braved out the old ballad, and laughed his own applause. Yes, that was the way they had used to sing it, he and Dick, and he could remember their breaking out with it boisterously at a Christmas party, with Bob Blaber in the tightest of Eton jackets and the most polished of collars, looking at them superciliously over the top of a sofa. Afterwards, they had kicked his top-hat to disgraceful nothingness in the cloak-room. Supercilious little swine!

Yes, and it would appear that Robert Blaber was as supercilious as ever. He had allowed no memories to chasten him, though it was Suvla's experience that nothing changed men fundamentally; the white remained white, the yellow—yellow, though the yellow might grow more cunning and put on a false white smile. As for the grey men—well, they did not matter; they sold cheese and punched tram tickets, and assuredly Nature would grow very bored with them. It was better to be a Blaber, and to provoke in white men a desire to wring a neck.

He had an impulse of wicked mischievousness, and coming to the pond in the green bottom below Panhurst farm, he knelt down and played Narcissus. The water was very clear and still, for there were no beasts in the field to muddy it, and Suvla revised his toilet. He put on the eye-shade and knotted a dirty handkerchief round his throat. His cheeks were all black stubble, his face grimed, and when he had knocked his hat into a more dilapidated dreariness, and pulled it down well over his eyebrows, he fell in love with his own reflection.

"After all, men fail to see what they are not expecting to see."

About eleven o'clock a very slovenly looking tramp appeared in Feldhurst, walking heavily, and helping himself along with an ash truncheon cut from a hedge-row. His hairy face was very dirty; he looked spiritless and furtive, slouching along with his hat pulled over his eyes. The very stoop of him was typical, as typical as were his boots. His right boot was laced with string.

The tramp passed Feldhurst Green, and continuing up the hill in the heat of the morning he came to where the gates of Wynyats opened upon the road. The gates were of oak, hung on massive, free-stone pillars, and each pillar was capped by the figure of a seated lion supporting a shield. Old Blaber had had much trouble with Rollo Maunder over the stone lions; to the artist these stone beasts with their shields had set the seal of an absurd vulgarity upon Wynyats, but old Blaber had dreamed dreams. "Thou'll't see something on those shields soom day." His son was to be a states-

Suvla John

man of the Manchester persuasion, with a peerage to
follow. Hence the ready and prophetic shields.

On each side of this entry a neat square of mown
turf lay marked off from the road by stone posts and
chains. A pollarded lime stood in the centre of each
plot, shaped like an open umbrella, and throwing a
circle of shade. The tramp paused outside the closed
gates, and, stepping over the chains, sat down in the
shade of the limes. He pulled out a paper and a clay
pipe, and sprawling on one elbow tempted fate.

He had been there for half an hour when a voice
admonished him.

"If I was you, mate, I'd get off that bit o' grass."

A round, red face, and the end of a birch broom
showed between the leaves of the gate. The tramp sat
up and expectorated.

"Wa' for? I ain't doin' no 'arm."

"It be'nt the harm you're doing. But if the boss
catches you."

"This ain't private property. Posts or no posts, it's
part of the public 'ighway."

"Well, you tell 'im that."

"Don't mind if I do."

"Don't say I didn't warn you, mate. He'll be down
here on 'is horse any minute."

"Right'o. I'll ask 'im to lend me a tanner."

It was this derelict figure that Blaber saw, a scrubby
vagabond impertinently sprawling within the sacred
precincts of the posts and chains. The tramp appeared
to be asleep, the dirty newspaper spread over his face.
He snored.

Blaber pulled up.

"You there—get off that grass."

The tramp heaved. The paper was slid to one side,
and an eye looked up at the peremptory person on the
horse.

"Beg pardin, guvner?"

"Get off that grass."

The tramp sat up.

"I'm a bit deaf, mister. Got m'ear drums bust in
the great war."

Blaber called to the gardener who was sweeping the
drive.

"Banks!"

"Sir?"

Suvla John

"Turn this fellow off the grass. He says he's deaf."

The gardener looked frightened. He came and leaned over the chains, his broom trailing in one hand.

"Move on, matey. You'd better."

The tramp had been deaf to the master, but he appeared to hear the man. With some deliberation he folded up his dirty paper, put it away, rose, lifted a slow leg over a chain, and stood scratching the back of his neck.

"No 'arm meant, mister. Give us a bob. I'm an ex-sojer, I am."

Blaber looked down at him with infinite scorn.

"You look it! Every blackguard in the country spins that yarn. Clear out."

He rode on, turning in the saddle to see that the fellow obeyed him. The tramp was slouching off down the road, rounded shoulders and shambling feet suggesting a resigned sulkiness.

"Low beast," he thought. "A pity we have lost the whipping post and the stocks."

He went on up the road into the beech shadows, while Suvla passed down it, his heart full of laughter and of exultation.

3

Suvla entered the Green Man and asked for half a pint of "bitter." Mr. Higgs was still the lessee of the Green Man, the same round-headed Higgs with the depressed nose and the staring blue eyes, but to Suvla it seemed that he showed more waistcoat.

Higgs stared hard at him, and Suvla put down a shilling.

"Any jobs goin' round 'ere, guvner?"

"Want a job?"

"I'm asking you."

"Nothing in your style—I think."

Mr. Higgs had known Suvla for ten years, but there was no flicker of recognition in his eyes. All that Suvla saw there was frank surprise, the alertness of a man who had no reason to think too well of the world, and who had no intention of doing so. Mr. Higgs was a man of property and a good Tory, and he believed in the beneficence of beer.

Suvla John

He gave the tramp his drink and his change, and, moving to the end of the bar, resumed his share in a conversation that was being held in the Green Man's second sanctum. Suvla sat down on a form. He could see two pairs of legs protruding from behind the half-closed door of the inner bar, also the old open fire-place, the brass candlesticks on the shelf, and the end of an oak settle. Higgs had accustomed himself to doubling his personality; a part of him kept watch on Suvla, while the main part of him supervised the Green Man's gossip.

Suvla put his glass on the bench, lit a pipe, and pulled out his newspaper. Ulysses had not been recognized, and he sat and listened to the words of the men of Ithaca. They were speaking of Richard Shere and of Hengest's Farm.

"What I says is—why didn't he give 'em the land? He's got plenty."

"He's rented it to 'em pretty easy."

"Rent! Rent's rank robbery."

This was too much for Mr. Higgs, who always tried to be impartial.

"I don't follow you. That's Bolshie talk, sir."

"What if it is?" said the truculent person. "Landlords! There won't be any landlords in ten years' time."

The discussion grew noisy. Half a dozen men were talking at once, while Higgs frowned and rattled the money in his pocket. It appeared that the truculent person was a haulage contractor, and owned a small motor-bus and two lorries, and someone was asking him in a playful voice to explain the difference between the ownership of land and the ownership of lorries.

"All the difference in the world—you fool."

"Now then, gentlemen."

"I worked for my lorries. I didn't inherit land pinched from a lot of poor people. What price the enclosures?"

"Hold on. You called me a fool."

Mr. Higgs loomed over them.

"Gentlemen—this isn't the House of Commons. No quarrelling here—please."

"Righto, Mr. Higgs. But if Mr. Bloomer—here—will lend one of his lorries—same as Dick Shere has lent Hengest's."

"Stuff! I'm a working man."

Suvla John

"There be something in a gentleman's ways. I'd rather work for a gentleman—than some jumped-up cove."

"Bloomer hadn't any damned lorries before the war."

"That's right. Say I'm a profiteer."

"You called me a fool."

"Some people think like fools."

An old fellow stood up, bent down, and knocked his pipe out against one of the iron fire-dogs.

"What, going, dad?"

"I've got me pertaters to earth up. Pertaters don't take no account of politics."

There was a laugh, and Mr. Higgs used the laughter to spread an atmosphere of peace.

"That's real English sense. What sort are you growing, dad?"

"One of the new wart-proof warieties. Master Shere gave me the seed."

The man who had been called a fool turned upon the haulage contractor.

"Did you hear that, you—Bloomer? I'll have a can of free petrol, please, for my motor-bike."

Suvla did not hear the haulage contractor's reply, for he was out in the road, waiting beside a green and red lorry. When Mr. Bloomer came out he asked for a lift into Dorking.

"I'm not going to Dorking," said the lorry owner truculently: "and you can go to hell."

VII

I

MR. BLOSSOM left his hat and stick on the refectory table in the hall.

"If you will tell Mrs. Shere that I am in no hurry."

The maid smiled at Mr. Blossom, and opened the door of the library with "I'll tell Mrs. Shere, sir." Like the rest of the Feldhurst world she smiled at and with Mr. Blossom, for he was a person who invited smiles, more especially so since the war. He had a sandy coloured head, with a shiny bald patch over the occiput, a round pink face, and a Cyrano's nose. He wore gold glasses. His Christian name was Gregory. But the maid had smiled because of the nickname that had followed him back to Feldhurst, brought thither by some irresponsible child who had served in the R.A.F. The Rev. Mr. Blossom had gone out to the war. A rather priggish old maid of a man, he had found himself attached to the Air Force, dumped down among a crowd of wild youngsters who feared neither God nor Devil. His nose had been a banner to a fanfare. Instantly, they had christened him Grog Blossom, this most abstemious of men, and the name remained with him for ever. But the war and the flying boys and the brave, rollicking anguish of it all had worked a transformation in Mr. Blossom, and he had returned to Feldhurst with renewed youth. He danced; in fact, he had instituted winter dances at the church hall. He hit a harder ball at cricket. He had lost his pulpit voice. Even his choir boys called him "Old Grog Blossom," but they were words of affection, and if Feldhurst smiled at its parson, its smile was human and possessive. Mr. Blossom was a character; he belonged to them; they would not have changed him for anyone else.

When Sybil Shere came into the room she found Blossom with a book in his hand, one knee on the red cushion of the window seat. He pivoted and gave her a smile.

and a little bend of the body, for his ecclesiasticism had grown gallant.

"I am afraid you must think me a terrible nuisance——"

She was gravely smiling.

"Surely not."

"Coming at this hour. But I wanted to catch your husband."

She sat down in one of the Sheraton chairs, and Mr. Blossom took the window seat.

"Richard has gone up to Hengest's. He may be back at any moment. If you are busy—perhaps I can give him a message?"

Mr. Blossom was not busy, and he had a curious piece of news to impart.

"I'm in no hurry. But perhaps I am keeping you. The fact is——"

She shook her head.

"Something about the flower show?"

"No; nothing to do with the flower show. In fact—it is rather strange—and—rather sacrilegious."

"Oh?"

He was mysterious, and she could see that he was engaging the mystery. He produced a pocket-book, and laid it on his knee.

"The fact is—I went down to the church this morning. I took the key. I happened to go to the Shere pew, and I noticed something on the wall."

"On the wall?"

"Yes; just above the memorial brass to John Shere. Someone had stood on a cushion and used a pencil."

"Very extraordinary."

"Yes; I copied it down. Of course, it will have to be washed out. It was like this."

He opened the note-book at the place where he had inserted a slip of paper, and, rising, passed the book to her. She saw the cross with the question mark above it, and printed in capital letters: "Birdcage Walk—midnight. For what?"

Her face was both grave and puzzled.

"How extraordinary!"

Mr. Blossom removed his glasses and wiped them with his handkerchief.

"Very. There is more than a suggestion of blasphemy. You observe the cross and the question mark."

Suvla John

Sybil Shere was not concerned with the possible blasphemy.

"That was the name of the trench where he was killed."

"Birdcage Walk?"

"Yes; Mr. Blaber told us. I think it is a detail that is known only to ourselves and to the Blabers."

She stared over the note-book at a point on the Turkey carpet, and her eyes suggested a sudden inward reticence.

"Most queer. The church was locked."

"Yes; Newdigate had been scything grass all the day before, and Banks had not been into the church. I have questioned both of them. What is more, I was the last person in it, and, curiously enough, I looked at the brass—I sometimes say a short prayer there—and I'll swear there was nothing on the wall then."

"Either someone broke in, or——"

"I could find no sign of that. Nothing had been disturbed. There are only three keys."

"Yes, ours and the rectory key——"

"And Banks'. By the way—there was another key."

"Oh?"

"Banks lost a key a year or two ago. It may have been stolen, or found by someone. But even then——"

They looked at each other questioningly.

"Who is there—with a motive——?"

"Just so. Where is the motive? Your brother-in-law was very popular. Besides—that—suggests no malice."

"No—but rather—a cynical challenge—to fate. Oh, here's Dick."

Richard Shere came into the library with a frosty brightness in his blue eyes, a sure sign to Sybil that something had annoyed him. His temper was sanguine, like his nature, but so rarely did he lose it that few people ever discovered its existence. He glanced at his wife and at Blossom, and wondered what the mystery was.

"Dick, Mr. Blossom has come up to show us a queer thing he has found in the church."

She handed him the note-book, and glanced at the parson, who took up the tale. Shere, with that same angry brightness of the eyes, sat on the edge of the table and listened. Blossom's recapitulation explained the cross and the question mark and the words printed below them.

"There seems no motive."

Suvla John

Shere stared at the note-book, and then looked at his wife.

"No; nothing occurs to me. I should like to see this—in the original."

"Of course," said Mr. Blossom; "and then I thought I would rub it out myself. I have kept the church locked."

"Good."

They went down together, and Shere came back half an hour late for lunch, nor did he or his wife speak of the matter until the children had gone and they were alone. Shere, still trailing a preoccupied look about with him, got up and lit a pipe. Sybil waited; she knew her man.

"We scraped it out, Celli, or rather—old Blossom did. I wanted to look around by myself."

"Did you find anything?" her eyes asked him.

"How—whoever it was—got in? And that's one of the queerest things about it. John got in once in that very same way; one of his kid's adventures."

"How?"

"By turning back the lead of one of the old casements and taking out a lozenge of glass to reach the catch. There were fresh marks. And it was the same window."

"Did you tell Blossom?"

"No."

He was standing, looking out into the garden, and the obvious deduction came to her, as it had come to him.

"Someone who knew?"

"Exactly. There were just three people who knew of that escapade. John—myself——"

"And Elsie."

He turned sharply upon her.

"Celli, how did you guess that?"

"Inference."

Their eyes acknowledged the same intuitive thought.

"It was Elsie?"

"I don't know."

"But that's what occurred to you."

"Yes, but why—that?"

Sybil's face looked very serious and strange.

"Women—Dick—especially when they are unhappy. We do queer things. I know she goes there."

He nodded.

"A sort of obsession. A bit morbid, a mood that asks

68

questions, and then reaches the stage when it must chalk them up. Sort of protest against the way things happen. Of course, Blaber——"

"Yes, the man is responsible. And what is one to do?"

"Nothing," he said, and added: "If it were Elsie, do you think—yourself——?"

She answered him with a quiet and tragic simplicity.

"Dick, if I had lost you, and been married to a man like Blaber, I might have come to that anguish of loneliness—emptiness—when a woman——"

"Poor Elsie," he said.

2

Sybil Shere was a woman of wise reticences. She did not ask Dick what it was that had angered him at Hengest's Farm, where Merrow and half a dozen other men were putting an experiment to the proof, for Sybil knew that anything that was worth telling would be told her.

And John Suvla could have told her.

He had been drawn to Hengest's to see what the Shere of the day was doing there, and very early that morning he had taken the lane to the farm, which lay back among oaks and ash trees about two hundred yards from the road. At five o'clock in the morning no self-respecting, twentieth-century labouring man should have been out of bed, but coming out of one of the field gates opening into the lane Suvla had met a shortish man who looked as broad as he was long—David Merrow himself, ex-cowman and ex-soldier.

Merrow had seen a tramp, and nothing more than a tramp.

"Hallo, mate, what are you doing here?"

Suvla had turned on his snuffling voice.

"Lookin' for a job, chum."

Merrow had a shrewd eye and a sense of humour.

"At five o'clock in the morning—what? It won't wash, mate."

He had laughed, for the tramp needed a wash.

"You ain't got a job? I'm an ex-sojer, I am, and a bloke told me 'ow this was a farm for ex-sojers."

"So it is. But it's not like the army, where three men

out of ten did the work and t'other seven loafed. We're picked men."

"Thought you was socialists, Bolshies."

"And what's that?"

"You orter know, chum, downin' the idle rich."

"I know all about that. Me and my mates wanted our own show, and we've got it. It's no ca-canny stunt on this farm."

"Bought it?"

"We hope to, some day."

But Merrow had had other things to do, and he had given Suvla to understand that Hengest's Farm was not the heaven dreamed of by people with prehensile souls, so Suvla had turned about and retreated down the lane. Flanking the gate was a little coppice half open to the road, and Suvla had entered it and stretched himself in the hazel shade.

It appeared that Merrow and his brave men were developing a sense of property! They cherished their chickens.

Suvla went to sleep.

He woke some time during the morning to hear two horses coming down the road. The men who rode the horses were talking. They pulled up by the gate at the end of the farm road, and Suvla could hear all that was said.

"You are making a mistake, Shere, creating a bad precedent."

"I disagree. The precedent is a good one."

"Is it? Encouraging these chaps to think that they have some sort of moral right to your land? You are suffering from post-war sensibility. It's all very dangerous."

"I think you are rather prejudiced, Blaber. Isn't that so?"

"I respect my own property. You don't. Do you think your brother——"

But here Shere's voice had gathered heat.

"Look here, Blaber, I'll tell you how it happened. A year ago Merrow came to me; he's a good chap, the sort of chap one gets fond of. He said to me: 'We've come back different, sir. There are some of us who feel we want a bit of the land—our chance. I don't say that we might not make a mess of our show, but what we fellows do hanker after—is—our—chance. Do you think you could

Suvla John

help us, sir?' Well, look here, Blaber, I knew in my heart that David was right. A good man has his right to his chance. Why, damn it, how could I sit here—with all I've got—after that bloody war—and do nothing? I came back, but poor old John was killed. And he would have said to Merrow what I said, or what I felt I had to say. And I wanted to say it. 'You are quite right, David. I'll help you all I can.'"

Suvla could imagine the other man's sneer.

"That's nothing more than sob-stuff."

And that was how the white light had come into Shere's eyes.

"Sob-stuff be damned! You haven't the tradition, Blaber."

"Yes, landlords have always been altruists!"

"Some of them have been abominably selfish, others haven't. But that doesn't justify one in behaving like a cad."

VIII

I

JOHN SUVLA lay all day in the high beech woods above the manor.

Through a woodland window he could see Feldhurst house set in its green valley, and never had he loved it so well.

A change had come over him, and he no longer scoffed at the mystery of it or tried to thrust it off, for the sudden softness of his mood was England, an England such as this. Here life had a dignity, a goodness; there was something changeless about it, a beauty that still held in spite of machinery and the Sabbath swarm from all suburbia, the road hogging, the orange peel, and littered dirt. Airmen could fly over Shere Park, but as yet no motorist could drive through it.

Suvla thanked God for it. He loved the roads as the wanderer loves them. And these hustling, hooting, dust-raising swine! Progress! He knew it was inevitable, just as the war had been inevitable, a vast stupidity shot through with moments of splendour. Even the Sahara had been conquered! The camel would go the way of the horse.

Yet life had dignity. The peasant and the gentleman were conscious of this dignity; the commercialist was not. And it was with a kind of fierce tenderness that Suvla looked down on Feldhurst, and brooded over the tradition of it, this most English house in an English valley. There was nothing quite like it anywhere else in the world, nor was there any other man quite like the man who owned it. How un-American Dick was!

He rode his horse; he did not talk emotional slush to you, and then do his best to pick your pocket. He had a clean blue eye, not those glassy, bastard, surreptitious eyes.

A man to be loved.

Suvla lay there and smiled. He did not grudge Dick

72

Suvla John

Feldhurst Manor. On the contrary, he gave it to him with all his heart, knowing that it was part of the soul of Richard Shere, and that no man could fit it better. A tradition lived, and went about in old country clothes among country men, understanding their ways, aware of their troubles, keeping a wise and human dignity, kind but proud. Such men mattered. They would matter when all the demagogues were dead.

Yet, to Suvla the man, the mood of the hour held infinite and deep yearnings.

He could go away; he knew now that he would have to go away; the seemingly dead had no right to meddle with the living. Life painted its own picture; your interfering egoist splodging with a brush was the most damnable of fools. Life had painted the portrait of Richard Shere, and of Robert Blaber and of Robert Blaber's wife. There was inevitableness about it all; you might watch and wonder, you might allow yourself to prophesy, but—if you had a sense of humour and of pathos—you refrained from posing as Jehovah. Poor Elsie! In a way he felt himself responsible for her unhappiness, but what a tangle of responsibility would be his were he to be cruelly soft hearted.

Yet, towards Richard Shere he did feel soft hearted. He would have given much for half an hour with his brother; had Dick been other than he was, Suvla might have dared it. He remembered Dick's sensitiveness, and it was this very sensitiveness that put a barrier between them. He had come back as a ghost, to wander for a few hours, to see without being seen, and that was the end of it.

As he made his way back through the woods to Hackbury he thought of that Turkish hospital, and of the little German doctor, cropheaded and bespectacled, bending over him and displaying a bullet. The little German had been puzzled by the bullet. "It ees not a rifle bullet!" Later, they had worried him about his name, for the silver identity disc he had worn chained to his wrist had been appropriated by a stretcher-bearer. How easily he had given a false name. In a flash he had foreseen the possible grim jest. He had seen just that, and nothing else. It had all grown out of that one ironical impulse. One foresaw so few of the great game's twists and chances. But looking back upon it now he realized that he had said good-bye to his brother when he had given that false name, and had carried the imposture through until it had ceased to be an imposture, and had become a reality. John Suvla was the reality.

2

But when the sun had set, and the dusk began to cling to the Hackbury firs, Suvla grew restless beside his fire. For one hour he wanted to be near his brother, seeing but unseen, and to feel himself a ghostly part of the life down yonder. The desire was so strong in him that he climbed out of his hollow and went down over Hackbury and into the valley. He knew what he meant to do, and coming to the field gate above the decoy pond he climbed it and made his way across the meadow and into the park.

The old house piled itself in the dusk, and the cedars merged themselves into the darkness, and as Suvla stood there under an oak the "eye" of the house flashed out. It seemed to say to him: "Ha, you are there; I see you!" The turret clock struck the half-hour, and its notes seemed to fall from the branches of the cedars. A few stars shone. An owl hooted. And the smell of the place was in Suvla's nostrils, the perfumes of many memories.

The darkness was in his favour, and he made his way across the dry moat and up into the garden. Before him he saw the great lawn and the dim masses of the cedars. A bank of rhododendrons edged the sweep of grass, sheltering a stone seat, and Suvla, on his hands and knees, crawled in among the rhododendrons and lay hidden.

He had been there less than half a minute when he heard a woman's voice quite close to him.

"Dick!"

A voice echoed hers:

"Hallo! Where are you?"

"Here, on the stone seat."

"I'll bring a rug."

The moon was coming up, and a vague silveriness spread across the lawn towards the house. Suvla had a partial view of it through the foliage, and he saw Richard Shere appear at one of the long windows and cross the grass. Suvla's heart yearned towards him.

"What a night! Here, sit on this, Celli."

Suvla John

"You careful old thing."

"Of course. I have just been tickling John in bed. It always makes me think of the way old John used to tickle me."

Their voices were happy, the voices of two who were well mated and hide no secrets from each other. Suvla could smell Dick's pipe.

"We are rather lucky beggars, Celli."

"I think so."

"Partly—you know—because we want the same things." Her silence breathed the thought that she would always want the things that he did.

"It makes me feel strange when I think that Elsie might have been mistress here."

"Poor Elsie! Well, I suppose we should have had one of the farms. Not a bad life. Jack was a generous old beggar."

"I wish I had known him."

"So do I. To think that Blaber came back—and Jack was left out there! I had a row with Blaber this morning."

"O? Tell me."

"About Hengest's, and David Merrow. I'm afraid I lost my wig."

"Was it necessary, old thing, with Bob Blaber?"

"No, not really. But there are times when his hide bound superciliousness—— He's such a superior person."

"Dick—don't you know?"

"What?"

"Why he is so annoyed about Hengest's?"

"He wanted it."

"No. He was annoyed because the men came to you and not to him. He would have liked to have run that show, to have had the credit."

"You think so?"

"Quite sure. Blaber is like that."

There was a short silence, and the light of the moon lay more brightly upon the grass.

"I'm sorry I was short with him. I always feel that it reacts on Elsie."

"It does."

"He's a mean beast."

"He is made that way. I suppose he can't help it. So many things over which we have no control go to the making of us. He had that horrible old grandfather who

75

Suvla John

built a chapel, and made his money working wretched little kids to death. Then—there was the father."

"I preferred old Blaber to Bob."

"Less highly ornamented?"

"He was a boastful, vulgar old swashbuckler, but you knew where you were with him. He was quite frank in his attitude to us. We were to be slowly but surely effaced."

"And Bob was to do the effacing?"

"Bob and Bob's children. And there you are! That's how life has a man. Both of them wanted children."

"I wish Elsie had children."

Shere was smiling at her.

"Do you remember, Celli, that day on the river, just before I went out to France? You gave me a fright. Such a solemn young woman!"

"Life was rather serious then."

"And you told me your idea of hell was being a school-mistress, and that you loathed children."

"So I do. Half of them ought never to have been born."

"Which means that you loathe those who ought never to have been born."

"I think I loathe their parents—more. There is always something horrible about children who were not meant."

"Poor little devils!"

"Yes, my lad; and two or three generations of your poor little devils may bury Feldhurst under mountains of orange peel and beer bottles."

Shere laughed, but his laughter was not all clear moonlight. Sybil had a shrewder head than he had, and like many modern women she was mercilessly logical and quite fearless. She had dropped the sentimental pretendings; she loved what she loved, and she hated what she hated.

"I'm not an altruist—in that way. You can't sweeten people by feeding them on treacle. A good dose of brimstone is necessary."

"You incorruptible little autocrat," he laughed—and pulled her up. "What about some music? Half your hatred of the poor, raw blunderers——"

"Don't forget the rug."

"You hate the discords, the poor blatant—silly voices. Debussy's the magician!"

76

Suvla John

"I think it's arrogance I hate, Dick. I'm not arrogant."

"I know what you mean. Ignorance is arrogant, and sensitive people shrink. For instance—there's old Mostyn, the author chap. He won't go out of his garden on Sundays. Says the Lord's Day should be called the 'Lout's Day.' Come along."

Suvla saw them drift across the lawn together in the moonlight, and past the cedars to the house. He had said "Yea" to Dick's mate; she was made for him, for always the Feldhurst women had been a little longer sighted and shrewder than the men. They had seen things coming, and had fought them off, or forestalled them. They were honest with themselves, and had never pretended that they loved the other cat's kittens as well as they loved their own. The type appealed to Suvla. Richenda Lee belonged to it, a young woman who was not ashamed of a little fierce, human and wholesome egotism, and was proud of her claws.

They had entered the house, and Suvla followed them a little way across the grass, and lay down where the branches of a cedar brushed the turf. The window of the drawing-room, on the side towards the lawn, filled with soft light, and presently the sound of music came to him, a piece of Debussy's, impersonal, plaintive, mysterious. Sybil had an understanding of such music, and a most delicate touch; and as Suvla listened, a great peace seemed to come to him, for the music was not of the world or the flesh. It excluded all hate and strife and passion, and all the little earthly frettings, yet it spoke to this wild man of the things he knew. It was moonlight upon forests, and the singing of birds in the grey of the dawn. He felt that life was good here where such music was made, unlike the life in that other house of hatred and disillusionment. And Suvla was uplifted above the fierceness of his own scorn, and beyond the recoil of mere retaliation.

3

The spirit of Sybil's music was still with him when he made his way into the garden of that other house, and, keeping in the shadow of a hedge, considered Wynyats and all that Wynyats stood for.

Suvla John

Rollo Maunder's house spread its mock antiquity in the moonlight. It is possible that Rollo Maunder had had little joy in the creating of it; for from the beginning it had been a bastard house, the product of one man's skill and of another man's ignorant vanity. It had grown up in an atmosphere of contention. Maunder's art had squabbled with old Blaber's moneyed arrogance. Their quarrels had been a source of secret joy to the workmen, red-headed Maunder striding about like an enraged grandee, with old Blaber prodding him in broad Lancashire. Once, Maunder had thrown up the job—old Blaber had insisted on having the cupola of the clock turret painted a bright yellow, but Maunder had carried on upon a compromise. The cupola had been gilded.

Yet, even Rollo Maunder had been unable to save Wynyats from being a flagrant monstrosity. Old Blaber had been for ever foisting some new whim upon the original plan; he had wanted Flemish gables, high octagonal chimneys, Georgian windows, a double flight of steps to a Gothic porch. He had asked for a Moorish gallery and an organ. He had proposed to plant statues in the garden, impossible figures in quite impossible places. There had been a Venus, a shyly immodest Venus, and an Apollo brandishing a blue tin flag.

Rollo Maunder had been viciously ashamed of the whole business. He had known that half the country had been laughing at his rough and tumble with old Blaber, a scrimmage in æsthetics between a very vain man and a very vulgar one.

Wynyats was less vulgar now; Robert Blaber had seen to that. Some of the atrocities had been torn down, and the statuary banished, but in ceasing to be foolishly vulgar Wynyats had become supercilious and affected. It was a very new gentleman in new old clothes, and as Suvla stood and looked at it he smiled as a man smiles at a foolish cad.

It was a cad's house.

It raised the problem of caddishness in a particular form, a problem that was complicated by the fact that the cad had a wife.

Poor Elsie !

She had to suffer a man's spitefulness, to listen to his disgruntled sneerings; and Suvla, pondering her case, fell back upon some of the brutal truths he had discovered in the trenches. You handled men differently; you looked

Suvla John

straight into the eyes of the good man and smiled; you laid an affectionate hand on the shoulder of his courage. But you had to frighten the bad man, and by badness Suvla understood that which was mean. Mean caution, mean self-carefulness, mean shirking, the yellow grin of the mean egoist who would fool you if he could. In bloody and terrifying moments you may have had to show such a man the snout of your revolver. That had been mere justice, in fairness to the good.

Blaber was a coward, and there had been occasions when he had behaved like a mean coward. All men feel fear, but fear does not make all men mean. And it occurred to John Suvla that a dose of fear might so work upon Robert Blaber that he would shiver himself into a mood of humility. Well scared, he might grow a little kinder to his wife, because he might need the company of her kindness. He would want to come and warm himself at the fire of her humanity.

Wynyats showed Suvla two groups of lighted windows, two on the ground floor, and three on the floor above. The lower windows belonged to the billiard room, and in the stillness of the night Suvla could hear the click of the balls. He drew the little leather bag from under his shirt, and extracting something from it went slowly across the grass, avoiding the stop-netting and the iron standards of the tennis-court. Between the grass and the loggia ran a gravel path, and Suvla took off his boots here, and, carrying them, went forward in his socks.

The blind of the right-handed window did not reach the sill, leaving a gap as on that previous night when Suvla had watched Blaber and Gutteridge at their game. The window was open, and Suvla knelt down on the flag-stones. To-night Blaber was alone, moving from place to place about the table as he made his shots. Sometimes Suvla saw him in profile, at other times he saw his round face; but whenever Blaber's face was towards the window Suvla lowered his head.

Blaber was playing for a cannon from the top end of the table, when, following the sharp kissing of the balls, he heard something strike the polished floor. He turned sharply, and stood staring at the window, fancying that he had seen a slight movement of the blind. Cue in hand, he walked forward and raised the blind. There was no one there, nothing but the loggia pillars and the moon-lit garden beyond; nor could he hear any sound.

Suvla John

He dropped the blind, and in stepping back trod on some hard object that rolled under his foot. Bending down, he picked it up and let it lie in the palm of his hand.

It was a bullet belonging to the type of cartridge that had been used in a service revolver during the great war.

4

On Hackbury Suvla lay in his hollow, looking at the stars.

"One more day," he said to himself, "and then—the open road."

He turned on his right side and fell asleep, but at Wynyats Robert Blaber lay awake through most of the night.

IX

I

ELSIE looked out of the window at a sky that was grey. The weather had changed in the night, and this still, grey sky showed purple in the dim south-west. Hardly a leaf moved. The green of the grass and the trees was heavy and intense, and the very stillness listened for the rain. It would come, but not yet; some hours hence there would be a few pattering drops upon the leaves, and then a sudden downrush, heavy and straight. Feldhurst would be a little world of green and dripping trees, sad with an infinite and strange sadness to those who looked out of lonely windows.

The scents of the morning were subtly sweet. They spent themselves before the moist chill of the coming rain, and she responded to the languor of them as she pinned up her hair before the glass. Perfumes were part of the past; she had no hope of the day or of the morrow.

The breakfast gong sounded, and she became a creature of trepidation. Her husband never talked at breakfast, but he expected her to be punctual, sitting behind the tray and ready to pour out his tea. She was afraid of him, and the days when he looked up at her coldly over his paper or his letters were bad days, clouded and stormy. His irritability created such a restless and magnetic atmosphere, and poor, soft-skinned sentimentalist that she was, she had never grown acclimatized to all his frightening moodinesses.

Her hands became flustered. She hurried into a rose-coloured jumper, because rose was a cheerful colour, and Robert was supposed to like it. She forgot her rings, and left them lying on the dressing-table.

"I'm so sorry, Robert."

She came in with a stage smile, closing the door very gently. Blaber was at his place, with the paper propped against a bowl of roses, and she saw that he had poured out his own tea. He glanced up at her over the paper,

81

and it seemed to be that there was something strange
about his eyes. She was not an observant woman, and,
like a child, she reacted to mere surface impressions,
and the impressions she got of her husband was of a man
who was ill.

"I'm afraid it's going to rain. Oh, you have your
tea."

"Yes."

He lowered his eyes and resumed both his reading and
eating, while she sat down and dropped sugar into her
cup, and wondered what it was about his eyes that had
so startled her. Sick eyes. Yes, she could remember
him looking at her like that when he had been laid up
with appendicitis; he had been worried about himself.

She glanced across at him, and found him doing the
very same thing to her. Their glances fell away almost
guiltily.

He was eating like a man who had a train to catch.

"You have forgotten your rings."

He had noticed it, but he kept his eyes on the paper.
She gave a start, and spilled tea into her saucer.

"So I have. I was late. I'll ring for Parker——"

"Better get them yourself. It's silly to leave rings
about."

"Yes."

She rose with quick agitation and went to the door.
She had her hand on the handle.

"You're not ill, Bob?"

His face startled her. It seemed to grow more thin
and harsh. He looked suspicious.

"Ill! Do I look it?"

"I thought——"

"You mean you imagined. If you want to know—
that damned soup last night——"

"I'm so sorry."

"There must have been something in it."

"Something in it?"

"Yes, some filth. I wish you would tell that confounded cook——"

She trembled to appease.

"It had a rather queer taste. I remember. I'm so
sorry. I'll speak to Sarah."

"Do."

She went up and recovered her rings, and thrust
jerking fingers into them. When she returned, her

Suvla John

husband's napkin lay on the table, and he was standing by the west window, tapping a cigarette against his silver case. She noticed that he had left his tea unfinished. The feeling of tension in the room seemed to have increased, and like a flustered bird she blundered against the bars.

"Robert, what would you like? I mean—about lunch?"

"Oh, just anything. It doesn't matter."

"But you ought to——"

"Oh, don't fuss."

Her expressive face whimpered.

"I'm sorry. I didn't mean——"

She began to eat hurriedly. Buttered eggs and toast, and the buttered eggs were cold and flat. And it was going to rain, and Sarah had given Robert dyspepsia, and the roses were withering in the rose-bowl, and she had nothing to do.

"It is going to rain like hell."

He capped the prophecy with a little curt laugh.

"And the co-operative gentlemen have half their hay down."

She winced, though his malicious gloating might be nothing but congealed bile.

"Yes; they ought to have known."

"Farming by a committee of socialists!"

He lit his cigarette.

"I hope it soaks. Serve the fools right. I shall be able to chip Dick Shere. I think I'll ride over and see Gutteridge. He wants my advice about his trees."

"Yes," she said, saying the wrong thing—and realizing it when it had been said; "it will do you good."

He gave her an enigmatic look and walked out of the room.

2

Elsie finished her breakfast, and when she had finished it she idled to one of the windows with the feeling that she had nothing to do for the rest of the day. She was not responsible for anything, and she had begun to drift towards that emotional state when a woman is not

Suvla John

responsible for herself. Wynyats was full of servants, highly capable servants; and in the garden Tombs, the head gardener, exercised an autocratic authority, even supervising the cutting of the flowers. There were times when she had a bewildered realization of the fact that she did not belong to Wynyats, though she ate and slept in it, and was supposed to be its mistress. She was mistress of nothing, least of all her own clinging, sentimental soul. She was afraid of people, the servants, Tombs, Hulk, the chauffeur, and particularly of her husband. She breathed an alien air, she who had been brought up by a sentimental old man, and been fed upon novels of the rosebud school.

She stood at the window and looked towards Hengest's Farm. It suggested the Sheres and Feldhurst Manor, and the insidious dream—a day-dream—that was beginning to dominate her waking life. Things were so different down at the Manor; it was a happy house, and the people in it were always happily busy. There were the children. And Sybil had so much to do. You always found her hard at work in the garden or the house, and yet her grave, grey-black eyes had time to look at you kindly and to smile. Of course, she and Dick were such lovers——

Yes, life was all wrong. Her dream was of the life that might have been hers if John Shere had not been killed, and he had come back to give her children in the old house down yonder. If only he had given her a child, even though they had not been married! Yes, she had grown so bold in her dreaming as to dream herself beyond her gentle conventions. Then, she had married Robert Blaber. She had felt that she was echoing John's last words: "Look after Elsie." Her marriage had been a sentimental tribute to John; she had become a wife in order to feel like a widow.

Perilous pilgrimage! With Elsie Blaber it had ended in her being all widow and no wife. The cult of a dead memory had grown upon her till it had become a romantic obsession. She had read everything that was to be read on the Dardanelles campaign; the books were there in her sitting-room, though she kept them locked in a cupboard. In her bureau she treasured a few relics, for a part of John Shere's kit had been sent home, and from Sybil she had begged a few personal trifles, a pipe, a knife, two worn khaki handkerchiefs. These trifles, with the

Suvla John

letters that John Shere had written to her, she kept locked in a cash-box, the key of which she hid. Her obsession had grown careful and secret. It hid a tragic illusion in its bosom. Only when she was sure of being alone would she bring out John Shere's two photographs, the one of him in khaki, and the other that had been taken a month after they had become engaged. She would sit and stare at them with the brown melancholy of her velvet eyes; and sometimes she would weep a little and dry her tears with one of the dead man's handkerchiefs.

All this she hid from Robert Blaber with a frightened, sexual fierceness, though there was something maternal in it, as though the memory were her child.

On this grey morning with the west blue with the coming rain, she waited until she had seen her husband pass down the drive on his horse, sitting hunched in the saddle with his moody eyes looking towards Hengest's Farm. Then she went to her sitting-room with its window overlooking the Feldhurst Woods, and, locking the door, sat down at her bureau. She opened it, drew out the carefully secreted key, and, taking the cash-box from a drawer, laid it before her under her soft and ineffectual hands.

Someone knocked at the door while Elsie was in the act of unfolding one of John Shere's letters. She put the letter away, and closed the flap of the bureau.

"Yes—who is it?"

The person had tried the door and found it locked.

"A note from Mrs. Shere, madam."

Elsie unlocked the door and made a feeble jest of it.

"Thank you, Parker. How silly of me. I don't know what made me lock the door."

"The boy says there is an answer, madam."

"I'll see. Oh, yes. Mrs. Shere says a verbal message will do. Will you tell the boy to say that I will be there at four o'clock."

"Four o'clock, madam?"

"Yes."

Elsie returned to her bureau and reopened it, but the interruption had dispelled the atmosphere of her day-dream. The Sheres were having tennis, if the rain held off, and they wanted Elsie to make a fourth, though her tennis was vague and haphazard. John Shere had used to tease her about her tennis: "Now, then, Elsie, forget about that blackbird," for on a court she had a way of standing with a detached air as though she were listening for the note of a bird.

She decided to go for a walk. There was that sick woman down at Barley Mill, a thatcher's wife, rather a nice person upon whom kindness appeared to make a deep impression. So Elsie locked her bureau, went up and put on a Burberry hat and a light raincoat, and came downstairs calling to Tom the Airedale. Tom was a dog of moods, a surly and independent animal who paid court to no one, and did things in his own good time. Elsie had to ring for him.

"Have you seen Tom anywhere, Parker?"

"He's in the kitchen, madam."

Tom was produced. He gave Elsie a look from his barley-sugar eyes and a condescending twitch of the tail. If the woman wanted to take him for a walk—well, he supposed that she would have to be humoured.

Half-way down Panhurst Hill and in the thick of the hazel coppices the dog, who had been loping along at Elsie's side, stopped dead and stood sniffing the air. His hair rose; he began to growl.

"What is it, old man?"

The dog ignored her. With eyes fixed and nostrils twitching he went step by step towards the low grass bank and the hazel shade on the right-hand side of the road. He paused there, growling.

Elsie walked on. Whatever the hazel shade hid from her, she did not wish to discover it, nor were the dog's growls reassuring. She called to him as she hurried down the hill, glancing back over her shoulder.

"Tom, Tom, heel, boy!"

The dog was standing rigid and motionless, staring into the wood. He had ceased to growl, and suddenly he swung away and came loping after her, though her calling of him had had nothing to do with his retreat. She noticed that he kept looking back, that he drew rather closer to her than usual.

"What is it, old man?"

He gave her a momentary and surly stare as though he had cause to feel ashamed, and had no use for a fool woman who asked a fellow embarrassing questions.

"Something frightened you, Tom."

The dog was a particularly fearless beast, and Elsie decided that she would not go back by way of Panhurst Hill, but would take the park road up to the Green.

Suvla John

Gutteridge had called his new house "Fiesole."
That is to say he had accepted Clara Gutteridge's suggestion that it should be called by that Italian name,
for whenever Clara Gutteridge stood upon her little short
fat legs it was evident that her petticoats were mere
camouflage, and that underneath them she wore the
trousers.

It was she who took Robert Blaber over the new
estate, though George Gutteridge accompanied them,
stroking his blonde moustache and receding chin, polite,
and slightly apologetic. His wife apologized for nothing.
In spite of her brevity and her stoutness she wore a
white skirt chequered with black lines, and a white coat
embroidered with large blue and purple flowers. The
coat had come from Algiers. It suggested sunlight, and
above it Clara Gutteridge's swarthy, broad-nosed face
radiated energy. She had little, bright, dark, beadlike
eyes, and a powdering of black hair on her upper lip.
Certain types of men found her extraordinarily attractive,
perhaps because of her broad nose and lips, and her
air of devilish blitheness.

Blaber was attracted by her. He liked her hardness,
her vigour. She was such a contrast to his wife. Moreover, Clara Gutteridge knew the male; she was the most
expert of horsewomen. She flattered the creature, poured
out his whisky for him, and saw that the whisky equalled
the soda; she treated men as a world-wise and thoroughly
cynical barmaid treats them, but she made sure they
paid.

"Fiesole," Italianesque upon a Surrey hillside, and
looking like a block of chalk under its new red pantiles,
with blue shutters, window frames and doors, advertised
the modern spirit. It was a "poster" house. It had all
the glare, the falseness, the over-coloured artificiality of
the hoarding, of the picture postcard that takes an English
landscape and washes it over with arsenic green and
sparrow's egg blue. It appealed to semi-barbarous people
with raw appetites, who liked their motor-cars painted a
canary yellow or cerise. It shouted : "I'm here; look at
me. Mr. Balls, the famous architect, built me. I belong
to Mr. George Gutteridge. I'm some house—what!" It
was a child of the new England. You had not to hunt it

Suvla John

out in some green and white setting; it accosted you like
a chalk-faced harlot! And yet its blatancy was better
than the genteel affectedness of the Edwardians, their
niminy-piminy, paste-board villas, all barge-board, and
spots of plaster and imitation oak, coloured glass, and
simpering tricksinesses.

It had beauty of a sort. Like Clara Gutteridge it
was a healthy, vigorous animal of a house, sensual,
splendid company for a week-end. After that—you might
notice the paint. And Blaber, the Oxfordian, Blaber knew
that it was all crude flesh, and yet in his present mood
it attractea him.

Mrs. Clara was indicating a row of cypresses planted
at the base of the stone-faced terrace.

"The things you grow in cemeteries—what d'you call
'em?"

"Cypresses."

"Balls said we ought to have 'em. Talked about
vertical lines of green breaking the yellow and white
horizontal, whatever that means."

"They have them in Italy."

"What, the same sort of tree?"

"No. The Italian cypress won't grow here. Those
are Lawsons or Frasers."

George Gutteridge caressed moustache and chin with
a hollow hand.

"Tivoli, my dear. You remember Tivoli?"

"What—the Tivoli?"

"No, no; near Rome."

Blaber smiled his first smile of the morning.

"If you have been to the Italian Roof Garden——"

"O, that jazzy place! Rather! Yes, Balls said we
ought to have vines and that mauvy stuff."

"Wistaria. Glycine."

"Glycerine? Why not paraffine? Villa Paraffino,
Georgie, what!"

She roared. Their money came from paraffine.

Blaber liked her laughter, and the provocative crinkles
on her broad face. A woman who could laugh like
that——! Made you forget things, morbid things. She
was so furiously real, and as reassuring as bacon and eggs,
or a bed at the end of a long day's motor drive.

He laughed.

"Madame Sans Gêne."

"What's that?"

Suvla John

"Don't give me away, old man."

"Say, it's going to rain. What about going in and having a little 'wet'? You look a bit off colour, Bob."

"My cook."

"O Lord; aren't they terrors! We had a lady cook for a week, and then she chucked it. Most superior young person. We had a row, didn't we, Georgie?"

"We had," said Mr. Gutteridge politely.

"And what do you think she called this house?"

"What?"

"Jazz Villa! I told old Balls, and he looked down his nose at me."

"I expect he did."

"Anyway—I gave him a stiff drink. Best thing for a man who's peeved. And George gave him a cheque."

"He went away satisfied?"

"Giggling, and with eyes like a sheep."

A treasure of a woman! How could you worry about your sore soul when she laughed, and glittered her wicked little eyes at you, and floated along with that pleasant little shiver of the hips? Blaber felt reassured. He had spent half the night wondering how a revolver bullet had come to be dropped on his billiard-room floor, a bullet of the same sinister size as the one——! He had been scared. He had tried to fit every sort of explanation to the incident. No one else knew; no one else could know. And even supposing that he had talked in his sleep, that would have been two years ago so far as Elsie was concerned, for they had occupied separate rooms for the last two years. If his wife suspected anything, why had she waited for two years?

Unable to explain anything, he had put the bullet away, and set himself to regard the incident as one of those unexplainable things. But it had scared him. He had an emptiness within him, the same sort of dropping of his organs that he had felt under shell fire.

Clara Gutteridge was pouring him out a whisky. She looked at him over the top of the glass, and her broad nostrils and bright eyes belonged to the solid, comforting, material world.

"It will do you good; a nice stiff one."

The tips of her fingers touched his as she gave him the glass.

"Cheer-i-o."

Suvla John

He rode away from "Fiesole" feeling that he had attached an absurdly serious significance to a quite trivial incident.

4

Beyond Panhurst Old Forge the road dipped into a wood of beeches, old trees well spaced, and hiding the sky with solemn spread of their greenness. At the bottom of the hollow the Panhurst brook crossed the road, a little secret shimmer of brown water appearing out of the beech gloom and disappearing into it again. Here, the air was always moist and still, and the light diffused and dim.

Blaber had reached the place where the water drifted across the sandy road when a voice called to him somewhere out of the beech wood. It was a man's voice, deep and resonant.

"Only one more hour, Blaber. Cheer up, man. We shall get off safely. Cheer up."

Blaber stopped his horse in the middle of the water. He looked this way and that, but he could see nothing, nothing but the grey trunks of the beeches, the dark spread of the boughs, the blackish earth below, and the foliage above. In the dim light his face seemed to take on a greenish tinge. The silence was unbroken.

Again he heard the voice, that familiar, gaillard voice.

"Birdcage Walk at twelve o'clock on a December night. A wooden cross stuck up against the round moon. Suvla—Suvla Bay!"

The voice seemed to come from somewhere on the right of the road, and Blaber pulled his horse in that direction, and, spurring him, dashed in among the trees. He saw nothing but the trees. He wheeled his horse this way and that, making futile and desperate attacks upon the green and empty stillness of the wood.

He was sweating, and his scared horse trembled with his rider's fear. He turned back to the road and dismounted. The green silence lay so heavy that his heart cried out against it.

"Damn you, whoever it is, come out!"

From the distance a faint sound of laughter drifted to him through the trees.

90

X

I

IT began to rain when Suvla had been an hour upon the road, and he drew in under a hedge to pull his ground-sheet from the canvas bag and to loop it over his shoulders. He could see Hackbury and Panhurst through the haze of rain, and as he took leave of them before topping the rise that would hide them from sight he bethought himself of the first glimpse he had had of the hills from the mouth of the old chalk-pit. His eyes smiled, for in saying good-bye to these Surrey uplands he knew that they had put a spell upon him. For the moment they had tamed his wildness, and imposed upon him a mood of magnanimity. All that lay beyond them was a dream redreamed.

"Yes, we English are bad haters."

The rain came down on his ground-sheet and dripped from the brim of his hat, and it seemed to Suvla that the soft and kind eyes of this northern sky spoke of nothing but resignation. This climate was like an irresponsible and incalculable woman; it was useless to quarrel with it; you shrugged your shoulders and accepted this tyranny of tears. The smile of one day's sunlight fooled you, and you let yourself be fooled.

"For," said Suvla to himself, "life is like that. The whole thing is illusion. When we are practical and full of our affairs, we pretend that life is solid and real. We drink our beer and know it to be beer. But sometimes—most of us—see over the top of the beer mug, and become conscious of the illusion. We feel like disembodied children, ghosts. An uncomfortable feeling, shivery! We want to get in front of a fire and huddle close to other humans; but even then—we hear the wind in the chimney."

He smiled at the wet sky.

"Nothing matters and yet we pretend that it matters. We have to pretend. And it is good for the world that

Suvla John

it should forget that it is pretending. And yet—perhaps
—things do matter! No one knows."

His thoughts were with those people on the other side
of the streaming hills. It had seemed to him that his
brother had found life good and convincing. Could anything seem more beautifully real than the life in and
about Feldhurst Manor? And then poor dreaming Elsie,
lost in a dead illusion because of the destruction of a live
one! And Bob Blaber, hatchet-faced, voracious, biting
at life as he bit at his thin moustache, never happy, never
satisfied, riding his egotism into a thin sweat! Why had
he spared Blaber?

But had he spared Blaber? Had not his revenge sub-
tilized itself, and fleshed its teeth more delicately in the
path of the other man's cowardice?

"I gave him a hell's own fright!"

His mouth twisted as he repictured Blaber blundering
about among the beech trees, trying to catch a voice, and
finding nothing but his own fear. Blaber's conscience did
not matter. What did matter was that he had left the
other fellow feeling horribly scared and wondering whether
he had been found out.

Cruelty! Yes, cruelty could be good. Everything had
its virtue, its own particular, potent taste; bitter and
sweet, the eternal and wholesome contrasts. They kept
life—or the illusion of life—sane and vivid. What a de-
cadent, milk-and-water affair it would be if one could
never spit one's scorn down a cad's throat! Cads had
their uses. The cad in each and every man was a pro-
voker of contrasts. Universal beneficence was the dream
of a weak-kneed world.

Suvla reached the Hampshire town of Alton that night,
and since the rain was still coming down, and his boots
were full of it, he found a bed at a little inn. It was a
dirty rest-house for indifferently clean people, and Suvla
had to show his money before its dirtiness was put at his
disposal. In fact, when he had seen the bed, the soul
of him spurned its nastiness. He asked if they had a
stable.

"I'm used to sleeping rough. Sheets ain't in my line."

There was a stable, with an old black horse lodged in
it, and Suvla climbed a ladder, and poked his head into
the loft. Half a dozen trusses of clean hay were fra-
grantly welcoming.

"This'll do me proud, guv'nor."

Suvla John

"Please yourself," said the sodden-looking person who kept the pub, and who was accustomed to rough customers; "but don't you pull the hay about, nor light no matches."

"No need. I can bed down on a couple of trusses. What's the charge for a bed with the old 'oss?"

"Same as the room."

"Say, guv'nor, but you won't be havin' to wash the sheets!"

"That don't signify."

"I reckon it doesn't, not once a month. A bob for the privilege of bein' out of the wet, and me—a suspicious-lookin' character."

"You've got it," said the sodden man, with laconic candour.

So Suvla chose the hay and the near presence of the black horse, nor did he hanker after the foul bed in the attic, nor for the company of the humans who steamed and argued in the dirty little public bar. For such human cattle he had no use. A French peasant might keep his manure stacked under his windows, but he had a native intelligence, and his beds were clean. An Italian might breathe garlic at you, but he boasted a sort of historic picturesqueness.

"Hallo, old son," said Suvla, sitting on a truss and pulling off his wet boots and addressing the black horse below, "don't you find it a rum world? Anyhow, you don't drink bad beer and talk a lot of filthy nonsense, and go to sleep in a dirty bed. Each country has its own way of being clean and dirty, and while it is scratching its own flea-bites it is criticizing the foreign chap for harbouring strange vermin. I could understand God saying: 'I think I made a little mistake about Noah.' And yet you have to learn to laugh at your own scorn."

The smell of hay and a pungent odour of ammonia mingled in the air, and Suvla made ready to go to sleep. He could hear two drunken men arguing in the yard, and the silly, screaming laughter of a woman, but presently all was peace.

Suvla wished the black horse "good night."

"For you can't use silly adjectives—thank God."

Suvla John

In the Forest the world was very green after the rain, and it was along rainwashed roads and under dripping trees that Suvla came to Romsey. Here, addressing himself to a loafer in the centre of the ancient town, he had news of Richenda's people, and, making his way to a field on the outskirts of Romsey, he found the booths and the swings set up, and the steam merry-go-round flashing much gold in a stream of watery sunlight.

Here, one Tinto Smith, a swarthy fellow, shining with oil and sweat, was busy about the engine. Suvla addressed him, and Tinto looked at him over the backs of the horses, the whites of his eyes like china in the hot swarthiness of his face.

"Is this the Lee show, bor?"

The engine man allowed that it was.

"Is Miss Richenda this way?"

He had been looking for the green caravan, and had been unable to discover it. Tinto Smith regarded him closely. Gossip had been busy in this little community, and there had been talk of the tall gorgio who had fought for his place on Richenda's steps and had slept under her wagon.

Tinto wiped his hands on a wad of cotton waste.

"Name of Suvla?"

"Sure."

"No, she ain't here."

"She wouldn't be. Open country."

Tinto nodded. He was old enough to know that it was useless to push in between a man and a girl.

"Castle Malwood way or Rufus Stone."

"Thanks. Have a cigarette, bor. Not much weather for swing-boats."

Tinto reached over the backs of the wooden horses, and his black finger-nails were jet against the white paper of the cigarette.

"We don't take much count of the weather. It's all the same to her."

"I guess it would be."

Suvla shouldered his kit and returned to the road, and set his face towards Ringwood. It was late in the afternoon, and the weather was clearing, with a broadening sweep of blue sky and a glister of gold upon the trees.

Suvla John

The earth steamed. Far horizons were mysterious and
vaguely blue, and the wetness and the green smell of the
earth were a joy to a man's blood, and when Suvla came
to the high ground the day had taken in its linen, and
there was not a sheeted cloud trailing in the sky.

Beyond a dip in the road where a wood of beeches
made a wet stillness Suvla came upon a rough track,
and, standing in a little grassy space with bracken all
about it, he saw the green caravan. The steps were down
and Richenda was seated on them just as he had first
seen her, but with a book in her lap and her hair hanging
loose, for she had been washing it and was letting it dry
in the sun.

There was no stirring of her dark dignity. She sat
there, grave and unsmiling, watching his approach, her
eyes steady, the book lying face downwards on her knees.
She neither welcomed nor repulsed him. The proud
animal in her waited, and made no sign.

Suvla pulled off his hat. He was aware of her as an
enigma, a creature with unblinking, velvet eyes, calm
yet vaguely fierce. Whether she had expected to see
him again he did not know, but she could sit and gaze
and say nothing, and such women are rare.

He, too, said nothing. Her silence was a challenge,
and he met it—throwing his bag into the bracken and seating himself on the lowest step at her feet. He pulled out a
pipe, filled and lit it, and began to smoke. Neither of
them had uttered a word.

"This England!" he said presently, and pointed to the
beech trees with his pipe.

He was smiling, and her eyes absorbed his smile. It
was not for her. It was the sheen of some inward glimmer
of his spirit, ironical, tender, subtle; it included the sense
world and himself. It suggested an inward gentleness;
she felt this gentleness in him, the laughter of one who
laughs at the way things happen.

"Your job is done?"

He nodded his head, and remained silent for several
seconds, and she felt that life had surprised him.

"Yes—that's that. A Balaam's Ass of an adventure.
The angel with a shining sword—you know! Some day,
perhaps, I'll tell you all about it."

"Thanks."

He was full of long silences, and she did not disturb
him with chatter, but read her book, and paused in her

reading when he had anything to say. Sometimes it was she who gave a casual flick to this desultory conversation. She was thinking how queer it was that they should get each other's meaning so quickly and with so few words, and even the silences were a sort of stillness which they shared and understood.

"Going back is like getting out of your coffin."

"Presumably—dead?"

"I've been dead for seven years."

She considered the significant confession.

"A long time! And did it hurt?"

"A bit. In unexpected places, you know. Rather like going to a picture show——"

"But live pictures."

"Yes; that's the difference. Flesh and blood; flesh of your own flesh. Still—the picture-show is over; I had to sit in the dark, and sneak away without any of the people in the picture seeing me."

"It would not have done?"

"No. One can't play at resurrections. Too uncomfortable for the people who have settled down."

"And you wanted them to be comfortable?"

"Mostly. Bar one. I had my one good laugh. A month ago I thought that I might wring his neck."

She looked fiercely serious.

"You thought—that—when you left us that morning."

"I did. You're quick. You get me—like one of those thought-reading people."

They shared another silence, and presently Suvla came out of it, and tapped the dead ash from his pipe.

"I have a favour to ask you, Miss Richenda."

She waited.

"May I bed down here to-night? I can hand over my rations to Mother Beckett."

"Is that the favour?"

"No. Just look—will you?"

He was feeling for something, and he produced his little leather bag, and, untying it, he emptied the contents into his palm.

"Looks like the result of a successful burglary?"

Ironical, humorous, he watched her face. Her slow, dark eyes lifted to his.

"Yes; but it isn't."

"No."

"Well?"

Suvla John

"It seems rather mad my carrying the stuff about. Suppose I deposit the stones——?"

"With me?"

"That's the idea. You can give me a receipt or not, just as you please."

"You must have a receipt."

"All right."

"My bank is at Winchester. They could go in a sealed envelope, and be put in my deed-box."

"Splendid. Hold out your hand."

Suvla poured the stones from his own palm into hers, and in bending, a part of her loose hair slipped down along her arm and almost touched him. She had been using some perfumed soap, and he was aware of the smell of it.

"Count them."

"I shall make a list and give it you. That ruby!"

She held it up between finger and thumb.

"Yes, Russian. Which does one value most, the beauty or the market value of them? Sometimes one, sometimes the other! You had better keep the bag."

He gave it to her, and Richenda, holding it over her lap, poured the stones into it. Her face was as serious as fate. She had not exclaimed at his quixotry in trusting a woman who should have seemed a stranger, for she knew that she was no stranger, and that his faith in her was the product of one of those quick and inevitable impulses. He gave and she accepted; neither of them felt the need of the why or the how.

"I shall go over to Winchester to-morrow."

"What it is to be a woman of property!"

She tossed back her hair, leaving him a trace of the smell of it.

"I wonder!"

3

Suvla took his supper with Richenda and her people, and in old Mother Beckett's beady eyes he divined the grudging acceptance of him as one of the fraternity. She growled at him: "You sleep rough, but you'd like to sleep soft." And Suvla, smiling at her, said: "I'm a gorgio, but my prejudice is as good as yours, mother. Something for nothing is no motto of mine."

She watched him all through the meal, nor could he

Suvla John

look at Richenda without the old woman pulling his look to pieces as though to find the honey or the poison in it, and later, when Suvla crawled under the green caravan to spread his ground-sheet on some armfuls of litter, she hung close, peering at him through the wheel spokes.

"You need not mis-wish me, mother," he said. "I have eaten your bread."

She put her face close to a wheel.

"You have a power of pride. Your bed would look as fine under my van."

Suvla, kneeling, showed her an open hand.

"Read it—if you will. Kings lie where they please."

"Kings!"

She growled, but it was a growl of acceptance.

"A mumperly tramp."

"More—or less. Perhaps—more, mother. Ever heard of King Cophetua—or rather—of the beggar maid? Or a gentleman called Ulysses?"

"Satan take your big names."

"Let him, so long as he leaves me my boots."

The night was warm and still, for the chill of the rain had passed, and Richenda, lying awake, heard Suvla moving below her. For an hour or more he had made no sound, and she had thought him asleep, though her own wakefulness seemed centred about the little leather bag fastened by a piece of ribbon and lying in her bosom. Whether it was a "lucky bag" or not she did not know, neither did she care; it had come to her and she accepted it, fatefully, yet with a sudden secret leap of the heart.

She heard the creaking of the steps, and a slight movement of the caravan. She sat up, confronting an abrupt thought, neither welcoming it nor trying to put it aside, nor shirking the human issue. If it would happen, it would happen. But, in her heart, she wished that he would not touch the door, not because she would say him nay, but because of his imagined pride and its comradeship with hers.

There was no further movement. Her bleakness grew less tense, and she laid a hand over the treasure he had trusted to her, and in her way—she prayed. Presently she heard the striking of a match, and the faint smell of burning tobacco drifted to her. He was sitting on the steps, smoking, wakeful, silently restless. Neither of them had been able to sleep.

Suvla John

She pushed back the clothes from her feet, and gave way to an impulse.

"John Suvla."

"Hallo! Not asleep?"

"I heard you moving."

"Sorry. I did not mean to disturb you. Do you feel like sleeping?"

"Not yet."

"Then come and help to put the devil out of me, Richenda."

She got up at once, slipped on her stockings and shoes, and buttoning a heavy coat about her, she opened the door. He was sitting on the lowermost step, but he stood up when she appeared.

"Richenda."

Her words fell upon him with a sudden fatefulness. She was ice and fire.

"Why did you come back?"

"Here?"

She shook her head.

"I have not asked you that. But—to England."

They stood close, she above, he below.

"I have not talked my heart out for seven years. I have had no one to talk to but myself. I am beginning to think that's bad."

"You trusted me with that bag," she said.

He had one of his silences, and she was still as the night.

"Richenda—will you sit down?"

She seated herself on the topmost step, with her back against the closed door.

"Thank you."

He sat at her feet, but a little nearer than before, and she felt his hand touch her left foot with a touch that was purposeful and gentle.

"Good. Sensible wench. Shoes on. Well—why did I come back?"

She looked down at his dark head.

"That means the whole tale."

"Every precious stone of it!"

"Every precious stone of it—lying here."

He glanced round and up, and saw her hand on her bosom.

"You were meant," he said, "somehow. It's a long tale, my dear."

99

Suvla John

"So is life."

"No—it's short—absurdly short. Unless, of course, one believes in Theosophy! Seems I have been kicked back to learn to scorn my scorn. Girl, what's the difference between disdain and scorn?"

"Is there a difference? Yes—I see. Disdain is higher than scorn. It goes up to the tops of the hills."

"You're great," he said.

She felt his hand touch her foot and rest there, and she drew one deep breath, for in the touching of her foot there was a movement of homage.

"How long ago was it?" she asked.

"About seven years."

And so he told her the whole tale, and for an hour Richenda sat very still, turning over the strangeness of its telling, and growing big with unasked questions. For Suvla explained nothing. It was "I did this—and this," but he gave her no why or wherefore. Parts of the story she understood, her wildness leaping to the reckless and gaillard happenings, but parts she did not understand at all, nor the apparent perversity of his silences. And yet it fascinated her. There were moments when she had spasms of jealousy, for this man had lived and loved fiercely before he had come into the young world of her liking.

There was no moon, but the night was bright with stars, and Richenda looked up at them and felt that her head was as full of questions as the sky was full of stars.

"Well—that's the yarn. Believe as much of it as you like."

She was aware of the challenging tilt of his head. He was filling another pipe.

"You know that I believe every word of it."

"That's more than most men would do."

"I'm not a man. But I want to ask questions."

"Fire away."

"Why did you go on pretending to be dead?"

"Why, don't you see the grim jest I had up my sleeve?"

"Yes—for that beast. But—then—there were others—the woman."

"Richenda—I thought that if the woman cared—she would wait a little while."

"How long did she wait?"

"About a year. And then she married that chap, and I got the news in a frayed old paper that had been smuggled in."

Suvla John

"And you laughed?"

"How do you know?"

"I can hear that laughter. You were a bit of a brute, John Suvla."

He laid a hand on her knee.

"Thanks. I was. I have got a lot of the fighting brute in me, my dear. Cruel—yes, a little. There are times when it is good to be cruel. Any more questions?"

She laid her hands on his.

"O—hundreds. But—not—to-night. I'm like a child who has heard a ghost story."

"And you will keep those stones for me?"

"Yes—I will keep the stones."

4

Suvla had gone to his place under the caravan, and Richenda was back in bed, but for a long while she could not sleep, for her thoughts kept her awake. And yet, she was more a mirror than a lamp, for the extraordinary vividness of Suvla's story reflected itself in her consciousness, and the scenes repeated themselves like pictures on a screen.

Moreover, his personality had penetrated the whole telling of it, and with the sweep of a few simple words he had made her feel the fear and the hate and the tenderness. And sometimes his voice had laughed, and sometimes it had grown mocking.

"Yes, my dear, it was hot that August day. Our old men had made a fine mess of it, sitting on their hunkers, afraid to take any risks. There were the sand dunes, and the salt lake, and the sea and Sari Bair and Tekha Tepe, with Ismail Oglu between, and Little and Great Anafarta, all waiting for us to take them. Raw—oh, yes, we were raw. And the old men made a mess of the water arrangements and we had no guns, and they fooled us about till we were mad with thirst. If we could have pitched a few of the old men into the sea, and gone ashore like a lot of pirates, I'll swear we could have taken those hills and held them.

"Well—that's history. I had two days' beard on me, and a hell of a temper inside, and a thirst. I shan't

Suvla John

forget that sunset in a hurry, as though the gods were pouring blood into a purple blue sea. We were being shelled, and the men were done up and jumpy, and suddenly what must Master Blaber do but begin blubbering. Yes, in front of the men whose lips were none too stiff. I knew that I had to do something, and I was pretty mad, so I got up and walked over to him and pulled out my handkerchief—"Come here, my poor darling, and let me wipe your poor wet darling nose!" A yell went up. But there you are, my dear; I had to be cruel to stop the rot, and of course the fellow hated me. He always had hated us Sheres, but that sort of hate never troubled me. I had got in his way; he wanted the woman I was going to marry; and Dick and I were what he wanted to be—and couldn't be. No, Eton and Oxford left him a little Lancashire grabber. Queer—too—that I should have had him with me that last night. There was a moon, but a haze dimmed it; we were the skeleton screen, while the evacuation went on. I had Blaber with me and a platoon; we were strung out, keeping up the illusion until the hour fixed for us to bolt. It was a huge game of bluff. And then—Blaber got jumpy. I took him away from the men, up an old sap, where a little old wooden cross stood up at the back of the trench. I could hear his teeth chattering, and I told him to cheer up—and that we would be off before the morning. He must have hated me. And then —some imp of mischief made me get up on the parapet and wave my cap at the Turks. One or two shots came over. Yes—that was a lesson. You should never show off with a clever little devil hating you behind your back, and with a sting ready in his tail. Blaber got me. That was where his cleverness came out. I expect it was part impulse; he had wanted to kill me for months, and when his chance came he was on it like a good scrum-half. I happened to glance over my shoulder before jumping down, and I saw Blaber with his revolver out and his teeth all grinning and white. He got me in the back—but the fool ought to have made sure. I suppose he scuttled back to the men, and told them that I had climbed up on the parapet and been potted by the Turks. Anyhow, I was left there for dead, my dear, and dead I ought to have been, and I knew nothing much about life for the next few days. The Turks treated me well, though one of them pinched the silver disc I had chained to my wrist, and that gave me my inspiration. And a little German doctor man pulled me through. Blaber's bullet had gone clean through me, and was pouched in the skin over one of my ribs. The German removed it, and made me a presentation. That's how it happened."

The sound of Suvla's voice was in Richenda's ears when she fell asleep. She had told herself that she had many questions to ask him—questions that he would have to answer.

XI

I

AT seven in the morning Richenda sent the Beckett lad to Romsey for her dog-cart, telling him that she would meet him in the Romsey road, and that he was to go with her to Winchester. She breakfasted alone, and Suvla copied her aloofness, taking his plate of bacon and his cup of tea to the shade of the beech wood, while old woman Beckett muttered to old man Beckett, and watched both the caravan and the beech wood. The separateness of these two suggested a quarrel, and the obvious and likely cause of the quarrel had put the gipsy woman in a dark temper.

"The gorgio lied to me. And she—put him in his place. You see, dadda, to-night he won't be sleeping under her van."

At eight o'clock Richenda came down out of her caravan and walked towards the road, and Suvla, watched by Palmyra and her man, got up and joined her. She gave him the merest flicker of a smile. "Man, this is more serious than death," her steady eyes said to him; "do you understand me?"

His smile was more open than hers, but quite as solemn.

"So—the bargain holds?"

"I keep my word."

He put himself at her side.

"May I come a little way? Last night I did all the talking. The day is yours."

"It will take more than a day."

"To ask me all the questions you wish to ask?"

"To think over the answers."

He gave her a quick and approving look.

"That is sound. Well—Richenda, if it is going to take so long we had better begin at once."

"One question at a time. Why did you wait seven years?"

She saw him smile.

Suvla John

"My dear—that's shrewd of you. You begin with the most difficult question of the lot. Sometimes I have asked myself the same question, and by all that's holy—my own answers have not been convincing."

"But there are reasons for everything."

"Are there? I wonder! Sometimes—our impulses are such queer, dubious things——"

"Then—you were different from what you are now?"

"How?"

"Because—the man who sat on my steps last night would not have waited seven years."

He pulled up and stood still, and his serious face had lost its look of defiance.

"Now—that's true—but how you came to know it is beyond me. Wildness! Yes—I was wild. England did not pull then, nor the people in it."

"But later?"

Her eyes demanded a fierce sincerity.

"I wanted to see my brother."

"Is that all?"

He looked at her quickly.

"It is all. Not her. And that other fellow? I thought that I would have the devil's own game with him. I liked the smell of revenge. Say, Richenda, do you know those lavender bags some people used to carry about with them? Well, my revenge was rather like that. But, in a way, I must have got used to the scent of it—and then——"

"Perfumes lose their power. Your little packet of revenge——"

"Exactly. I ran wild about the world, carrying that nice little talisman about with me. And my swashbuckling life was so good. Wherever a row was on, I had to be there. There came a time when there were no rows, save the usual filibusterings in Mexico. I tried it, and it was too dirty, even for a reckless old blackguard like me. And suddenly the smell of that lavender packet got me."

She answered him instantly.

"No, it was more than that."

"You think so?"

"Yes, it was something in your blood, blind things calling out, the things that are in all of us. You used to laugh——"

"True, O—queen," he said, and she saw the deepness of his eyes; "I was a beast of a boy playing with a toy pistol. But life gets you in the end. That's the devil of it. I don't quite know how deeply it has got me."

She walked on in silence for some seconds.

"You have got to find that out, John Suvla. That is your share of the bargain."

He accompanied Richenda along the road until young Loverin and the trap appeared in sight, and for a minute or more they stood together by the side of the road. Richenda watched the approaching trap, but Suvla's eyes were on the horizon.

"You fight like a white man, Richenda."

"Do you call it fighting? All your thoughts are of fighting."

"My dear, less than you think, since I saw the old place. And to-night you will be ready with another question?"

"I shall."

Loverin and the trap arrived, and Richenda, after glancing at the horse to see that beast and harness had been turned out to please her dignity, climbed in, with Suvla spreading an arm to keep her skirts from the wheel. She felt the brush of her clothes against his arm, and there was a sudden softness in her eyes. She glanced down, smiling.

"Good-bye."

Bareheaded and silent, he answered her smile with a steady and proud look.

"I shall spend the day preparing my catechism."

She took the reins from Loverin, and drove away, and while Suvla stood watching her a passing motor-car, furiously driven, and hooting blatantly, involved her in a cloud of dust.

"Beast!" said Suvla—and laughed, remembering her accusation. "All your thoughts are of fighting." But he knew that there would be occasions when Richenda would not quarrel with him for fighting, and that by fighting he had won his place on the step of her caravan.

He turned back, and avoiding the camp, went deep into the shade of the beech wood.

"It's like life," he thought. "She's right about the deeps of it. I haven't yet seen half the trees."

Suvla John

Suvla came back from the Rufus Stone as the sky was reddening, to find that Richenda had returned.

She was exercising her imperiousness upon Palmyra Beckett, who was full of ancient presumption, and Richenda was angry, and when Richenda was angry Palmyra grovelled. Suvla stood off, liking Richenda's fierceness, for he wanted no tame woman, a creature of giggles and sensibility. Richenda was a "person" set apart from the machine-made crowd.

She called to him.

"Supper is ready."

A table had been set on the grass beside the green caravan, and Palmyra, darkly obsequious, was laying a place for the gorgio; and it was Palmyra's assumption that Suvla would not sit at that table that had roused Richenda's anger. Times had changed. Miss Lee had been to school; she had ceased to sit down cross-legged on the ground, like her illustrious grandmother; she had no liking for roast hedgehog; Palmyra was forbidden to tell fortunes.

Suvla joined her. Her eyes had ceased their flashings, and had become velvet, but she looked consideringly at his clothes.

"Here is your receipt."

He took it and sat down on a stool that Palmyra had placed for him.

"Thank you. Clothes make the man. To-morrow it will be my turn to go to Winchester."

"You need it."

Her frankness was significant, suggesting pride and the notion of permanency.

"I like reverence. The master should be dressed like a master."

She caught his smile.

"Master is no word for these days."

"Yes—and that's the pity. The crowd has got to relearn the duty of obeying."

"You rule your people, Richenda."

"And why not? I have the strongest will; I know more and see more. And you——"

"Well?"

"You are not my idea of a Robot. The social slave!"

"A most modern lady!"

Suvla John

"I'm serious. We are making a silly, smug god of equality, when we should make a religion and a cult of inequality."

When they had finished supper she dismissed Palmyra and brought out her queer little pipe.

"Does it offend you?"

"It would—in any other woman."

Her eyes glimmered.

"There are two deck-chairs in my van. Will you get them. Yes, and let's face the afterglow."

Suvla brought the chairs, and placed hers before opening his own. She sat down, and withdrew into a deep silence, while he lit his pipe and waited upon her silence. Her silence was as individual as her pride.

"When—you saw your old world," she asked suddenly, "what happened?"

He did not hurry to answer.

"Some of the old Bible phrases. My bowels yearned."

"Had you expected it?"

"Not—as it happened. But—does one? And then I knew——"

"That the John Shere of seven years ago—had committed suicide."

He glanced at her with homage.

"You arrive like a flash of light. Yes—I saw myself dead——"

She paused to think.

"I suppose you never saw that play of Barrie's? No. People—dead people—should not come back. You realized it—and when you had realized it—did it hurt you?"

"Yes—devilishly."

"Hopelessly?"

"No. I felt cut off. When—I saw Dick bathing—and heard him talking to his wife——"

Her voice softened.

"You would. So you came away. You did not feel greedy?"

"No, not greedy. I felt gentle, Richenda, strangely gentle. I felt that I could leave Dick and his—my blessing. He is a better man for that life than I should ever be."

She nodded a grave head, while he sat and considered her and the real meaning of her to him and to the world. Was she a beginning or an end, or like himself a proud recusant, fastidiously fierce, disdaining the

many, and keeping her warm-heartedness for the few?
He likened her to Cassandra. Were she to prophesy, no
one would believe her, save the wild and the solitary
few, for the modern prophet—to be believed—must be
a pleasant and ignorant liar, truckling to the mob.

Yes, Richenda would always be a creature of solitudes,
holding herself aloof, a woman of beautiful disdain. In
her way she was even less conventional than he was.
She surprised you. She put out a finger and it touched
your heart.

"So you saw them all?"

"All—who mattered."

"Her?"

"Yes."

It was growing dark, and she looked him full in the
face.

"How much happiness?"

"Not much—I think. Poor Elsie, made to be a
mirror."

"And when you were younger you saw your vanity
in her."

"My dear, perhaps. But vanity is a cheap word. I
prefer the 'consciousness of power.'"

"Male energy?"

"Yes, if you like."

"And now—the mirror?"

"Let's be kind," he said gently; "you would be kind
to her, Richenda. Such a little mirror, a little sentimental bit of glass for a boy to look in. Why, if she
could only realize it, she was lucky to lose me. She
could not have reflected the whole of me."

"Is that arrogance?"

"No, wisdom. I should ask my mate to find in me
a mirror big enough for her to see in me her whole self.
Of what use is a marriage of one room, with all the rest
of the house shut up? A comrade, or nothing. I'm not
a nursery man."

Richenda brooded.

"Poor kid. She made you feel sentimental?"

"She made me feel sorry."

"For the might have been?"

"No. That I—had—in a sense—messed up her little
life. Like wringing a bird's neck—you know. One can't
put a patch on the past."

"Nor attempt it?"

Suvla John

"I don't want to attempt it. That is a brutal fact."

"Less brutal than it seems. She would not be strong enough. And so, you frightened the man."

"I let him off."

"But—did you?"

"Some men, Richenda, are better for being scared. I thought he might be a little kinder to her."

"Does she want him to be kinder?"

"What do you think?"

"She wants to cling, you say, and a woman will cling to a thorn bush—but to a man of cold slime! I should say she hates him, as much as that sort of woman can hate. How did you see her, and where?"

He told her, and she seemed to darken.

"Living on an illusion?"

"Well, isn't everything illusion?"

"No. But even if it were, we should have to pretend——"

And then she got up and walked a little way apart, and stood there, absorbed and mysterious. His words had gone deep, and the depths of her enveloped them.

"I don't know," she said, and came back; "I can't quite get the answer to it all. One has to get an answer. And you——"

"Is there an answer?"

"O, it is not that—only. Perhaps—you'll feel—— Later—— Some things draw one. Are you adrift? I wonder!"

He paused before answering her.

"You mean—I shall feel the draw?"

"Perhaps. Something incomplete. I can't quite put it into words."

"Meanwhile?"

"Yes, meanwhile?"

"Can you find me a job, Richenda? Or, I'll make one."

"We'll make one between us."

3

Suvla had a couple of five-pound notes sewn up under the lining of his coat, and he came back from his day in Winchester wearing new boots and a rough tweed suit

Suvla John

of a greyish-green. His hat was not quite new, but all the better for that. He opened a parcel and showed to Richenda a pair of knickers, two pairs of stockings, three pairs of socks, three shirts, six collars, six handkerchiefs, and a tie.

"The biggest wardrobe since the war!"

The Becketts had watched the return of him, and had commented on his clothes.

"He's cadged the money off her," quoth Palmyra, Old Beckett was less sure. Richenda was not a young woman to be fooled, and this John Suvla was very much a man.

Richenda was planning something. When supper was over she took her seat of state, red-cushioned on the topmost step of the caravan. Whatever her impulse might be she was its mistress.

"They say you are cadging from me, my friend, and that a man has put the blinkers on me. Will that worry you?"

"The remedy is obvious. You can use your tongue."

"On you?"

"Why not?"

"That's humbug. It's not my way. No—full partnership."

She sat intent and slightly frowning.

"My people are a jealous lot. You know something of horses?"

"I was in a saddle at five. I lived with horses; I used to break my own."

Her dark eyes cleared.

"I've got it. My father used to do some horse dealing; I suppose there is less money in it now, but does that matter? And one or two of my men have been giving trouble. Suppose you take over the men and the horses?"

"Transport and remounts. You are making it too easy for me, Richenda."

"You may find it a tough job. But you like them tough. There is one fellow, Kid Stanley, whom you may have to thrash. He is a good deal above himself."

"And supposing that Mr. Stanley should appeal to the police?"

"He won't. I'm the court of appeal. We settle our own cases."

"But I am not putting any capital into the show."

"There is enough there already. Call it a six months'

trial. Naturally a man would want to see how the profits work out before putting down his share."

"And my capital consists of those precious gimcracks in your Winchester bank."

"I would take them at a valuation. What do you think they are worth?"

"I don't know. I got an old Russian Jew to look at two or three of them. They are genuine. But look here, Richenda——"

He stood up. She might be the most unusual and the most potent young woman on the face of the earth, but her bigness was not a thing to be played with.

"You have had my history."

"Yes—I know about your wildness."

"It has been a fairly clean sort of wildness, but there it is."

"I'm not blind."

"You'll risk it?"

"All but one thing."

"Out with it."

"Wildness about women."

He looked her full in the face, and its passionate austerity had the clearness of white light.

"I'll make you that promise. As a matter of fact, it is easier for me to make it than you imagine."

"Why?"

"Part of it you might guess. The other part of it is that I'm through with women. And when a man feels like that, before——"

She nodded gravely.

"I don't give easily. I despise easy givers. But there is quite a long road yet."

"I'll travel it. And, what is more, Richenda, you are thinking of the possible cross-roads."

"Mine and yours."

"Yours too?"

"Why not. I have a feeling that your past is not behind you yet."

"And until it is?"

"I want it rounded off. I'll help you to round it off. Feelings are queer things—John."

"Tell me."

"I can't—yet. Something is coming to me, but what it is I don't quite know. It may come to you first. You see, I don't take life like sugar. I'm out for complete-

Suvla John

ness; I like a rough edge tackled and smoothed off. There is still an edge somewhere."

"And you are feeling for it?"

"So are you. Do you not know it? Always, there are queer things passing inside us, and suddenly they break out, and we wonder why we did not feel them before. I'm not sure yet whether you ought not to go back again."

He looked at her intently.

"There?"

"Yes."

"For good?"

"No—that's impossible."

"Then for what?"

"That is what is going to come to me, and to you."

He looked at her as he had never looked at any other woman.

"I did not think your sort existed, Richenda. I stand with my hat off."

Matters moved swiftly when they had come to this decision, for Richenda was all for swiftness when once she had pondered a thing out. She and Suvla drove into Romsey next morning and held a tour of inspection in which every detail was gone into. The horses were led out, and Suvla examined each beast, with the eyes and the hands of a horse-master. They went all over the carts and vans, and Tinto Smith had to report upon his engine, and all that concerned it. Richenda's people were left in no doubt as to John Suvla's share in the show, for though Richenda explained nothing, she left nothing that needed explaining. The Lee caravans were to have a master as well as a mistress. Again, more swiftness. They were to pull out of Romsey and take the road on the following morning, with Wimborne for their destination, and at this point Mr. Kid Stanley contrived a piece of sauciness.

"I told yer Bobbo has a sore shoulder. What about it?"

Bobbo was one of the horses responsible for drawing the wagon on which the swing boats travelled, and Stanley saw an opportunity in Bobbo's shoulder.

"Let's see the horse's collar."

Suvla passed the order, and Stanley ignored it, looking insolently at Richenda. He had a vicious leanness, a half finished mouth, and a blackguard's eye.

Suvla John

Richenda ignored him.

Suvla smiled.

"A little deaf, my lad! Well, we'll assume that the collar is at fault. The next time you let a collar get worn and chafe a horse's shoulder, we'll put the collar on you."

"It's a lie," said Stanley.

"That's up to you."

Stanley went for the collar, even though it was doomed to convict him, for he was seeing red. And a disgraceful piece of cobbling Suvla found there.

"So you put that on a horse, my lad?"

"I did that. I ain't one to go cadging a woman's money when I can do a job myself."

"To be sure. And a darned bad job you have made of it. You are no saddler, Stanley. I'll look over your harness each week myself, and there'll be trouble if you chafe another horse. There's no need for it, man. It's just laziness, and lack of sympathy."

Richenda had turned away as though to leave Suvla his full authority, and Stanley, watching her out of the tail of an evil eye, spat his defiance.

"Suppose yer think because you've bin——"

But he did not finish his filthiness, for Suvla with a fierce swiftness crammed the horse-collar over the man's head, and, getting him by both arms, forced him behind one of the vans. They stood there a moment, breathing hard.

"Let go o' me, and fight, you——"

"I am going to lick you, Stanley, and then we shall know each other better——"

And Kid Stanley had his licking, with half Richenda's people looking on and wishing Suvla the best of luck, for Stanley was a quarrelsome beast and a nuisance to the community. When it was over, Suvla picked him up and told him to go and wash his face and to keep his mouth clean for the future in the presence of his betters.

Stanley was cowed, and from that day forth he gave no trouble.

"I'd have done it myself, bor," said Tinto Smith, oily and smiling, "but he's ten year younger than me. And he's got some nasty tricks."

"Well, I can throw one better trick, Tinto," and Richenda, who had held aloof, came back and joined them, with one swift look at Suvla's face. He was untouched, unruffled, and her pride was satisfied.

"If Stanley would be as kind to his horses as Tinto is to his engine."

Tinto showed all his teeth.

"Not one breakdown in three years. Me and my oil can, Miss Richenda."

"You are a good man, Tinto, and I know it. Mr. Suvla, shall we want another horse?"

"Bobbo is not fit to pull. He'll have to run loose, and I'll vet that shoulder of his."

"We have two spares, but I don't think they are big enough."

"I'll manage," he said, and met her smile.

"I'll leave it to you," she answered.

XII

I

AT Wimborne Suvla's memory was of sitting with Richenda in the nave of the empty minster, the sun shining through upon the Norman greyness, and falling upon Richenda's face and hands. She sat beside him with a great stillness, and he, looking up into the misty distances of the roof, felt that her silence was a blessed refuge from the world's chatter.

They were there without speaking for the best part of half an hour, and then Richenda, sitting very straight and stately, turned a head and gave him the deeps of her dark eyes.

"It's good to be where other people are not."

She spoke in an undertone, and with hands clasped over one knee; he nodded a grave head.

"Not easy—in these days. I wonder how long it will be before the crowd gets sick of being a crowd? You are not a crowd-woman, Richenda."

"I am myself."

"Queen of the solemn, silent night. You would like the desert, my dear."

"Perhaps we shall go there, some day."

"A tent, two palm trees, and a thousand stars."

"Aren't the Arabs noisy?"

"I suppose they vary. But I have been in Arab crowds and Arab market places, and it is a people of dignity. No, not noise. Not like the raw, English voices."

"Most English voices are ugly—or silly. I mean—the intonation. Listen to two common women. And yet England has this—and a beauty——"

"This—belongs—to the few, Richenda. And the common Englishman had nothing to do with England's beauty, save in doing what he was told to do. Oh, let's get away from the crowd, and even from talking about it."

"You are a bad citizen, John Suvla."

Suvla John

"Not in my own country, my dear. And can I see you in Peckham, or teaching stuffy-nosed little children who smell of mice? We are an arrogant couple!"

"Is it arrogance?"

"No; fastidiousness. We can't chant with the crowd. We don't read our daily paper. Oh, let it be!"

She smiled deeply.

"Always fighting—something."

"Not this—or you."

"So I am a piece of old ecclesiastical architecture!"

"You are you. There is nothing in you I want to fight, just as there is nothing in this old place I need quarrel with. I'm quarrelsome—or was—because there is so much to quarrel with, faces and stomachs and feet, and silly shibboleths, and machine-made sottishness——"

"There you are——!"

He laughed softly and took one of her hands.

"It's like holding on to life, this. Deep and cool and strong. Away from the monkey-cage, my dear. My dear old dad was a bigger man than I am."

"Why?"

"He could pity people, make allowances. He used to say: 'Remember their ignorance and be gentle.'"

"I think I'm with you, Suvla. I am in favour of wise justice and a whip."

From Wimborne they went to Dorchester, and so to Bridport, Beaminster, and Crewkerne, and the hill country, and to John Suvla the life had a Biblical flavour. He rode at the head of the company, beside Richenda and her green van, on a nag bought from a Dorset dealer. The column of transport trailed behind, five caravans, seven wagons, two spring carts, an old water cart, and one or two odd vehicles and odd horses. There were men, women, children, dogs, a cat or two, and Mrs. Tinto's parrot. Tinto, and his engine pulling two heavy vans, were sent on ahead. Richenda had instituted a pleasant autocracy, and she had disproved the modern assumption that the suffrage killed the autocrat. True, she had had some trouble with the younger men, but after Suvla's thrashing of Kid Stanley there was no more questioning of the fact that some men are born to be masters.

Often Richenda would mount one of the saddle horses and ride on with Suvla to the next halt, and arrange for the camping ground. She was known all through the south, though she and her people never went north

Suvla John

of the Thames or the Avon, and her word was good enough for any man. There would be brisk work when the community arrived, and all the fun of the fair was got ready for Dorset men or Wiltshire men. Red-and-white booths went up, the swings, the roundabout, the shooting-gallery, the coconut alley, and what not. Mrs. Tinto and her girl managed the shooting-gallery, Stanley ruled the swings, Tinto the wooden horses. Richenda was never seen on the ground when the show was in progress, but Suvla was astonished at her command of the whole business. She paid her people well, but every coconut and cartridge was accounted for. And she was hygienic. The show carried a couple of spray-baths, which were erected everywhere, and used. Suvla teased her about them. "Well—that is autocracy! You could bathe a man by order in the army." "Washing is the first lesson," she retorted; "to be clean, inside and out, is more important than being able to read." Her school was another surprise to Suvla, for one of the vans was fitted as a schoolroom, and in it Miss Tinto Smith, a certificated teacher, carried on the good work even when they were on the march.

So, lazily and pleasantly, they passed through Somerset into Devon, and it was in a Devon lane some-where beyond Exeter that Suvla captained Richenda's people in a fight that was never heard of by the police. It arose out of a meeting of Richenda's vans with a char-a-banc full of South Wales miners, women, and beer-bottles. The lane was narrow, and it was impossible for either party to pass the other at the spot where they had met.

Suvla sat on his horse in front of the char-a-banc and held the road, while the convoy crowded itself behind him.

"I am afraid you gentlemen will have to back."

The driver of the char-a-banc had imbibed much beer.

"Not much, dook. You pull into a field—or some-where."

Suvla, sitting at ease, produced a pipe and proceeded to fill it.

"I have some ten or twelve vans and wagons behind me. I'm in no hurry. We can't turn back, so it's up to you."

He lit his pipe, and the driver, knowing that he would have to reverse for a quarter of a mile, let himself loose.

Suvla John

"You oughtn't to be on the road, you and your damned clutter——"

Suvla smiled at him.

"These roads were made for horses. Bad manners won't make them any wider."

And then the beer and the tongues of two or three excited women began to turn a ridiculous situation into a steaming brawl. One or two of the miners came climbing down. Someone threw a beer-bottle, which broke in the road close to Suvla's horse. The lane began to fill with ugly, jeering voices.

Suvla looked hard at the driver.

"You had better back out."

A woman answered him, a woman with her hat all awry, and a face like a rotten plum.

"And who are you, giving orders? We're as good as you, and a bit better, you saucy scum."

Another bottle was thrown, and Suvla got off his horse. Richenda's people were crowded beside her van, the men to the front. Richenda herself sat and looked at the char-a-banc crowd with tranquil disdain.

More miners climbed down. They may have numbered a baker's dozen, and Suvla had about eight men, young and old, behind him. He turned his horse, and threw the reins to Richenda.

"Gentlemen," he said to the beer party, "if this is part of the day's sport you can keep your bottles. We don't like them. It is a pity that good beer should breed bad manners."

He was pretty sure that they were in for a fight, for he saw the drink beast in the eyes of the Welshmen. A man pulled off his coat. He came sparring up to Suvla, and Suvla smiled in his face.

"You silly fool."

The storm burst, but it was soon over. There were three or four fierce fighters in Richenda's crowd, men who could use their fists, and with Suvla to lead them they made a quick end of the beer party. In two minutes the Welshmen were scrambling back into the char-a-banc, and the driver, accepting fate, began to reverse his load of screams and profanity. Suvla and the vans followed them up, until the char-a-banc was able to insert itself into a gap where a farm road opened, and Richenda and her people went by in triumph. A last bottle was thrown at one of the caravans. Mrs. Tinto's

Suvla John

parrot, greatly excited, and bobbing up and down on his perch, screamed : "Rats—rats ! "

No more was needed, though an urchin, perched on the watercart, took leave of the beer party with thumb to nose and fingers spread.

2

It was on Dartmoor, close to a little wayside grave, that Richenda and John Suvla talked heart to heart.

The "show" was at Bovey Tracey, Richenda's caravan in a field on the edge of a wood, and some time after noon Loverin had come to Suvla's tent.

"She's wanting you and the horses."

They had ridden up to the moor, and in Suvla's eyes there was a restlessness, and for many days Richenda had been aware of this restlessness, and she had been in like mood herself. The something that she had searched for had come to her, as she believed that it had come to Suvla.

They had tethered the two horses, and had spread themselves on the grass close to a rough stone wall. The day was windless and clear, and over the green fern the blue sky met the moor, and even the tors looked gentle. A few sheep grazed, and this vast sweep of open country was empty and mysteriously serene. Suvla lay on his back and stared at the sky. Richenda, knees drawn up and arms clasped round them, watched the lights and the few cloud shadows. Her eyes were grave.

"It's not savage to-day."

He turned his head to look at her.

"You have seen it savage ? "

"Devilish. I was lost for a whole night here once as a child. A sudden mist. I huddled up under a rock, and kept two or three stones ready."

"To throw ? "

"Yes."

"At what ? "

"Anything. There are people here, strange old people."

"You thought so then."

"I think so now. Do you know what father used to say ? "

"What ? "

120

Suvla John

"When he was on the moor and talking—he felt that he ought to speak in a whisper."

"Why?"

"Because something was always listening."

She pointed to one of the tors.

"People swarm over that. They bring tea-baskets, and leave bottles and orange-peel. But they never see it at night, or when it is savage. And there is mockery, too, though whether it is worth the old folks' while to mis-wish such people——?"

"But you do."

"I have done."

He rolled over and lay prone, with his chin on his crossed wrists.

"It's fine country—but it does not pull me like the old place."

"No."

Her eyes were quick and deep.

"So, it is pulling? I thought so. You know, last night, when we went wandering down that lane——"

"You were silent."

"With you—I can be quiet as midnight. And then— we heard that woman crying in a cottage, though what she was crying about we shall never know. Did it say anything to you?"

"Some fool man."

She stretched out a hand and let it rest on his shoulder.

"It sent my thoughts back. You've been restless, John."

"Not with you."

"Is it the old place?"

"No, not the old place in itself."

"You are not satisfied. I want you to tell me how you feel, for I have been feeling something."

"I feel as though I had left something behind."

"So you did—fear."

"In a way."

"Yes, as though you had shot at the fellow from an ambush, and left an arrow sticking in him. I have been asking myself whether it was worth while."

He raised his head and smiled at her.

"Is that all?"

"No. Is it with you?"

"I have wondered whether it hasn't hurt her more than him."

Suvla John

"The same here. I knew that I had to get right to the heart of it. I'm made that way. And I wanted you to be made that way. It seems a pity——"

"Shoot straight."

"It seems a pity to make two lame lives still lamer."

Suvla turned and sat up.

"That's how you feel?"

"I do."

"You are a great woman, Richenda. I suppose you have made me feel like that. It came gradually—the thought that I had been nothing more than a mischievous beast."

"My dear," she said, "you were more than that. You are so big at times that you don't realize how easily the little people get hurt. You could give up everything to your brother, and then——"

"And then?"

"You throw a stone at a cur. If you had thrown that stone seven years ago—it would have been a right action, but after all these years!"

"Richenda, I shall call you the Iron Virgin."

"Am I right? Think right back. Was it for the woman?"

"Not wholly. Yes, I'll confess; I liked to think of him with a sore spot in his soul."

She was silent awhile, but she held his hand.

"My dear, was it worth while—for you? I have no morals—in the tame social sense. I'm fastidious; I have a personal pride. I know that half the things we pretend to believe and to do—well, it's just social humbug. Civilization has to strike an average, and put up notice boards. I go by pride, my own sense of completeness. If you had shot that cur I should have nodded my head and understood, but knowing you I should have wondered whether it was worth while."

His grip of her hand was strong.

"And you would have shut your mouth? And the Law could have gone hang?"

"Of course. There are times when one goes against the social contact—brushes through it. What is a policeman to me but a necessary social bug-a-boo? I'm more fastidious than the Law."

"You step over it."

"There might be occasions when I should choose to be quite alone. Everyone has that right."

Suvla John

"Not everyone, Richenda. Only the very few. The tame man has to wear some sort of uniform, and be given a palm branch or an idiotic red flag. The naked souls are pretty rare."

"Perhaps I am one of them," she said.

3

The day that followed was grey with a soft greyness, windless and still, and yet as Suvla and Richenda climbed to the top of a wooded hill, a sudden breeze came out of the west and ruffled the foliage. The trees raised gentle and protesting hands. There was a murmuring, a movement of unrest.

Richenda turned aside to a field gate hung upon rough stone posts, and below her the crumpled green valleys were deep and dim. Leaning upon the gate she looked at the vague sweep of the distant moor, sunless to-day, and mysteriously brooding, and her face reflected some of the moor's mystery.

"You see," she said, and pointed.

Suvla's glance came back from the moor to her serious face. Never had her eyes looked so black in the warm brown glow of her. Her lips were firmly set, and she held her head proudly, defying some vague menace.

"Yesterday was a good day."

"This green sadness—this England. It turns one to tears."

"You!"

"We sensitives wear armour. We put it off with the few."

"Is your armour off, Richenda?"

"Yes. And yours?"

"Laid at your feet. O, woman of completeness, you have put a spell upon me."

She gave him deep soft eyes.

"What spell?"

"You know. And your passion for completeness! To round off a thing till it looks like a perfect fruit, glossy and unmarked. Why should one wish for it?"

"Pride."

123

Suvla John

"O, something more than that. The old mad knight of Spain! You cannot reason it out. Life cannot be reasoned out. So, you want completeness?"

She bent her head.

"I do. It is a sort of passion I have. I want what is ours to begin like a perfect fruit with no other poor fruit lying rotten and unhappy."

"Can one cure unhappiness?"

"Have you thought what you can do?"

"Can one think out other people's lives? It is a problem."

"Something for you to fight, John Suvla. I feel that you should go back."

"I am going back. But, my dear, it is kinder to be dead."

"To her. Yes. But this arrow is a wound."

"The strong hand will pull it out?"

"Your hand would. And if such a *beau geste* cannot bring a man to his knees——"

"He will hate me the more."

"But will he? You cannot tell. Besides—one must act up—not down to a man."

"Coals of fire! Subtle retaliation."

"No. Not for you. If he cannot rise—well, that's his fate."

He drew closer, and his arm lay gently across her shoulders.

"Richenda, when you stretch out a hand to a bad dog, you are never quite sure whether he will cringe or bite."

"But—you stretch out your hand. That's completeness. Besides, badness is relative. If a man has had poison in him for seven years, and you neutralize that poison——"

"Yes—I see. I give him a second chance—with her, and to her. But—my dear——"

He looked at the distant moon, and his eyes were deep.

"It may not work, or it may work quite differently. Life is rather like the old alchemy; you mix your stuff, and it may blow you through the floor."

"But they mixed the stuff."

"They did; brave old dreamers."

"And so will you."

He drew her closer.

Suvla John

"But—how? Well, that's the adventure. Seems I shall have to lie out on Hackbury again, and get the feel of things. And you?"

"I shall not be far away."

"Great woman."

"We will turn back to-morrow."

"Eastward ho!"

XIII

I

IT was at Shaftesbury that Suvla left Richenda and her people, marching down out of the old hill town by way of the steep grey street under the abbey wall. Richenda went with him, a very solemn Richenda, sending her man upon the last adventure that he would dare alone. Suvla was gaillard, and upon the road he rallied her on the dear seriousness of her face.

"You look deathly solemn, Queen!"

"Does it vex you?"

"A walk to the railway station, a third-class carriage, a ten-mile tramp in the dark. Is it so serious?"

"Why should I feel that things might go amiss?"

"They might. But what is there that can hurt us?"

"I don't know. One does not know. It is just a feeling. I ought not to have said."

He held her arm.

"No secrets, girl. I think you trust me."

"It is not that. Perhaps I am growing sentimental!"

"I began it—long ago. Why worry?"

They walked on in silence for half a minute. Suvla with a pack upon his back, and looking like some hardy country lover on a walking tour; and Richenda glanced at his pack.

"You will be there to-night."

"On Hackbury."

"We shall move at once. It should take us five days. I shall leave the 'show' at Farnham and come on alone. You will have four days with nothing but that pack."

He smiled at her.

"Does that worry you? You should have seen me at Suvla during the great storm, all mud and misery, and feeling that I had no feet. Nowhere to lie down for three whole days—except in a sort of frozen quagmire. Hackbury—after that——!"

Suvla John

She answered his smile.

"You shall have a six-course dinner on the day that I arrive."

"All cooked by you?"

"Perhaps."

"And coffee?"

"And a liqueur. And perhaps——"

They gripped hands for a moment, with arms touching as they walked.

"Richenda——"

Her colour deepened.

"Tell me—you said Panhurst?"

"Yes—try Panhurst farm. The old chap there has a wild field or two on the edge of the woods. He would rent you a standing. Bulmer was his name; I think he is there still."

"I'll remember. But supposing I have to go elsewhere?"

"Well, in that case—let's say Panhurst Mound at ten o'clock. The Mound is on the high ground above the farm. It has five or six old Scotch firs on it. Anyone will tell you."

"I'll remember."

A little way from the station she paused, and held his hand for a moment.

"I am going back—now."

Their eyes held and hid nothing.

"You great woman," he said; "I want you, as I have never wanted anything else."

She stood and watched him walk away, and when he was out of sight, her face became overshadowed. She questioned something, herself, life.

"Is it fate?" was her thought; "and what is fate? How can any harm come of it?"

2

High upon Hackbury among the pines in the hollow below the round barrow Suvla lit his fire. The night was warm and dry, and an overcast sky held off the fall of the dew. Of fern there was plenty, and he had cut swaths of it and made a bed under the shelter of an old yew.

Suvla John

Alone with the night and his fire he let his thoughts go where they pleased, and the height of their pleasure was Richenda. She was the mistress of his maturity, queen of all his vagabond wisdom; and all his wanderings seemed to lead up to her, the woman on the hilltop. Her inevitableness was supreme. With a pointing hand she had sent him to Hackbury, and bade him look down upon the complex of things below, but she had changed the temper of his vision, and he gave her his thanks for it.

For with all her pride she had that most precious of powers—the power of understanding, and it seemed to him that her understanding justified her pride.

Completeness! Yes, that was a good word, a master word, a symbol of power. Not the sentimental resignation of a beautiful sad body hanging on a cross—but accomplishment, proud self-expression. He stooped to recognize his own incompleteness. In Richenda he had found that other completeness, something that was guiding, stimulating, mordantly tender.

"She's great," he thought, spreading his hands to the fire.

With that he fell to thinking how few were the things that he had respected. Courage, yes, and a high sort of recklessness, strength, laughter, but always he had lacked just that something which Richenda gave to him. She was clean, a new blade cutting at life. And with her how absurdly simple life seemed. What a solemn hash he had been striving all these years, letting his life centre about the memory of a little cad who—in a moment of hysterical and vicious frenzy—had fired a bullet into his back.

"Why—I owe the fellow my thanks."

He smiled at the fire, realizing that hatred is a fatal flame. It consumes the hater. Disdain is the most a man should allow himself. Richenda had taught him the kingliness of disdain, the high indifference, the magnanimity that has a downward smile. It seemed to him that this adventure was on the way to an easy completeness. He had but to catch his man alone and speak a dozen words. Forgiving meant the end of his responsibility.

But did it? For there was Elsie. Her weakness had been a sentimental weakness, her unhappiness a kind of fragrance cherished from the past. Just like

Suvla John

that spray of honeysuckle! Richenda had warned him, and Richenda's reading of Elsie had been a revealing of herself, a steady and proud tenderness.

"Leave her the illusion. Some women are made to kneel at the foot of a cross."

Yes, Richenda was right. He had to keep away from Elsie, and leave her her illusion. Blaber would never tell. That he would be kinder to his wife was the thing to be hoped for.

And again, Richenda had spoken deep words.

"Kindness comes of itself. You cannot coerce it—John. It is not born of fear."

So much for Richenda's plan, wise, generous, and sincere, ready to fly like a winging bird, while in the dark valley down yonder a hired American "tin pan" rattled Robert Blaber from Shottesford station. Blaber had told the man to stop at the bottom of Feldhurst Hill—"I'll walk the rest of the way"—and by the old toll-house he climbed out and paid him.

"You have got another mile and a half, sir."

As if Blaber did not know, and had not planned the stealthiness of the last mile!

"You are a new man here."

"Yes, sir. Took on with Mr. Mason last month."

No more was said, and Blaber attacked the hill, while the taxi-man drove back, thinking—if he troubled to think at all—that the gentleman had a reason for slinking home on foot. To walk in a dark lane on a summer night just for the pleasure of it, was beyond the motor-man's appreciation of things physical. Of course —if there had been a girl!—yes, that was understandable, something to cuddle.

Blaber went on into the secret night, under the black sweep of the beech boughs. He walked quickly and once or twice he paused to listen, but there were no woodland sounds, and his restlessness was peculiar. His right hand, tucked into a side pocket of his coat, appeared to grip something. An occasional quick turn of the chin betrayed uneasiness.

"It was six weeks ago."

He was startled by his own voice, for the thought had translated itself into sound. He had caught himself talking to himself. "Like any village idiot," as he put it.

Yet, he felt chilled. The mood of the last six weeks

had reminded him of those hours of vile tension during the war when some ominous adventure had been in the air, that feeling of nausea without a stomach, those moments of abysmal gloom, and those other moments when he had felt mad with a kind of futile madness. Anything to get out of it! Who cared? Just silly butchery! What were five thousand pounds a year worth if any fool in a brass hat could send you out to face a machine-gun? How he had hated any man who had been in a position to give him an order! How he had hated——

He drew a sharp breath.

"Why the devil doesn't something happen?"

That was the abominable part of it. For six weeks he had been waiting like a man shut up in a black and silent room, knowing that an enemy was in it, a man with a knife. And nothing had happened. It was absurd.

For all the rage of the war had gone, and for years he had been living as though the war and its violences had never happened. He had been plunged back into the evil dream of it, and there were times when it seemed like a dream, absurd and unreal.

His fear had tracked out every possible explanation. Perhaps some blackguard soldier, who had been in Shere's platoon on the night of the evacuation, had turned black-mailer, and had come very near to imagining the truth. Then, six weeks of silence had ruled out this hypothesis. A blackmailer would have followed up the first attack, and not have waited.

Blaber paused under a beech tree, and felt the silence of the woodlands round him, a silence that was familiar and friendly. The fear that had come back into his life seemed to struggle with this silence as it struggled with the irritable yet cold complacency of his normal self. Had the thing happened? Had he really fired that shot? Or had he imagined it all on that night of terror? Had he imagined the voice in the beech wood?

He put his hand to his head.

No—the first part of the picture was real. But what of the rest? Did things come back to haunt a man and drive him mad? Was this the beginning of insanity, and that voice the first of a whole string of delusions? There had been no insanity in the Blaber clan, those hard-headed, evangelical people who had believed in

Suvla John

Jehovah and scoffed at ghosts. They had been clean-living people.

But—then—that bullet! He had picked it up off the floor and locked it away in his desk. Had that been another delusion and was there no bullet in his desk, but only the imagined shape of one?

He had not unlocked the drawer since the night when he had hidden the thing away. Perhaps there was no bullet there? He would go and look before he went to bed.

Blaber walked on, remembering why he had come back before Wynyats expected him, and why he was walking that last mile of the road. He was supposed to be in town, staying for a couple of nights at his club, with some real or imaginary affairs to be dealt with, and a sudden gust of suspicion had swept him out of town. His whole life had begun to move against a background of suspicion.

At Wynyats most of the lights were out, and to Blaber, passing in by way of the side gate towards the stables, the house looked to be at the end of its working day. He stood where a path opened in a mass of flowering shrubs, and his scanning of the house revealed one window on the ground floor where lights still burned. The blind was up and the curtains but half drawn, and he could see some of the detail of the room, patches of colour, the pink shade of an electric light upon a writing-desk. It was Elsie's room.

He crossed the lawn, diverging towards the left and drawing nearer to his wife's window. A brownness that was a head showed close to the pink shade of the lamp. A little half of circle of turf reached to the window between two beds of hybrid teas, and the light from it lit up the greenness of the grass, and striking upon the scattered roses, turned them to points of red and white and carmine. The interior of the room had a soft brilliancy. His wife's bent head was surrounded by the delicate sentiment of her treasures, books, pictures, photographs, a blue bowl full of roses, a high-backed chair with a black velvet cloak thrown over it.

Blaber came to a pause. The soft sensuousness of the room, the woman's head with the light falling upon its hair, the white curve of the forehead seen below its wreath of shadow, stirred him to sudden self-pity. This woman belonged to him. His old desire for her returned,

131

but it was no mere physical yearning. Sympathy, a woman's hands, to feel less horribly alone in the warmth of her human nearness.

He wondered what Elsie was doing. Writing letters —perhaps? Her bent head had a peculiar stillness, and he saw a moth flutter in and circle about the lamp. It seemed to pass and repass behind her soft hair, like some silvery shuttle weaving ghost thoughts. She did not move. His self pity had made him forget for the moment why he had come back to Wynyats when no one expected him, but his suspicion revived, to link itself with his sudden desire for her. He wanted to discover why she sat there alone. His sense of possession—ever a dominant force—urged his right to see and to feel. Why should this woman be anything but his—even in her secret moments apart? What was she doing—dreaming, thinking?

He approached the window, moving across the grass like an ape, crouching and using his hands. He reached the broad band of light where the grass was green and the roses regained their colours. He could hear no movement, and very slowly he raised his eyes above the sill of the window and looked in.

Her face was downturned. He saw the pretty spreading of her hair, the white streak of her forehead, the eyebrows and lashes, the little line of her nose, her soft chin. She was holding something in her hands, and seemed lost, absorbed in regarding it. The moth was making a soft flutter against the globe of the lamp.

Blaber's eyes were fixed upon the thing she held in her hands. It was an oblong piece of pasteboard, obviously a photograph.

A moment later her startled eyes were looking into his—for she had become suddenly aware of a presence. Her eyes looked big and black, and that expressive mouth of hers had a wounded and frightened piteousness. She did not utter a word.

Blaber leaned over the sill and took the thing she held out of her hands, and she sat like one paralysed, unresisting.

He glanced at the photograph.

"I thought so."

His face looked frozen. He had the air of a man trembling with violent impulses, but unable to put them into expression. When he laid the photograph down

Suvla John

upon the desk he did it quite gently, but to the woman his gentleness had a quality of horror.

"You are madder than I am," he said.

She stared, feeling helpless. His mouth was all awry, and she could see his teeth.

"Adultery, a queer sort—with a dead man!"

Her eyes grew wide.

"Don't—— What do you mean?"

"Take it to bed with you, damn you."

He flung round and disappeared, and presently she heard him in the house, and the violent banging of a door.

3

Elsie came down late to breakfast, fearing to come at all, and yet afraid to stay away.

Her husband was at the table, with the usual paper propped up against the sugar bowl, nor did he look up when she entered.

Elsie sat down, and not until she had seated herself did she notice something in the middle of her plate, a bullet set on end. Her surprised stare flicked into a sudden glance at Blaber. He was watching her, and their eyes met.

"What's the matter?"

"This—thing on my plate."

He half rose, and looked down over the big bowl of roses and the silver teapot and jug.

"What?"

His eyes bewildered her.

"This. Did you put it here?"

His retort was still more astonishing to her.

"There's nothing there. I tell you. Haven't I eyes? Don't be a fool."

She stared mutely and then fell to pouring out her tea. For a while she feared to move the thing that Blaber had refused to see, but presently she smuggled it away under the edge of her saucer, while his face was hidden behind the paper. She did not know what to think or what to do, whether he was serious or making a bitter fool of her, whether he was mad or cruelly sane. She helped herself from the silver dish, and with her eyes on the plate she tried to eat as though he was not there. Her scared eyes hid themselves until she felt constrained to look across the table to see whether Blaber was watching her.

He was. His glance met hers over the top of the paper, and she had a feeling that he had been watching her ever since she had removed that thing from her plate.

Her plaintive mouth grew tremulous.

"Aren't you well, Robert?"

"Well! What do you mean?"

"I always say the wrong thing."

"You do."

He got up with the paper in his hand and began to fold it and refold it with nervous, jerky movements.

"I want your keys."

"My keys?"

She looked bewildered.

"I suppose you have got all sorts of sentimental stuff hidden away in that blessed bureau of yours. Well, I'm going to clear it out. Our life's been nothing but the darned dream of a dead man."

Her helplessness was obvious, and so was her fear.

"Only a few old letters and things, Robert. All that was before—— You knew——"

"Did I know? Anyway, I'm going to kick this dead man out of my house."

"You can't," she said, suddenly desperate before a rush of tears.

Her words seemed to strike him with peculiar significance. His narrow face looked all edge.

"Is that a threat?"

"I don't understand——"

"I said—a threat. Give me your keys."

She rose, and pushing the chair aside, backed away from the menace in his eyes.

"I don't understand. Why is it you are so strange——?"

"I want those keys."

"They are upstairs."

"Get them."

She went, with wet eyes and a bewildering sense of tragedy, like a child weeping and unable to understand. It was as though he suspected her of something. And all these poor little relics, her letters, her very diary, he would find them, read them. It was an outrage, and suddenly

Suvla John

she felt it was an outrage, an abominable invasion of a sacred memory. Why should she submit? She would not submit. She would go back and tell him.

Half-way down the stairs she saw him standing below her in the hall. She paused, leaning against the rail.

"Robert, you have no right——"

"Have you got those keys?"

"No. I won't——"

It seemed to her that something mad and violent looked up at her out of his eyes. They were all red.

"All right. A poker will do. Keep your damned keys."

He went quickly across the hall and into her room, slamming the door after him. She heard the key turned. And then there was a sound of things being smashed.

A scared maid came down the stairs.

"What is it, ma'am?"

Elsie steadied herself.

"Nothing, Parker."

She went slowly down the stairs and out through the door into the garden. The sun was shining, and as she stood on the ground of the drive she heard blows and the splintering of wood.

"Oh, how could he!"

Her bewilderment was like a sudden blindness. She seemed to go gropingly across the grass towards the shadows of the trees.

"What does it mean, what does it all mean?"

XIV

I

A HEAVIER greenness filled the valley, but when Blaber's wife stepped through one of the long windows into the Manor garden, July wore a cloak of many colours. Somewhere behind her a servant's voice was offering guidance. "You'll find Mrs. Shere there, ma'am. By the sweet peas, most likely." Elsie did not seem to hear. Her emotions were afloat upon this sea of colour where Sybil's love of riotous splendour had overborne old surly Thomson's orderly niceness. This garden dreamed; it was old and it was young. It smelt of mignonette with the dew upon it, shy, unbrilliant reseda, scenting the petticoats of more flamboyant beauties. So beautiful was it that it brought a little, choking pathos into Elsie's throat, self, pity, intimate and wounded. "Mrs. Shere." How often had she dreamed that she was Mrs. Shere, walking in this very garden, a soft creature with large, soft eyes, while up at Wynyats a raging man had broken and scattered the sacred relic of a dream.

She came upon Sybil, or rather—Sybil came upon her, emerging suddenly through a cleft in a yew hedge where purple phlox and yellow achillea rose bosom high. At a glance Sybil saw tragedy, the tragedy of a childish poignancy in the child's face of Elsie.

"My dear——!"

"Oh—I'm so unhappy——"

"Poor Elsie; let's go this way."

She left her basket of sweet peas forgotten in the sunlight on the broad turf path, and thinking of the most quiet corner of this little garden world, she took Bob Blaber's wife to the little Georgian garden house at the end of the terrace above the moat. Water and lilies lay on two sides of it, and from its low stone steps the grey paving of the terrace spread a stately solitude.

Suvla John

There were chairs in the garden house, old wicket chairs—the same as ever. One of them had a lame leg and a memory attached to it.

"Not that one, dear; it's broken."

"I know. Everything's broken——"

She was in tears now, seated in that familiar chair and remembering how it had come to possess a lame leg one night in June.

"Bob's broken everything."

"Tell me."

"He found me looking at John's picture. He said a horrible thing, and this morning he asked me for my keys. I wouldn't give them. He went into my room and broke things open——"

"Unpardonable!"

"Sybil, I think he's mad."

She pressed a handkerchief to her mouth and looked at Sybil with wide, wet eyes.

"The last few weeks—it has been ghastly. He's always watching me. Not saying anything—at least—not till last night. He does such extraordinary things."

"Tell me."

"It sounds absurd. I found a bullet on my plate at breakfast."

"A bullet!"

"And when I showed it to him he flew into a rage and said there was nothing there."

"My poor dear. But—why——?"

"Oh—I don't know. I can't understand. I suppose —it may be—because—neither of us have been happy— and I—I couldn't forget. He always had such a strange temper; it frightened me from the very first——"

Sybil sat very still. How could it help matters to call a cad a cad, or to dilate upon the obvious? The things that she might have said she knew to be answerable; moreover, she had not forgotten Elsie's obsession, the wedded widowhood, the eternal illusion, the strangeness of the writing on the wall in Feldhurst church. Even a cad must be allowed his provocations, and Blaber had had them. His sin had been that he had snarled, where a bigger-hearted man would have healed the past with a patient tenderness. It would have been so easy to have healed poor Elsie.

Meanwhile, something had to be done. Wynyats, with an evil-tempered man raging and breaking a child's toys, was no place for Elsie—at least, not till Robert Blaber had come to his senses. Sybil was a resolute creature with a gift for making swift and sound decisions. Dick, playfully protesting, had sometimes called her "the little colonel."

"You must stay to lunch, Elsie."

"Oh—but if I don't go back—he will——"

"Let him."

"I ran down here—just as I was—without a hat. I felt that I had to run somewhere——"

"Quite right. You will stay to lunch—and I shall speak to Dick."

"But what can Dick do?"

"My dear, we regard you as part of the family. We have a right to protest—on occasions."

"It will only make him angrier."

"Perhaps not. Anyhow, no man has a right to unlimited bad temper. I'll go and find Dick. Dick has a way with people."

"But Robert——"

"He hates Dick. I know. It is not Dick—but the Shere in Dick he hates. You won't be bothered here, dear."

Sybil left Elsie there and went in search of her husband. She found him in the walled fruit-garden, helping old Thomson to net some of the peach trees.

"Dick——"

She waited at the end of a box-edged path, and understanding that she had something to tell him that was not for old Thomson's ears, he left Thomson to a restrained and puritanical struggle with the netting and came towards her.

"Wanted?"

"Elsie's here."

"Oh! Anything wrong?"

"Very wrong. Blaber seems to have been behaving like a beast. She came flying down here without a hat."

"What has Blaber been doing?"

"He seems to have got in a rage over her cult of poor John. Broke into her room—and smashed or tore up all her treasures."

"What a cad!"

"Yes, I know. But a cad may have excuses. Elsie thinks him mad."

"A man in a blind rage is mad."

"She has been telling me one or two queer things."
His blue eyes questioned hers.

"Well—poor old Elsie—herself—— I'm not blaming her; she can't help it——"

"But—if—what she told me is true—someone up there is not quite sane."

Dick listened to all that she had to tell him, his face taking on that expression that Sybil knew so well. She called it his "knightly face," a bleak kindling of it, an angry radiance, something finely ominous in the blue eyes.

"He ought to see a doctor. Where is Elsie?"

"In the garden-house. I am keeping her to lunch. I thought——"

"I'll go up and see Blaber. It is supposed to be a fool's game, interfering between husband and wife. I'm one of the fools."

"There is a use for such folly, dear man; I like it. This sort of thing can't go on."

"Exactly. It is just as well that Blaber should know that Elsie has friends and that a man can't do just as he pleases. But I want to be fair."

"You always are. A man can say things to another man. It all depends——"

"On Blaber being anything of a sportsman. In case of trouble, Elsie can come to us. I'll tell him so—frankly—if he shows his nasty teeth."

"I fancy he is better at showing them at Elsie. That is what I loathe about a man like Bob Blaber. A regular Furioso—in the nursery or the drawing-room, or to people who can't answer back."

"I'll go up now, Celli."

"Why not wait till after lunch? Give him time to cool."

"Wise woman. And Elsie——?"

"Leave her to me."

2

Richard Shere walked up to Wynyats after lunch.

An open car was waiting in the drive—Blaber's car—and as Shere came to the open door he caught sight of Robert Blaber in the hall. A leather attaché case lay on the gate-legged table, and Blaber, turning to lift the lid

Suvla John

and place some papers in it, saw Shere standing in the porch.

His narrow face reminded Shere of a pale and sinister face looking out of the faded gloom of a Spanish picture. There was a moment of hesitation before Blaber closed the attaché case with a click of the catches and pushed it across the table. To Shere the whites of Blaber's eyes looked peculiarly brilliant.

"Come in."

He glanced at his wrist-watch as Shere entered.

"What can I do for you? I have five minutes."

Shere laid his hat on the table.

"Off somewhere?"

"Town."

"I see. Well—I wanted a few words."

Blaber's face was in half profile, a sidelong face, giving the impression of distortion.

"I suppose my wife scuttled off to you."

"Yes. She can stay with us if necessary."

He glanced at the open door of the dining-room.

"Shall we go in there?"

"Thanks. There is nothing to discuss. Elsie's nothing better than a prostitute."

He spoke with such viciousness, his whole face flickering with a kind of white anger, that Shere began to wonder whether Elsie had not realized the truth.

"There is no need to talk like that, Blaber. People have ears."

"Let them hear. I'm off to town for a night or two. I can't divorce her for carrying on an affair with a dead man, but I've torn up and burnt all her letters and photos. You can go back and tell her so."

Shere sat down sideways at the table. It was no use losing one's temper with a man who was in an emotional frenzy.

"Isn't it rather a pity, Blaber?"

"I don't want pity. I can look after myself."

"You mean—that it is hopeless?"

Blaber glanced again at his watch.

"One moment. You can go back and tell Elsie that I have done away with all her sloppy truck. She can come back here—if she wants to, and try and behave like a wife."

"You offer nothing?"

"I offer to—let her behave—as a woman should."

Shere rose from the table.

"She's rather a child, you know, Blaber. One ought not to frighten a child."

"Shut up. I don't want any advice from you, Shere. You can go to——"

He snatched up the attaché case, and picking up a coat from a chair, flung it over his shoulder. His face still wore that look of distortion.

"She can come back or stay away. If she's wise she will come back. Anyway—she won't have me here for two or three nights. That's the lot."

He passed round Shere and went out into the porch and, like his wife before him, he had forgotten to put on a hat. The chauffeur was standing beside the car. He opened the door with a glance at his master's bare head.

"The station, Cox."

"Very good, sir."

Shere came out into the porch, and with a conscious-ness of his failure as of something inevitable and beyond him, he watched the car pull out, with Blaber sitting stiff and strange beside the man. But half-way down the drive Shere heard the squeal of the brakes and the throttling down of the engine. The chauffeur came running back to find Shere still in the porch.

"Forgotten his hat, sir."

The man's eyes were interrogative, and Shere nodded at him.

"All right."

He walked out into the sunlight, wondering how far the forgetting of a hat justified him in suspecting another man of being not quite sane.

3

Elsie chose to go back. It was an emotional choice, and neither Sybil nor Richard Shere attempted to oppose it.

Sybil walked up with her to Wynyats by way of the park, and at Wynyats Elsie went straight to her own sit-ting-room, glancing back over her shoulder, and uttering the one word, "Come." Servants had been busy here since Blaber's going and had cleared the burnt remnants out of the grate; but there was the smashed flap of the bureau and the broken drawers to prove to Sybil that Elsie had not dreamed.

Suvla John

"You see!"

She faltered about the room, seemingly afraid to go to the bureau, like a bird avoiding a rifled nest.

"You go. I suppose he burnt everything."

And that is what had happened. Sybil turned down the split rosewood panel and drew out drawer after drawer; the bureau was empty; even the unused notepaper, the pens, pencils, and all the odd clutter that a woman loves to collect had disappeared. A black smudge trailing down one wall showed where Blaber's furious hand had sent the ink-pot crashing.

"Everything's gone, Sybil."

Her voice was a hushed wail. She sat down on the rose-coloured sofa and gazed blankly at the blue-black stain on the wallpaper. She looked like a pathetic child whose nursery had been ransacked and all her beloved toys smashed.

Sybil Shere felt fierce, but her anger veiled itself in gentleness.

"Some men are cads. No man has a right to do such a thing."

She closed the drawers and tried to shut the broken flap, but it would not close.

"You mean to stay—after this?"

"It doesn't seem to matter."

"It does matter. You have got to make up your mind about it, Elsie."

A glance at Elsie's face brought to her the realization of her friend's emotional helplessness.

"What ought I to do?"

"Has he ever been rough to you?"

"Only with words."

"My dear, they can be more cruel than fists. Shall I tell you what I should do?"

Elsie's eyes were big and scared.

"Well——?"

"Directly he comes back you should leave the house and come and stay with us. Leave the next move to him. Let him come to you. He cannot bully you in our house. Then—you will have to state your conditions."

"I'm such a coward."

"If you like—Dick or I—will act for you. Robert has got to do more than say he is sorry; he will have to promise certain things. What is more—we will have them in writing."

Suvla John

"But will he?"

"We shall see. I'm not a lawyer, but in these days—I believe—that if one of the partners is too beastly to live with—you can claim to live by yourself. Do you want to?"

She sat down beside Elsie, and put an arm round her.

"It is up to you, dear, to choose. Life isn't all logic and common sense. It depends on how you feel."

"I want to go, Sybil."

"But you feel you ought to stay?"

"Yes—somehow. I—did—promise. If I had promised John—I can't put it into words. John always used to despise people who could not play a losing game."

And Sybil understood. She drew Elsie to her—and kissed her.

"That's true. I won't argue against that, at least—not yet. He ought to feel it—if he can feel anything. And—we—shall be there."

4

Sybil and her man talked it over that evening in the garden.

"What a woman does—she does. But I think the chap ought to be watched."

"It is Elsie's risk, Jack, and if she cares to take it. Women do take risks, risks of the heart."

"Instinct?"

"Oh, sometimes—it's our way of winning through."

"I suppose you are right."

While, somewhere in the garden a man listened to their voices, hoping that they would come nearer to him, but not too near. It had been an empty day for Suvla John. To catch a man alone was not so easy, especially when the catch had to be made in some lonely place, and the only glimpse that Suvla had had of Robert Blaber was of his being driven in a car under the broken light of the Feldhurst beeches. Suvla had waited for an hour, and had seen the car come back empty.

XV

I

ELSIE dined alone, with a sympathetic maid trying to persuade her to eat more than she had the heart to eat, as though a well-filled body could make her forget an empty soul.

"I'm not hungry, Parker."

"Cook's made you your favourite fruit salad, madam."

"How kind of her. I will have just a little."

At the end of the solitary meal she went out into the loggia, and, sitting down with her face to the sunset, waited for Parker to bring her coffee. She was still suffering from a feeling of bewilderment; the sanctuary in which she had lodged her illusion had been sacked and desecrated. She had one of those child natures that attaches itself to objects, cherished trifles, little symbolical relics, and all her relics had been destroyed. She had been shocked, and left trembling, but the dominant idea remained. Already she was beginning to collect herself about it, and to search in the wreckage for any relic that could be salved.

Parker appeared with the coffee. She was an austere woman of five-and-forty, with patches of red on her high cheekbones, and reserved brown eyes. Thin and tall, she held herself very erect, and she had need of this erectness. Her enemy was man. She had suffered, and she had never forgiven.

"White or black, madam?"

"White, Parker, please."

She watched Parker's capable hands with their big red knuckles. In winter Parker was subject to chilblains. Always, she had stood a little in awe of the woman, but to-night, in her loneliness, she felt to Parker as she had felt to her old nurse. Parker was severe, but beneath her severity was a body of strength upon which a weaker woman could lean.

Suvla John

"I am afraid—you have had—a rather upsetting day, Parker."

The maid stood holding the tray.

"Not for myself, madam."

"I don't want you to leave, Parker."

"I may say that I have no thought of leaving you, madam."

There was a pause, and Parker held her ground, rigidly loyal to this other woman.

"We found one or two things, madam."

She saw her mistress flush.

"They belonged to poor Mr. John Shere—who was killed——"

"Among the ashes, madam, we found the bowl of a pipe, a key, and two brass buttons. I cleaned them. They are in my work-box."

"Thank you, Parker."

"Shall I fetch them, madam?"

"Please."

Parker disappeared. For the moment her antagonism to everything that was male had concentrated itself against her employer, and in rescuing those trifles she had felt herself registering a point against him. She returned with the key, the charred bowl of a pipe, and two military buttons on the silver tray she had used for the coffee.

Elsie's eyes glimmered.

"You have cleaned the buttons, Parker."

"Yes, madam."

"They are quite bright."

She took them in the palm of her left hand, and her face dreamed.

"Bright as the poor gentleman's courage, madam. I have heard it said that Mr. Shere did not know what fear meant."

"He was very brave, Parker, too brave. If he had not been so brave——"

Parker gave a stiff bend of the head. She understood. She, too, had been a fool about a man, but her mistress's folly—if folly it was—had left her with a consuming and sacred memory.

"Perhaps, madam——?"

Elsie's eyes were large and questioning.

"Yes, Parker——?"

"I might keep—those things—for you?"

Suvla John

"Thank you, Parker. How kind. But—I must keep them myself—somewhere."

"Very good, madam. Is there anything else? I will put a hot-water bottle in your bed."

"Thank you, Parker. I am glad you are going to stay with me."

Parker left her with these trifles lying in her lap, a key, the charred bowl of a pipe, and two brass buttons. The key was big and heavy; it fitted the door of Feldhurst church, and had been lost by the sexton two or three years ago, though he did not suspect that a lady had stolen it. It had been plucked surreptitiously out of the church door by a woman whose one adventurous theft was unique and solitary. She picked up the key and looked at it. Yes, this key did symbolize the preservation of one doorway opening into her world of dreams; it had been one of the most cherished of her treasures.

She sat and watched the sun set behind Hengest's Farm, silhouetting the trees and one big chimney-stack, and she remembered how her husband had grudged the land and the house to those other men. He was selfish, possessive, a man who coveted the whole landscape. But she shrank from the thought of her husband, for her fear of him was the fear of a child that runs away and hides. Escape had come to her always by way of her dreams. So she hung up her dreams against the afterglow, while all the trees grew black, and the dew began to fall, and the lights went out in the coloured lamps of the flowers. There would be a moon, a great white moon in the clear sky, and moonlight made her restless, as though it created a more mysterious world in which she could wander.

Moreover, there was no one to watch. Robert had gone away, and she had a sure feeling that he would not surprise her again to-night. He would think that there was nothing else for him to discover and destroy.

The church key lay in her hand. It was magnetic. She rose up in the cool and scented gloom, and, entering the drawing-room, rang the bell.

"Oh, Parker, I am going to stroll down to Mrs. Shere's. I'll take the key."

"Would you like anyone to go with you, madam?"

"No; it is so quiet through the park. I don't suppose I shall be gone more than an hour."

"You had better have a cloak, madam. And shoes."

"Yes, my black velvet. Will you ask Mary——?"

Suvla John

"I'll fetch it for you, madam."

So Parker, the austere woman, sent Elsie forth on the first of one of those most tragic nights, when death and life were to come together. It was warm and still with the deep stillness of the woodlands, the great beeches masses of black silence, with the stars dusted above their tops. The grass was wet with dew, and from the earth and the green growth of it rose a moist fragrance. The slopes of Feldhurst Park were a sheeted greenness, and far down in the hollow the lights of the manor hung like points of gold.

Elsie knew every path here. She did not go as far as the gate by the lower pool, but turned up over the hanging hill under the beech gloom, for the fear of darkness and of lonely places was not with her. Moreover, as she reached the gate opening into the lane the first rays of the rising moon struck through the trees. Even as a child she had spoken of the earth's satellite as "Friend Moon." Two hundred yards farther on the lane met the high road, and almost opposite hung the white gate where the path went down to Feldhurst church.

Elsie loitered for a moment at the gate, watching the moon rising above the trees. There were towering spruces here, and delicate tasselled larches, and beyond them the solemn domes of the beeches. The valley below was full of the moonlight, and as Elsie descended into it she saw the shingled spire of the church like a big white ghost among the elms.

How often she had wished that John's body had been brought home and laid to rest in Feldhurst church. Somehow, it would have given her a more sure sense of possession. She had that type of mind that finds a happiness in putting flowers on graves. As it was she had nothing but that tablet of brass upon the wall, the letters he had cut as a boy in the old oak, and the remembered presence of him, tall and convincing and smilingly ironical. She had never discovered his irony, because a strong man does not look ironically into the eyes of a child.

Elsie walked on down the path under the high thorn hedge, the white cap of the church rising as she descended. She could sit for half an hour in the Shere pew, before hurrying on to the manor.

Suvla John

To Suvla the day had brought nothing but the realization of the fact that the opportunity he was in search of might prove more elusive than he had imagined. The return of the empty car had made it obvious that Blaber was not at Wynyats, though whether he would be absent for an hour, a day, or a week, John Suvla had no means of knowing.

He lay in the woods till dusk before making a move that brought him down to the high road above Feldhurst church, and here he sat for a while on a rail fence under a beech tree, and smoked his pipe while he considered the situation.

His thoughts went back to Richenda and her passion for completeness, and he was bound to admit that the day had been complete in the matter of self-denial. His food and drink had been bread and cheese and water from his water-bottle; his tobacco-pouch was nearly empty; the final stage appeared to be a tramp back to Hackbury and a bed in the fern.

"Seems—she has spoilt me a little," he reflected. "One is not quite so ready to play the hermit."

He uttered her name—Richenda. Had any woman ever been more fitly christened, or given a name that was more personal and convincing? Complete. Yes, she was superbly complete, a world in herself, a world that a man might explore and ever find new country. She was deep, and always there would be deeps, wild country, the sense of space. In the most intimate moments there would be a little streak of strangeness.

She would be on the road—now, or rather—drawn up for the night on some spot where she would sit on the steps of her caravan and smoke that queer little pipe of hers, a woman apart. Their mutual apartness had drawn them together. He was impressed by the seeming inevitableness of it. Fate, a foreordained affinity—what you please. He wanted her, and he felt that he would go on wanting her to the end of his days, even as a man desires life and self-expression, for he would express himself in her, and she in him. Her blood was as restless as his, but richer in the things that make for inborn wisdom. He felt that she would never tire. Such a woman held you for ever by reason of her passion and her completeness. She was like life; full of unexpectedness, deep, true to the things that are true, instinct with fine passion.

"I have not deserved it," was his thought. "Does one ever deserve the great things? Perhaps not. Wisdom lies in realizing their greatness."

He smiled at the unexpectedness of his own humility, but it was a consenting smile. An impulsive romanticism had coloured his vagabondage, and though he had laughed at it, the impulse of his romanticism had never failed. Realism was too much a thing of the gutter, and when you can smell white thorn in blossom, or a bean field, or Persian roses, why hold your nose over some unseemly human stench? It was the essential clearness of Richenda that delighted him, her cool and fastidious nakedness, her hatred of soiled conventions, and it was his inveterate romanticism that inspired the idea of an hour's vigil in Feldhurst church. He would sit in the Shere pew under the tablet that commemorated the death of John Shere, and he would give thanks to God for life and for Richenda.

So he walked down to Feldhurst church, and using his knife as he had used it before, he made his entry into the dim interior, and seating himself in the Shere pew, let himself think of life as it might have been and as it was. He gave thanks for Richenda, and in remembering that other woman he thought of her with self-revealed pity. Elsie would have been no mate for him, nor he for her. She would not have held him as he knew that Richenda would hold him. His recklessness had been blind but merciful.

The silence and the darkness enveloped John Suvla, but presently a greyness spread over the east window above him. The pew had once been a chapel, projecting beyond the line of the chancel wall, with the old entrance from the south aisle bricked up and plastered over. It had two windows, an east and a south, and it was the east window that showed the silver of the moonlight between the black mullions and the tracery. The light poured through, falling upon the white wall and the tablet of brass, and upon Suvla himself as he sat below the tablet. It silhouetted his head upon the plaster.

"Same old moon as at Suvla Bay," he thought. "How we used to curse you—sometimes!"

And then he heard a little, unexpected sound snapping the profound silence, the sound of a key turning in a lock. Hinges creaked. He heard someone enter the church,

Suvla John

a few soft footsteps, and then an interval of silence. Presently the footsteps began again. They came up the nave, and turned towards the Shere pew.

Suvla sat absolutely still. War and a wild life had taught him the protective uses of such stillness. His eyes looked straight forward across that part of the nave below the chancel steps, and this space was in deep shadow, for the moonlight had not reached it. The footsteps had ceased. Someone was standing there in the shadow within a few yards of him, but he could detect only the vaguest of outlines.

He wondered who the person was. Anyway, it was a singular hour for visiting a church. And it was probable that he was visible to the visitor, unless his stillness made him seem part of the oak wainscoting.

For some moments the silence held. It was broken by a curious and stifled cry. The footsteps were in retreat, like quick, frightened breaths, receding down the nave towards the porch. But Suvla had heard another sound, a rustling movement that warned him that the visitor had been a woman.

"She saw me," he thought.

He waited. He heard the porch door closed, and the key turned.

"The caretaker—I suppose. The woman may have left something here—and come to fetch it."

He allowed ten minutes to pass before he made his way to the window, and climbing through it, closed it noiselessly, and stood leaning against the wall. There was not a sound. He picked up the glass quarry and replaced it.

"That was a near thing. I shall have to be more careful."

Taking the warning to heart, he cut across the north portion of the churchyard, and climbing over the wall, made his way down the valley. He was alone here with the moon and a few sleeping cattle, but even in the moonlight it did not occur to him to think that he had been taken for a ghost, the ghost of his old self.

XVI

I

SYBIL SHERE sat reading, her back to the shaded lamp
and her chair turned to the open French window. Dick
was up at Hengest's, sitting in council with Merrow
and the men of the co-operative farm, for though these
Surrey labourers were running their own show they had
discovered that a gentleman may have his uses. There
had been arguments, quarrels, threats of secession. Agri-
cultural depression had set in, and though these co-opera-
tors had separated their eggs by adding dairying and
market gardening to ordinary arable farming, they were
finding the business more complex than it had appeared.
A monthly share-out had replaced regular wages, and the
share-out was proving less solid than some of the men
had expected. There were bills to be paid to the detested
but ubiquitous middlemen.

Richard Shere had provided the capital, but he had
also given something less tangible and almost as important, the balanced wisdom of the gentleman. He and
his forbears had known for a couple of centuries many
things that the labourers had not begun to learn. Merrow,
the inspirer of the scheme, had realized this difference.

"They are like a lot of children, sir. Their idea of
arguing is shouting. There are one or two who are greedy.
Some of 'em are jealous of me. I've been told not to put
on side. I have given one or two of 'em a pretty rough
dressing down, but they simply cheek me. ' Who are you
talking at, Tom Merrow?' It's the young ones. I want
you, sir, to act as a sort of chairman."

"Won't they rather resent that, Merrow?"

"No; I don't think they will, sir. At least—not the
ones who matter. If the two or three young louts clear
out, so much the better. They talk more and work less
than the older men. I wish you'd do it, sir. I have talked
it over with several, and they are with me."

So—Dick Shere had gone up to teach his political

Suvla John

equals that good manners, and self-restraint, and a quiet voice are of more value than noise and a sort of sprawling self-sufficiency. Moreover, he knew. He loved the land and all that belonged to it, and his love had understanding.

Sybil laid down her book, and fell to contemplating this modern phase of social England. She was more conservative than Dick, and yet more far-sighted. She came of Anglo-Indian stock, and had inherited some of its beliefs and prejudices, but she agreed that the English labourer was not a Hindoo peasant. Nor was he a Frenchman. He would never work so hard, even for himself. The man with a passion for independence does not talk of an eight-hour day.

"Of course they will fail," she reflected, "all—except Merrow."

Her eyes were turned towards the open window, their glances going out into the darkness beyond the little carpet of spread light. She had heard nothing. She was unaware of the window save as an empty frame, and suddenly the frame was filled by the figure of Elsie, an agitated Elsie with a face that was strangely white.

"Sybil—I have seen his ghost."

"My dear!"

She rose and made a restrained movement towards the figure in the black cloak.

"You startled me. Come in!"

"Sybil, his ghost!"

"Whose ghost, Elsie?"

"John's."

She came in, white and round-eyed, with a quality of exultation in her fear.

"John's ghost! My dear, sit down. Tell me."

She touched Elsie's arm, and with a hand laid along it pressed her gently towards the sofa. The emotional significance of the incident was conclusive; if Blaber was not quite sane, neither was his wife.

"Tell me about it."

"It was in the church. I had gone there; I have a key. You won't tell anybody, Sybil, about my key?"

"Of course not."

"It was only about half an hour ago. The moon was shining—and I was going to sit in the Shere pew. I go there sometimes; it seems to help. But when I got close to the pew——"

"Yes."

Suvla John

"I saw a man sitting there, just under John's tablet. He sat absolutely still. The moonlight was shining through the window on him."

"Supposing it was a man——"

"But it was John's head; I haven't forgotten the shape of it. It was his ghost, sitting in the old pew under his tablet."

Sybil did not contradict her, but she asked more questions.

"Did you speak to it?"

"No. It was such a shock—that I ran away."

"And locked the door after you?"

"Yes. You see, Sybil, the church was locked, and only a ghost could have been in it. Oh, my dear! Often and often I have felt that his spirit would come back to me."

She rested her forehead on Sybil's shoulder, and Sybil's hand stroked her head.

"You have been thinking a great deal about John lately?"

"Yes."

"That may account for it."

"But Sybil, does a ghost cast a shadow?"

"A shadow? How do you mean?"

"I saw the shadow of John's head on the wall; I saw it quite plainly."

Sybil's hand remained resting on Elsie's head. She was thinking of that curious incident of a few weeks ago, and of Mr. Blossom's discovery of the writing on the wall. There was something queer about the whole business. If the man seated in the pew had thrown a shadow on the wall—then—the shadow suggested physical solidity. But had Elsie seen a man in the Shere pew, or had she imagined it after the stress of the day's emotion? An unhappy and emotional woman visiting a church secretly at ten o'clock at night might be expected to see that which was dominating her own mind.

"I think someone ought to go down to the church, dear."

"Why?"

"To make sure. I'll ask Dick. He should be back at any moment. And I will walk back with you to Wynyats."

Elsie accepted these suggestions, for her emotional exaltations had begun to spread an aura about the night's happenings. Her obsession had found itself miraculously

Suvla John

justified. Her dead lover had appeared to her; she wished for no other explanation; the spirit of John Shere lived.

"I am sure it was John."

Sybil did not contradict her.

"Dick will go down——"

"But—you see—Dick may not be able to see what I saw."

She was looking at Sybil with wide, childlike eyes, in which a personal and possessive love exulted. John Shere had appeared to her. No one else might be able to see him, or he might not wish them to see him. He had come to her—Elsie, and had given her a proof of his great love; he had known how she had cherished the thought of him through all these years, and all the while—perhaps—he had been near to her. And, at the last, he had come to comfort her for what Robert had done.

"I wish I had spoken. But it was such a shock."

"Of course. Ah—here's Dick. Shall I tell him, dear?"

"No—I'll tell him. For dear John appeared—to me."

2

Shere went to Feldhurst church with an electric torch, and Elsie's borrowed key, while Sybil walked back with Elsie to Wynyats. Dick had promised to call for her at Wynyats after he had visited the church.

Nor did he discover anything of significance in Feldhurst church, and though he was no scoffer, he had no meeting with Elsie's ghost. The moonlight was shining upon the brass tablet, and Shere stood on the seat and examined the wall, half expecting to find some scrawl there. But the wall was innocent of any such message. He searched the pew, and turning his torch upon the flags of the church floor, he searched for traces of footmarks and found none.

An examination of the window in the chancel where John had made his adventurous entrance left him puzzled and undecided. He went and examined the window from the outside, and though there were indications of the lead having been tampered with, he could not swear that the quarry had been removed a second time.

At the end of half an hour he locked the porch door and walked up to Wynyats. Sybil had persuaded Elsie to

Suvla John

go to bed, but she appeared upon the stairs when she heard Shere's voice.

"Did you find anything?"

"Nothing."

She came down to him, wrapped up in a dressing-gown, her feet in pink slippers.

"But—that—proves nothing, Dick. I—saw—him. Perhaps he meant me to see."

Her voice was softly exultant.

"Have you my key?"

It lay in Shere's pocket, who was tempted to keep it, but a promise was a promise.

"Here."

"You won't tell?"

"Of course not. But—I should not go down there too often, Elsie."

Her answer nonplussed him.

"Why—how could John's spirit do me any harm?"

Shere took his wife back through the park, and in the moonlight and under the deep shadows of the trees they went arm in arm trying to disentangle the meaning of the experience. That it might be very serious in its reactions upon Elsie, was obvious to both of them, though whether the whole mystery was due to some psychical aberration of Elsie's they could not decide.

Shere believed that the whole mystery was of Elsie's making.

"I'm not being hard on Elsie, Celli, but one has to look on this affair as a doctor would look at it. It's an obsession."

"Supposing it to be an obsession, she believes everything."

"She may be lying. The best of women invent—when they get into a semi-hysterical state. Put a woman of Elsie's temperament—in an empty church—at ten o'clock on a moonlight night——"

"You would expect her to see anything?"

"She might see what she wanted to see. Self-suggestion, you know."

They had reached the gate by the lower pool, and Sybil paused here, with one hand on the gate.

"But there are one or two curious details. She said the figure cast a shadow."

"Yes—that is rather queer."

"You would not expect her to imagine a shadow, or to

suggest it to herself. Besides—it surprised her. And then—that piece of glass in the window. You remember —we thought at the time——"

"Just so—if Elsie had a key—why should she repeat John's old trick?· Unless—it was another example of suggestion."

"Rather far-fetched. And that scribbling on the wall?"

"I can only put the whole thing down to Elsie. She goes about in a kind of somnambulistic state—or whatever the psychologists call it. And she carries out certain suggestions from a part of herself, the part that is obsessed by her memories of John."

Sybil stood deep in thought.

"There is one possibility. It has just occurred to me." He leaned with his back against the gate.

"Has Bob Blaber anything to do with it?"

"Blaber? But where is the motive? At one moment he is behaving like a sot, smashing Elsie's treasures, and the next he is sitting in Feldhurst church—and being taken for a ghost. It does not explain anything."

They walked on across the park, and, entering the garden by the bridge, loitered to watch the moonlight on the water. They stood with shoulders touching, hands crossed upon the stone coping of the balustrade.

"Elsie will need watching, Celli. That's the only decision I can come to. If there is madness in it, she is a dear, harmless lunatic."

"I am wondering whether she ought to be alone."

"You can go up and see her to-morrow. The fact is I'm pretty tired."

"You must be, dear old thing. I have never asked you how the meeting went."

"Oh, quiet as a funeral. I had no trouble."

"Not even with Merrow's louts?"

"They are not bad chaps, Celli, only ignorant and rather full of the new democratic self-importance. One ought to have enough poise to be unaffected by that sort of thing."

"Yes, of course."

But she realized how few men had that poise; it was part of the large-heartedness that enabled her to believe that her own husband was like the house they lived in. To Sybil there was no other house like it in the whole world.

Suvla John

3

Elsie knelt at her bedroom window, a white figure with the shadow of her hair upon her shoulders, and her face raised to the moon.

For the happenings of that night seemed to her to be the culmination of all her years of loyalty to a dead man's memory, the pale and mysterious flower of all her pain. Her mood was one of ecstasy, as poets and priests have understood it. The supernatural had broken through into her world of dreams.

"Dear John—I always felt that you would come back to me. I prayed God to send you back, and He has heard me."

To Elsie the dim figure seen in Feldhurst church was the divine proof of consummation of all that she had prayed for. She had no doubt at all as to the reality of that figure, and her love had recognized the very shape of the head, even the shadow of it. That she was not quite normal was a debatable question. Normality demands limitations.

"How foolish of me to be frightened of you, John."

She smiled at the moon, and her eyes were luminously large.

"The next time you come to me I shall not be frighttened. Come soon, John, come soon."

And up on Hackbury her ghost-man was falling asleep on his bed of fern, little thinking that he had given such strange and perilous joy to a woman.

XVII

I

ON one of the great green chalk-hills above Salisbury, Richenda had drawn up for the night. The green van stood backed into a hollow that had been a chalk-pit, and from the steps of the van Richenda could see the spire of Salisbury, a thread of blue in the valley haze. A belt of beech trees had been planted above the hollow, and through them a wind blew, for on these uplands air was moving and the breath of it stirred in the beeches. The hollow itself was very still and full of the evening sunlight, and on one side of it the Beckett woman had lit a fire, and old Mother Beckett had a pot and a kettle slung on two iron hooks.

Richenda sat and surveyed the valley. She knew all this rolling country very well, but to-day it had a strangeness even though it was the same, for it was she who had changed, and her inward eyes saw the world anew. It was a richer world, but more perilous; its shadows were deeper, its sunlight more vivid. The wind moved more swiftly; she felt the troubling of the beech trees as a stirring of something inevitable within herself, a haunting tenderness laughing in the eyes of her pride.

The fire was on Richenda's left, and old Jenny Beckett, squatting over her pots, threw at Richenda many furtive and sidelong glances. And Richenda knew what was passing in the old rogue's mind. Jenny had hopes of Suvla's badness. She wanted to be able to say: "He's a bad lot. Didn't I warn ye?" There would be rejoicing among the Becketts over Suvla's badness, for he was a gorgio, and a new master, an inconvenient devil whom nobody wanted. Jenny called him a sponger, a flash blackguard who was after Richenda's money.

Richenda rose and came down the steps. Mrs. Beckett, peering into one of her pots, emitted a surprised grunt, a sound that was intended to attract the queen's attention.

"Dearie me! Bless us——"

Suvla John

"What's the matter, Jenny?"

"Nothing, my dear. But I did see something queer in the pot."

Richenda stood over her.

"Old women see what they wish to see."

"God forbid, dearie. What's black needs no soot, as the saying is. I couldn't help seeing your Mr. Suvla any more than I could help seein'——"

"Jenny, if you try your nonsense on me, you will go back to Brighton."

"Nonsense, my dear! Don't mock at what the spirits send. If I did see Mr. Suvla's face—and a young woman's face alongside it——"

Richenda gave her one steady look.

"Mr. Suvla has gone to buy horses. We shall be at Romsey to-morrow, and after that at New Alresford. The show will stop at Farnham, and you will stop with the show, Jenny."

Mrs. Beckett held up her claw-like hands.

"There, now, you be vexed with me. All because I saw two faces in a pot of water, and me not bein' able to help seein' what I have to see."

"You will stop at Farnham. I am going on alone with my van."

Jenny's cynical eye veiled its full meaning.

"Well, I hope you'll find him, my dear, and the horses. Real beauties—for all the money you must have trusted him with, and he——"

"You can go back to the show to-morrow, Jenny. I will have Sinfi with me. She has some sense."

And then Mrs. Jenny grovelled.

"Don't say it, my dear. I'm a silly old woman, but a silly old woman as loves you. Sinfi ain't fit to clean your shoes, a feather-headed wench. I know my tongue does travel——"

"It can travel with the show, Jenny. That is settled."

Richenda left Mrs. Beckett to her pot and kettle, both equally black, and wandering up one of the green bluffs into the eye of the wind, she stood and let it blow through her.

"Clean, clean wind," she thought.

The grass bent with it, and the flowers trembled. Her skirts were blown against her straight, boyish legs, and she felt the stir of the wind in her bosom, and its fresh breath upon her forehead. A wide world lay at her feet,

Suvla John

spacious and splendid. Clouds travelled fast, white and flocculent, sending their shadows before them, and Richenda watched those sweeping shadows and the sunlight following behind them.

"Little stuffy souls," she thought, "the souls that are hatched in little stuffy houses. I must get rid of Jenny. In taking the one you surrender the many."

Following the crest of the hill, she crossed the road into a plantation of beeches, and passing through it came again to the open grassland where a solitary red brick tower stood in windy isolation. Richenda knew the tower and its history. Gossip had christened it someone's "Folly," for such things seem foolish to the common people. The tower had no uses—in the eyes of the utilitarians—and yet Richenda had understood the building of it even when she had passed that way as a child. It was the tower of a man who had wished to be alone; and to be sure of his solitude, while he had looked out over these rolling hills under a hurrying northern sky, he had built this tower. He had a door to shut against any chance intrusion. He was there, closed up happily with his self. At night he may have gone there to look at the stars; he would have had that leisure of mind that goes with star-gazing and bird-watching. A solitary soul, gently disdainful, shutting out the chatterers.

Richenda sat down on the grass at the foot of the tower. Hitherto she had thought of the builder of it as coming here alone, but on this windy July day she doubted the tower's meaning. There may have been times when the tower had held two instead of one. If so, then the builder of it had been happy in his mate, a woman who could sit, and watch, and remain silent, while the clouds and their shadows went by, or the constellations rose and set. Happy silences, in the midst of solitude, with this red-brick building like a pivot round which the whole world swung.

"Yes—that's marriage, two in a tower."

She accepted the symbolism. She was ready to enter the tower with her lover, and to close the door upon the rest of the world. She understood the risks that every woman takes, and more especially the woman who has loved and thought apart.

"At least—our tower will be a moving tower."

She smiled.

"And sometimes he will want to run it up against

Suvla John

some walled city and go scaling the battlements. And if I am his mate, I shall hold his shield. I think he will go on wanting me. A woman who has ceased to be wanted may as well jump over the wall."

She was looking towards the spire of Salisbury when she heard voices and discovered a party of motorists approaching the tower by way of the track beside the wood. Richenda recognized them as citizens of God's own country, three women and two men. The women looked like black bundles; each vast and sallow face carried tortoiseshell-rimmed spectacles. The men were like the women, with huge chins and rolling foreheads. They talked loudly as though the world was their stage.

"Say, that's a queer notion—putting a tower just there."

They stood in a group and discussed the old red relic, and one of the women, waddling towards Richenda, appealed to her for an explanation.

"Say—can you tell me—who built this tower—and why?"

Richenda rose with the gravity of a prophetess.

"A man built it for his wife."

"My! Is that so?"

"Yes; she had such a tongue and such a temper that he shut her up there."

The American looked suspiciously at Richenda.

"I guess you are telling me a tale."

"It was my great-great-grandmother, so, you see, I ought to know."

"Well, if that isn't fine. Say, Cora, I have just been hearing a bit of history——"

Richenda left her to repeat it to the others, and letting her long legs carry her downhill, she went like a skimming bird with her face towards the sunset.

"Some tower! Yes, one would want—some tower—my dears—in these days—to get away from your voices."

Old Jenny, seeing laughter in her eyes, thought that the scolding she had received from Richenda might be treated as a yesterday's camp-fire.

"Supper's ready, my dear. Sinfi's no lass to be cooking for you."

"I shall do my own cooking, Jenny. What I said still holds."

But when the night fell a mood of restlessness came with it. She left the Becketts sitting round the fire, and as she went up into the darkness Richenda could hear

161

Suvla John

old Jenny's voice gathering shrillness and courage. On the ridge Richenda paused, and stood looking down into the hollow, where the fire seemed to float like a flame-coloured flower on the surface of the darkness. She could see the old woman leaning forward, pouring her grievance into the family pot.

For a moment Richenda watched the group.

"Yes," she thought, "you follow me because I feed you, and when you have been fed—you begin to feel indispensable. It is your form of vanity. It is all as old as these hills."

She went on to the tower, and, sitting down on the grass, she felt about her the calm and the strangeness of these upland solitudes. The wind had dropped. The moon was rising behind her, and in the valley she could see the faint glow where the lights of Salisbury clustered about its spirit. The hills were vastly silent, and she was glad of their silence. Her thoughts were with John Suvla among the pines of Hackbury. Two days ago it had seemed to her so easy to be generous, but now she felt less generous, not because she had no faith in her man, but because of an intuitive disquietude that had taken shape since she had been alone. She had begun to question the rightness of her decision in sending him back among those other people, and yet what had she to fear? Some echo out of the past—but what echo could there be? Yet Richenda was disquieted. Life can be so incalculable. Suvla himself had been surprised by it, by the unforeshadowed spell of a house, a garden, a green valley, some mysterious reincarnation of old memories. There is so much old self below the surface of the immediate consciousness. Vaguely, she was aware of the anxious instincts beneath the mental skin of the woman who was called Richenda. The Richenda of yesterday was like that orderly, glimmering town in the valley; the Richenda of the moment was the sister of these primæval hills.

She realized that she was jealous of John Suvla's past, most fiercely jealous of it. Her love went armed like a huntress. She wished that other life of his to be dead; she herself was ready to bury it in some hollow cyst in these chalk hills. She had talked to him of completeness, and as the moon rose huge and white she realized that all her passion for completeness was but life's vital egotism.

"Because it matters—to me," she thought, "and matters so much, it is the only thing that matters."

Suvla John

In the Panhurst woods John Suvla had spent an empty day, watching a strip of road for the passing of Blaber's car.

At nightfall he was no nearer to the rounding off of the adventure, and if he was beginning to lose patience with it he let his impatience reach out towards Richenda. "Oh, Queen of Completeness, at your bidding I lie in the underwood, tormented by flies, and feeding on bread and cheese, because you have set me a task. And the days of visiting-cards are over." But he could lie and think of the green caravan rolling over the Wiltshire hills, and so on into Hampshire. Richenda would come by way of Romsey, Winchester and Alton to Farnham, and at Farnham she would be very near. If Blaber still stayed away, what did it matter? He would catch him some day, and offer his fear the choice of forgetfulness.

"We'll run wild," he thought, "she and I. She shall see the house of the Sheres, and sit in the Shere pew in Feldhurst church. A kind of ghost holiday by moonlight. Two wild lovers in a caravan. Richenda goes awandering with the ghost of John Shere."

The fantastic play of the impulse pleased him.

"It is a pity I cannot take her over the old house in the dead of night. But we will walk in the garden, and my lady shall eat of the Feldhurst fruit. She shall stand on the bridge and look down at the lilies in the moat."

He was led aside by other wandering thoughts.

"Richenda Shere! She would have made as fine a portrait for the long gallery as any woman that ever lived. How would she have liked it? But little. She would rather hang up her real self in a tent in the desert. Feldhurst would be too tame and easy."

It did not occur to him that a woman might be jealous of a house or a memory, or of those dim figures in the world of his past. She had sent him to seal up this past, nor had she felt jealous of it when she had sent him. That was a thing that came afterwards, when she was quite alone with herself, and Suvla had not seen it. He might never see it. Her pride did not wish him to see it.

When the moon rose Suvla found himself in one of the hanging woods above the Feldhurst valley where it sloped to join the park. He had promised himself that he would take a walk in the Wynyats garden, and listen for the clicking of billiard balls. If Blaber had returned, then—he might get some such evidence of his return, and perhaps the chance of a meeting.

Meanwhile, he discarded the steep bank where the beeches grew and found himself by the gate where the valley path entered the park. The lower pool lay close to it, very dark and still, but touched here and there by the fingers of the moon. Suvla walked to the gate and rested his arms upon it. He could see the lights of the Manor, and his desire was to watch them for five minutes before going up to the Wynyats garden.

3

Elsie stood looking at the moon. Its light lay sheeted upon the dew-wet grass. It made a broad walk of the lane, until the branches of the trees came together and roofed it with black foliage burred with points of silver. There was a great stillness here, a sense of mystery, and to Elsie the whole world had become mysterious and full of miraculous chances. The thing that had happened once might happen a second time, and the supernatural would become the natural.

She was sure of it. She believed all that she wished to believe, and as she went down into the moonlit woods her eyes were the eyes of a credulous child. Her love and its illusion were mixed up with her religion, and since she believed in God and had prayed to Him, and God had sent her the spirit of her lover, the marvellous had become the real. After all, it was a ghost tale proving itself true, her own dear ghost story, and in Elsie the woman and the child went hand in hand. The child would make statements which the woman had no wish to criticize or to contradict.

"If John was in the church—he can be in other places," said the child.

"Yes, one of our dear places," the woman answered. "Ghosts attach themselves to the people and places they have loved."

"Let us go and look for John."

"Yes, on this beautiful night. It was just such a night as this. He kissed my hair. We stood by the pool gate

164

Suvla John

and looked at the lights of the house. We played at count-
ing them. There were seven. The 'Seven Sacred Kisses,'
he called them. He gave me seven kisses."

"Perhaps we shall see John to-night?" said the child.

"I shall speak to him. This time I shall not be afraid.
He will want me to speak to him. Poor dead John."

"Why has he come back?"

"He has come back because I am unhappy. God let
him once. I asked God to let him come."

She passed through one gate, and, loitering there for a
few moments with a large-eyed expectancy, she went on
down the valley path. No, this gate was not so dear as
the other gate; it opened to let in less precious and intimate memories. The gate of the Seven Kisses was the
gate of Elsie's city of dreams. She wandered down to it
over the grass under the hanging branches of the beeches,
passing from light to shadow, and from shadow to light.
The moonlight seemed to tremble, as though stirred by the
tremors of her own expectancy. She was a spirit, a frail
breath of love, drifting, to meet another spirit. The
moonlit world was both unreal and beautifully real.

Some fifty yards above the pool she paused. She could
see the gate as a black criss-cross of bars, for the moon
had cleared the trees, and the shadows had passed to one
side. Her eyes were big and luminous, her mouth slightly
open as though about to utter a cry.

There was something there, a figure, leaning upon
the gate. She drew a quick breath. Her feet made no
sound upon the grass, and the figure remained motionless,
with its back towards her. In that moment of wonder
and exultation she saw that the figure threw a shadow.

She came upon him with arms folded over her bosom, a
hand upon each shoulder.

"John, dear John, I am here. I am not afraid."

XVIII

I

SUVLA turned quickly with one hand still resting upon the top bar of the gate.

Elsie was standing within six feet of him, wrapped in her black cloak, the moonlight glimmering through her hair, her face a whiteness, strange and uplifted. He saw the shine in her eyes, and her mouth as a little curving shadow.

And instantly, he was conscious of a sense of tragedy, though how tragic her surprising of him would prove he did not know.

"Elsie."

He saw her smile in the moonlight, and there was something in her attitude of dreaming mystery that gave him the impression that she was not real. She stood there shadowy and still as a ghost, with that whitely radiant face, and her hands upon his shoulders. He could remember some nursery picture of an angel standing thus, bright and exultantly serene.

"John—I knew you would come. I have been so unhappy. I asked God to let you come—and when I saw you in the church——"

She spoke in a whisper with the voice of one who prays, looking up into his grave and silent face. He was silent because he could not think of what to say to her, and the emotion that he hid was anger against himself. He had been guilty of being taken unawares, and for the moment the shock of it had left him helpless; for a shock it was, not unlike those under concussions of the war, but more spiritual and less selfish.

"You saw me in the church?"

"Yes—I often go there, and sit under your memorial tablet, John. It helps me. Oh, I want to talk to you; there is so much——"

"Talk to me, Elsie."

She came a little nearer, still looking up at him.

Suvla John

"You have grown a beard, John. I suppose you grew that before you died?"

And suddenly he understood. She thought him dead, or rather—she believed that his body was dead, and that she was talking to the ghost of John Shere. He stood back, leaning against the gate, all the cleverness of him confounded, and his sense of the adventure's tragic possibilities growing urgent and inexorable. Here was the woman he was to have married, looking up into his face, and talking as though he were her ghost lover come back to speak with her. Was she sane? What did she expect of him? What had her life been all these years? And how was a man to handle such a situation, such a complex of moonlight and tears, of resurrected memories, and of incalculable emotions?

To tell her truth, at once and quickly? And in a moment of tense self-questioning his hand went to the side pocket of his coat. He was unconscious of that hand's purpose. Should he tell her? The situation was tragically absurd.

He heard her give a little surprised and delighted laugh, like the laughter of a gentle child.

"Why—do ghosts smoke? Yes—of course—I have read about Raymond——"

That hand of his had carried an empty pipe to his mouth. Rigid, momentarily undecided, he stuck it between his teeth, and then returned it to his pocket.

"Seems so—Elsie. But tell me——"

He needed time to think things out, to try and adjust the rough human reality of his living self to this little woman's fantastic illusion. He was suddenly aware of her as a creature to be hurt, and hurt most damnably. He realized that his imagined death had hurt her far more than he had believed. Also, he realized that he ought to have told her years ago. It was possible to sin against a child, and he suspected that his silence—reckless and wanton—had been a sin against a child. He had despised her for marrying Blaber, but then—he did not know all the circumstances of their marriage.

"Your voice is just the same, John."

"I suppose it is. How did you find me here, Elsie?"

"I felt that you would be here at—our gate. You came first to the church. But can you remember things—John?"

"What things?"

Suvla John

"Our things. Do you remember what we called this gate? The Gate of the Seven Kisses."

He remembered it very well, and the past stirred in him with a movement of pity. Had it meant so much to her? Did it still mean——?

"Seven kisses. We were very young then, Elsie."

"But I'm not old, John. But can you remember everything?"

"Everything."

"And you have been near me—all the time?"

"No, not all the time."

"But you knew that I was very unhappy."

"I have come to tell you to be happy, dear."

She came yet nearer, and Suvla's hand was feeling behind him for the latch of the gate. If spirit she believed him to be, then spirit he would remain. The inspiration came to him as he stood looking down into her dim, adoring face. What were they but ghosts? His part was to disentangle the live man from her illusion, and to leave the ghost man in her dream.

But it would be fatal if she were to touch him.

"You are to be happy, Elsie, happy."

"Are you happy, John?"

"Happier than I deserve."

He had his hand on the gate latch, and was ready to swing it back.

"Did you know, John, that I had married Robert?"

"Yes."

"You weren't angry with me, John?"

"No."

"Because Robert brought back your last words—and somehow—I felt—it was your wish——"

"My wish is for you to be happy."

"I'll try, John; I'll try very hard. I had all your letters—and other things—but two days ago he burnt them all. He's so strange—now. But if he knew——"

"He must not know."

"No—you are mine, John. Say you will come again—often and often."

He looked down at her steadily, and in these few moments he saw the past as he had never seen it before, as an irretrievable act of cruelty towards this child. And yet—was the fault his? He had thought her so easily consoled, and in those more brutal days his opinion of women had been different.

Suvla John

"Elsie—what were my last words?"

"Have you forgotten them, John?"

"There is a blank—just there."

"You said to Robert: 'Look after Elsie for me.' And he was kind, John, at first."

"He will be kind again. Pray for him, Elsie, and for me."

"John, you are not going——?"

He held out a hand—as though both to bless and to repulse.

"Yes. There are laws for us—as for you, dear. Be —be happy."

He swung the gate back—and then the tragic thing that he had feared happened. She made a despairing and appealing rush at him as though to clutch a substanceless shadow, and her hands touched the live and solid man.

2

Suvla found her clinging to him, as though the shock of her discovering his liveness had left her nothing but a pair of hands.

"Oh—John, you are alive."

His impulse was to break away and to leave her to re-gather the fragments of her dream, and one moment of merciful harshness might have gone far towards saving the face of this disastrous night. The gate had swung back and was pressing against him. Her hands held fast, not heeding his passivity. She clung with a wild and exultant eagerness.

"John, you are not dead."

He saw her wide eyes and her tremulous mouth like a wounded shadow. The fierceness of her emotion astonished him, for after all these years he had presumed her love for him to be dead, or to have faded to a mere sentimental memory. And he was shocked by it, by the sudden possessive grasp of her two hands, by the urgent and live woman in her.

"Elsie, this ought never——"

"John, hold me, I'm——"

His first chance fled from him, and he had to hold her or let her slip to the ground, for her arms trailed with a sudden limpness on his shoulders. She had fainted, leaving him with the problem of her in his arms.

"Good God!" he thought, "what a devil's mess!"

She lay in his arms like a child, eyes closed, her face turned to the moon, and as he looked at her and cursed his carelessness, he was moved to think of her as a child. What was one to do with such a child? Lay her gently down at the foot of a tree and vanish, leaving her the bewilderment and the fragments of an illusion? He thought of Richenda. In fact—like a big boy he called on the spirit of Richenda—the mother spirit. "Queen, for God's sake, tell me what I ought to do?" Completeness! How—the devil—was completeness to be perfected in such a case as this?

Supposing he left Elsie and her problem at the foot of a tree, and fled to Richenda, would not that be cowardice in the face of life? To blunder is human, and to run away may be human, but would Richenda be proud of his running away? Suvla, the tough, the ironical vagabond, sneaking away from a girl in a faint!

"Life may be a silly business," he thought, "and a man never so great a fool——"

He felt a stirring of her body, and it quickened his tense contriving. The enemy had come over his parapet. This limp, white-faced thing was the enemy! What nonsense, and yet life can be nonsensical. Bayonet and bomb—and an emotional woman! He had got to see it through, lie to her, tell huge—compassionate lies. She was a child, a sentimental child; he must complete the romance and vanish from the stage with a last gesture of pathos and renunciation.

Yes—that was it. Elsie—the Elsie he remembered—had been a dear creature of convention. His part was to play upon the conventions, leave her a secret, a dear secret, like the brass plate in Feldhurst church. Women love secrets, even secret wounds.

The light of the moon seemed needlessly bright, persuading him to carry his catastrophe into the shade of the trees. Her eyes were open, and as he stood hesitating, she put up a hand and touched his face, nor was it a mere touch, but a soft feeling of his features.

"Dear John!"

He looked down into her half-closed eyes.

"Elsie—you will have to forgive me."

"What have I to forgive?"

Suvla John

"My infernal carelessness. To stay away all these years—and then to get caught like a fool boy up an apple tree! How is it with you?"

"Did I faint—John?"

"Well—I don't wonder. I thought that I could get away without you touching me, and leave you thinking me a ghost."

He made as though to set her on her feet, but her body betrayed an unwillingness to leave his arms.

"No—hold me, John."

"You dear baby."

He smiled down at her, but her shadowy face was serious, nor could he judge how serious it was.

"I'm not a baby."

"You are Mrs. Robert Blaber."

"Don't," she said—almost sharply. "I'm a woman, John. I want you to talk to me. There is so much."

"So much—and yet so little."

He set her down, but one hand slid softly along his arm, and remained clasped upon his. She stood close in, touching him. Her silence waited, and possessed him while it waited.

"Shall it be here?" he asked.

"What better place, John, close to our gate."

"A closed gate—now."

He put an arm about her, a consoling and reasonable arm, unaware of her emotional obstinacy. She stood very still.

"I don't know. It is as though one had died and woke up in another world, John. There is the moon and our gate. It might be that night when——"

He began his attempt to hold her to the conventions.

"Elsie, we must try and keep our thoughts off that."

"Can we?"

"Necessity, my dear."

"Can you?"

She was looking up at him watchfully, and it seemed to him that the child in her had disappeared.

"I learnt that—seven years ago."

She drew a deep breath, and then—out of the darkness —her questions began to grope like an eager hand.

"Did Bob lie to me?"

"He thought me done for. It was not his fault."

"What happened?"

"I don't remember much of it. The Turks gathered me

171

up next morning, and a little German doctor pulled me through."

"But—why—didn't we hear?"

"I suppose there was some infernal mistake. Some kind soul took a liking to that silver identity disc I wore. The Turk is a casual beggar. I was huddled off to a prison place——"

"But you wrote——?"

"Of course."

"But what became of the letters?"

"Ask the Turks, little girl. And of course I got no letters. I had no news until——"

She drew even closer to him, and he felt the pressure of her body.

"Until?"

"Oh, a chance old newspaper smuggled in, and a piece of news——"

"My marriage?"

"Exactly. It changed my outlook upon things."

He knew that she was looking up into his face, but he kept his eyes on the dark trees across the valley.

"Did you hate me, John?"

"No; I think I understood. It was just the perversity of things."

"You thought of me as Bob's wife?"

"Yes."

"And happy?"

"And happy."

"I have never been happy—never."

He glanced at her to find her face like a dim but naked light. It streamed candour, the candour of the elemental and obstinately emotional woman.

3

That was the first phase, and Suvla felt it moving rapidly towards its second aspect in which the lights were still vague and dim. Certain unequivocal necessities formed the background. He had to send Elsie back to her husband, or back to a life in which she should cherish a romantic memory. He had to persuade her to keep his secret, and especially must she keep it from those dear people at the manor.

Suvla John

"Tell me about it," he said.

He was not so much concerned in listening to her tale of past unhappiness as he was in his inward contriving to save her from future pain. His compassion put on a protective gravity, but as he listened to her poor confessions, his anger against Blaber became once more a live anger. What an inevitable cad the man was!

"So you see, John—I have paid for my mistake. It does not seem wrong—my telling it to you."

She was facing him now, and standing close to him in the shadows, and something about her made him feel that she wanted his arms about her.

Instead—he took her hands.

"What a mess that bullet made of it. If I had known——"

"You would have come back—before?"

He was silent—and she asked him a second question.

"Why did you come back?"

"Ghosts walk, Elsie. They revisit the old places. I had been away all these years."

"And you wanted——"

"Well—yes, to look at the old house—and the people —like a ghost that no one sees."

"But I saw you."

"I'm sorry for it."

"But I'm not sorry. I think it was meant. Some things are meant, John. Don't you think so?"

He stared over her head and smiled.

"One gets surprises. One has to make the best of the surprises. Knocking about the world—all these years——"

"But you ought to have come back. Yes, in spite of me. What were you doing?"

"Fighting—mostly, sharing in other people's quarrels."

"But—why?"

"Because I liked it."

Her voice took on a tinge of reproach.

"You ought to have come back. I cannot understand your giving up so much——"

"Dead men are best out of the way."

"But you were not dead, dear."

"I was to you. And when I had been dead—say— three years, don't you see—that I was dead for good?"

He felt the pressure of her hands.

"No; I don't see it. Feldhurst belongs to you, though Dick and Sybil——"

Suvla John

He realized his chance and seized it.

"That is the very reason why I can't come back, even if I wanted to come back——"

"Oh, John——!"

"It is a fact. Dead men ought not to come to life again. Think what it would mean. You know what Dick is. He loves that place; he has had seven years to to grow into it; it's his. How could I arrive and turn him out? He would be justified in hating me."

She held obstinately to her point.

"But Feldhurst belongs to you. I'm sure that Dick would be the first to realize——"

"He will never have to realize it. That is where you have to make me a promise, Elsie."

Her face was half averted.

"What am I to promise you, John?"

"To keep my secret. We'll share it—you and I."

She stood as though considering the effect this promise would have upon her life. The secrecy of the compact pleased her, as Suvla had believed it would. Her sharing of the secret assumed a dear intimacy; she was a fellow conspirator, a trusted comrade. She reacted to the challenge, but her reaction was to swing farther than he imagined. In winning her to his view and to a promise of secrecy he was putting a lighted torch in her hand.

She raised her face to his.

"I'll promise, John."

"That's brave of you."

She waited, expecting him to kiss her, but when no kiss came she drew her hands away and seemed to be searching for something in the darkness beyond him. She had become aware of his passivity. She had to explain it to herself, for to the woman his passivity was a challenge. Was it apparent or real? What inspired it? Did he wish to have her in his arms as hotly as she desired to be there? She was conscious of the beginning of pain in the bewildering exultation of the night, and as this little red blur of pain glowed in the flesh of her soul it set fire to the stored and hidden passion of seven years.

XIX

I

THERE was an interlude of silence. Elsie had moved into the moonlight, and, after standing for a moment, had seated herself upon the grass. Her pose was both contemplative and questioning. The dark figure of had made a little pool of shadow, and her face was turned towards the trees on the farther side of the valley. Her silence was tentative. It made Suvla wonder what was passing in that little head, and behind those largely luminous eyes and poignant mouth. He seemed to have gained his point so easily, and her surrender to his call for secrecy had made him wonder what the surrender implied.

It was she who drew the curtain and called up the next phase.

"You are going away again."

Her voice suggested that she had come to an emotional conviction and that she would hold to it with passionate obstinacy.

"There is nothing else for me to do, Elsie."

"Without seeing Dick or anyone?"

"Of course. That would be fatal."

Pausing, she glanced round at him; she was waiting for him to join her.

"It's great of you to give up so much. Doesn't it hurt?"

"Less than you think—perhaps. I made a new life, and I am used to it."

He had come out into the moonlight, and was standing beside her. The risk of their being surprised here at this hour was very slight, and when she touched the grass beside her, and looked up at him with an air of mystery and of appeal, he threw himself down beside her.

"This new life, John, tell me about it."

Prone, and resting on his elbows, he gave her one of his old, ironical glances.

Suvla John

"It is not the sort of life, my dear——"

"You mean—it is not like the life here?"

"Hardly."

"That might be an advantage."

He was a little puzzled, and therefore more on the alert.

"It is life for a rough man, a devil-may-care ruffian."

"Adventure."

There was a little thrill in her voice, and instantly he realized the need of dissipating the illusion that might have inspired that thrill. She looked on him as a romantic figure.

"You can call it adventure—but it's not nice, bookish adventure. Tramping, living and sleeping in all sorts of odd places—ditches and stables. Not much washing—sometimes, and your toes through your boots. Adventure may be a dirty business."

In turn he had given her something to puzzle over. She believed that he was over-colouring the picture, and that he had reasons—romantic reasons—that concerned herself. Her hero was the beau chevalier, a man of wonderful renunciations.

"But how do you live?"

"Mostly by fighting, hiring myself out to quarrelsome people. I was a colonel in Denikin's army; the Chinese only made me a major. In Mexico—I was a sergeant."

"But you can't always be fighting, John. Do they pay you for it?"

"Of course. And there is such a thing as loot."

"Loot! But I don't believe that, dear. And when you are not fighting?"

"I have been a sailor, a fireman, and a ship's steward, a horse-breaker, a tramp."

"You must have been all over the world."

"Most of it."

She sat awhile in silence, as though absorbing the rather shocking strangeness of this life of vagabondage. It excited her. But she divined the gaps in this Ulysses story. There was one most obvious lacuna; he had said nothing about women.

Had there been women? Feeling towards him as she did, Elsie realized that there had been other women. And suddenly she was furiously and ravishingly jealous. Of course—if a man—a fine man—could not get the woman he wanted, he might fall to other women. Her jealousy ex-

cited her; it was pleasurably painful; it fired her eagerness to possess and to be possessed.

"So—you are going back to that life, John?"

"I suppose so."

"The same sort of life?"

She had turned, and allowing herself to sink on one
elbow, she was nearer to him.

"Not quite so rough—perhaps. You need not pity me,
my dear."

Her voice grew very soft.

"Oughtn't we to pity each other? You are thinking
of me all the time as Robert's wife."

"I am facing a fact."

"For my sake?"

"For your sake, Elsie."

It seemed to him that her breathing became deeper.
She was close to him, lying like a young girl, her head on
her hand. The other hand was pulling aimlessly at the
grass. Her silence had a quality of exultation; he felt this
exultation, sensed it like a perfume, and became wise as
to the danger. She lay there in the moonlight, smiling
to herself, eyes overshadowed, exulting silently over some
passionate and secret conception. When she looked at
him her face expressed mystery, a kind of tender slyness.

"You have done so much for my sake, John."

"Less than you think."

"I am Mrs. Robert Blaber. You don't know what marriage is—or may be?"

"That's true."

"When we are young we are told such lies about
marriage. I have had to find out. I married Robert because I thought I was carrying out your last wish."

Suvla let his chin rest on his crossed wrists.

"Damned sentimental people! Blaber might have left
my blurtings behind. Of course—he wanted you, and
why shouldn't he want you? And he is your husband."

She answered him with silence, and behind it lay
the climax of the revelation she was holding over him.

"Am I? I don't feel that I am his wife. Why should
I? He was never kind to me after the first year. He
loves being cruel. He was cruel because he knew that I
did not want to forget you."

"Much better to forget some things, my dear. I'm
not worth remembering. Stick to the conventions. They
are much more comfortable."

Suvla John

"But you have not followed them, John."

"Yes, I have—for you."

He was lying very still, and as she leaned over to him he seemed to know what her words would be.

"John—I don't want to be conventional. I'll go away with you—live your life, dear. No one need know. We'll just disappear like two—two ghosts. I know that you would never have asked me to do this, dear. You are too unselfish. Oh—John—my darling, we can be so very happy."

2

The man in Suvla knew what the woman in Elsie expected of him, and as he turned over and sat up and looked at her pale and tenderly exultant face he was touched to the deeps. For she was offering to him all that she had to offer, this douce and conventional creature who had suddenly turned rebel. He was astonished at her courage and the vehemence of her recklessness, and as he saw her—poised—waiting to fall to the full consummation of the night's emotion—he was conscious of anger and self-disgust. He deserved to suffer for his carelessness. He became grossly impatient of the playing of a part of the fooling of this child. He was the merciful humbug, the very brand of hypocrisy that he despised. He had believed always in hard knuckles, and a merciless but unmalicious tongue; he had never been a truckler to women, a slimy, sensual liar.

But this little war of emotional surprises was like the great war—for however much your gorge might rise, the only male alternative was to see it through.

"Come here, little thing."

He drew her to him with a large gentleness, and held her close, with her head on his shoulder and her soft hair against his cheek. She came to him gladly, with a little breath of deep delight, and her infinite contentment hurt him. For he knew now that he had to hurt her far more bitterly than he had foreseen. Also, he understood that no lie mattered, provided that there was any healing grace in it.

"I have got to talk to you like a big brother, child."

"I mean every word of it, John."

Suvla John

"I know you do. You want to sacrifice yourself for an impossible idea."

She made a little, protesting movement.

"No; it is not impossible. I want to make it all up to you for all that you have suffered."

"My dear heart," he said, "when we think that we can alter the past—the past that is ourselves—we make for tragedy. I am not the John Shere of seven years ago."

"To me—you will always be John Shere."

"Listen. I shall have to tell you all kinds of beastly things. I am much rougher than I was; I have lived a rough life; I have been all sorts of things to all sorts of people. You are much too sensitive and gentle to understand——"

There was obstinacy in her voice.

"But I do understand."

"How?"

"You are trying to tell me, dear, that there have been —other women. Do you think I am so innocent that I could not guess?"

He was astonished by the swiftness of her intuition, and by the calm candour with which she met his adventure into realism.

"There have been other women, Elsie."

She looked up into his face.

"I forgive it. It was my fault. It was because I did not wait. And now—we are quits, John."

Again he was vividly conscious of her expectant devotion. She tore down every barrier as he tried to erect it, and her hands were the hands of a woman whose one obstinate obsession would not suffer itself to be set aside. For the moment he thought of telling her of Richenda, but he had not the heart to do it. He would compel her to realize that he was not going to let her jump over a cliff with him.

"Yes, quits, little girl, but that does not alter my view of things. I am going to be rather hard in order to be honest."

"You are not to think of me, John. I want you to be selfish—so selfish. Don't you understand? I'd love to be hurt for your sake, to have to bear all sorts of suffering——"

"Dear—and do you think I am going to let you bear it?"

"If you love me—as I want to be loved."

179

He turned her face so that he could look right down into her eyes.

"I won't do it, Elsie. I have knocked about the world enough to know what life is. You are too generous to understand what life is—my sort of life. That's final, little girl."

"John, you don't know what I want."

"My God, dear—but I think I do. And I won't do it. Oh, I know we are right down in the deeps of things. I'm not going to talk a lot of religious tosh, but even a man like I am has a sort of religion. You are like a rose bush rooted in a quiet garden. I'm a sort of storm cloud——"

She clung to him.

"John, my roots are in you. I want you—as part of me. All these empty years——"

3

Parker, that unemotional woman, was going round pulling down blinds and drawing curtains, but she left one of the long windows of the drawing-room open and uncurtained, for her mistress was out there somewhere in the moonlight. Parker paused by the window. She stepped in through it, and stood in the loggia, looking out across the moonlit garden, for Parker had her moonlit moments. She put a long thin hand to her cheek, and seemed to listen.

She was listening to the voice of her own thoughts, or to what passes for thought in the brain of a lonely woman.

"With her looks she might get a lover."

Sex had caused Parker to suffer. It still lived under her starched apron of repression, and as she stood there she made a movement of the hands as though smoothing out a crease in the white linen, and erasing an unpleasant and suggestive emotion.

"I've got over it, and so will she. Beastly nonsense. All the trouble comes of making a romance of it. We get over it pretty quickly in my class; housework and too many kids soon take the ice off the cake. We sweat our souls out over washing-tubs and frying-pans, and our men go to the pubs and round the corner. There are always the girls growing up, and it doesn't matter how old a man is—he can't keep from hankering——"

Parker knew her world; she had five sisters who were married, and the only happy one of the five had no children and a husband who had been a successful tradesman in a small way and whose passion was gardening. The other four were grim women who had ceased to nurse any illusions after nursing too many children.

"Beastly brats! You haven't the time or the strength to be romantic unless you are a lady. Like having your breakfast in bed, and all that. But she's a dear soul."

Parker stood reflecting upon Elsie, for Elsie was all that she was not, and contrasts are provocative. It seemed to Parker that Wynyats would be a very pleasant place if there were no man about the house. She had her philosophy, the wisdom of the woman who had spilled her share of raw bitterness and had mopped it up, and gone on to clean, satisfying, sexless living. She knew how much more comfortable a woman's little world can be when man has been eliminated, man—the irresponsible and untidy boy and the persuasive liar. Parker had grown to love her work. There are satisfactions in touching beautiful glass and silver, in a serene and laborious orderliness, in the nice hang of a picture, the shine on old wood, the colours of old china. She knew the extent of her responsibilities, and their blessed limitations. She felt herself better off than all her sisters. Proud of being wives and mothers were they? They might put on the rather crumpled apron of matronly pride, but she knew that they envied her.

Parker's philosophy included Elsie.

"Yes, I'd allow her one child, one healthy child. And if we could get Mr. Bob out of the way—we could be very comfortable here. She'd learn in time that a free woman can enjoy life and make a better business of it. Marriage! What humbugs we are! As if having a thing in trousers always about—— That's a man's idea. Sacred trousers! She'd be as happy as anything here —in time, with that blessed memory of hers, and flowers, and little jobs to do, and no wondering what a man's temper was going to be like. Why not? I'd know he'd be hankering after some baby-faced little wench round the corner."

The Wynyats clock was striking eleven. It occurred to Parker that her mistress might have walked down to the Manor. If so, someone would walk back with her; Mr. Shere most likely. Parker approved of Richard Shere. He was one of those rare and comfortable men with whom a woman can sit down reassuredly for the rest of her life. Parker decided that she would leave the lights on and the windows open. She had a book to read, and cook and the other girls had gone to bed.

She was crossing the drawing-room when she heard a car coming up the drive.

"One of those Ford taxis," she said to herself; "that means—him—from the station."

Her austerity stiffened. She went out into the hall, and stood by the oak cupboard, in rigid readiness for the return of the man. He could open the door for himself.

She heard the "bundle of tin" shake itself and clatter off down the drive. Mr. Blaber appeared to be a long time in making his entrance, and then she heard footsteps in the drawing-room. He came upon her quite suddenly, and she knew by his voice what sort of temper he was in.

"What are you doing here?"

Parker had never given him any excuse for finding fault with her.

"I was expecting someone to ring, sir. I heard a car."

"Where's your mistress?"

"I think she has gone down to Mrs. Shere's."

Blaber flung a coat upon the table.

"Hang that up, will you? And you can go to bed."

Parker hung up the coat in the oak cupboard.

"You will wait up for Mr. Shere, sir?"

"I suppose so."

He stood waiting for her to go.

"Another time—you had better shut the windows. Anyone might stroll in."

"Yes, sir. Can I get anything for you?"

"Nothing."

He was more abrupt than usual, and as she passed through the doorway leading to the servants' quarters Parker found him watching her with an air of suspicion. She had hidden her hostility, but he seemed aware of it. His sharp and rather Jewish profile, like a face cut out of cardboard, remained half turned towards her until she had closed the door.

"Enough to give one the creeps," she thought.

Suvla John

After seeing that the lights were out in the kitchen, Parker climbed the back stairs to her room on the second floor, and closed the door with more noise than seemed necessary. Blaber was still in the hall. He appeared to have been waiting for some such sound as the closing of Parker's door; it released him from the stiff attitude of the listener. He had left the porch door open, and turning out the hall lights, he went and stood in the porch.

Meanwhile Parker had slipped off her dress, and put on a dressing-gown. Opening her door cautiously, she crept out on to the landing carrying a bedroom chair, which she placed behind the big linen cupboard. Parker sat down. Her hostility was on the alert. She had no intention of going to bed until she had heard her mistress come in and go to her room. For Blaber's face had suggested the viciousness of the evil-tempered dog waiting on the end of a chain, ready to leap out and snarl.

"If he snaps at her," thought Parker, "I'll go down. I don't care what he may say about it. I can say I thought I heard strange voices."

She sat erect, like some image in a temple, screened by the outjutting cupboard. The house was very silent. No sound came to her from below.

"If she has been at the Manor—Mr. Shere will come back with her. That—will keep him from snarling."

Presently, it occurred to her to wonder whether her mistress had gone down to the Manor. If not, where could she be at this hour? Was it possible——? And Parker left her chair, and going silently down the stairs in her stockinged feet, made her way to Elsie's bedroom. She flashed on the light for a moment, and made sure that it was empty.

Returning to her chair on the upper landing, she sat down to listen and to wait, her sense of loyalty to this other woman giving her a pleasant feeling of triumph over man.

XX

I

THERE were two timber seats in the neo-Gothic porch
of Wynyats, and Blaber took one of them.

Like Parker, he was waiting for the return of a
woman, though his motive was less definite than Parker's.
His mind was obscure, shadowy with vague and sinister
intuitions. Unable to explain things to himself, he had
fallen into a state of abnormal and restless wakefulness,
mind-wakefulness, of uneasy and suspicious tension, the
jerky alertness of a frightened sentry on a dark night.
He had begun to imagine things. Trivial incidents, even
the details of the day's happenings, had come to have
exaggerated and distorted significance. Why this—why
that? What had been the esoteric meaning behind such
a phrase? Life had become full of terrifying innuendoes,
of ghosts lurking in dark corners.

So Elsie had gone down to the Sheres. These ironical
and ubiquitous Sheres! He had never been able to get
away from them. Dispose of one, and you were confronted with another. Even his savage stealing of John
Shere's wife had left him fooled; there were young
Sheres, but no young Blabers.

And Elsie was down there! Of course, she would
be down there, feeding on the Shere sympathy, and
telling them tales about her husband. He felt that he
hated her, and that he hated everybody; that life had
bested him at every turn. He despised most of his
fellow humans, and yet—with all his cold astuteness he
had failed to impress himself upon the people he despised. The war had been responsible for his failure,
that crude period, full of raw emotional excitement, a
vast and sentimental melodrama favourable to village
heroes. He had been nothing of a hero. The whole
business had thrown him off his balance and left him
cringing before hearty fools, loathing himself and them.

Suvla John

He had been unable to lose himself in being a good fellow to other men. A Blaber was a good fellow only to himself.

Various possibilities occurred to him as he sat there in the porch. Elsie might be down at Feldhurst—but also she might be in the garden or the house, and he went upstairs, and finding the door of her room unlocked he flashed on the light to discover an empty room, with the bed-clothes turned down and Elsie's night-dress and lace cap laid ready. Evidently Parker expected her to return. But he did not trust Parker, that grim woman with the wooden face who never allowed herself to lose her temper. The servants sided with his wife; he was well aware of the fact, and it exasperated him. It was a conspiracy.

As he descended the stairs he remembered the open window, and the way Parker had met him in the hall. Had Elsie been in the house, and on hearing the sound of the car, had she fled out of the house to take refuge with the Sheres?

Damn the Sheres.

He went out into the garden, and wandered through it, keeping as much as possible to the grass, and frequently pausing to listen. In the pergola a swinging rose shoot caught him across the forehead, and the thorns drew blood. He swore. He emphasized the fact that he kept three gardeners to look after the place, and that the swine were too lazy and careless to tie up the roses. He decided to sack them.

But Blaber did not find his wife, nor had he had any great expectation of finding her, and as he returned by way of the rhododendron walk he became more and more conscious of the night's profound stillness. He had begun to grow afraid of these listening silences. He had felt more at ease in London, in the thick of the anonymous noise of it. He had come back because he suspected Elsie, and because he had a feeling that she had to be watched. He believed that—somehow—she had come to know of the thing that had happened in that trench above Suvla Bay. He had enemies—shadowy, unseen enemies. He had ceased to be able to reason calmly, or to analyse the situation and to reduce it to its practical possibilities. He was growing as fearful and as superstitious as a Louis XI.

Blaber returned to the porch. The turret clock struck

twelve, the hour at which ghosts are supposed to walk, and his own particular ghost was moving in the moonlight. It was not remorse, but the fear of being found out.

Well, he would stay there until the clock convinced him that his wife had no intention of joining him at Wynyats. That would be one definite detail in the damnable obscurity of the situation. He could regard her as an enemy, perhaps as—the enemy.

He felt for his cigarette case and matches. He had a cigarette between his lips, and had struck a match, when he thought that he could hear voices somewhere in the garden.

He blew out the match.

2

Suvla held Elsie in the hollow of his arm.

They had taken an hour to walk from the lower pool in the Feldhurst valley to the gate of the Wynyats garden, for there had been hesitations and pauses, and little poignant conflicts. Elsie's obstinacy had seemed to catch at the very moonlight, and to cling to the shadows under the trees. Always, there had been the steady and compelling pressure of Suvla's arm.

"I am going to take you home."

Nevertheless she had protested that Wynyats was not home, and that it never would be a home. She had begun to talk less of self-sacrifice, though the whole of her effort was gathered to resist the assumed spirit of self-sacrifice that she discovered in John Suvla. She had struggled with it, betraying a pathetic and increasing frankness. Desperately, like a woman throwing off every concealment, every little shred of veiled convention, she had sought to weaken his decision. She was ceasing to argue; her persuasion had begun to use more elemental appeals. Nor did it seem to occur to her that Suvla's opposition was anything but a romantic renunciation of that which they both desired. She assumed him to be feeling all that she herself was feeling, and that he must want her as she wanted him.

There had been a little, breathless struggle at the gate.

Suvla John

"No, no—I'll not go back, John."

"Child—you must."

"Don't call me child."

"Dear heart, I must not call you anything else."

"I'm not a child. That's why I can't go back. I don't belong to him; I belong to you."

He had had to force her into the garden, hurting himself as he hurt her.

"You belong to yourself, my dear."

And suddenly she had grown docile, or rather—she had ceased to resist.

"You are being cruel to me, dear."

"I'm being kind, Elsie, kinder than you know."

Their voices made a murmuring in a far part of the garden where a group of young cypresses threw up their slender finials. There was a seat here, with a grass walk running from it between broad herbaceous borders, and Elsie drew him to this seat. She still held his hands.

"You need not be afraid."

He was listening.

"I have to be afraid, my dear."

"But—he—is not here."

Recklessness stood concealed behind her assumption of meekness. She did not care whether her husband was there or not; nor was her recklessness blind; it was looking beyond the moment towards an occasion when discovery might involve them both in a dramatic climax. He would have to stand by her if Blaber caught them. She was beginning to ignore the consequences to others in her impatience to compromise her lover. For she was on the edge of realizing that only by compromising him might she be able to make him hers.

Her seeming acquiescence was a mask.

"Oh—this tortures me. But I will try to be good, John. I—I can't make up my mind to-night."

"You must, dear."

"But I can't. I've been through so much. I'm so tired."

"Poor little girl."

He put an arm round her.

"You think me a pious brute. I'm not. I want you to be happy. Jumping over a cliff doesn't mean happiness. Now, go to bed, and have a good sleep, to-morrow you will wake up——"

Suvla John

"Then—we shall have to go over it all again, John, because——"

"Dear, the safest thing would be——"

"Oh, I know what you are going to say. But I don't think you understand women——"

"Perhaps not."

"Well, I made you a promise, not to tell anybody."

"And you'll keep it?"

"Yes, but you will make me a promise—in return."

"It depends on the promise."

"Such a small thing."

"Out with it."

"You were away from me seven years, John. I'll ask for one day for each year, and that will only be part of a day, an hour or two. Seven short hours. It does not mean much, does it? And yet, it will mean so much——"

He sat very still.

"Elsie—when one picks up a hot coal—the best thing is to drop it."

She freed one of her hands, and laying it along his chin, turned his face to hers.

"John—you have been bullying me, making all sorts of solemn speeches. It is my turn to bully you a little. I want my seven days——"

"Oh, yes, I'm in your power, my dear."

"John, how dare you! I am trying to be good and patient—at the end of these seven days——"

She drew her fingers down his cheek.

"Why think of that? Why shouldn't we treat it as seven days' leave—like those seven dear days before you went. I had to let you go then, didn't I, John?"

"True."

He sat considering this most elusive of problems. She had the power to wound herself more deeply than she knew, and yet it seemed to Suvla that if he humoured her he might be able to bring the relationship to a happier end. He believed that he had persuaded her to take the path that he wished her to take. She had entered upon it. She was merely asking him to go a little way with her before he turned back.

Moreover, he was thinking of Richenda. In another day or so she would be with him, and he had need of Richenda. A man's fingers might be too big and fumbling for the unravelling of such a knot.

Suvla John

"Supposing that I promise, little girl?"

"I'll promise to keep your secret for ever and ever."

"Where shall we meet?"

"You know the dell, just below the spruce wood, at the end of the wild garden?"

"I should know it!"

"There—after dark."

"And supposing—your husband——?"

"I doubt whether he will come back, or not for a long time. But even then——?"

"You will try——"

"Of course. And where shall you be?"

He reflected, holding her head against his shoulders.

"O—somewhere in the woods. I have to be very careful. I can get a bed at Guildford. Don't worry your head about that."

He rose, drawing her with him.

"I'm being weak, my dear."

"No—no."

He kissed her—and when he had kissed her she clung to him for a moment.

"That's the first time, my dearest."

He was wondering how he could make it the last.

3

The listener had come as near to them as he had dared to come, or as the setting of the garden permitted, and he had stood there under a golden catalpa, gathering an occasional desultory word.

So—his wife had a lover.

Presumably, the discovery of such a romance should have provoked anger and jealousy, but its effect upon Blaber was rather more complex, and yet quite simple. He was conscious of a sense of relief, for here was a definite factor in the problem that had puzzled him. He was in touch with a motive, a live and human impulse. It could be used to explain certain incidents that had seemed unexplainable.

As to the lover's identity he had to confess himself surprised by it. He had managed to pick up a few odd words, but it was the voice that had made him wise. The voice belonged to a Shere.

Suvla John

The pieces of Blaber's jig-saw puzzle were fitting into their proper places. That the voices of a dead man and a live one should have resembled each other was not a fact to be reckoned with. Blaber was concerned with the live man.

"Well—I'm damned!"

The discovery produced a grin upon the face of his cleverness. Nothing is surprising to the man of forty; a shrug and a laugh may be all that he will allow himself, and Blaber shrugged his sloping shoulders.

But Dick Shere.

Well—really—this was magnificent!

Richard Shere, the irreproachable, the ideal husband, the man of sensibility! The devoted father, Feldhurst's admirable gentleman! But why not? It only went to prove the ubiquitousness of the sex adventure, the thing the English tuck away in the cupboard, though the cupboard is less secretive than it used to be.

Blaber was conscious of sardonic exultation. He allowed these lovers their cleverness, a really artistic handling of the romance. Yes—who would have thought that fool wife of his capable of creating such a nice atmosphere? Pretending to dote upon a dead man while she was concerned with a live one! Those pilgrimages to Feldhurst church—that sweet friendship with Sybil, those brotherly courtesies, those seeings-home by a devoted husband!

He thought that he understood. These two had been playing a game with him, a rather grim game. They had dressed up a ghost with which to frighten him, but he had discovered the candle in their turnip.

Excellent!

He felt grossly elated, immensely relieved.. He had his weapon, his coat of mail. His self confidence returned. This was the sort of situation that piqued him, the kind of trench-raid that did not find him with chattering teeth and a void in his stomach. It might be an amusing affair, laying this ghost of theirs.

And then he was conscious of a gust of rage, and of snarling vindictiveness. These Sheres! He had dealt with one brother, and the other had bobbed up and borrowed his wife. But a complacent fool was needed to make such a situation successful, and Blaber did not feel like a complacent fool. At last he had a chance to get a thrust in upon one of these fine gentlemen.

Suvla John

The whole thing was now so obvious. Shere had been in the house when he—Blaber—had returned. Parker was in the plot; the wooden-faced woman had had her douceur. She had been set to waylay and detain him while those two had slipped out into the garden.

He knew what to do. The more deeply he let them compromise themselves, get stuck in the mud, the more sure would he be of controlling the situation.

Bland innocence!

The old Italian delicacy!

4

Blaber saw his wife before she saw him, or, at least he saw the reflection of her in the long mirror opposite the open window. She entered by the window while he sat deep in one of the big, brocaded arm-chairs, a book on his knees, and his eyes on the mirror. She paused for an instant by the window, and her face had a dreaming ecstasy, and her mouth remembered other lips.

And then she saw him, and her face seemed to fall from heaven into hell. She was afraid; she shrank back a little, one hand feeling at the curtain.

Blaber jumped up.

"Hallo, Elsie, I'm glad you are back."

He was smiling; his figure had a certain awkwardness, an apologetic slope from the hips.

"Parker told me you were down at the Manor. So— I sat up. You haven't walked back alone?"

She nodded. He had surprised her both with his presence and his manner of meeting her, and his voice and manner were conciliatory. Even the quality of his awkwardness, a subtly suggested embarrassment, added to the impression he gave her of having returned as something of a suppliant.

"I think Shere might have walked up with you."

"It was so late—I——"

"All the more reason. I would have come down to fetch you—if I had known."

She closed the window and drew the curtains, and he understood that she was making an opportunity to draw other curtains, and when she turned to him again her face had a white blankness.

"I did not expect you, Robert."

He gave her a self-conscious smile.

"I don't wonder. I have been sitting here for an hour, thinking things over. I'm sorry, Elsie."

Her eyes were large and watchful, like the eyes of a shy animal.

"Sorry?"

"Yes. I behaved like a pretty average beast the other day. I don't know whether you——"

She shrank into a chair, and her expressive mouth grew plaintive. She could detect no trace of irony in the make-up of his attitude towards her. He looked sorry, awkwardly penitent. And yet——

"You hurt me rather badly, Robert."

"It shan't happen again."

He met her veiled eyes.

"I mean it. I dare say you don't believe it. That's understandable. The fact is—I have been living in a sort of vicious circle—but that row—the other day——"

He wandered across the room, and coming back, stood looking at her feet.

"Well—I'm sorry. I think I have broken out of the circle. I have seen the evil beast in myself. Can you understand?"

His eyes touched hers.

"What I mean is—that I don't expect you—to forgive me—all at once. There is too big a gap for that. But I won't interfere; we'll go quietly along, until I can convince you——"

She stood up, her face quivering and averted. She had reached the climax of one emotion, and to have a second emotional experience thrust upon her in one night seemed to her more than she could bear. Life had been so violently unexpected. She felt that if she tried to lie to him she would burst into tears.

"Robert—I can't promise—but——"

She made a movement of escape towards the door, and quickly—and with an air of conciliatory eagerness he went to open it for her.

"I don't expect you to promise, Elsie. I don't deserve any promises. You are perfectly free——"

She paused for a moment in the doorway, her head thrown back, arms rigid.

Suvla John

"Thank you, Robert. I—I'm rather tired——"

"Of course," he said; "that's my fault, Elsie. I won't worry you. Go to bed and get some sleep. I haven't slept much—myself—these last few nights."

He followed her to the foot of the stairs, and waited there till he heard her door close. He was smiling, his head tilted obliquely, one half of his face in the shadow.

"Movement number one," he thought.

And while he was closing the porch door and switching off the lights, Parker had taken up her chair and was softly closing the door of her bedroom.

XXI

1

SUVLA walked seven miles that night, and about three o'clock in the morning he lay down and slept for three hours under a hedge. During his wandering life he had learnt to wake at what hour he pleased, and about half-past six he caught a sleepy-eyed train which landed him at Basingstoke. Here he breakfasted in the station refreshment-room before catching a train to Winchester, and he was in Winchester by eleven.

His need was Richenda. He had calculated that the "show" would trek out of Romsey that morning, pulling out about nine o'clock on the road to Winchester. Romsey and Winchester were ten miles apart, and the caravans moved slowly.

He had time to be clean.

The barber who shaved his cheeks and upper lip, and who trimmed his little pointed beard, and shampooed him, discovered in Suvla the abrupt reticence of a man who would not be bothered with small talk, and the barber was relieved. It was the garrulous man-in-the-street who had created the myth of the loquacious barber. Suvla and the cutter of hair exchanged some six sentences, all of them intimately connected with the business in hand. Suvla walked from the hairdresser's into a tobacconist's. His route lay up the steep street and through the grey gate, and he held to the Romsey road until he came to a point where the road could be held in view for a couple of hundred yards or more. He sat on a bank, under a thorn tree, with his feet in a dry ditch. He lit a pipe. His brown face had not the glimmer of a smile anywhere. Life and Richenda was as serious as fate.

For in a night Suvla had grown more human. That a man should discover occasionally his limitations and be able to think of himself as a fool, is a fine necessity, and Suvla felt something of a fool. The kind fool! And he had run away from his own kindness, to appeal

194

Suvla John

to a woman to help him out of this quagmire of soft-heartedness. Richenda was to hear and to judge, and there were moments when he was a little afraid of Richenda.

"Well—a man must be afraid of something!"

Perfect love casteth out fear, yes, but a man should fear to appear trivial or mean in the face of his love. Weak he may be, or too easily generous or angry. The woman will always stoop to the impulsive boy in man, and Suvla had gone back ten years.

"I ought to have laughed in the child's face," he thought, "and told her I was married, or as good as married. This sentimental storm in a tea-cup would never have happened. Why didn't I tell her?"

Something green was moving about the curve of a hedge, the top of Richenda's caravan, and hardly had Suvla realized its nearness than he saw the head of the white horse that drew the caravan. Horse and caravan rounded the corner. A woman was seated under the projecting curve of the roof, the reins held lightly in one hand. A girl with a red handkerchief fastened over her hair was walking beside the white horse.

Suvla stood up. He knocked his pipe out on the heel of a boot, and looked down the road towards the slowly moving caravan. Life and Richenda were approaching.

He saw that she had recognized him, and even at a distance he felt her eyes fixed upon him with a questioning intensity. He remembered how rarely he had seen Richenda laugh. She was not a woman who laughed easily. He stood still, waiting, his old ironical self like a Samson with shorn locks. He had made a mess of the adventure, and the tale he had to tell her would have no swagger.

When the caravan had come within thirty yards of him he saw Richenda turn her head to speak to the girl Sinfi, and Sinfi dropped behind. Richenda's convoy was trailing half a mile behind her caravan. The white horse's head went up and down as he breasted the long hill, and Richenda, leaning forward slightly, seemed to Suvla all silence, steadfast and sombre eyed.

She pulled up and made room for him on the seat, and with a flick of the reins sent the white horse plodding upon his way. She had given Suvla one searching look, but now her eyes gazed ahead over the white horse's ears.

"Been waiting long?" she asked him.

Suvla John

"No; half an hour." And then he added: "I have made a devil's own mess of the business. I want to tell you."

She pulled the white horse to the near side to let a hooting car go past.

"That's—rather—a new experience—for you!"

"You may rub it in."

"Am I that sort? What happened?"

She seemed curiously aloof from him for the moment, and he made no attempt to challenge her aloofness. They sat a little apart, looking straight ahead, and Richenda's face made him think of the chilly freshness of the dawn. And he was glad of her dignity, for dignity gives a rhythm to life in an age of jerkiness and of cheap discords. Richenda was a woman apart. She did not speak before she was ready to speak; she was in no hurry to please; she spoke a different tongue from the language used by a world torn between class-hatred and futile good nature. She was a person. She went her own way, completely and surely herself, disdaining the crowd, acknowledging the few. If anybody had asked her—"What's wrong with the world?"—she would have replied that there was nothing wrong with the world. There were too many people in it—that was all.

"There is a man in you," he said.

She gave him the faint freshness of a smile.

"That means to say——?"

"You are going to listen to an old woman in me."

"There is an old woman in all of us. Supposing we leave her out? What happened?"

He gave a toss of the head.

"I let myself get caught."

"You?"

"Dreaming like an ass with his head hanging over a gate. Don't laugh—my dear."

"You want to laugh at yourself, and so—you warn me against doing that which I have not the slightest intention of doing. When a man asks you not to laugh at him——"

"He is no better than a hyena!"

"Who caught you? It must have been a woman."

His eyes crossed hers.

"Why?"

"Because—the person who caught you—seems to have had rather the best of it. And a man——"

196

Suvla John

"A palpable hit. You can't use your strength on a woman."

"Can't you? Doesn't that depend on the woman? You men like to think of women—as clinging—and sweet —and then—on occasions—the woman gets you in your own net. And you deserve it."

"Well—I'll tell you."

Even while he was telling her the tale of how a woman had caught a ghost and discovered that the ghost was real, he was wondering how Richenda would accept Elsie and Elsie's embarrassing tenderness. A jealous Richenda might prove catastrophic. Her potentialities were beyond those of other women. And yet for shame he could not tone down the story, or shrug his shoulders over Elsie's obsession. A less courageous man might have turned it into ridicule, and attempted to appease one woman by laughing at the other. He was conscious of Richenda sitting there very still, and looking out over the white horse's ears at the rolling country. Her face had a listening austerity.

At the top of a steepish hill she pulled up at the side of the road to let the white horse rest. Moreover, they were within a mile or so of Winchester, and Winchester would prove quite superfluous in the middle of such a confession.

"What a pity it wasn't the man who caught you."

She was far calmer than he was, and he had no way of telling how she was feeling about it, but it seemed to Suvla that her pride would always hold itself very straight.

"Yes—Blaber would have been easy. But how the devil was I to know that—all these years—she had been making a little sentimental god of me?"

"Didn't you feel flattered?"

He answered her with a touch of fierceness.

"Strange to say, no. There are occasions, my dear, when one's silly self-love hides under the bed. I hadn't so much to kick it as to tell it to keep quiet. A part of me was scared."

"I'm glad of that," was all she said.

He could not decide what her "gladness" portended, nor what her solution of the affair would be. At all events he was sure that it would be neither obvious nor cowardly. Yet her silences troubled him, for no other woman's inward thinking had ever mattered as did Richenda's.

Suvla John

"So—there you have it," he said. "The fact is, I ran away. I wanted—you——"

He met her level eyes, and deep down in them he divined a hidden anger. He was baffled. Open anger would have been understandable.

"So—you came to me!"

"I am not ashamed of it."

"It is not a question of shame. Besides, you have told me too much."

"My dear—I had to tell you."

"Your—sense of honour! That's a subtle point, John Suvla. Men are like dogs—they must yap. Now, women are more like cats!"

"I don't take you."

"No? It is difficult to explain—atmosphere. The cat is a creature of dignity; why should she be compelled to scratch the fool dog's nose? Or—to use her claws—and her fastidiousness——?"

She threw him the reins, and, climbing down, stood in the road with her gaze going downhill. Suvla, sitting sideways, had a view of her haughtiness and of her wild woman's pride. Somehow, she felt fiercely offended, though he could not gauge the deeps of the offence. She was deep. And he loved her for it, as he loved her aloofness and her pride.

"What's doing?" he asked her.

She kept silent a moment, and then he saw her wave a hand.

"We shall have to drop—all superfluities, you and I. I'll leave Tinto in charge."

The head of the procession had appeared, and to her came young Loverine and a rough pony.

"Loverine," she said, "I am going on ahead. Tell Tinto to take charge. Wait, he'll need money."

She entered the caravan, and reappeared with a small packet of notes.

"Twenty pounds. The route remains the same. New Alresford, Alton, Farnham. Tell Tinto to remain at Farnham until he hears from me."

Loverine nodded. Richenda Lee was a woman who did not stoop to explain, and the lad turned his pony and rode back, while Richenda reascended to the driving-seat of the caravan.

She took the reins from Suvla.

"That—seems to be my fate," she said.

Suvla John

Her voice had a tinge of passionate arrogance, and he sat beside her, questioning and immensely serious.

"I'm sorry, my dear. Man is—the fool dog——"

She did not look at him.

"Just one thing. You promised to go back?"

"Does such a promise——?"

She made a movement of protest.

"Don't talk. We'll get through Winchester, and up on the chalk hills. I've got to think."

2

It was to take them the best part of an hour to thread their way through the city, for Richenda pulled up where the main street broadened out and left Suvla in charge while she bought fruit and vegetables and other things that she needed. Suvla sat regarding the statue of King Alfred, another hero who had attained disgrace over burnt cakes. He saw nothing of Richenda, but he heard her return once or twice and open the door at the back of the caravan. She was stowing away her stores for the journey that was in front of them.

"She's angry," he thought, "and yet not angry. Anyway, her anger is better than any other woman's smile. But where was I wrong——"

Reappearing suddenly, she took the reins from him without a word, and drove on, pulling aside to let the white horse drink at a water-trough. Suvla's silence waited upon hers. He sat and smoked as they went on over the bridge and began to climb the steep and winding road, but here she ordered him out.

"It is a pretty stiff pull for the horse."

He descended without a word, but with a smile deep down in his eyes, and, going to the tail of the van, put his right shoulder to it. Richenda was the first woman who had given him an order. The thinking part of her went just one step ahead of him, and he was not piqued by it. His maleness uttered no protest. He had begun to allow that in some ways she was stronger and more clear-sighted than he was, while there were certain activities in which she would have to give way to him. But the day was hers; she dominated it; she was oracular, and he stood between the pillars of her temple.

Suvla John

"Mush," he thought, as he helped the white horse up the hill; "she doesn't give one mush. And yet she's so human. She's greater than the Queen of Sheba. King Solomon would have boasted of nothing——"

He watched the near back wheel revolving. The white horse was a gallant beast, and Richenda would not ride behind a beast that was not gallant. She had no great use for weaklings, or anything that was indifferently bred. The world needed weeding, and a purblind and sentimental democracy was refusing to hoe its own weeds. But the patient wheel ceased to revolve. Richenda had pulled up where the slope of the road flattened itself, and the white horse turned his head as though to say: "How's that—for a pull? Thanks—all the same."

Suvla came round from the tail of the caravan.

"May I get up, Richenda?"

There was faint irony, a lover's irony, in his eyes.

"No," she said, "not yet. Walk."

And Suvla walked.

There followed another half an hour's silence, Richenda sitting with her elbows resting on her knees, and her eyes following the road, while Suvla swung along beside the white horse. A breeze played upon the chalk hills, and the white clouds went over them. They passed a number of very new and dreary little buildings, the probable homes of post-war "back-to-the-landers," and Suvla noticed that Richenda looked at them with pity. She seemed quite unaware of him trudging beside the horse.

Presently the country mellowed. They came to a spot where old thorn trees and bracken broke the ordered monotony of the road, and Richenda pulled the caravan on to the grass. A nose-bag was slung under the van. She climbed down and unslung it, and, passing it to Suvla, left him to give the horse his dinner. She disappeared into the caravan, to reappear with a white cloth, plates and glasses.

Suvla took the things from her.

"Shade or sun?"

"Sun."

He spread the cloth, and arranged the plates and glasses, and going to the rear of the van took such things as she handed to him, fruit, bread and cheese, two bottles of cider, a bag of cakes. They sat down opposite each other, with the white cloth between them, and the tall

Sulva John

fern throwing flickering shadows. The horse was busy
with his nose-bag. An occasional lorry thundered by.

Richenda ate bread and fruit. The silent fit was upon
her still, a mood that was not to be meddled with, and
Suvla left her to her aloofness. She would come out of
it when she chose, but not before, and he did not wish her
other than she was. There was nothing in her that he
wished to change.

Presently her little amber and meerschaum pipe came
out. Her fingers were deliberate as she filled it, and
then, with elbows on knees, sat smoking, her eyes
watching the smoke, and the light and shadow amid
the fern.

"What does your watch say?"

He glanced at his wrist-watch.

"Ten past three."

"It is dark about nine. That gives you six hours."

He watched her face, but she kept her glances from
him.

"So—I am to go back?"

"Why not?"

She baffled him. Her pride was so calmly impartial.
She betrayed neither prejudice nor passion.

"I don't want to go back."

Her glance crossed his—like a sword.

"If I thought you wished to please both of us!
Perhaps you do."

"It is a question of not hurting—someone."

This time she gave him a clear and steady glare.

"I see. She is so hurtable. The only one? No, let
it be. I'm the queen on the chess-board. You want me
to move and get you out of check."

"Is that cowardly?"

She sat, considering.

"You don't see all round things," she said presently.
"In the beginning you just saw the immediate adventure.
And then—you saw me. The trouble begins when you
start mixing your adventures, or mismanaging them."

He made a movement of protest.

"But you sent me back."

"I did. Because—it seemed to me—that you had left
a lot of loose threads hanging."

"Your precious completeness——!"

"I hate frayed ends. I sent you to tidy things up—
inside and outside. And the tangle——"

Suvla John

"Ten times worse I admit it. If a man's fingers are all thumbs——"

"He runs to a woman. Is that fair?"

He looked at her as he would have looked at a man.

"That's a question to be answered. It's fair—because—you—are what you are—to me. I don't want to go back—but if you tell me to go back——"

Her eyes gave a queer, dark flash.

"Idiot! No—not quite that. But you men—even you—make me angry. Why—should I have the job——?"

She got up, and, walking across to the white horse, removed the empty nose-bag, and fondled the beast's ears. Her back was to Suvla, a passionate and protesting back. She gave him the impression of being on the edge of some fierce outburst, and that she was holding herself in.

He turned on his side.

"Richenda."

She did not move.

"I won't go back. That's the best way out of it—after all."

He saw one of her hands pass slowly down the horse's neck. Her head was very high. And then she turned slowly, and looked down at him.

"You told me she made you promise."

"That's true."

"And you made her one—in return."

"True again."

Her eyes were profoundly fierce.

"You want me to tell you to break your promise. I'm not that sort of woman. Go back and keep it like a man."

3

She became strangely inscrutable yet serenely frank. She let him get up beside her on the caravan, but when he tried to speak of the one thing that mattered to him he found himself easily repulsed. She held him at a distance. Her smile had come back, but in it there was something incomprehensible and dangerous. It had occurred to him to suspect her of jealousy, but she was not behaving like a jealous woman, or like the jealous women he had known.

Suvla John

His feeling was that he had failed her in some way, and that he was still failing her. What had he done that had caused her some wound of pride or of prejudice? Or was she playing a mysterious game with him? Inscrutable Queen! She sat there beside him, holding the reins, suggesting a calm defiance.

"Woman," said he, "why do you beat me with whips?"

She laughed, a little silent laugh, but she showed him no mercy.

"What time is it?"

"Nearly four."

"Five hours. You will have to hire a car. No—you need not pull on your war-face. I'm serious."

She was. He divined her seriousness, and it baffled him. What did she want him to do? Why this fierce austerity?

"Very well; I'll hire a car."

"We can pick one up somewhere, perhaps at New Alresford. If it drops you within five miles——"

He had a fit of silence, and she did not attempt to break it, and yet—after they had been so near to each other—this silence seemed to him exasperating and absurd. He had lost the power to move her, to make her answer him out of her heart.

"And the rest of the plan?" he asked her at last.

"What plan?"

"What happens—when you have dropped me overboard?"

"I keep my promise."

"Panhurst Farm—and all that?"

"Unless—you wish it changed."

He flashed out at her.

"Changed! You are a devil, Richenda, a dear, damnable devil. I can't get you—but—by God—I will."

She smiled straight into his eyes.

"Less of a devil than you think, my man. Find out. I have not ceased to be an adventure."

XXII

1

ROBERT BLABER looked out of a window.

In the soft glare of a July afternoon the shadows of the trees lay with a pleasant solidity upon the grass, so that green joined gold along the lace-like edge of the shadow pattern. There were patches of dim sunlight scattered here and there, patches that seemed to breathe and blink when a casual wind stirred the foliage. Also, he saw the curved red streak of the hammock under the big chestnut tree, with a white outline filling it like whipped cream upon a plate of fruit. The hammock swayed slightly. The highly coloured cover of some magazine lay on the grass beneath it.

Blaber strolled out, and across the grass. He approached from a flank, and not being heard he was able to gain a vivid impression of the thing the hammock held. His wife's dark head lay on a red cushion. Her clasped hands were under her head, and her eyes looking up into the hollow dome of the great tree. She was in white, with touches of cerise. One white, shoeless foot hung over the red edge, and about the curve of the leg a little froth of white lace protruded.

Blaber stood still, a dozen paces away from her. She was quite unconscious of his nearness, lying dreamily relaxed, lap and bosom open to the strong scattering of sunlight through the leaves. He saw a burr of light playing upon her hair. Her relaxation suggested to him an innocent wantonness, the languor of sensuous dreams, and of rich anticipation.

He moistened his lips, and smiled.

"Elsie."

Her hands came from under her head. There was a jerky movement of the hammock. She half turned, and the shoeless foot was withdrawn.

"Sorry. Were you asleep?"

Suvla John

He came and stood beside the hammock, but slightly behind her.

"Not quite. You made me jump."

"Sorry. I have had a note from the Gutteridges. They want me to go and dine."

He saw the trembling of her lashes.

"Well—you'll enjoy it."

"Do you mind? I wondered——"

He was as conciliatory as a cat in quest of milk.

"You like the Gutteridges——?"

"Yes—but I wondered—if you would care——"

"I feel so lazy in the evening."

He accepted the excuse instantly.

"I don't want to drag you out. I only wondered. I feel I have been a bit of a hermit-crab—you know. It has occurred to me—do you mind?——"

"Well?"

"We ought to entertain more. I have made things rather dull for you here. What about having a few people up to tennis?"

"Just as you like."

"No, that's not it. As—you like, Elsie."

She lay very still for moment, eyes half closed.

"Who shall I ask?"

"O—Blossom—I suppose, and his sister."

"Yes."

"And the Anstruthers."

"If they are home."

"And Dick and Sybil."

"Of course."

"I might get the Gutteridges. But they bore you."

"No. Ask them."

"Thanks. So you won't feel hurt?"

"Not a bit. We agreed—didn't we?"

"That's good of you, Elsie. A man likes to be taken at his word."

Stooping down he picked up the magazine, and offered it to her, making some jest about the sensuous young woman on the cover, but she told him she had finished with it.

"Right—I'll borrow it. Tea—as usual—I suppose?"

"I told Parker—in the loggia."

"I'll try a little literary strawberries and cream in the loggia—till tea-time."

He withdrew, leaving her to sigh out her relief and

Suvla John

to clasp her secret exultation. His sudden, seeming kindness troubled her a little; she did not need it; she resented it; it was as though someone had asked her to join in a hymn tune when she was in the midst of a rhapsody. All day she had been thinking how she could elude him that evening, and now the Gutteridges had asked him to dinner. She blessed the Gutteridges and the vulgar and hospitable glare of "Fiesole." Robert admired Clara Gutteridge, and Elsie knew that she would feel grateful to Clara Gutteridge if she were more than kind to him.

She made a soft, writhing movement in the hammock. To-night, in the warm darkness——! The smell of the fern in "Mab's Dell." He had promised, and she did not doubt but that he would keep his promise. That beard of his would make kisses different—and yet—of course—how different would their kisses be! She knew things that she had not known before.

"O—John—hold me——"

Blaber had returned to the loggia. He had the magazine on one knee, and was staring at the cover. His eyes glanced from it to the white figure in the red hammock.

Strawberries and cream! Yes—that was just what she was, what every pretty woman was at the ripe and psychological moment. Shere was to enjoy her. And probably he had not enjoyed her for very long, for it seemed to Blaber that the affair had come just to its fruition. That look on Elsie's face? O—yes, there was no doubt about it.

He felt vicious, triumphantly vicious. He had gone pretty far with Clara Gutteridge, and this affair of Elsie's provoked him to desire much more than he had been given. Gutteridge was a bore and a fool, and Clara a woman of the world. But—first—he would wring the neck of Dick Shere's reputation.

It occurred to him that it would be as well to have a witness. Yes—but there was plenty of time for that when he was sure that the birds were in a trap.

Tea arrived. Parker arranged the oak table and two Dryad chairs. She never once looked at Blaber.

"Tea, sir. Shall I tell Mrs. Blaber?"

"Thanks. I'll call her."

He stood up, still holding the adventurous magazine. "Elsie—tea."

She sat up in the hammock, slipped out of it, and

206

came slowly across the grass, her secret big in her. She did not realize that she had changed, and that the subtle glamour of it was obvious to her husband. Even her walk was different, expressing an excited languor, sensuous self-consciousness.

At tea she forgot that he did not take sugar, and gave him two lumps, and Blaber let the error pass.

His comment upon it was private.

"I suppose that is Shere's usual allowance."

2

It was half-past six, and as Blaber came out of his room he saw his wife emerge from the bathroom at the end of the passage. She was wearing a cerise coloured wrap; some white undergarment trailed from her arm.

He smiled as he went down the stairs into the hall. Every little sensuous detail had its significance.

He rang the bell, and looked with sarcastic interest at Parker's wooden face.

"Bring me a cocktail—please."

"What will you take, sir?"

"Oh, bring me a gin and vermouth."

Parker disapproved of cocktails, for they seemed to her a male drink—and therefore unnecessary. Blaber was in the drawing-room when she came in search of him with a glass on a silver tray.

"Thank you, Parker. By the way, no one need sit up. I expect I shall be late."

"Very good, sir."

"I am sending the car back. I shall walk home."

She gave him a veiled and suspicious side-glance as she went out of the room, for his "niceness" filled her with mistrust. Parker had served in Robert Blaber's house for three years, and his goodness of heart had never been greatly in evidence. Atmosphere—a frigid atmosphere—cannot grow genial all in five minutes without some artificial stimulus, and Parker's hard eye searched for a motive. When a man like her master became polite, conciliatory, and considerate it behoved one to think less well of the world.

At seven o'clock Blaber's car was waiting for him, but Elsie had not descended. He idled about, adjusting the white silk scarf over his collar and shirt front, and Parker—divining his necessity—came to help him on with his coat. She was withdrawing when a door on the upper landing opened, and Elsie appeared on the stairs.

She bent over the rail, and her husband looked up at her.

"Just off, dear. Hope you won't feel lonely."

The hollowness of the words was lost upon her, for she was so alive with rich anticipation that nothing could seem hollow and unreal. She came down the stairs. She was wearing black, and out of the black sheath her throat and shoulders swelled smooth and white. And she brought a perfume with her, subtle yet penetrating, and from her eyes distilled the fragrance of desire.

"I hope you will enjoy yourself."

"And you?" he thought with a sudden savage envy. for in that moment he saw his wife as a woman to be desired.

"Don't wait up."

He was pulling on a glove, and his teeth showed under his little black moustache.

"I expect I shall go to bed early. These hot days are rather tiring."

"They are. Night night, Elsie. I won't forget to ask the Gutteridges for to-morrow."

3

Elsie sat and watched the last sun rays burning upon a bed of purple phloxes and rose and yellow snapdragon. They glowed like lamps, and then faded to a gentle dimness.

She rose, entered the house, and ascending to her room, looked at herself in the little Sheraton mirror, touching her hair with white fingers. Her eyes were deep with desire. A powder puff brushed her soft skin, and she scattered a few drops of perfume on her bosom.

The little mirror gave place to the long glass in the door of her wardrobe. She put her hands behind her head and stood at gaze, loving the woman who was to be loved. A black velvet cloak and a little black lace wrap hid her white neck and shoulders, there being a meaning

Suvla John

in the veiling of the body, for where there is no veil there is no mystery in the surrender.

She went downstairs, and out into the garden. A soft greyness was spreading like water, and all the world was very still. The grass, moistening with the dew, was a carpet of romance, and as she passed among the flowers and under the shadowiness of the trees she felt that the flowers and the trees understood her happiness and were glad.

A winding grass path brought her to a gate of larch wood, and beyond it lay the wild garden. She stood here awhile, soft-eyed, conscious of a new strangeness in beauty. Here, purple willow herb and golden rag-wort made a dim splendour in the dusk, and the curving fronds of the fern seemed to spread their hands over hidden treasure. In the beyond towered dark spruces with little crevices of gold plucked from the fading afterglow.

She opened the gate and passed through. A clock struck nine deep strokes, and the air about her seemed to tremble. Some big insect went booming by on heavy wings. She came to the gloom of the spruces, and paused at the head of the narrow path that plunged towards the dell. She listened; her eyes looked back for a moment.

How slow had been the coming of the darkness, and yet when she entered the wood of spruces night seemed to fall. It was like going down into deep, cool water. Below her she saw a little lingering greyness in the green smother of the dell. It seemed still as death, and for a moment she was afraid.

Again she paused to listen, with the bracken brushing against her cloak. A piece of the dead wood cracked under her foot when she moved on, and the silence and her heartbeats were startled. Was he here? She felt a sudden passion to be sure, to feel herself held in the deep waters of this solitary place, to know that life lived.

Everything looked dim. And when she saw something move, a vague and shadowy outline, and she seemed to float towards it swiftly through the fern, she realized the substance of her love, the dear reality of her most dear ghost.

"John——"

She came to him with a little sighing, face upturned, and eyes half closed. Her hands went to his shoulders.

"John, my beloved——"

He held her. He was conscious of the soft warmth and perfume of her. She was woman, yet all the world of woman was Richenda.

4

Suvla went with her as far as the gate above the wild garden. They stood here for a minute holding hands.

"To-morrow——"

She had not told him that her husband had returned. She had meant to tell him, but the dear deceit had been conceived in a moment of chagrin when she had realized that everything was not to happen on that first night. And suddenly she had grown reckless, but there were motives behind her recklessness.

He opened the gate.

"You must go—now, Elsie. We have had an hour. I have to think——"

She clung to him, wondering why he did not answer her with all that fierce impulsiveness. All the while he had seemed to be holding himself in, and she was saying: "He thinks it is for my sake."

"To-morrow——"

"Yes."

With a hand on her shoulder he seemed to impel her gently into the darkness, and when she had gone he stood leaning upon the gate. He felt tired, most strangely tired, as though the effort of seeming her lover had exhausted him. He was conscious of anger, and impatience, and compassion. The situation seemed to him utterly false, for his heart and soul were full of Richenda.

Hell—but why had she sent him back? Was it for this very reason, that he should be made to feel how wholly and rebelliously he was hers? Had she been able to foresee this reaction? Had she any pity for the other woman? Was she thinking of the other woman?

And what did she imagine that he would do?

Break away and go back to her?

But she had told him to keep his promise, and he began to understand the vagueness of the promise. Its very vagueness left it perilously open. To him it might seem one thing—but to Elsie—and to Richenda——?

He returned to "Mab's Dell," and pushing through the fern and the tangle of green growth he made his way out into a strip of meadowland that lay secretly between two woods. He knew how the ground lay, and following the meadow, he came to a gate opening into a farm track. Hackbury lay more than a mile away, and he felt like a tired man after a forced march when he reached it. He lay down in the heather, thinking of Richenda, and of the time that would elapse before the green caravan would climb Panhurst Hill.

5

It was about midnight when Elsie heard a door slam, and knew that her husband had returned.

She lay looking at the outline of the window, and her whole consciousness was full of the to-morrow.

Her recklessness had hardened. She was passing beyond the convention of excuses. She had come to the point when the rebel refuses to make excuses.

She was ready to exult, and to defy.

She met the daylight with a smile. The sun was shining.

Her husband was up before her. He was smoking a cigarette, and looking at an impression that had been left in the fern on the slope of "Mab's Dell."

XXIII

I

BLABER stood at his dressing-room window. He was fastening the buttons of his flannel shirt, and looking down at the tennis court, where a gardener was mending a hole in the stop-netting. The court was all sunlight, but beyond it two or three trees threw a pleasant shade. Chairs had been placed there, and Blaber noticed that there was no wind to stir the striped canvas. The net with its white band hung absolutely still, as though it were a pattern marked upon the grass. The whitened lines of the court were precise, clean cut, and symmetrical. Bees were working in the honeysuckle outside the window. The landscape had the placid and green solidity of a perfect summer day.

Solidity, orderliness, comfort, the tranquil atmosphere of an English country house. Blaber stood fingering his shirt. He was going down to play tennis on that court with people who would laugh and rally each other on their bad shots. It would be very indifferent tennis, but then—indifferent tennis is enjoyable. There would be tea under the trees, and later, Parker would bring out a tray of glasses, and cider-cup and lemonade. Someone would call for a men's four, and they would go on to the court and try to impress the women. Blossom would dash about, and bounding for high balls at the net, would hit them on the wood or miss them completely. And Shere, with those easy and graceful drives of his and his kicking service, would be on the winning side—as usual.

Blaber watched the gardener looking for other holes to mend.

He realized the bland stillness of this summer day and of this English landscape. It was so quiet, and until a month or so ago Blaber had understood that life grew more and more quiet as you grew older. Even

Suvla John

the war had never equalled the sensationalism of the highly coloured magazines, and few exciting things happen outside the criminal court. Life here had seemed so secure, and then—suddenly—it had grown full of an absurd yet disquieting sensationalism.

It was as though the war feeling had returned. He was being reminded of the fact that in a moment of savage spite he had committed murder. Almost the memory of it had ceased to be red, and had faded to a comfortable greyness. He wished the redness back again, and yet did not wish it. He was both a coward and spiteful.

The gardener had found another hole in the netting, and Blaber watched him cut off a length of tarred twine and draw the meshes together. The man was in no hurry; he knelt there as though life held nothing but the job in hand; he pushed back his hat and scratched his head. The man was real, the garden was real; the tennis court suggested pleasant realities and people who had no serious troubles, and to Blaber it seemed incredible that he should be going down on to that grass to watch two lovers, guilty lovers. The quietude of it all was deceptive.

Downstairs in his den he took his racquet out of its press, and opened a box of new balls. The smell of them suggested other summers, and jolly, heedless games in other gardens, and as he stood there he wished it were possible to go back ten years. But no, not to go back, but to alter the way things had happened. It seemed to him that he had wanted the wrong things, or that he had mismanaged the getting of them.

A yellow car passed the window and he realized that the Gutteridges had arrived, and as he went to meet them he felt less piqued by the thought of Clara Gutteridge. She—too—was inclined to be sensational and disturbing. How was it that he had not understood the preciousness of quietude and security?

Clara Gutteridge was wearing a yellow jumper, and it made her look sallow.

"Well—well, squire—feel in form?"

She had a trick of calling him "squire," and Blaber resented it, because he knew that he was no more than the son of a manufacturer come south. He had not the touch or the feel of the countryman.

"I don't know how the court will play."

Suvla John

"Ours is a nightmare. The turf they put down was a disgrace."

Gutteridge was taking off his coat. His stupid and kindly face was as placid as a sheep's, and to-day its stupidity seemed to Blaber to be more comforting than the wife's animal energy.

"Aw—plenty of time—my dear; we'll get it right—next year."

Elsie came gliding out in white and cerise. She smiled. She had a secret look as though she had some happy secret hidden within her, and yet her happiness was less exultant and less sure than the happiness of yesterday. For she had begun to wonder and to ask herself questions, and haunting thoughts kept starting up like ghosts, and sometimes her eyes had the shadowiness of these thoughts. It had seemed to her that her warm ardour had encountered a sense of resistance, and that her dreaming recklessness challenged a spirit that was vaguely unwilling. She went about among these outward voices, while a voice within her would not be silent. "Why does he hold back? Why does he not take anything? Is it—that he does not care quite as he used to care?"

She was smiling at Frederick Gutteridge. His bland and heavy face was not exacting.

"I'm afraid our court has not been played on this year."

He bent towards her like a polite shopwalker.

"Aw—it can't be more—surprising—than my bad play."

Mr. Blossom arrived on his bicycle. He wore a sweater under his coat, and looked hot; in fact, he always looked hot—and yet he always wore a sweater. His racquet was about five years old, and his trousers were too big for him.

"Splendid weather. Afraid I'm late, Mrs. Blaber."

She was a little more shy of Mr. Blossom, for his rosy face represented the conventions, and she felt like a child who had stolen forbidden fruit.

"No—you are not late. O, here are the Anstruthers. That means you will be able to have a men's four."

To her the afternoon was as unreal as it was to her husband. It seemed to her that the world had ceased to belong to her, and that she had left a mere empty voice in it. She was sitting in one of the chairs under

Suvla John

the trees between the Gutteridge woman and Grace Anstruther; the four men were examining the height of the net as though it required the whole four of them to assume its accuracy. Blaber threw six new balls on to the court. And then the Sheres arrived, appearing as they always appeared—like two bodies and one inseparable soul.

Elsie jumped up. She was aware of a little heartpang as she looked at Sybil. What would Sybil think—if——? What did it matter what Sybil might think? And yet—it did matter.

"Elsie—I'm afraid we are late."

"O, no, you are not, dear. We want Dick to play."

Elsie insisted upon a man's four.

"It's so hot; we women can play after tea. Will you arrange it—Robert?"

So, Dick and Mr. Blossom faced Gutteridge and Anstruther, while Clara Gutteridge talked to Grace Anstruther and tried to draw Blaber to the chair beside her. Sybil and Elsie sat a little apart, and Sybil had the demure look of a woman who was exploring a situation. Elsie's letter had said very little when she had written asking them to tennis—but Elsie's husband had returned, and in Elsie herself Sybil divined an emotional excitement. It appeared that there had been a rapprochement.

They watched the tennis, and the game brought out the characteristics of the four players. Mr. Blossom ran and jumped on every possible occasion, and got redder and shinier and still wore his sweater, and shouted "Shot!" whenever his partner scored. Anstruther was nervous and apt to be cross with himself. Gutteridge missed most of the balls that came his way, and stroked his moustache and smiled apologetically. "Aw—I'm sorry, partner. Aw—bless my soul!" Shere was the only one of them who knew how to play the game and could play it with the satisfying ease and cleanness of a man who was good at all games. His skimming drives and crisp volleys, and graceful backhand shots across the court made the other men look clumsy.

Elsie was watching him without realizing that she was watching him with more interest than she gave to the others. For it was pleasant to watch him—and was he not a Shere, and John's brother? She hugged a secret. She felt a queen of mystery. How she could astonish all

8

these people! And once or twice she applauded the Shere shots.

"O—well played, Dick."

Some instinct made her glance along the half circle of chairs, and she caught her husband in the act of watching her. Two moody eyes, and a narrow and clouded forehead! He turned his stare from her directly her eyes met his, and leaning back in his chair, put a hand up over his little black moustache. But his glance had surprised her. She had a feeling that he had been watching her for quite a long while without her suspecting it, and his eyes had faltered when she had surprised him in her turn. There had been something very disturbing in his eyes, curiosity, a peculiar cynicism, the shadow of a threat.

She turned to Sybil and became aware of another sort of watchfulness, of eyes that were wanting to ask—"How is it with you, my dear?" And her self-consciousness became flooded with sudden, sensitive timidity. Her dream state dissolved in an abrupt and vivid appreciation of the realities. She had a feeling of sitting there naked.

At tea she was nervous and distraught. Her hands trembled and became so clumsy that she took an unconscionable time in filling the cups. The men stood round, waiting, and she was so bothered by them standing there that she grew more nervous, and felt sure that her trembling and incoordinate hands were betraying her emotion. She wished that she had arranged for Parker to pour out the tea.

Shere, quick in his intuitions, took possession of the milk jug and the sugar bowl.

"I'll take these round."

She gave him a look of thanks, and reached for the hot-water jug to refill the teapot. Someone was standing at her elbow, and in glancing up she met her husband's stare.

"I'm thirsty. Mayn't I have a cup?"

He was smiling, but his smile made her afraid.

"I'm sorry, Robert."

Her hands became more out of control. She did not appear to be wholly conscious of what she was doing, and while one hand was opening the lid of the silver teapot, the other was tilting the water-jug. The steaming water splashed over her left hand.

Suvla John

She gave a little cry.

"Oh! How silly!"

The pain of it seemed to steady her.

"I'm afraid I have scalded myself."

She managed to laugh, but Blaber had taken the hot-water jug away from her, and was staring at her hand.

"You had better do something——"

It was Sybil who intervened. She had been watching Elsie and her fumbling agitation, and now she put her cup aside and took control. She ignored Blaber, for it seemed obvious to Sybil that Blaber was the cause of his wife's panic. She took Elsie's arm.

"You must have something on it—dear."

She carried Elsie away from an atmosphere of sudden and embarrassing sympathy. They went up to Elsie's room, and Sybil made her lie down on the sofa while she powdered the reddening skin and wrapped up the hand in a silk handkerchief.

"How's that? It must smart."

"Better, dear, thank you."

"I'll get Robert to send for Dr. Warburton."

"Oh, no."

"But it ought to be dressed—properly."

"Sybil, it is only a trifle."

But Sybil believed that the scalded hand was a mere part of the pain, and that the real source of anguish lay deeper. Mental anguish, with a husband who could smile in public, and say cruel things when no one else was there. Nor would it be a disadvantage to have a doctor about the place for the next few days.

"Lie down, my dear, and stay there for half an hour. I'll go and see to things."

She returned to the group under the trees, and, taking Elsie's place at the table, she became the woman in control.

"A nasty scald. More tea—anybody? I have made her lie down."

She looked at Blaber in a way that made him understand that she had a message for him. He came to the table as though to have his cup refilled.

"I think Warburton ought to be sent for."

She was a little puzzled by Blaber's eyes, for behind their seriousness she seemed to divine ugly and cynical laughter.

"I'll see to it."

217

Suvla John

He put down his cup and walked towards the house, wondering if Mrs. Richard Shere would be so sympathetic if she knew why Elsie's hand had trembled.

Scalded fingers! Sybil Shere was in danger of a far worse scald than that.

2

On Hackbury John Suvla lay watching the far hills growing clear and blue. The weather was changing, and this blueness of the hills and the sunlit flash of some church spire warned him that the eyes of the West were filling with tears.

But he was not thinking of the coming rain, or of the sodden night he might have to spend in the fern before Richenda's caravan reached Panhurst, for Richenda's van might not mean shelter from the rain. She might let him sleep between the wheels, or she might not. It would depend upon how a man had handled his pity.

Nevertheless, he could not think of one woman without considering the other. Richenda seemed above pity, and as he pictured her seated behind the white horse and looking along the road with her steady and sombre eyes, he felt that he understood her as he had not understood her yesterday. Her pride was against all makeshifts and compromises, and Suvla had tried to compromise with his own heart.

"Well—after all," he thought, "it is very simple, and it would have been still simpler if I had treated Elsie like a man. Because a creature wears petticoats, and has long hair and a soft voice, why should one assume that she is incapable of hearing the truth or of bearing pain? And yet—telling the truth to a woman seems to require more moral courage than most men possess."

Yes, it was very simple. He had run away from an emotional woman, and had appealed to another woman to ask her to help him. And Richenda had received him as she would have received a coward. He had deserted his trench, fallen back on his supports, and Richenda had refused to go up and take over the trench for him. Richenda was right, but hers was the added rightness of having spoken hard words to a man. She had told him off as he, Suvla, would have told off another man under similar conditions. "Am I to take on the unpleasant jobs for you? Go back and stick it." It requires another sort of courage to say the unpleasant thing, and Richenda had that courage. Perhaps women had more of it than men.

Obviously, every man was a bit of a swashbuckler. He liked to return with tales of the enemies he had humbled and the wild beasts he had slain, and the woman would listen and ply her needle. Her man might be a physical marvel, energy personified, but she would know that there were certain delicate and more subtle problems that he would shirk. The boy in man loves to be dramatic, to create a sensation. But were women different?

Suvla lit his pipe. He felt that he was getting a grip upon something. He was climbing above the mere sex idea. For to man sex is an affair of incidents.

Were women different?

To women sex meant children.

A different outlook? Of course. Women had to think of security; they might have had to develop another sort of courage, the courage that sits still and faces unpleasant facts. While her man was spreading himself in an ale-house, full of yeasty babblings, she might be at home explaining to the rent collector why the rent was not forthcoming, or telling the milkman that the milk was watered. Did men leave it to the women to deal with the world's watered milk?

Richenda had the woman's outlook. Her man might be a tremendous fellow; she could leave to him the killing of lions, but when it was a question of telling some little wench that she was a slattern, or warning the grocer that he has charged twice for a pound of sugar, then the killer of lions ceased to be the hero. Man cannot deny himself the self-encouragement of seeming generous. He must appear the good fellow. Hence the mean little scuffles of life have been left to the woman. It is she who has carried on the obscure, guerilla warfare against mean and petty enemies, while her man has hidden in the tent under his lion's skin.

Suvla had glimmerings of all this. Seven years of adventurous life had needed the culminating experience of Richenda. It was not that she was wise as to men; she was wise as to one man, and she had found him telling the usual romantic and self-concealing lies to a woman.

He sat cross-legged amid the fern, looking through the fronds at the blue horizon. The horizon was Richenda.

Suvla John

Somewhere—away yonder—the white horse was plodding along between the hedgerows.

"That's her completeness," he thought. "She had more courage with me than I had with Elsie. I wanted to say the soft things; she said the hard ones."

What was it but vanity, the wish of the male to look well in the eyes of a woman? It had hurt him to think of hurting Elsie by destroying an illusion, for he was the illusion, and Richenda had made the illusion look no better than a scarecrow.

"She has taught me something. Obviously I have got to go down to-night and tell Elsie the truth—yes, before Blaber comes back. Not the truth about Blaber, but the truth about myself. Blaber can wait till to-morrow."

3

Warburton had dressed Elsie's hand, but for the dressing of sore hearts there is only one sure balm, the truth, or what we humans agree to call the truth. We fear the smart of this most potent of dressings, and yet there is no healing without it.

In her own way Parker understood this. To cut out of your life all that which is tainted and useless; to apply a plaster that will bring away moribund dreams; to concentrate upon the compensating realities.

She would like to have said things to the other woman who was her mistress, for to Parker Elsie was something of a child.

"Dainty food is good, madam, and sleep in a clean bed, and flowers about you. There's something—I don't know what—in getting a polish on furniture. And feeling that you have dropped the hot coals of life, and that they won't burn you any more. A fire to sit by is different. Hobbies, too! Why, didn't I know one old lady who was quite happy on a wet evening, cleaning up all the snails in her garden? Your marriage is never going to amount to anything. It never does in most cases, not in my class, anyway. Your man's no good. He's not the sort of man any decent woman could settle down with on the other side of the fire. You've tried marriage. Why not try doing without a man? It's all a matter of getting used to things—but you'll never get used to him. He's never got used to himself—somehow. There are people like that. Wretched, spoilt children."

When Elsie said, "Parker, I don't think I'll go down to dinner," Parker replied, "Certainly, madam; you shall have it up here." She had the look of the austere but kindly aunt. She went down and confronted Blaber, who had had a bath and a change, and was standing moodily in the loggia.

"Mrs. Blaber will take her dinner upstairs, sir."

"All right."

"Will you have yours served, sir?"

"Yes."

Parker detailed one of the under-maids to wait upon Blaber while she cared for the wife. Elsie's left hand was bandaged, and Parker stayed to cut up her meat for her, and found pleasure in the doing of it.

"I hope it won't keep you awake, madam."

"It is much easier now, Parker."

"If you should want anything in the night—I wake up very easily."

"Oh, no; I'm sure it will not be necessary. Thank you all the same."

When Parker had brought her coffee, she sat in the cushioned window seat and wondered how she was to find some excuse for wandering down to Mab's Dell. She was surprised to find that her recklessness had diminished. The idea of going to the dell filled her with fear, and this fear was a complex emotion. It included her husband, and it included her lover. She felt tired. She found herself shrinking a little from facing the decision, whatever it might be. She was afraid that John Shere might refuse to jump over the cliff with her, but—also—she discovered a slight shrinking from the edge of the cliff. She was not used to such storms of emotion; she was a frail thing; her petals were beginning to wilt.

She felt hot and tremulous. She began to wonder whether she would be equal to so wild an adventure, to cutting herself adrift from the familiar surroundings. Even with John? But what was the reason of this sudden shirking? Had she failed to convince herself that her recklessness of yesterday could count as an answering recklessness in her lover? Had she not divined a something, a holding back? His kisses had not satisfied her.

She drank her coffee, and mused. Her consciousness

had recovered some of its little conventional attitudes. As a woman she was more sentimental than passionate.

She realized that she was afraid of people, of Sybil, Dick, even the rubicund Mr. Blossom. She clung to the familiar figures, the people whom she knew; and suddenly she came to the dark moment when she realized man as a stranger, the man to whom she had offered everything. He was not the John of seven years ago, nor the John of her dreams.

But how horrible of her to feel like this!

How was it that the exultation of yesterday had become a sudden shivering abstraction dressed in a damp sheet? And John had been so splendid; he had renounced so much, given up the Manor to Dick, and left her to what he had believed to be a happy marriage. No, she must keep her promise and go down to Mab's Dell.

XXIV

I

ROBERT BLABER sat in the loggia, and watched the sun sink into a mass of purple cloud. A little melancholy wind had risen, and begun to play in gusts among the trees, ruffling the foliage for a moment, and leaving a moment of silence and of stillness behind it. The evening grew grey. It made for restlessness, and Blaber felt restless, for on an evening such as this a man's unhappiness goes out to meet the melancholy of a trembling and ineffectual twilight.

The gusty wind blew into the loggia and made it chilly, and Blaber abandoned his chair, and stood leaning against one of the pillars.

"Nothing can happen to-night," he thought; "they can't meet every night. Excuses are limited—and Shere was here till seven."

He stepped out on to the grass, and as he did so a light was flashed on in a room up above—and a moment later he saw Parker at the window pulling down the blind. It seemed that Elsie was going to bed. The blind showed up as an oblong and faintly yellow patch in the grey twilight, and it suggested to his clouded and unhappy mind that light—even artificial light—was preferable to the melancholy of the dusk. He felt the need of letting his restlessness spend itself, and a minute later he was in the billiard-room with all the lights turned on and the red and white balls skimming cheerfully over the green cloth.

The click of the balls carried a message upwards, and between the little complainings of the wet west wind Elsie heard her husband at his game. She knew that on some evenings he would spend two hours in the billiard-room, absorbed in the play of the balls. It seemed to fascinate him. He was an expert with the cue, and it may be that Blaber found satisfaction in making three ivory balls do what life had not done for him. His egotism dominated the green table. Here most of his shots came off and no human chance interfered with them.

Elsie took her black velvet cloak from the wardrobe, put it on, and slipped out. She met no one. She made her way into the drawing-room and turned on the lights. A novel that she had been reading lay on a table, and she opened it, and placed it on the sofa so as to give the impression that she had been sitting there reading. One of the long windows hung open, and she passed out into the garden and into the greyness that was troubled by the gathering sadness of the wind.

The wild garden waved dim colours. She went through it into the gloom of the spruces, and beyond them lay the deeper gloom of the dell. On the lip of it she hesitated, listening, looking back. It was early and he might not be here, and now that the emotional crisis was upon her she began to tremble.

As she paused there against a little patch of pale sky she was visible to Suvla where he sat in the hollow of the dell among the bracken. The figure was hesitant and frightened; it looked back; it seemed to shrink a little from this dark place where life might be too deep for its ineffectual spirit. He was conscious of pity.

Poor, fluttering, ineffectual bird! She was made for a cage, and as he rose and went towards her he realized that there are many people who are happier in cages. Only the few have the strength and the right to be free. She wavered there in the dusk, and he came quite close to her before she became aware of his presence. He met her sudden, frightened eyes.

"John! Oh, you are there! He—has come back."

He saw the bandaged hand.

"What's that, child?"

"Oh, nothing. I scalded myself a little. We had people to tennis—and I was talking—and not thinking what I was doing."

She moved nearer to him, but the impulsiveness of yesterday had left her.

"I ought to go back, John. I have been thinking, and thinking—has made me afraid."

He stood over her, looking down.

"Elsie—he hasn't——?"

"No—he has been quite kind. He said he was sorry."

"I'm glad. Perhaps he is sorrier than you think. Men are—sometimes."

Suvla John

He laid a hand on her shoulder.

"My dear—you are trembling."

"Am I, John? I'm frightened."

"Of me——?"

"Of everything. I don't know why. Yesterday, it seemed different. I thought——"

He was looking at her steadily.

"Elsie—I am going to send you back—but before you go—I want you to be kind to me."

Her large, soft eyes met his, but they had the quality of troubled water.

"Of course, John. But let's go a little farther—where it is darker. What is it?"

"I have something to tell you. No, don't shake so. There is nothing to fear. But I have not been quite fair to you, Elsie."

They moved into the deeper shadow, and there—looking up at him like a pathetic child, she surprised him as she had surprised him before.

"I think I know what it is, John."

"You do!"

"You can't take me away with you because——"

"My dear, listen——"

"Because you don't care quite as you used to care."

There was a moment of silence, and he put his hands on her shoulders.

"Can you forgive me, child?"

"It was my fault," she said.

He had expected tears, a storm, but though she trembled she seemed calmer than he had expected. The complexities of her emotional state were beyond him. He was wondering whether he had hurt her beyond forgiveness, while she—in a spasm of self-pity, and struggling with a sense of her own helplessness—was conscious of a little tremor of relief. She had become suddenly a child, a pathetic child. She wanted to run to some woman, a woman who would pet and soothe her.

"Sit down, Elsie. The whole fault has been mine."

But she would not have that. She sat down beside him in the ferns, and held one of his hands.

"Of course, I ought to have known—that after all these years—things couldn't be the same."

"It was my fault that you know. I ought not to have come back here. And if you can forgive me for coming back—will you keep my secret?"

Suvla John

"Of course I will keep it, John."

He raised her bandaged hand and kissed it.

"Some people get all the wounds, dear. Do you know that you are making me feel rather a beast?"

"You have never been a beast to me, John."

"Thank God—for good women. But it hurts me, little girl, that you should be unhappy. You were made for happiness."

"I think the chance of it died when you died, John."

"No, no. It is giving in to such thoughts that makes unhappiness. Isn't it possible for you to be happy?"

She mused a moment, looking into the shadowy fern.

"Oh, I don't know. Life's so queer. I think that if you had really died, and that we had been married before you went—and that you had given me a child."

He was silent, and she let her head rest for a moment against his shoulder. Even in her longing for a child, the dream child of a dream husband, she was the sentimentalist.

"Why haven't you had——" and then he stopped himself, and pressed her hand. "No—that's beyond me."

She raised her head with a little, lost smile.

"Yes, they say it makes such a difference. We haven't had a child. I think he hoped for one; though—or—I don't know. Have you any children, John?"

"No."

"But some day——"

"Elsie," he said suddenly, "I wish you knew the woman I am going to marry."

Next moment he realized that she was in tears, but they were the quiet tears of a gentle nature that consents. She was weeping over unutterable things, and the broken toys of her dream. And Suvla drew her head back on his shoulder, and knew that there was nothing that he could say or do that would alter the little tragedy of her life. That was the pity of it. His adventure had fallen most heavily upon the creature who seemed least able to bear it.

2

"I must go now, John."

She had dried her tears, and as he helped her to her feet she gave him the ghost of a smile.

Suvla John

"I am going to be brave."

He bent down and kissed her forehead.

"I know you are. You have been very generous to me, Elsie."

He went with her as far as the gate leading from the wild garden, and they paused here to speak the last words.

"I suppose you are going away, John."

"It is better."

"I know. But shall I ever see you again?"

"Perhaps."

She passed through the gate, and, closing it, stood looking up at him.

"Life has been rather cruel to me——"

"It has."

"I had my dream, and even that has gone. There seems nothing——"

He was greatly moved.

"There will always be what others think of you, my dear. I wish to God——"

She put up a hand as though she were thrusting something away from her, and then she turned and fled away into the darkness, leaving him standing there with a sense of shame. How easy it was to play with life and to break life in the doing of it. He had thought himself so strong, such a tremendous fellow, and at that moment he felt himself to be the sorriest of swashbucklers.

He turned away from the gate. He felt that he wanted to be hurt as he had hurt this child, and that the self-anger that was in him could find expression only in self-pain. A bare back and the lash! Yes, as he had seen men whipped in Russia, torn to tatters, with their blood running down into their boots. The swagger had gone out of life. He thought of Richenda as the woman with the whip. Perhaps she would give him his scourging?

But how useless! There was a finality about things, and when you had smashed a child-soul's toys, the toys remained broken. You might try and compromise with your own conscience by assuming that new toys could be bought, and that the broken ones would be forgotten.

But in this case Elsie had made and furnished a dream doll's-house, and he had put a careless foot upon it. Mere sentiment, but—good lord—what was life without sentiment? Mere hog-wash.

He felt savage and ashamed.

"Am I to leave the mess I have made, clear out, and

227

do nothing? What a confession of failure! To be beaten by a child's tears?"

He found himself plunging through the fern, with hazel boughs striking him across the face. It seemed good. He welcomed the sting of the branches.

"I have been so damned cocksure, taking things as they come. Incidents! Just hitting things and laughing when they fell over. I suppose no man knows what he is going to feel like when he knocks a child over—until he has done it. Well—now I know."

It began to rain soon after he had climbed Hackbury Hill, and he sat with his back against the trunk of a fir tree and let the rain soak into him. He was glad of the rain. Any sort of discomfort seemed right and good to him on that wet summer night.

3

When Elsie re-entered the Wynyats drawing-room she found her husband standing by the sofa with the book that she had left there in his hands.

They stood quite still, regarding each other.

"You have been out."

She had to lie to him, but in her hour of disillusionment it seemed to her that no lie mattered.

"My hand hurt so. I went out into the garden."

She waited, aware of his sombre face, realizing that—somehow—her life and his had been linked together, and the thought of it filled her with a dreary despair. She would have to go on living with him to the end of her days, dreamless, lonely, unsatisfied.

He threw the book back on to the sofa.

"You had better go to bed," he said.

"I think I will."

"What about the pain?"

"It is better now."

His voice was toneless. He did not say that he was sorry for her pain, and she was quick to feel that he was not sorry for it. His protestations of yesterday seemed to have been forgotten. Once more he was the man as she knew him, queer, self-absorbed, uncertain as the weather.

Suvla John

She felt lost, helpless. All these years she had clung to the figure of a dream, and now she had nothing to cling to.

"I'm going to bed, Robert. Good night."

"Good night."

He turned his back on her, and appeared to be looking at the books in the case beside the sofa. She hurried out, closing the door, and wishing that she could close a door on him and their life together. Her tears came again. She went upstairs, weeping.

And at the top of the stairs she met Parker, a Parker who had been to her room and had found it empty.

Parker's wooden face seemed to soften and to become yielding.

"Why, madam—I thought——"

"My hand was so painful, Parker, I had to go and walk about."

"Dear, dear——"

"It's better now."

But Parker understood that there was some other pain that had not died away. The easy and selfish tears of a child would not have touched her, but the tears of this grown child were different.

"You ought to go to bed, madam."

"Yes, Parker."

"I'll help you to undress. And Dr. Warburton left some aspirin."

She followed Elsie into her room, and as she moved Parker's rigid body betrayed a new fluidity. She closed the door, and pushing an armchair forward, stood waiting.

"Sit down, madam, I'll take off your shoes."

She knelt down at Elsie's feet, and suddenly the thought came to Parker that she had found her child, a child utterly unlike those raw and semi-savage little brutes —her nephews and nieces—but a gentle child, sensitive, rather helpless, clinging.

She stroked one of the small feet.

"You'll feel better soon, madam."

She raised her face, and these two women looked at each other.

"Oh, Parker, I'm so unhappy—— "

A moment later her head was on the austere shoulder, but it was the shoulder of a woman.

"There—there, little lady, you just leave it to me. I've had my own troubles. I know what men are,"

Suvla John

"Oh, I want someone to be kind to me, Parker."

"It's woman's kindness you want, my dear. Now I'm going to be your old nanna. I'll brush your hair for you and put you to bed, and if you want me in the night——"

"You won't go away and leave me, Parker."

"I'm not that sort, my dear."

XXV

I

THE white horse and the green caravan moved slowly along the crest of the Hog's Back, and Richenda saw all the rolling country blue with the rain. The smell of it and the freshness filled the air; the grass and the hedges were wetly grey, and the west wind blew softly. Beyond the white horse's bobbing head the road ran straight, a black and shimmering line under the drift of the clouds.

Richenda sat leaning forward, with her elbows on her knees, and the reins held slackly. The soft melancholy of this green blue land seemed to spread itself about her thoughts, and to form a background to her purpose. She went forward like a young figure of fate, deep eyed, austere, mysterious, sure of her purpose because her purpose was her self. Life might have its byroads and its blind ends, but Richenda's road went steadily over the hills, and neither her pride nor her compassion would choose to turn aside from it.

She had been on the road for twelve hours, and the white horse's ears showed that he was tired, and as they descended the long slope into Guildford she decided to put up there for the night. One of the inns in the steep main street received her, and in these anonymous days she was no more than an eccentric young woman who preferred a caravan to a car. The place was full of motorists, and when Richenda had seen both the inn yard and the coffee-room, she knew that she preferred the men who drove and washed the cars to the people who owned them. The aristocrats of Richenda's world were few and rare. Her duke might be a shepherd, and her Christ a carpenter. It did not matter. All that she knew was that she had no use for the fat and the greasy.

She dined at a little table in a corner of the coffee-room. Three sorrowful pink asters in a vase kept her

231

Suvla John

company, and the vase was short of water. She filled it, and discovered that a "grossness" at the next table was interested in her. The "grossness" had the back of a whale, and a face that was longer from nose to chin than from nose tip to the crown of the forehead. She stared it straight in its blurred eyes until its fatness quivered and melted under her disfavour. The room was full of flies.

Afterwards she went out to see that the white horse had had its supper and clean straw. He was a clean beast and he carried no fat. She liked leanness; none of her aristocrats ran to fat. A stableman, hanging about for a tip, looked at her curiously, and wondered what manner of young woman this was who travelled alone in a caravan. She had locked the door of it, but the man had been peeping through the window, and had seen the luxury within.

"Would you like the van washed down, miss?"

"Yes—you can wash it down. Early to-morrow will do."

She stroked the white horse, and her silence was part of the dusk. She went out past a group of chauffeurs who stared at her far less rudely than the "grossness" had done, and wandering downhill she came to the bridge over the Wey and paused there. A light rain damped her green woollen coat and her splendid hair, but rain was better than the fustiness of closed rooms. Her life was a thing of the open air. She breathed it fastidiously, not liking to share her breath with people who overfed themselves and had frowsy souls.

But the rain made her think more intimately of John Suvla, for somewhere over yonder in those dark hills he should be getting a wet jacket. She wondered how he had fared. She was keeping a cool hand on her heart.

"You shall beat as I please; not as any man pleases."

She knew that she might have much to say to John Suvla, and what she would say and her saying of it would depend upon what sort of story he would tell her. She did not think that he would tell her a lie, but that if he did she would know it. She had sent him away from her rather red about the ears. He should have no cause to mock at her "completeness."

The dark water went under her feet, and as she watched it she thought of Astolat and Elaine and all those strange old sadnesses of the shadowy green world of a poet's dreaming. She knew that she could dream, but that when her moment came she would be wide awake, flame, and not the vague smoke from a poet's fire. Sex in her went armed, and its arms were bright.

Two lovers paused near her in the darkness, blurred figures leaning over the bridge, some servant girl and her man. The girl's arm was round the man; he smoked a cigarette, and was casual and complacent.

"O—Bert——"

Her poor silly voice was servile. Her tenderness truckled, edging close, accepting his cigarette smoke when he puffed it in her face.

"Blast this rain," he said; "let's turn in somewhere."

She giggled.

"The 'pictures.' It's dark in there—Bert."

"Oh, all right."

"I'll pay."

They moved off, leaving Richenda watching the river.

"Yes—you'll pay—you poor thing!" she thought. "What fools we are! Hold a knife at the throat of your love."

Richenda woke early to the sound of the traffic in the street, and she lay awhile listening to it, and thinking how much better it would be to wake up on the edge of a wood or in the desert. Why all this noise and hurry? Moreover, the bedroom offended her. The quilt was not as clean as it might be; the tooth glass was smeary, and behind the paper screen in the grate she had noticed a collection of matches, cigarette ends, hair-combings and torn envelopes. The window showed her a blue sky full of huge white clouds; rain and sun were there together; it was a sky such as she loved, full of sudden shadows and of great bursts of sunlight. She saw the wet roofs glistening, and an old red chimney trailing a plume of smoke.

By nine o'clock she was on the road, having escaped from Guildford before the daily disorder of its High Street had expressed itself. She chose to go by way of the downs, and here on the chalk hills the day was superb. Splashes of sunlight, and sudden scatterings of rain from mighty, blue black clouds, and the hills the colour of amethyst. Everything was wet and glittering, and as she walked up the long hill beside the white horse she felt her heart full of the day's freshness.

Before noon she was in John Suvla's "England," and

Suvla John

she understood why this country had called to him. It would call to him again and again, and Richenda knew that she too would answer to the call of it, and that from the desert or the mountains she would come back to dream in one of these green valleys. As she walked beside the white horse she was receiving the familiar impressions of a hundred familiar appearances, and yet with each year the impressions seemed to grow more vivid. She—felt—the country. Its memories were born afresh each spring. It lived. She saw herself and the past and the future in it, in the high shade of the valley beeches, in the play of the sunlight under the trees, in the green life of the hedgerows, in the climbing of the bryony and the rose. All the strange, intimate, beautiful things, the colour, the gestures. Each tree had its own soul, and each soul was different. The living tapestry was ever the same, and yet, whenever it was unrolled before her eyes, she saw something new—a bird skimming from shadow to shadow like a living shuttle, a deeper silver in the bark of a birch, some new beauty in the texture of a leaf, a patch of willow herb against the gloom of pines, loose strife in a ditch, elder flower in an old hedge, sunlight in the cleft of a green wood, a pool swelling like quicksilver. She was this England. She might wander, but she would come back to it with the birds in the spring.

In one of the Feldhurst lanes Richenda pulled aside on to the grass, and seeing the decoy pond shining below among the oaks and alders she went to draw water for the horse. Moorhens were busy there, and she stood for a minute watching them, while a sudden shower came on, the rain falling through the sunlight and making a grey blur of the glassy surface of the pool. The place was extraordinarily peaceful, and Richenda loved rain in the woods, the beautiful, clean, silencing rain, driving away human discords and silencing the ugly voices of children. She went back, carrying her bucket, the rain playing upon her face and hair. While she was giving the white horse his drink, a labourer, who had been cutting the rough grass under the hedges, came down Feldhurst way for a glass of luncheon beer.

She spoke to the man.

"Am I right for Panhurst?"

"Straight up the hill, miss, and take the first on the left."

Suvla John

He looked at her curiously. She appeared to be a lady, and he had never seen a lady watering a horse.

"I suppose this is Feldhurst?"

"Feldhurst woods, miss."

"Mr. Shere's estate."

"Yes. You can see the manor house over that there gate."

The man walked on, and Richenda put down the bucket and wandering on up the lane found the gate he had referred to, a field gate opening into a meadow. Feldhurst Manor faced her between the outlines of the trees, its redness overshadowed by the great cedars. She rested her arms upon the top of the gate, and looked long and steadily at this house of the Sheres. It was both friend and enemy, and she found herself wondering whether she would ever covet such a house and wish to make her home in it.

But it was the peace of the place that impressed her most strongly. It seemed to her that on this rain-washed, summer day no untoward event could happen here, and that that wise old house could find an answer to every human question : "What to do? Why—nothing. Things happen, but the happening of them passes. Wise men and horses let them pass." She returned to the white horse and the caravan, and set out to climb the hill to Panhurst, the raindrops from the overhanging branches of the beeches making a pattering upon the roof of the van.

2

At Panhurst Great Farm they told her that she could park her caravan in the orchard, but when Richenda had seen the farm house and its master she chose The Mount for her camping-ground. It was a knoll or barrow covered with Scotch firs, standing on a piece of waste on the edge of the Panhurst beech woods. The Mount and the woods near to it went with the farm, and when Richenda made her choice she was thinking of John Suvla.

For the tenant of Panhurst Great Farm proved to be a young man, and not old Bulmer, who had held it in John Shere's day.

"Please yourself," he said.

Suvla John

He had self-assertive and adventurous blue eyes, and he was more than ready to be familiar.

"Can I put the horse up here?"

"You can. Shall I send a lad up for him?"

"I'll bring him down. I am much obliged to you."

He tried a friendly smile.

"That's all right. Bad weather for camping—though. I prefer a roof and a bed."

She ignored his freshness, effacing it with the calm casualness of her indifference; but when she returned from the Mount bringing the white horse with her, the man was waiting at the yard gate. She knew that his waiting was deliberate, and it annoyed her.

"Thank you. What shall I owe you?"

He took the white horse, and smirked at her.

"O, we can talk about that later. Staying long?"

She avoided the question.

"My husband joins me for week-ends."

And she left him to put the horse in the stable.

The Mount was half a mile from the farm, and as Richenda sat on the steps of the van and looked about her across the heather and fern she realized that she was restfully alone. The trunks of the firs were dark and wet with the rain. The bracken was drenched with it. A canopy of blue-black cloud was ready to spread another downpour, and down below in the valley the red roofs of the farm and its buildings were touched by transient sunlight. She would have no neighbours save the birds and the rabbits. And all about her she saw the dark fringes of the woods, grey-trunked against the gloom.

"Solitude," she thought. "It will be easy for him to come here. How many hours have I?"

She glanced at her watch.

There were seven hours of daylight before her, for Suvla would not keep their tryst until dusk fell, and when the clouds began to empty themselves again she lay down on her bed with a book, and listened to the rain on the roof. Her reading was desultory. She was in no mood for other people's stories. Her thoughts were with Suvla somewhere in the rain.

At five o'clock she made tea. The sky had cleared again, and she sat on the steps and watched the woods, knowing that they held a secret. Would he come to her soaked and subdued, or would he appear as his own old gaillard self? Had the thing been serious enough to make him suffer? If not, then she would have to make him suffer.

Towards sunset more clouds loomed out of the west and spread a smother of blackness against a sky of wet gold. The sunlight, shining under the edge of the clouds, lit up the trees, the fern, and the heather with an extra-ordinary brilliance. Purple and green met gold. The shadow spaces between the trunks of the trees became filled with an intense blackness. The wet world glistened. In a little while all the colour and the splendour would melt into a gradual greyness.

Richenda lit her pipe. She sat on a red cushion at the top of the steps, and her eyes were turned towards the woods. They seemed to grow more deep and dark. So, in times of old, man passing that way would have seen her as a young sibyl, enigmatic, austere, with the tall trees like a canopy above her head, but her lore was human, for it was the lore of her own heart.

3

It was growing dark when she became aware of a figure drawing towards her over the waste. She heard the brushing of its feet through the heather. A few drops of rain had begun to fall, but Richenda was sheltered by the projection of the roof. The caravan was in darkness, for she had lit no light.

She made no sound. Her heart seemed to quicken like the quickening rain upon the roof. Her woman's crisis was upon her.

He drew out of the darkness.

"Thank God—for you—Richenda."

He was very wet, soaked to the skin, but his wetness did not concern her for the moment. It was his voice that mattered. It had a new quality, deeper vibrations and at the sound of it the tense austerity of her softened His face was a mere dimness.

"I have been here since two o'clock."

"I know. I was over there among the trees."

"I am glad you waited."

He was standing close to the foot of the steps, and he made no attempt to come nearer.

Suvla John

"Oh—yes—I waited. Perhaps that may be allowed me as a sign of virtue! Lying in the fern like a rabbit."

"You must be pretty wet."

"I'm wet enough, Richenda, wet enough to please any woman. That's nothing. Most completely wet—my dear!"

His humour had an ironical pathos, but behind the irony of it she felt the liveness of the man. She could picture him in the war, soaked and muddy and either cursing or making a jest of it, shaking life from his strong shoulders, but now he was different. She divined in him a gentleness, like the sudden gentleness of a hard man who has been ill.

"You had better change," she said.

He had brought out a pipe and a box of soaked matches.

"I have had twenty-four hours of it. I'm acclimatized. But I would sell my soul for a match."

She smiled in the darkness, and her heart went out to him.

"I had dry clothes ready. Go in and change. There is no war on."

He looked up at her in the dusk as she rose and made way for him, and she felt that he knew his need of her even as he knew his need of dry clothes.

"You are a great woman, Richenda."

"You will find a candle and matches inside the door."

She resumed her seat on the red cushion while he was changing into dry clothes, and her deep eyes envisaged all the significance of this wet night. He had come back to her with a touch of half-unrealized humility in his voice. He had ceased to storm life like a captured city. His very wetness had cried softly—"Richenda, I want you." She was glad.

She heard him moving within. Presently the light was blown out, and opening the door he joined her on the little platform at the top of the steps. For a moment he stood looking out into the night, and then, seeing that she had moved aside to make room for him, he sat down. But the seat he chose was at the bottom of the steps, and close to her feet.

"It is wet there," she said.

"It is not raining now."

She passed him her cushion.

"Take it. You are not a boy."

Suvla John

He accepted the red cushion, and began to fill his pipe.

"The tobacco in my pouch was the only dry thing on me. The matches ceased to strike yesterday. Nearly a whole day without a pipe!"

"Has it ever happened before?"

"Not for many years."

He struck a match and held the flame to the bowl. His face was lit up by it for a moment.

"Oh—that's good. Well—I told her."

He drew up his knees and rested his elbows on them.

"I washed the illusion off the slate. I always flattered myself that I was a hard devil, Richenda. I'm not a sentimentalist. I have no use for babies and all that sort of thing, like the Yankee who holds his handkerchief in one hand and picks your pocket with the other. But wringing the neck of a little woman's illusion——"

"It hurt?"

"What part of me did it hurt?"

"That depends. If it was your self-love——"

"My dear, it wasn't. There was not a shred of the sex vanity in it. I felt that I had broken up a child's doll's-house. It hurt. I felt that I wanted to be hurt. Do you know, O queen, it came to me suddenly—that I needed hurting. I needed one good punch over my soul's solar plexus."

"Could a little woman hit so hard?"

"Ah, that's it. She didn't hit me, Richenda. She just went away like a bewildered and broken child. Oh, not the ordinary hard-faced, self-assertive kind who deserves nothing but a smack across the mouth. I had made up my mind that the only straight thing was to tell her."

"What did you tell her?"

"That I didn't care as I used to care."

"Was that all?"

"I told her there was someone else."

There was silence for a moment, and during that silence neither of them moved. Suvla's pipe had gone out, and he sat holding it in his hand. His thoughts seemed to be gathering in the darkness, like ghosts.

"Queen. I've killed men, and thought nothing of it. I have taken what women chose to give. Just—adventure, a world of adventure. All this—was only an adventure, but when I got back into this little bit of England—I

239

seemed to grow soft. The wet, grey eyes of England, you know."

"Well—why not?"

He half-turned to her.

"My dear—I needed something. I suppose you would say——"

"Completeness!"

There was a tremor of deep laughter behind it.

"You minion! Don't laugh at me, my dear, the old blackguard turned sentimentalist! I've got green sap in me instead of Spanish wine."

"That's England. And why not England, slow, sleepy, swearing, swilling, kindly England? And perhaps——?"

"Oh, perhaps——"

He gave a twist of the shoulders.

"There's more in it than that. I have found a woman who can lay a stick across my shoulders."

His hand went out in the darkness, and hers met it. "Hold fast."

"Hit hard. There's more to talk of—yet. The doll's-house is smashed."

"That troubles you?"

"Tell me, Richenda, is it self-love that makes me wish to try and mend it—before we go?"

"Yes—partly."

"You inexorable one! But am I no better than a sentimentalist?"

"Better and worse. But then—I'm with you. But how can one mend such things?"

"Ah—how?" he said. "That's where life rubs it in."

4

There was much talk between them in the wet darkness, and Richenda grew oracular, with her man's head resting against her knees.

"You have been nothing but a big boy, and life was your game. Just an adventure. That's very well for the man. But for the woman——?"

"The game has been rough at times, my dear. I admit it."

Suvla John

"Yes, and the moral is——"

"You may rub it in."

"You know that I have no more morals than you have. We are not social people; we make our own laws. But what I mean is that the strong should not play rough games with the weak. It is fair to neither."

"Not even to the strong?"

"Of course not. Weakness is infectious; like democracy—it tends to drag down. But I am being pompous, my dear. What matters is—how to give Elsie back her doll's-house."

"Can it be done?"

She mused, letting her hand lie against his cheek.

"Women like Elsie Blaber ask for so little. Chocolates in one form or another, and children. No, I'm not being cynical. She would make most decent-tempered men happier than they deserved. This particular man missed drowning when he was a pup. What are we to do about it?"

"Does he matter?"

"Of course he matters. In a conventional home he is the little essential god. If the little god could be made to smile, instead of looking as though he had an inward pain——"

"You mean—that if he were kind to her——?"

He felt Richenda's fingers grip his hair.

"Kind! What a word! A cad's kindness. Don't women deserve something better than that? And—after all it ought to be so easy to be kind to a pet gazelle. I suppose—because she was the gentle sort he felt that he had the right to feel bored, and to bully her. By God, John Suvla, I could frighten him into being kind to her —yes, more than kind."

Suvla clasped her wrist.

"Be it known to you, O queen, that your fingers are stronger than you think. But—come now, that's an idea. Can one scare a man into being a passable husband——"

"Be quiet," she said. "I'm thinking."

He remained mutely at her feet while she sat looking into the darkness of this unhappy marriage. The first drops of an imminent shower began to patter upon the roof of the caravan, and at first Richenda did not heed them. But the scattered drops grew into a rattling downpour. She stood up.

Suvla John

"Enough for to-night, John. And you have had no supper. I'll light the lamp."

He had risen with her.

"Hunger is an adventure, my dear. And afterwards if I may borrow an old driving rug or a coat——"

She touched his cheek.

"The heather is all wet under the van. Let's go in and light the lamp."

XXVI

I

BLABER strolled through the Temple. It was with pleasure that he found himself in that particular little court where Dodson, Fagg and Chesterton had their offices. When the plane tree that grew in the courtyard was in leaf, the soft and austere gloom of the place was deepened. The light seemed to take on a greenish tinge between the dark Georgian walls and the pale blue sky above stretched like a velarium, looked far and remote. Robert Blaber had no sense of colour, and the particular atmosphere of the place made its appeal to his individual prejudices; he felt pleasure in it because it was cool and secure and practical. There were no extraneous details, no clutter of romanticism. Moreover, when he walked into the offices of Dodson, Fagg and Chesterton, the commissionaire with the huge black moustache would rise and greet him with deference. Blaber could hear the man saying to himself: "Mr. Blaber, of Wynyats. A five thousand a year client. Good morning, sir." The legal atmosphere flattered him. It assumed him to be a man of substance, able to will this and that, to dispose of considerable favours, to say yea or nay with formidable finality. Blaber felt himself a person when he walked into old Dodson's room, and old Dodson stood up and showed his artificial teeth, and waved him gallantly to a chair. He was allowed to smoke in Dodson's room. In fact, Dodson would go to a cupboard and produce a box of cigars.

Blaber paused in the archway opening into the court. He looked at the plane tree and the familiar and discoloured walls. He did not try to explain to himself why he felt spitefully self-important; the feeling was there, and was as much a part of him as the plane tree was part of the courtyard. His egotism was rather like that tree; it had grown up in a confined space; it had never been able to push its branches quite as it pleased, or to get its top clear of the chimneys. Other people had built walls round him. The Sheres had been responsible for the most offensive of these walls, and Blaber had discovered that it had a weak point in its foundations. He was malicious. "I'll show the chap up." He had spent hours going carefully over all the peculiar and personal aspects of the affair. Two people had conspired against him, and he was going to kick their conspiracy to pieces as the Sheres had once dealt with his Etonian hat.

His consciousness had narrowed to a little slit of spite, yet, half an hour later, he was discovering in old Dodson a lack of enthusiasm in the sharing of this peep-hole.

"As a man of the world, my dear sir, as a man of the world. One needs to be very sure. Besides, I prefer persuasion——"

Old Dodson's smile was less gallant than usual. He sat cross-legged in his chair, tapping a knee with his pince-nez, eyes downcast. Almost it would seem that Blaber irritated him.

"But your own man—when he was down the other night."

"Yes, certainly; his evidence was very strong—but in these cases——"

He raised his eyes and looked at Blaber. Mr. Dodson had kind eyes; he had seen so many shipwrecks, and he hated shipwrecks. He had known Robert Blaber for twenty years, and he knew Blaber's wife, and beneath the legalities his sympathies were with the wife.

Blaber betrayed impatience.

"Do you mean to suggest that I should shut my eyes to the affair?"

Old Dodson tapped with his glasses.

"No—no—no. But I have always found that when a woman like your wife——"

"Well?"

"You must forgive me, Robert, but I try to look at the human side of things. As I was saying, when one party to a contract begins to falter, one has to ask oneself: 'What are the reasons?'"

"Reasons?"

His stare caught the curve of Mr. Dodson's gold watch-chain.

"Justification! Is it a hint?"

"My dear man, I have seen other people sitting in that chair trying to sin against their own happiness.

Suvla John

Tragedies. I hate tragedies, especially sordid tragedies; I try to prevent them."

Blaber was biting the end of his moustache.

"I have always regarded you as my legal adviser."

Old Dodson gave him a faintly humorous smile.

"Well—why not? There is humanity behind the law; we are apt to forget it. Now, when a little woman like your wife——"

"Where does my wife differ——?"

The old blue eyes looked at him protestingly.

"She ought to differ. Surely? Now, look here, Robert, before you plunge, just ask yourself a few questions. A man ought to have the courage——"

"Is it your suggestion that I am partly responsible?"

Old Dodson nodded.

"Well—yes. Faults, little omissions on both sides—you know. Nothing happens without a cause. And when a woman like your wife——"

"Damn it, Dodson, you seem to think my wife——"

"I have always thought her a charming little lady. When such a woman turns elsewhere—it suggests——"

"That the husband is to blame!"

"Let us say—rather—that she is unhappy."

Having made his point, old Dodson put on his pince-nez, and pretended to look for something on the table. He was aware of Blaber as an evil presence, a man with an obstinate and malicious purpose, the raw male squealing with jealousy and sore self-love. That morose little moustache and ungenerous mouth! He could remember old Blaber bringing the boy into his office twenty years ago, a rather sullen youngster, both complacent and reserved. An opinionated kid, not above correcting his old father. Dodson had never warmed to the owner of Wynyats. He had been a little surprised when he had seen Blaber's wife. He had wondered how she would get along with him. And now——!

He glanced across the desk at his client.

"Why not think it over? As man to man——"

But Blaber had risen.

"You ought to be a parson, Dodson, or a professor of psychology. I want this thing put through."

Once more old Dodson removed his pince-nez, and began to tap with them.

"I don't like it," he said. "And I am not in a position to make it necessary for me to like it."

Suvla John

"Very well—you throw up the case?"

"Not at all. But before we go farther—I should like to interview your wife."

Blaber looked at him, and turned towards the door.

"All right. I suppose——"

But at the door he hesitated. Old Dodson was watching him.

"You think—I shouldn't win?"

"I don't say that. But I do suggest that—later—you might be sorry."

Blaber went out, but turned and spoke before closing the door.

"Well—you have the evidence. I'll think it over. Possibly—I may tackle the thing myself. Good morning."

He closed the door, and old Dodson sat reflecting, with his pince-nez poised between his fingers.

2

Elsie was sitting in one of Sybil's brocaded chairs, for Sybil was trimming a hat, and the whole sofa was sacred to the undertaking, and littered with material that seemed sufficient for the trimming of twenty hats. A curved black plume was being attached to the brim of the "shape," and when the feather was sufficiently secure Sybil stood up, and, putting on the hat, studied its reflection in the Empire mirror over the mantelpiece.

"H'm——"

Human nature being what it is, Elsie should have been interested in the evolution of a hat, but she was looking out of the open window at the long border of asters, antirrhinum and verbena that trailed its brilliant colours along one side of the stone path. It had been raining, and here and there on the old worn stones little pools had collected. The flowers wore brilliants in their hair. Beyond this carpet of purple and red, violet, white and carmine rose the dense deep green of the yew hedge. Elsie was looking at the hedge, not as though she saw it, but as though it were a dark screen upon which her thoughts were projected.

Sybil removed the hat. She was worried about Elsie.

"Too much of that Oriana look, my dear."

Suvla John

She returned to the sofa and proceeded to put in the final stitches, glancing occasionally at Elsie, and thinking nothing but "Elsie." For it seemed to her that something critical had happened. Elsie's face had an emptiness. She sat there like a listless, melancholy child who had no toys to play with, and no playmate. Her hat had been put on carelessly; her hair betrayed a loose-endedness; she had taken no trouble.

"You had better stay to dinner," said the little mother on the sofa.

Elsie looked round vaguely.

"May I?"

"If Robert's in town—we'll assume him to be dining in town. How do you like my hat?"

She stood up and put it on, feeling that she was trying to amuse a sick child.

"Oh, I like it. Black always suits your hair."

"What about a touch of colour?"

"No, I'm not sure. I'm such a fool about hats."

She seemed to wilt.

"If there is no one to notice your hats—— Does Dick?"

"Freely and frankly. I allow myself to criticize his socks and ties—therefore——"

"Does he let you tell him——?"

"My dear, that is the essence of marriage. If you can't tell your husband that you don't like the colour of his socks, well—you are married to a bachelor."

"How funny you are! I can't picture myself telling Robert——"

"Try it."

"He'd snub me. He hates interference."

"It would be good for him. Besides, it does show—that one has an interest. If I were married to a bachelor-man I'd wear the most awful headgear until it penetrated."

"Till what penetrated——?"

"In some cases it might be the hatpin."

At a quarter-past seven Richard Shere was tying his black bow when Sybil wandered into his dressing-room. It was very untidy, but she had not come to criticize its untidiness; you must allow the beloved man some foible, and Dick was untidy in nothing else. Women did things for him, put the trees in his shoes, and reduced the dis-order among his collars and handkerchiefs and socks to some semblance of neatness. Women seemed to find a pleasure in doing things for him. He was the man child.

"I'm worried about Elsie," said his wife.

Dick was not having much success with his tie.

"Oh! Blaber again? I say, tie this for me, old thing, will you?"

"I don't know."

"Please."

"I meant about Blaber. It seems to me a pretty hopeless situation. I thought when he came back the other day—that they had patched things up."

"If I know anything of Blaber, Elsie would have to do all the patching."

She tied the bow for him, her finely sculptured lips pressed firmly together, her head held slightly on one side.

"It ought to have been so easy. What do men want? She's pretty; she had a most delightful nature. She's rather childish, I know, but she would have grown. It makes me savage to see her wilting. And then——"

She considered the bow, and gave the ends a final pull.

"Well, she strikes me as being—queer. John's ghost —and all that—and now—not a word. She gives me a feeling of secrecy. I can't explain it."

Shere slipped on his dinner-jacket.

"It is a pity they have no children."

"Children don't bring happiness. You men always seem to think——"

"Well—you look rather miserable——!"

"Be serious. I should have said most children, the unsmacked children. Elsie would spoil any child, utterly. She's made to be spoilt and to spoil. And married to that rat with a little black moustache. Dick—I hate meanness in a man; I would rather have him a blackguard than precise and mean."

"All right. I shall know. Personally, I may think Blaber a slimy cad—but be fair. Elsie would bore me into——"

"Dick, don't be cruel. You know that you are just as sorry——"

"But there is nothing to be done, my dear—at least— not at present. You can't kick a man into loving his wife. If one could—I would volunteer to kick Bob Blaber."

Sybil had moved to the window, and through the open lattice she looked down upon her beloved garden that had been refreshed by the rain. How elusive a thing was happiness! And yet she knew that she was one of the few fortunate ones who had attained happiness, that deeper happiness which feeds upon beauty.

"Dick, come here."

He joined her at the window.

"Isn't it lovely? The garden—not our garden. I hate people who talk about ' my flowers.' As though they had made them."

"That pet border of yours is like a Persian carpet."

"But it's alive. An hour ago I caught Elsie looking out into the garden as though the beauty of it hurt her. The great unhappiness that is bewildered! Do you know what I am afraid of?"

"What is it?"

"I feel that Elsie is one of those people who give up. Death—you know. It is so easy to give up when there seems nothing. She's impulsive. She ought not to be left alone."

"I'll walk back with her to-night. I wonder if it would be any use my tackling Blaber again?"

"I don't know. I think I would rather wait until I have got Elsie to talk. At present she is all closed up."

"Right, Celli. You know best."

3

Shere walked back with Elsie through the wet twilight. They took the path across the park, and through the gate by the lower pool. The beech gloom hung heavy here, and as Shere opened the gate for her he noticed that she glanced at the still, black surface of the pool.

He began to talk cheerfully of the family's summer holiday. They were going up to the Scotch moors where a friend of Shere's was lending them a cottage. The choice had lain between Deauville or Dinard and the moorland cottage, and Sybil had chosen the cottage for the sake of economy. Feldhurst, like most other estates, was suffering from over-taxation.

"You have better come with us, Elsie. Sybil would love to have you."

She said that she would like to join them, but Shere

felt that her thoughts were elsewhere, wandering in unhappy distances. She was an echo. She would agree with whatever he might say.

"Change is a great thing. I would rather have taken Sybil to some gay place, but she always says that their gaiety is so shabby."

"Yes, isn't it?"

"The world of fashion—you know, but Sybil will have it that she has never seen a hat to equal one of her flower beds."

When they reached Wynyats she asked him to come in. She did not know whether her husband had returned and she felt the need of support, someone to break the ice of Blaber's incalculable moodiness. Parker met them in the hall.

"Is Mr. Blaber back, Parker?"

"No, madam."

"Do come in, Dick."

He sat talking to her in the drawing-room for ten minutes, and when he rose to go he repeated his invitation.

"You had better come with us. There is room in the cottage. It will do you good."

She gave him a vague smile, and said that she would think it over; and when Shere had gone, she sat brooding, remembering the gate by the pool, and the soft dark sheen of the water.

4

Elsie was roused from her reverie by the opening of the door. She looked up, expecting to see Parker, but it was her husband who stood in the doorway.

He came in and closed the door. He was smiling, but his smile had a sharp edge to it.

"I did not know that you were back, Robert."

"No?"

He lit a cigarette.

"I came back an hour ago. I stayed out in the garden. A case of clairvoyance, you know!"

He gave her a shrewd look, and went and stood on the hearthrug, feet well apart, one hand behind his back. She looked at him; she seemed to notice things about him that she had not seen before. His hair was turning grey at the temples; his moustache looked ragged; he was slightly knock-kneed; his shoulders were like the neck of a wine-bottle.

"I have been up to see Dodson."

"Oh."

It meant nothing to her.

"Business, you know, domestic business. I suppose it is about time I told you, Elsie, that you have been found out."

She stared at him.

"What do you mean, Robert?"

He flicked the ash from the cigarette.

"O, come now! You know what I mean. I have had you watched. I have all the proofs I want. Well, what about it?"

She stared helplessly at his cold and amused face. She felt that he was enjoying himself, and her horror found itself confronted with a smirking and merciless mask.

"What do you mean?"

"When a woman has a lover——"

"But I haven't."

"Oh! What about Mab's Dell, and the moonlight—and all that?"

She sat very still, and her eyes looked blind.

"Yes—but I have no lover——"

"Shall I tell you his name? I may as well, because—when our divorce comes on——"

She rose with a sudden cry.

"Who——?"

"Why—the man who was in this room a quarter of an hour ago—that model husband, Dick Shere."

Her face expressed incredulity, bewilderment.

"What are you saying? It's not true——"

"Well—my evidence goes to prove——"

She ran to him suddenly—wildly appealing.

"Robert, it's not true. I swear it. You are making a horrible mistake."

He gave her a look that was an insult, and then they realized that the door had opened, and that Parker was standing there. She had heard their raised voices, and the horror of appeal and of protest in the wife's. Parker's wooden face looked all red, as though it had been scorched by the sun.

"Did you call, madam?"

Suvla John

She ignored Blaber, and her steady eyes were a refuge for her mistress. Nothing more was said, but Blaber saw his wife go unsteadily to this other woman, and take hold of Parker's arm. And he saw Parker's face, a transfigured face, tender, fierce, and compassionate.

She gave him one full stare as she shepherded Elsie out of the room.

"Beast," it said, "fool. You are not fit to have a wife."

She closed the door, and left him to think it over.

XXVII

I

WHEN Suvla opened the door of the caravan he saw that the sky had cleared. A great stillness prevailed. The early sunlight was making a golden blur of the tops of the Scotch firs, and lighting up the trunks of the Panhurst beeches. The wet world sparkled. The sheeted heather, and the green fern spread a magic carpet under the edge of the dawn.

"Dear God, it's good!" he thought. "This, and sunrise on the desert. Richenda must see the desert. We'll see it together."

He went down the steps and stood in the wet fern. His face had a luminous look; it had grown softer and less fierce. He saw that there was not a cloud in the sky.

"Yes," he reflected, "if things could be wiped out—as the clouds go."

He was watching the light on the beech woods when he heard Richenda speaking.

"John—how's the weather?"

He glanced up at the half-closed door.

"A queen of a day, fit even for you."

"That's good."

"I've been romancing."

"What about?"

"Dawn in forest country, or dawn on the desert. You have got to see the desert, Richenda."

"With you?"

"It's one of the prevalent crazes—they tell me. Sheiks —and all that—pronounced by suburbia so as to rhyme with 'shriek.' We'll rig up a little caravan of our own and go exploring. What do you say?"

He heard her stirring.

"We could go this winter. Put the 'show' away in cotton-wool, and take it out again in the spring."

He gave a toss of the head.

"You great woman. I'll sell a diamond or two."

Suvla John

"I pay half."

"All right. What about breakfast? I'll be mess orderly this morning."

Richenda was sitting on the edge of the bed, slipping her feet into her stockings.

"No risks," she said; "remember."

"There is not a soul about at this hour. I am going to wash. Is there plenty of water in your patent tank?"

"It's full."

"Righto. If you'll pass out the stove and things, I'll get the kettle boiling. You haven't seen me fry bacon and eggs."

"I'm learning."

"The smell of bacon frying always makes me think of the war. What ho! for a savoury smell! It shall lure the queen from her bedchamber."

"If you can fry bacon as well as you can talk about it——!"

"Now, now, no sarcasm at six in the morning."

Richenda came and sat on the steps and brushed her hair while Suvla was busy with frying-pan and kettle. He had extracted the collapsible table and two canvas-seated chairs from the locker under the caravan, and had set them up on a little patch of turf amid the purple of the heather. Meanwhile, he had many glances for Richenda sitting there brushing her hair. It was of a wonderful smoky blackness, and fell well below her waist.

"*Madame, le dejeuner est servi.*"

She came down from her throne.

"I'm hungry. It is good to be hungry. And you have forgotten the honey."

"Never mind the honey. You try my rashers."

He was busy with a fork.

"My lady ate six rashers for her breakfast, and the poor dog had one."

"Chatterer!"

"O—we are in one of our Sybilline moods! Well, you are right, my dear. After the bacon—the philosophy. Will you handle the teapot?"

"I will."

They sat facing each other across the table, looking into each other's eyes and into the eyes of the morning, and Richenda spoke of the debonair young farmer of Panhurst Great Farm.

Suvla John

"I snubbed him—but he may come strolling up here. Some men have to be snubbed daily."

"What a prospect for me!"

"Be serious. The fellow might know you—and we haven't decided yet——"

He became as serious as she could wish.

"One thing is inevitable. At least—that is how it appears to me. I must see Bob Blaber."

She nodded a solemn head, and told him to fetch the honey.

"Yes—but what is the objective?"

"It gives us the pistol, and the right to dictate terms. I am thinking of his wife."

He brought her the honey-pot, and as she spooned out the amber-coloured syrup her eyes grew set in a thoughtful stare.

"I wonder," she said presently.

She passed him the honey, and his eyes waited for her to go on.

"I wonder how it would work? He is the sort of man who responds to fear."

"He did."

"And to generosity? Generosity and fear—mixed. I have never heard of a case in which a man was scared into being a passable husband. Besides, does she want him? Would she ever want him?"

Suvla was looking at the honey.

"That's beyond me. If there is anything that she wants—I should like her to get it. Seems to me we could do that."

Richenda was musing. She looked at the woods and the sky, and presently her glance came back to the table.

"More tea? It is not easy to make life up for another woman. It depends—on the sex idea, if she can get free from the sex obsession, and give up feeling about man."

"And if she can?"

"Then—there's hope. Some women never become themselves till they become spiritual spinsters. It's all relative—of course. Giving up the jam pot in order to appreciate clean bread and butter. It's a delicate business."

Suvla was feeling for his pipe.

"Richenda," he said; "I take it that this is no problem for a mere man. It's a partnership job. Now—I think I could deal with the man."

She accepted the suggestion.

"And leave me the woman?"

"I leave you the most difficult part of it. Are you game?"

"I think so."

But she sat considering the problem, with deep eyes and serious forehead.

"The thing is—never to meddle unless you can meddle to some purpose. Life is like dyeing; when you mix your colours you are never quite sure how the final colour is going to turn out. Irresponsible meddlers ought to be drowned."

"Then—I ought to have been drowned in the English Channel. But I have taken on responsibility, my dear."

"You have."

She smiled at him.

"We have a whole day to think it over. If one could get at the inside of Elsie's head——"

"Or heart——"

"Or heart."

"And make Blaber a sportsman."

"Exactly. But can a leopard change his spots? This is not an adventure, John."

"I agree," he said; "utterly and wholly. But if we can do anything, for God's sake let's do it."

2

Elsie's dawn was very different.

She had gone to bed in a horror of bewilderment; she had slept a little, to wake and return to her horror of bewilderment. If her husband had got it into his malicious head that John was Richard, then what was she to do?

John had gone. He had disappeared into the unknown, and she did not know where to find him. If she went to Blaber and told him the truth he would not believe it, and she would break her promise to John. Meanwhile, the horror stood big-eyed, watching her. There would be denials, wild protestations, anger. And there would be Sybil. The thought of Sybil threw her into a panic. Yet, surely, Sybil would not believe——

Suvla John

At six she left a restless bed and got up and dressed, and sat at her bedroom window. The garden was all peace and early sunlight and dew, and as her bewilderment looked down upon it she felt that she could ask for nothing better than a garden such as this, some quiet corner where no violent things happened. She wanted to escape. She had come by a sudden horror of man and man's attributes; she recoiled from the sex in herself, and put up her hands to thrust it away. Peace, ever a delicious monotony! Her illusion of years was dead, and she felt like a widow. If life would only let her alone, if she could go away with Parker, with someone who would be kind to her. She did not ask now for wild kisses; she asked for kindness.

Meanwhile, this horror sat big-eyed, watching her.

She had to do something—but what?

Should she go down and confide in Sybil, after making her promise not to tell Dick?

But how would that help things? The telling of the truth to Sybil would not persuade Robert to stop his legal proceedings. Old Mr. Dodson knew. The scandal was like a fire that had begun to spread, and with agitated hands she wished to smother its flames, and she felt helpless.

Yet her very helplessness forced her to evolve some inspiration. She had to protect Dick and Sybil, to keep this infamous thing from them, and she had her promise to John. She must have the courage to face her husband and compel him to pause or to turn aside.

Her courage shivered, but it held.

She would ask Robert to let her go away. She would promise to do anything if only he would agree to believe her about Dick.

She was puzzled in wondering how he had come to imagine it was Dick. She supposed that he had been watching her. He might have heard John's voice. Yes, and the voices of the brothers were much alike.

Well, anyway, she would face him and compel him to believe her. He must believe her. Towards her own self she felt strangely numb, as though it did not matter to her what happened so far as she herself was concerned. She wanted to get through with it and to escape from this impossible entanglement. She supposed that Robert might strike her, but she was not afraid of blows. They were mere physical effects, and she had Parker to run to,

Parker who called herself "Old Nanna." But to push the horror away from those two at the Manor, to divert it, to save them—at any cost—from the silly and cruel shame of it——

3

Blaber was surprised when he found his wife waiting for him at the breakfast-table. She had an appearance of calmness; her courage had the white fragility of delicate china; that left hand of hers was still bandaged; her right hand was holding the silver teapot.

"Tea, Robert?"

"Thanks."

He took the filled cup and carried it to the other end of the table, and she noticed how steady his hand was. She was in a hurry to begin, but something held her back, a dread of showing emotion before him, perhaps because she realized that he would enjoy her emotion. "Hysterics on toast"—she could remember him saying that. She held herself in

Blaber was helping himself to scrambled eggs. He glanced at his wife's plate.

"Have some?"

"Thanks."

He passed her the plate, and her eyes avoided his.

"Ha," he thought, "I've got you; I've got both of you! I suppose we are going to have melted butter."

For two minutes neither of them spoke, and then Elsie, with her eyes looking glazed in a face of china, opened the parley.

"I want to talk to you, Robert."

He glanced up, biting toast, and grunting.

"Expect so."

"Were you serious last night?"

"I should think so."

"You really have been to Dodson and told him——"

"I have."

She gave him a glance of child's hatred and scorn.

"You told him it was Dick?"

"I did."

"What made you think it was Dick?"

"I am not going to give my points away. It was Shere."

Suvla John

She drew a deep breath.

"It wasn't. How could you believe it? As though Dick and I—and Sybil—— Such a monstrous thing!"

"These things are apt to seem monstrous."

"But it isn't true."

"Indeed!"

"You are making a very terrible mistake, Robert."

She was looking at him quite calmly now, and her unexpected calmness angered him.

"Rot! I know what I'm doing. I suppose this affair has been going on for years, and all that stunt about poor John was camouflage. You two thought you would have a game with me."

"I don't know what you mean."

"Oh, yes—you do."

"It wasn't Dick——"

He looked at her savagely.

"I suppose the next thing will be—your swearing that there was no man with you down there——"

"Yes, there was a man."

"Oh!"

"But it wasn't Dick. You are on the wrong scent, Robert."

He swore at her.

"Then—who the devil was it?"

"I shan't tell you."

Her dignity and her calmness were new to him. She was frightened; the brown flicker of fear was in her eyes, but she sat there, coolly hinting to him like a woman of the world that a wife does not betray her lover and that outraged husbands must find out. He glowered. He could not be sure as to whether she was bluffing him or not, and he rose and crossed towards the door.

"I shall assume Shere to be the man unless you tell me——"

"It was not Dick, and I shall not tell you who it was, Robert."

He locked the door and pocketed the key.

"Very well, you'll stay here until you tell me the man's name——"

But the melodramatic gesture failed him, for she rose and made a sudden glide towards the open french window, and being nearer to it that he was she escaped into the garden.

XXVIII

I

BUT here her effort seemed to exhaust itself. She vanished. Like a frightened deer who has heard the hunt go astray she lay hidden, trembling after the effort she had made. She was lost to the world for the next ten hours; no one saw her, and no one knew her hiding-place.

Very early in the day Parker intervened. She came to the library, where Blaber was pretending to write letters.

"Can you tell me where my mistress is, sir?"

She began with politeness, grim politeness.

"I don't know."

"I can't find her, sir."

"She went out into the garden."

He spoke to her over an impatient shoulder, making it very plain that he was being disturbed, and Parker, having made her first raid, vanished, only to return.

"Mrs. Shere is not in the garden."

Her tone was more aggressive, but Blaber went on with his scribbling.

"Probably Mrs. Shere has gone out."

"She wasn't dressed to go out. She had her house shoes on, and all her hats are in her room."

He turned angrily.

"What's all this fuss? I suppose you have counted the hats!"

She threw back his sneer.

"I have, sir."

She stood there between the writing-table and the door, menacing and austere, and quite unafraid of him. In fact, she showed no little dignity in her attack, and in her determination to have it out with him. She had ceased to be Parker the servant, and Blaber betrayed a lack of nous when he allowed himself to be sarcastic.

Suvla John

"I happen to be busy. Perhaps—if you will go and exercise yourself in the work you are paid to do——"

There was a short silence, and he waited for her to go.

"You ought to be ashamed of yourself," she said.

Blaber went a mottled red. She had thrown down the class barrier, and from that moment they ceased to be master and servant, and in their new relationship it was Parker who had the advantage.

"You had better go and pack your boxes."

"Mr. Blaber—I'm worried about my mistress."

"What the devil do you mean?"

"It is no use your losing your temper, sir. It doesn't frighten me. I'm afraid of something else—and so should you be——"

He stared.

"Since when——?"

"I know too much. I had to put her to bed last night —after the beastly things you must have said to her. I'm not mincing matters. I've got nothing to fear—from you. I'm afraid of the thing that has made her rush out like this—with her breakfast unfinished. Oh, yes—I saw her cup and plate——"

Blaber got up out of his chair.

"You seem to have lost your head, Parker——"

"Have I, indeed, sir! I have heard of people drowning themselves——"

"Rubbish!"

But she saw the narrowing of his eyes, and the look of oblique uneasiness on his face.

"Hysterical nonsense."

"I am going out to look for her, sir."

She left him, and he did not return to his desk. He walked up and down the room, and stood for a while staring out of the window, and his eyes were cynical and hard. Offending wives did not rush out and drown themselves; they fled to the other fellow; and his supposition was that Elsie had bolted to the other fellow—whoever he might be. The problem would solve itself—if he left it to solve itself. The austere Parker might go forth to hunt for an errant mistress, and make a fool of herself looking for injured innocence in this garden of intrigue.

Parker showed discretion. Her feeling of self-importance was personal, or rather—it approached a loyal sense of responsibility. She was not going to have gossip in the kitchen and at the back door of the gardeners' cottages; nor was she inclined to share her mistress's confidence with any little giggling wench. She put on her outdoor things and went down through the park to Feldhurst Manor. She asked for Mrs. Shere.

Parker's austere sincerity was her justification.

"I am worried about my mistress, madam. I thought —that—perhaps—she might be here."

No, Elsie had not been to the Manor, and Parker had to explain her case. She did it quite simply and without venom, leaving gossip aside, and keeping to the plain, human facts. Wynyats was an unhappy house, and Parker could say that she sympathized with her mistress.

"She's not made for hard words, madam; she is too sensitive. I'm afraid of her doing something dreadful."

Sybil remembered her feeling of the previous night.

"You were quite right to come here. Something must be done——"

"I did not want to make a noise about it, madam."

"Of course. I'll get my husband to go out. And there is one possible place. I will go there myself."

"Thank you, madam; I'm very fond of my little lady."

"And—Parker—if she comes back—you will let us know at once."

"Of course, madam. I shall go straight back to Wynyats. I don't want people gossiping. I shall look round the grounds."

"Good."

These three friends of Elsie's went different ways, Shere to the woods and the upper glades of the park, Sybil to Feldhurst church, and Parker to the fields and plantations lying about Wynyats. They did not find Elsie, and later in the afternoon Parker had a second interview with Blaber, a Blaber who had begun to feel cynically sure of his wife's flight to her unknown lover. Parker and her alarms were becoming a nuisance. He tried to rid himself of the woman by hinting at the truth. She had not told him that she had been to the Manor, and that the Sheres were her fellow-searchers.

"I don't think you need worry yourself, my good woman. I have my own reasons for believing that your mistress's disappearance will soon explain itself."

Yet—if the lover were not Shere, Blaber was somewhat puzzled to lay a finger on a likely man.

"I have been down to the Manor, sir, and I saw Mrs. Shere."

Suvla John

Blaber looked at her sharply. This woman's officiousness was getting beyond bounds.

"Just a few words, Parker," he said, "before you make a complete fool of yourself. This affair is going to be a case for the lawyers."

She did not or would not understand him, and when he hinted even more plainly at what he believed to be the truth, she flared up and would not credit it.

"It's not true, sir; she's not that sort. You are doing her a great wrong."

Blaber, resuming the reading of the book he had upon his knee, made it plain to Parker that he had set a limit to her meddlesome anxiety.

"That is no business of yours, Parker. By the way—that envelope on the table is for you. A month's wages. I suppose you have made your arrangements for leaving——"

"I haven't, sir."

"Very well. Unless you are out of the house to-night I shall have to take steps——"

"My mistress engaged me," she said. "I shall take my notice from her," and she went out leaving the money on the table.

Yet, in the cool of the evening Blaber's wife returned. She came across the sunlit lawn, and entered the house as though she had been out of it less than ten minutes. Her eyes had a set look. They were dark and obscure. She moved slowly with a suggestion of physical languor, as though the inward turmoil had left her body very weary.

She was half-way up the first flight of stairs when Parker came upon her.

"Oh, my dear little lady, where have you been?"

Elsie looked at her vaguely.

"Where? Oh, I don't quite know, Parker. I'm very tired."

"My dear—your shoes—and dress—they are all wet; mud, too——!"

"Are they? I think I will go to bed, Parker."

"You shall. Have you had anything to eat?"

"I forgot. Oh, yes—I had breakfast——"

"Breakfast! It's dinner-time. I'll have a tray got ready; I'll get it myself. But I'll put you to bed first."

As she was carrying the tray upstairs, Parker met her master coming down. Her eyes defied him.

Suvla John

"Hallo—who is that for?"

"Mrs. Blaber, sir. She is very tired, and I have put her to bed. She came back half an hour ago."

2

Dusk was falling when Richenda and her man came down through the Panhurst beech woods. They had locked the door of the caravan, but before leaving it Richenda had taken something that she thought might be needed, and had slipped it into the pocket of her coat. On such a night of adventure history might repeat itself, and Richenda went armed.

Suvla was in a silent mood. When they had passed the open woods, and come to the coppices that lay south of Wynyats, he went a pace or two ahead of her, holding back the hazel boughs until her outstretched arm was ready to shield her face. Once or twice she smiled at him in the dusk, or uttered a few words. They knew what had to be done, and they had laid their plans for the doing of it; all the rest was on the knees of the gods.

Suvla broke through into the little meadow west of Mab's Dell, and here they walked side by side over the grey grass. Richenda had her raincoat buttoned to her throat. She wore no hat, and only twice in his life had Suvla seen her in a hat. Her black hair was her headgear.

Above the dark trees he pointed out to her one of the flamboyant chimneys of Wynyats.

"There's the ogre's castle."

She paused and he paused with her.

"It's a still night, and voices carry. Now, is there anything we want to ask each other?"

"We open the game as agreed?"

"I shall keep in the background—unless—I get an inspiration. Or unless you say—'Richenda.'"

"Right. What time is the moon up?"

"In an hour or so."

"I don't think I shall trust the moon, queen. If I find my chance—I'll get him at one of the windows."

Smiling, he passed a hand over his chin, for before setting out on this last adventure he had shaved off his Spaniard's beard.

264

Suvla John

They went on, pushing through the thin hedge above the ferny slopes of Mab's Dell. Suvla led. He had to allow for the chance of Elsie having wandered to this old trysting-place, but the dark, bracken-filled hollow was empty. The spruces towered like the spires of a sleeping city. On the edge of the wild garden Suvla paused to listen, and Richenda stood close. Their hands touched. He looked into the two shadows that were her eyes, smiled, and kissed her mouth. He whispered:

"This is the first time that I have kissed my Colonel before going into action."

She laid her open hand on his mouth, and shook her dark head, and he kissed her fingers and nodded.

Willowherb brushed against them as they followed one of the paths of the wild garden. The larchwood gate in the hedge hung open, and the grass path brought them under a smother of rhododendrons to the lower lawn. From here they could see the south and west fronts of the house, with its windows lit or unlit, and the dim outlines of loggia and porch. Suvla stood at gaze, his left arm lying across Richenda's shoulders. Their figures seemed merged against the dark bank of shrubs.

Two of the lower windows grew dark while Suvla was considering the house. The lights in the drawing-room had been switched off, and for quite half a minute the whole of the lower part of the house was in complete darkness.

"No luck, queen; they are going to bed."

"Quiet! Look!"

He felt the pressure of her arm. Someone had come out into the loggia; the figure moved and then disappeared, though it was impossible for them to be sure whether it had re-entered the house or had become part of the deeper shadows under the loggia. They waited. Two lower windows on the south side of the house showed sudden light behind their yellow blinds, and Suvla's eyes were on these two patches of light when he felt again the pressure of Richenda's arm.

She was pointing towards the far end of the loggia, and he put his face close to hers.

"What is it?"

"Someone went out. I think it was a woman."

"I can see nothing."

"It has gone."

They stood at gaze. The night was very still, but

presently Suvla heard a sound that made him glance meaningly at Richenda.

"What is it?"

"Haven't you heard that sound before?"

"I can't place it."

"Billiard balls."

She felt the grip of his hand upon her shoulder, and she understood.

"If he is alone——"

Suvla walked slowly across the grass towards the house, and when he had gone some twenty yards Richenda followed him.

3

The billiard-room at Wynyats had sash-windows, and Suvla found the lower sash of the near window wide open. The bottom of the roller-blind did not reach to the sill, and Suvla was able to look into the room. He had seen a man's shadow passing across the blind, and the gap between blind and window-sill showed him Robert Blaber, cue in hand, contemplating the lie of the balls on the green table.

Richenda had joined him in the loggia. She was standing on the left of the window and close to the wall, and he pointed to one of the basket chairs.

"Sit down, queen; I am going to ring up the curtain."

He gave the blind a pull, and releasing it, let it roll up with a whir and a snap. Blaber was bending over the table in the act of making a stroke. His body remained bent. He looked round over his left shoulder, and for quite ten seconds he made no movement of any kind, the cue resting on the polished edge of the table, his oblique eyes fixed upon the open window. It resembled the frame of a picture, with the night for a background, and the live man forming the portrait.

XXIX

I

RICHENDA was something of a quietist, and as she carried the garden chair from the half-lit loggia to the dark lawn she remembered a saying of Suvla's about the war. They had been to a picture-house in some west country town and Richenda had been shown an American war drama full of mountings and posturings and magnificent emotion, and she had come out from it with a look of questioning scorn in her eyes.

"Was the war like that?"

Suvla had laughed.

"Oh, the American part of it—perhaps, but not ours. The big things are so quiet. The machinery made plenty of noise."

"But the men were quiet?"

"I'm thinking of the wounded," he had said, "and the men in the trenches. The tame man has to be a sensationalist; it is his emotional drink and tobacco. But when you have seen the real thing! Life's most dramatic when it's most quiet."

She had placed her chair in the shadow, well away from the tongue of light from the window; and between two pillars of the loggia life was staged for her. Suvla had rung up the curtain. He was in the billiard-room, and she could see him standing by the door; he had locked it and had the key in his hand.

"It is better that we should not be disturbed."

She glanced at the other man. He was leaning against the billiard-table, the point of the cue resting on the green cloth. She saw him in profile. His face appeared to her to be quite emotionless, a colourless mask, but she knew that he was afraid.

These two Englishmen looked at each other. Suvla had a smile in his eyes. She saw him put the key in his

Suvla John

pocket and bring out his pipe and pouch. He stood filling his pipe and smiling. The other man remained as before.

"Where is Elsie?"

Blaber put down his cue and rested his hands on the polished edge of the table.

"My wife has gone to bed."

"Which room? It is better that she shouldn't hear us—yet. You understand."

"She has the room over the hall."

"That's on the other side. Good."

Suvla struck a match and lit his pipe. He perched himself sideways on the billiard-table, and picking up one of the balls, rolled it towards one of the corner pockets. It missed the pocket, and, rebounding, struck one of the other balls. The struck ball came to rest close to one of Blaber's hands.

"You used to beat me at this game, Bob."

Blaber was staring at the red ball as though he saw his whole life symbolized in that red sphere. A strange inertness seemed to possess him; he managed to hold himself up, yet his immobility suggested immense effort. A puff of Suvla's smoke drifted across to him.

"What do you want?" he asked.

His voice was flat and casual. He glanced momentarily at Suvla under drooping and melancholy eyelids.

"Is it money?"

Richenda smiled. She saw Suvla pick up another ball and trundle it across the table. She heard the soft whir of its passage.

"Why say the wrong thing? I haven't changed. You always thought—Blaber, that you could do things with money. You can't. You couldn't bribe shells. Well —I have seen Elsie."

Blaber's head drooped a little.

"What do you want?"

"Can't you guess?"

"To get your own back."

Suvla's head went up, and in his eyes there was both pity and mockery.

"On you? There was a time—— But that has gone. Seven years ago—my friend. It was a dirty trick you played me, and yet—I don't regret it. I say—I don't regret it—for my own sake——"

He was looking at Blaber's rounded shoulders, and the narrow black head between them. He saw the face

Suvla John

foreshortened, the thin nose, the ragged moustache, the sharply-pointed chin. He seemed to know that the other man was paralysed, that he was holding himself up on those two stiff arms. His white shirt bulged through his black waistcoat.

"I suppose I suffered a bit. And so did you."

There was a short flicker of angry denial in Blaber's eyes.

"O, yes, you did, Robert. I dare say you are one of those who are rather clever at covering up dirt—but you couldn't cover up the smell of it."

"I'm waiting to hear——"

"There's no hurry. I suppose I ought to tell you all my adventures. They began after I had seen the notice of your marriage. So you told Elsie my dying words!"

The knuckles of Blaber's hands showed white.

"Anyway—I got her."

"Don't boast—Bob. I came back——"

He saw Blaber's eyes thrust the mute and sullen question at him, the inevitable question.

"Yes—why did I come back? That is what you have been asking yourself. To show you up—or for blackmail? Such obvious motives. Life is not so obvious; I have found that out. Well—I'll tell you why I came back."

He paused, looking out of the window, and Richenda knew that he felt her there.

"I came back for the sheer, devilish fun of the thing. I thought of scaring you to death, Robert. Please remember I'm dead."

"Dead?"

"Exactly. We will come to all that presently. But get that into your head and keep it there. It was mischief—and a little reckless malice. I came here and I played ghost. I wanted to see certain things again, but—then—you see—I did not grasp the possibilities of what I might see. For instance——"

He paused again, to press the tobacco down in the bowl of his pipe.

"I saw Elsie. Well—what do you make of that?"

He saw Blaber's shoulders heaving slightly as though some unbearable weight were pressing upon them.

"So—that's it," he said.

"Well?"

"You want to get back at me—through my wife."

Suvla John

Richenda was leaning forward in her chair. Through the oblong of the window she had her view of these two men, the one so sure of himself, so ironically gentle, the other crouching under the shadow of his fate. Dramatic— yes, but so quiet. They might have been discussing a point in the game, arguing about it. She saw Suvla glance towards the window. His face had a look of dignity, half humorous, half tender.

"Wrong," he said, "quite wrong. You are rather bad at guessing. It happened like this. I was playing ghost, and Elsie caught the ghost and found that it was alive. I'm sorry it happened, and yet not sorry in a way, for I found out something."

With an effort Blaber straightened himself.

"So—she knows. Get on with it."

"She does not know that I was not shot by a Turk."

"You didn't tell her? I don't believe it."

"No?"

He looked steadily at the man across the table.

"You would have told her if you had been in my place. Is that it? Well—perhaps you would. But when I realized what a mess you had made of Elsie's life—it seemed to me a pity to tell her. One should take care of one's emergency rations, you know."

He got off the table, walked to the window, stood there a moment, and, turning suddenly, caught Blaber's eyes fixed on him with peculiar intentness. He understood the look. It brought the ironical smile to his face, and the smile caused Blaber's glance to fall.

"No—Bob, history does not repeat itself. My wife is outside there, sitting in one of your chairs. And this is not Birdcage Walk."

2

From that moment Blaber appeared to acknowledge the full measure of his helplessness. He had an air of sullen expectancy. He was tied up and waiting upon the whim of this ironical enemy whose motives seemed to him so inadequate and so baffling.

"Well—what next?"

He went and stood on the hearthrug in front of the empty grate. Suvla was still by the window, and looking out into the darkness.

Suvla John

"Richenda," he said.

She came into the path of light, her face serious as fate. She looked in at the man on the hearthrug.

"Blaber—this is my wife. She knows all that I know. I think that she can help us."

He gave Richenda his hand. She climbed in, and stood a moment between the two men. She looked at Elsie's husband, and he made a sullen and ineffectual attempt to meet her look. She did not mean him to meet it, and she saw his head go down.

"I am more bitter against you than he is."

That was all she said for the moment, and passing to the end of the room she seated herself upon the raised settee that ran along the end of it. To Suvla she had her air of oracular calm. She was a figure of Justice, the woman above them both, serene as the night, though she had confessed to bitterness. And with her coming the room seemed to fill with a deeper meaning, some purpose that waited before going steadily forward.

Suvla leaned against the table.

"Now—I'll come to the point. It is very simple. It concerns Elsie. She's pretty miserable, and I suppose you know it."

"If she told you that"—and he gave a little flick of the head—"what is the use——?"

"You admit her unhappiness?"

"Oh—I suppose so."

"It doesn't worry you?"

"A little."

Richenda was watching Blaber, and her eyes troubled him even more that Suvla's did. Moreover, there was something here that he did not understand, why they had come and what their object was. He grew impatient.

"Why all this mystery? Who is to prove——?"

"My word against yours. Is that it?"

"It might be."

"Hardly. Don't take that line, Blaber; it won't pay you; it's bad business."

"That's a matter of opinion."

Suddenly Suvla grew fierce.

"Man—haven't you a drop of red blood in you? I don't ask you to say you are sorry that you shot me in the back. I don't ask you to tell lies. But listen here— I know you must have hated me pretty badly, and that you shot me on impulse. Let's leave it at that. I could

271

give you shot for shot—but I'm holding my powder, and for other reasons. Doesn't it occur to you to wonder why?"

"I'm afraid I'm a cynic, Shere."

"You miserable devil."

It was here that Richenda intervened. She sat very straight and still, the priestess on the throne, looking down upon the old hatreds of these two men. It was an open book to her why Blaber had hated Shere, and Shere had despised Blaber. Men were big children. She had had to handle them and to scold them; some were bigger and more generous than others, that was all.

"John."

He turned to her.

"I think that you are using a language that Mr. Blaber does not understand."

"Well—will you try?"

"I think so."

She was deliberate and calm.

"You two began wrangling when you were boys. You would always wrangle. It is in the nature of things. But to-night—neither of you matter."

She faced Blaber.

"It seems to me that your trouble is that you cannot say that you are sorry. Whether you have ever felt sorrow I do not know. That is the pity of it so far as you are concerned. Sorrow would have saved you so much. But we did not come here to trouble about your soul. I have sat and listened to you, and all the time I have been saying to myself: 'This man is impossible. He is like wet wood that nothing can set alight.' Let us leave the human and generous side of it alone. Let us treat it as a matter of business. You may understand that."

She paused for a moment, looking steadily at Blaber.

"Your father was a business man."

He nodded, sulkily alert.

"You inherit it. Very good. Let us look at it as a business transaction. Seven years or so ago you brought off a lucky stroke. You put a rival out of the way—and married the woman you wished to marry. Had you made the woman happy——! And yet—how could you expect to make her happy? Even—though you may have felt meanly exultant—like a little greedy sneak of a boy. The thing that matters to us is that your wife is unhappy."

She glanced at Suvla.

Suvla John

"He knows—and I know it. Just think—for a moment —you two men. Who has had to bear the burden of it all? Who has suffered most from your hatreds and your scorns? The woman. And why? Why should it be so? Why?"

Blaber had moved to a chair—and was sitting there, staring at the polished floor. He was beginning to understand.

"Did you love her?"

She was standing, looking down at him.

"Answer me. Was it love—or the mere desire to possess, to snatch something—from another man?"

He did not answer.

"Something of both—perhaps. And then—when you had played with your toy it began to bore you. It made you remember; it was for ever hurting your complacency. It is not in you to be big, big in hate or passion or remorse. Always you have been feeling the pulse of your cold little self. Yes—words are useless."

She turned again to Suvla.

"That is why we came—was it not?—to see whether we should find a man who could respond to a generous gesture. We were ready to say: 'We will keep this thing secret. We give you your second chance for the sake of the one who has suffered most. We ourselves are happy. Life is good. The happy ones should bear no malice.' But—you—it seems—do not understand such things—for you do not feel them."

There was a pause. She went a little nearer to the man in the chair.

"And so—it seems—we must impose our terms on you. We might say to you: 'You are better dead. Choose between death and exposure.' Do you realize that we have the right and the power to say that?"

He moved uneasily, and glanced up at her.

"O—yes, you have me in the pillory, I am not going to snivel."

She saw the vicious twist of his mouth.

"Quite. But I am not a sensationalist, Mr. Blaber. In this—I can be as cold as you. We might send you out there into the darkness with a pistol. No one would know. And your wife would be free."

She stood over him, and it seemed to Suvla that the man shrank a little and grew more withered. He could not contend with her, and he was afraid.

Suvla John

"Your wife would be free."

She repeated the words, letting them fall like drops of metal.

"Freedom. Freedom is something to a woman. But what sort of freedom? The freedom to be fooled by some other man, or the freedom to go where she pleases—to live as she pleases, to be herself. Do you see whither we are tending?"

He nodded a consenting head.

"What does she wish? That is what it is our duty to find out. If she desires freedom, we shall give it to her."

She paused again, silent, like fate holding a sword.

"You will give her her freedom. It will be done quietly—with a few strokes of the pen. Your promises will be on paper, and we shall hold those promises. We shall keep your secret just so long as you keep your promises."

She turned to Suvla.

"Have you anything to say—John?"

"Yes—the promise must include—the concealment of the fact that John Shere is alive. My brother must not know."

"You grasp that fact? We won't explain it."

"Oh—of course."

Richenda's eyes seemed to soften.

"Very good. Then—I think the moment has come when we can see your wife. Will you go and find her? She will not be told—anything—of the past. She shall be asked to tell us her wishes."

XXX

I

SUVLA unlocked the door, and they watched Blaber go out. It appeared to them that he went unwillingly, like a man uncertain of his purpose, holding something concealed. He had touched insignificance in being confronted with the impossible. He could rise to nothing higher than a futile cynicism.

"What a specimen!"

He had left the door open, and they heard his footsteps in the long passage, and they were like the shuffling and uncertain footsteps of an old man.

"No guts, my dear. He never had. Just a boiled shirt and a sneer."

Richenda was thinking. She moved to the table and rested her hands upon it.

"I wonder——?"

She looked full-eyed at Suvla.

"He may not come back?"

"I think he will. Such fellows always come back."

"But the shame of it. I have never had to swallow shame; I don't know the taste of it."

She put back her shoulders and moved her head as though freeing herself from some sense of oppression.

"Such people stifle one. I longed to blaze out—but was it worth it? In the old books the good old-fashioned villain could tear things to tatters."

Suvla had picked up Blaber's cue. He tried a shot with it and missed.

"Villains, my dear! There are only selfish men, and weak ones. The chap was good at this game."

"He would be."

She was listening, her eyes deep and curious, while Suvla stood holding the cue as though it were a sword.

"I wonder," she said, "which road will he take? The man's road? Or will he come back with that little sneer —to save himself behind a petticoat?"

Suvla John

She glanced about the room, at the old-fashioned hunting pictures on the walls, the pictures of men riding.

"He was never any good on a horse. A flincher—you know."

"That might mean nothing. But, John—I shall want to talk to the wife."

"I think that's wise. I'll take the fellow outside."

"Search his pockets."

He looked at her, smiling.

"No—I don't think that he will try to repeat history —just for spite."

"I don't know. He is beyond me. An incalculable sort of cur."

"Right—I'll keep him muzzled. But he is rather a long time——"

"Listen," she said, "I hear someone——"

2

Blaber had hesitated at the foot of the stairs. A light was burning in the hall, but the upper part of the house was in darkness. He looked at the light like a man besotted, unable to realize himself or his surroundings. In the room, before those two, he had shown no emotion, for he had felt no emotion, save a kind of fatal fear. He was inarticulate. His consciousness was nothing but a cold mirror reflecting incredible things with the vividness of a dream.

He leaned against the post of the stair-rail. It was solid. He felt its solidity. He touched it with his fingers. John Shere was just as solid. And that young woman, that terrible young woman with the remorseless eyes. How had it all happened? Why hadn't he fought? What was there to fight?

He felt weak. His self had crumpled, and he had nothing else to lean upon. He stood and wondered what was in the minds of those two. They had sent him to fetch Elsie, but did they expect him to return with her? She—too—would be against him.

He had been a lonely man, and hitherto his self-sufficiency had saved him from realizing his own loneliness, but now he was aware of it as he was aware of the dark stairs. They led upwards yet nowhere, to nothing that mattered.

What a fool he had been to shoot!

What a greater fool not to have made sure!

Yet self-pity ever was denied him, for in the midst of his weakness he had a clarity of mind that denied him the right to self-pity. His own logic was against it. Those two had got him in a cage. They could open the door or keep it closed. It depended on Elsie.

His wife!

He began to ascend the first flight, helping himself up by the handrail like a man enfeebled by sickness. He was conscious of physical distress, and with it came a little tremor of emotion. Such emotion as he had known in life, and especially in his hatreds, had been self-inspired, and it was so now. This preposterous entanglement, in his own house, this English house! How absurd it all seemed. That fellow Shere, cocksure as ever, bobbing up suddenly out of nowhere, despising him as he had despised him in the war. He felt a sudden flare of hatred, but it died down in the darkness and flickered out like the flame of a candle.

He paused, leaning against the rail, and searching, as a man who has always loved himself too carefully must search for some self-applauding thought. Strange justifications drift into a man's mind at such a moment. As an Oxfordian and a casual student of history he had pretended to admire the Florentines of the Medici period, their craft, their subtlety, their using of the rougher men, the soldiers. Craft, in politics and in games, had always appealed to him, the sly move, the delicate touch. Like most physical cowards he had used his wits.

A deep fellow, a mocker, a master of craft! Those sentimental people! Shere the swashbuckler posing as a Bayard. They had come to bargain with him for his wife's freedom. As though it mattered! Very well— he would treat with them as though it mattered, and play them at their own sentimental game.

He remembered old Dodson and the unfortunate accusation he—Blaber—had fastened upon Elsie. Of course, John Shere had been the man. Perhaps Shere's comforting of Elsie had gone farther than that black-eyed young person—Shere's wife—imagined? Well, anyway, he would have to apologize to Elsie. He would have to persuade her to promise to say nothing about the affair, to drop all such embarrassing confidences. But, after all, would not Elsie's tongue be tied? She could not go down and elaborate a hypothetical intrigue in the presence of the other man's wife.

He felt more comfortable.

Elsie should have her freedom. He would make an appearance of generosity, and gamble on the chance of these two romantic people keeping their promises.

The landing above him was in darkness, but as Blaber reached it he saw a slit of light broaden out suddenly far down the corridor. A door that had been left ajar had swung open. He saw a woman's figure in a grey stuff dressing gown, with the prim hair plaited under a white cap. The inevitable Parker was standing on guard.

He cursed her to himself, but put on a smooth look as she came down the corridor. She switched on a light.

"It is all right, Parker."

"I thought I heard voices, sir."

"Yes—two old friends have turned up. They are on a motoring tour and had a breakdown. They looked in —while their fellow is getting things right."

Parker's face was an enigma.

"I hope you won't wake my mistress, sir."

"Sorry, but I must. They want to see her."

"She was worn out. I put her to bed at nine."

"Oh, that's all right, Parker. She would be sorry to miss old friends."

He was damning the woman, wondering how he was to get rid of her, for it was more than probable that she would follow them downstairs. Parker was the sort of woman who would listen at doors. He would have to get Elsie to send her to bed.

"Can I get your friends anything, sir?"

"No, thanks. They have dined. If they want drinks —I can manage it. I won't keep your mistress up more than a quarter of an hour."

"It will spoil her sleep."

"She would be hurt if I let them go without her seeing them."

He walked along the corridor to his wife's door and knocked, while Parker stood watching him.

"Elsie."

His voice was cheerfully ingratiating.

"Elsie, are you asleep? There is someone to see you."

Suvla John

Getting no answer he knocked more loudly, and then tried the handle of the door. The door was not locked. He opened it, and saw a curtain waving against the greyness of the window. He had a feeling that the room was empty, and its emptiness frightened him. He closed the door, felt for the electric switch, found it, and turned on the light. The room was empty. The bedclothes were turned back, and there was a depression in the middle of the pillow.

He searched the room to make sure of its emptiness. Yes, it was empty. And he was on the edge of a panic, yet able to think. That damned woman was out there in the corridor, and she must not know that Elsie was not in bed. He began to talk, standing at the bottom of the bed, facing the mirror in the wardrobe.

"Too tired? All right—don't bother. They are putting up at Guildford—and I dare say they will be able to run over to-morrow."

He saw himself reflected in the mirror, a chalk-faced figure with lips moving. Good lord, did he look like that?

"Good night. Sleep well."

He walked to the door and switched off the light. He made a great effort to control the panic feeling that was sweeping over him, for he was realizing that he had lost his hostage. Where was she? Had anything happened? He withdrew the key, opened the door, and stood close, feeling for the keyhole.

"All right. Don't worry, dear. I'll look after them. What? Oh, yes, they will be all right."

He had managed to lock the door and to secrete the key. He was trembling. He felt that Parker was somewhere behind him, and when he turned from his wife's door he found her at the head of the stairs.

"Mrs. Shere's too tired. No, she wasn't asleep. I have left her. She says she feels like sleeping. I shouldn't disturb her, Parker."

"No, sir."

"Get to bed. I'll persuade our friends to come over to-morrow."

He passed Parker, and went down the stairs, listening for any sound from above that would assure him that Parker had gone to bed and was not attempting interference. He heard nothing. He remembered noticing that the infernal woman was wearing felt slippers. He turned and went up again; he could pretend that he had forgotten his cigarette-case.

The light disappeared suddenly before he reached the landing. He crept up the last few steps, in time to see a door closing far down the corridor and a streak of light shut out. Parker had swallowed his bluff; she had gone to bed.

He turned back down the stairs.

What the devil was he going to do?

3

Blaber sat down at the foot of the stairs, elbows on knees, a fist pressed over each ear. He was trying to think, to escape from the panic mood that was rising in him like water. He felt himself being submerged beneath this flood of fear; it was blotting out his power to think, and reducing him to a thing that struggled to escape from being submerged.

Was he going back to those two to tell them that Elsie was not in her room, that he did not know where she was or what had happened to her? They would ask questions. He would have to lie, and he began to realize that he could not lie very effectively. They would say: "We do not want your excuses; we want to see your wife."

It was like the war over again, and those days of damnable fear when he had sat in a corner somewhere, unable to speak or to move, suffering from the stupor of extreme terror. He remembered how he had squatted in a dugout while the shells were bursting in the trench above; he had tried to light a pipe, and his hand had trembled so violently that he had not been able to bring the flame of the match to the tobacco. He had thrown the pipe away like a furious and hysterical child. He had known the trembling busy terror, and the terror that sits still, rigid, fixed, not daring to move. He felt this rigid fear upon him now; he felt unable to get up and walk to the billiard-room.

His impulse was to run away. There had been an occasion when he had gone plunging in panic down a

Suvla John

muddy communication trench, and only the luck of things had saved him from awkward questions. Should he run for it now, and leave them to do what they pleased?

But where was Elsie?

Had anything happened?

How impossibly melodramatic it all seemed. But, like the war, it was so real. It scorched the live core of your inmost, selfish, secret self.

He had his head on his hands now. And suddenly, he had a feeling that he was being watched; he had had the same feeling in those panic moments during the war. He withdrew his hands, and looked slowly round over his left shoulder.

There was someone standing beside the grandfather clock with its brass dial and oak case. Shere's wife; she was looking at him attentively with eyes that were neither scornful nor pitying. They made him think of a dark night into which you looked and saw nothing, nothing but the enigma of darkness. He had a sudden feeling that she had been there a long time, watching him.

She was speaking.

"You cannot find your wife?"

He heard his own voice answering.

"No; she is not in her room."

"She has gone away?"

"I don't know."

"But you are afraid. There is something—— Tell me. It is better that you should tell me."

He looked up at her. She seemed as tall as the clock, and her eyes never moved from his face. It was as though fate had come, mysterious, compelling, to stand over him, without pity or anger. He felt that he was at the feet of his own fear.

"I'm afraid—— I—I had frightened her. I thought —I didn't know—— She was meeting a man——"

He broke down. He was shaking.

"Tell me."

"I accused her—of—the voice—you know the voices are so alike. How was I to guess——?"

She stood over him.

"Be quick. Blurt it out—the whole beastliness of it. You had accused her of having a lover."

"Yes."

"When did you accuse her?"

Suvla John

"Last night."

"Who was the man?"

"It was the voice. I thought it was John's brother She would not say——"

But Richenda was calling to her man.

"John—come quickly. I want you."

XXXI

1

THE two of them stood over him. He was half lying across the stairs, his right arm covering his eyes. His head ached. There was something wet on his forehead.

For there had been a moment of violence. He had been caught by the collar, lifted up and thrown against the stairs.

Richenda had intervened.

"Why waste time? It may be precious."

Then had come more questions which he had tried to answer, though he felt sick and bewildered. When had he last seen Elsie? Had he threatened her? Had he taken any steps to make the affair public?

They stood over him, but they were looking at each other. He heard what they said. Shere was the Shere of Suvla Bay, fierce, swarthy, a man who carried his head as though he knew himself to be taller than other men. Blaber had seen him like that, with dead men at his feet, men who had died horribly. And he, Blaber, felt that he was no more than a carcass at this man's feet. The two of them seemed to have forgotten him. They talked nakedly—as though he was not there.

"I see it all. He must have said things. Vile things——"

"Yes, but the question is——?"

"Where? I know. She may have gone down to the Manor. It's just a leap in the dark for us—anyway."

"Well, let's go. Is the garden worth trying? You remember—I thought I saw someone."

"How long now?"

"An hour—perhaps."

"Let's try the garden—first. The moon should be up."

They went away without looking at Blaber. It was as though he were dead. He had expected some threat, some last scorching word. They did not even ask him to help them.

He sat there for a long while, holding his head in his hands, alone with his naked shivering self. There was nothing left to him at which he could sneer. Their anger, an anger that had ended by ignoring him, had stripped him of all his illusions, his little, cold complacencies. He was conscious of shame.

Out there in the garden Suvla and his mate were calling.

"Elsie—Elsie."

The moon was up, rising huge and yellow in a deep blue sky behind a wood of pines. The sheeted grass glimmered with dew. White flowers showed up like ghosts, and this garden of Wynyats smelt very sweet with scents that mingled in the still, fresh air. Tobacco plants, stocks, honeysuckle, mathiola, white jasmine— all these were scenting a darkness that was becoming suffused with moonlight.

Richenda stood by the blue cedar on the lower lawn listening to Suvla's voice. He had gone down to the wild garden and to Mab's Dell, and she heard him calling, but in a little while he was back with her, and she saw his profile against the moon.

"Nothing. We had better try the park. It seems rather hopeless."

The hazels were scattering light and shadow in the lane to the upper gate, and as Suvla swung it open he paused with a hand on Richenda's shoulder.

"Intuition. If one could be clairvoyant!"

She stook looking into the valley.

"To feel what the other woman is feeling. An emotional impulse. Unhappy women fly to the water."

"By heaven!" he said. "Of course! Come."

They went down into the valley. It was in the shadow, with the moonlight striking obliquely across it and touching the tops of the trees on the further slope. Holding hands, they ran, and as they ran Suvla jerked out his thoughts. He told Richenda of the Gate of the Seven Kisses, and of the pool lying there under the fringe of the beeches. "Stoop down to the water, Melisande." He felt that they would find Elsie near the pool.

"Like a child she'll go back to the old places Yes, when one feels like dying——"

"One's heart goes back. Things call. Emotions move in a circle."

She was aware of the grip of his fingers.

"Queen—if we find her there—too—late—I shall go back for that undrowned cur."

"Would it be worth it?"

"To me—yes. I'll bring him down here by the collar and make him jump, or throw him in. He can choose."

She let his anger spread its wings, but she was thinking of the woman.

"How far now?"

"Quite close."

She dropped to a walk, checking his haste.

"I can see water. Softly—man. Sensitive things must not be hunted."

He fell back beside her, his eyes at gaze.

"I understand. You are right."

The moon, swinging higher, and shining through a cleft between the trees, threw its light full upon the pool and upon the path and gate beside it. The great beeches with the swelling curves of their foliage resembled a huge and shadowy wave about to break in the trough of the valley. Somewhere in the woods a night-jar uttered its queer rattling cry. Richenda and her man paused on the slope of the hillside. Both of them were looking at the white bars and cross-bars of the gate. Both of them saw something dark there like a cloak hanging upon the rail.

"It's Elsie——"

"I'm not sure——"

"Go first."

She followed some twenty yards behind him, and his long legs seemed to carry him over the grass without a sound. She was watching that dark patch against the white gate. Was it a mere shell, a woman's cloak, or did it hold the woman? She paused, eyes wide, waiting to see if it would move.

She heard Suvla's voice. He was very close to the gate.

"Elsie."

Richenda's heart gave a leap in her, for the dark shape moved. It was alive. She saw the two figures merge. She walked on with the moonlight in her eyes, and in her throat a tremor of emotion.

Suvla John

Suvla had taken Elsie up into his arms, and when Richenda came to them Blaber's wife was clinging to him in silence.

"That's all right, Elsie; that's all right. Everything's straight and clear now."

She broke into weeping.

"O—John, I couldn't find you. He had said terrible things——"

"There—there—Richenda's here—my Richenda—and yours. We've seen Robert. It's all right."

Her skirts were wet to the knees, and as he held her Suvla felt them and understood. What a piteous thing! She had been in that pool, had waded into it, and then her heart had failed her. She had all the anguish of her despair, and the added anguish of failure.

He looked at Richenda.

"Mother——"

She came. She touched Elsie's hair with her fingers.

"My dear, it is all over——"

She saw Suvla's right hand making a movement. It held the lower folds of the wet skirt, thrusting it out meaningly for her to see. She touched it.

"Take her, mother."

Richenda held out her arms.

"Come. I'm strong. That's it; hold on to me. John wants me to hold you."

Elsie did not resist, and, holding her, Richenda drew apart with a look at Suvla. "Leave her to me," it said, and he went and leaned upon the gate with his face towards his old house. He could see a shimmer as of glass and the outline of a chimney.

Feldhurst was asleep, a happy house sunk in the shadowy embraces of its wooded valley. And yet how near to it trouble had come, the vexed ghost of an imprudent adventure.

He heard the voices of the two women, but turning about he could not see the two, for Richenda had carried Elsie under the trees. She was sitting among the spread roots of a great beech, with Elsie on her knees, while Suvla stood and wondered. He realized that women had been kind to him, and that he had had more kindness

Suvla John

from them than he had deserved, and that like most men
he was a woman's debtor. What would Richenda say to
Elsie, and Elsie to Richenda? How little one could foresee things. Yet, as he listened to the two voices he felt
that the tragi-comedy of life was out of his hands.
Richenda had taken it into hers, and he knew how capable
her hands were.

It seemed to him that he had stood there by the gate
for the best part of half an hour before Richenda called
to him.

"John——"

He walked towards the tree from which her voice
seemed to come.

"Yes."

"Elsie and I have talked our hearts out."

"Wonderful woman," he thought, and stood to serve.

"We are walking back together. Will you go on
ahead?"

"Of course."

"And tell—Mr. Blaber——"

Her voice paused, and Elsie's voice broke in. She
was calm now with Richenda's calmness.

"John—I want to see him to-night. I want to get it
over."

"What shall I tell him, Elsie?"

"That I want to go away. I must go away, with
Parker. Parker is kind. She'll help me to gather up
the loose ends."

"You'll start afresh, Elsie?"

"Yes."

"That's plucky of you. What else?"

"I want to be free, to have peace, to be able to live
somewhere—quietly."

"What sort of freedom, Elsie?"

"O, just to be by myself—with Parker, who will be
kind to me, and to know that he won't come in and look
at me and say sharp things. I would like a house and
a garden. But I want him to promise that he won't come
near me, unless I ask him to."

"Right. He shall promise that."

"But can you make him promise, John?"

"I can."

"O—how good you are!"

He was smiling at the two invisible women.

"You may call Richenda good, my dear, but I'm like

Suvla John

the curate's egg. Well—I'll go on ahead, and see your husband. And Dick will not know."

"Never. I'll keep my promise, John."

"I know you will," he said.

3

Suvla kept to the grass when he had entered the Wynyats' gate, and cutting diagonally across the upper lawn he saw that the only lighted windows were the windows of the billiard-room. The climax of the affair was not complete, and he was wise as to Richenda's forethought in sending him on ahead, for Elsie's husband had had time to think. Suvla had seen all sorts of men in all sorts of stiff corners. The coward was a man to be treated carefully, and to be watched, and if Blaber had had time to think he had also had time to act.

But Suvla had his own mind-picture of the master of Wynyats. There was nothing of the "braw fighter" in Blaber, nor would he squat on his haunches and show his teeth like a trapped rat. Richenda, with her pride, had wondered whether a man could make terms with himself after such a night of ignominy; she could see him shuffling off into the great darkness, and leaving the road open for others. Suvla thought otherwise. There are men who love themselves so dearly that they will pick their precious bodies out of the mud and scrape them tenderly with a potsherd.

It was as he thought. He made his way silently across the grass to the loggia and the two lighted windows. The blind of one of them was up, as he had left it, and he was able to see Blaber sitting in one of the big arm-chairs. He was sunk deep in it, a hand across his forehead shading his eyes. He had the inert air of a sick man waiting for bad news. His clothes looked crumpled, suggesting that he had crawled from the place where Suvla had left him.

Suvla approached the window. He saw Blaber drop his hand and glance round fearfully, the whites of his eyes glistening. His mouth hung open. He raised himself in the chair.

Suvla stood at the window, looking in.

Suvla John

"We have found her," he said.

Blaber's lips moved.

"Is—is she——?"

"Alive? Yes—she is coming here with my wife. We found her down at Feldhurst Pool, Blaber. She had been in the water."

Blaber's eyes fell. He bent over the padded arm of the chair so that his face was in the shadow.

"I'm glad."

"Of course. You would be. It was your last chance. For I can assure you—that if I had found her—in the water—I would have taken you down there—Blaber. We will leave it at that."

He climbed through the window, and leaned against the billiard table, but his eyes never left the man in the chair.

"We know now what Elsie wants. I have come on to state her terms. She wants her freedom, the right to live her life in peace. We will arrange that for her."

Blaber's head remained down.

"Does she know——?"

"She doesn't. We know it, and that is sufficient. How much are you worth—Blaber?"

"Worth?"

"Yes—money."

"O, somewhere about a hundred thousand."

"Well—you will settle thirty thousand on Elsie."

"Thirty thousand!"

"Unconditionally—absolutely. You understand?"

"Yes."

"You will promise never to see her unless she wishes to see you, to leave her in peace. She will have a place of her own; she will leave here to-morrow and take Parker with her. You will go up to town to-morrow and see your lawyer, and arrange for a deed of gift. Also, you will deposit with Elsie a written promise—not to start any proceedings for restitution—or anything of that kind—at any time."

"Yes."

"We shall stay in England, Blaber, till all this is settled. I shall let you know where I may be found. You will come down and report to me. You will produce all the necessary papers. My wife's lawyer-men will see that they are in order."

"Yes."

Suvla John

Suvla turned his head as though to listen.

"I think I hear their voices. By the way—you will want a cheque-book. Elsie will need a round sum to carry on with until the capital is made over to her. We will go and write a cheque."

He walked to the window.

"Richenda."

"Yes——?"

"Mr. Blaber and I have one business detail to see to. Will you bring Elsie in here. We'll be back with you in a minute or two."

XXXII

I

WHEN Suvla brought Blaber back to the billiard-room he had some papers in his hand. Richenda and Elsie were on the high settee together, but Blaber did not look at his wife. He crossed over and stood by the open window with his back to the room. Elsie, wide-eyed, had given him one glance, a look that had touched him swiftly, and then shrunk away.

Suvla gave her the papers.

"A cheque, Elsie, to carry you on. Your husband knows that you are leaving to-morrow. He understands the conditions and he accepts them. You are to have thirty thousand pounds—and complete freedom. It is written on this paper."

She glanced at the papers.

"And I am to have Parker?"

"Yes. The lawyers will settle all the details. And now for a witness."

He took Richenda aside into the passage, and while they stood there talking in undertones Elsie read what her husband had written. Blaber remained by the window, looking out at the moonlit grass. Once and *once* only did his wife glance at his enigmatic back. She seemed about to speak; her eyelids flickered; but the impulse died away. The final silence was like an invisible wall between them.

Suvla and Richenda returned, and Suvla, standing between the two women, spoke to the man at the window.

"It is necessary that Parker should know these conditions. We cannot be present at this interview, but we shall listen to it outside. Will you go and wake the woman and bring her down. She must not know that anyone else is here."

There was a slight movement of Blaber's head. He turned and walked to the door. He did not look at his wife or at the other two; he was both furtive and sullen;

Suvla John

his self-consciousness was brittle as thin ice. And when he had gone Elsie began to speak, a little breathlessly, as though some oppressive thing had passed but would return.

"You won't leave me——"

"We shall be out there. Take Parker to your room afterwards. Let her sleep with you. There is nothing to fear. But she must not know of us."

Richenda kissed her.

"I'll write to you, my dear. We'll share this secret. You are not alone. Think of us as being somewhere near."

Elsie followed them across the room, plaintively, with that wounded wideness of the eyes. She was like a child who was going to be left alone, and ready to cling to anyone who was kind.

"Richenda."

They held each other for a moment.

"My dear, go through with it; don't flinch——"

Suvla was in the loggia.

"Queen—no risks."

She kissed Elsie a second time, and climbed out; and Suvla, with his hands on the window sill, saw Elsie for the last time.

"Go through with it," he said; "and then try to forgive me."

They did not see what happened in the room, for they were standing together pressing close against the wall, but the voices within made those last happenings vivid. Parker, roused from sleep, and dragged down to take her part in this last phase, a Parker who wondered, but who shrewdly held her tongue, and laid austere and loyal hands upon her little lady's freedom.

"Parker, Mr. Blaber and I are not going to live together any more. I am going away to-morrow. Will you come with me?"

They heard Parker's answer, and in her way she showed herself a woman of the world. It would appear that she and Blaber had fought some sort of fight on their way downstairs, and that there was no protest left in him.

"I take it, sir—that there will be a proper arrangement?"

Elsie was thrusting the papers into Parker's hand.

"O—yes——"

292

Suvla John

But Parker had her master under examination.

"It is all going to be legal and proper?"

His toneless voice touched sarcasm as he answered her.

"Yes—of course, a mutual agreement, with the money settled. It is written on that paper. Any other questions —Parker?"

She was holding the paper in her bony and long-fingered hands, and reading it at her leisure, she humiliated him with her deliberation.

"I see. You have signed it—but does it follow——?"

"It does follow. That is a private agreement between my wife and myself. The lawyers will do what is necessary."

"I'll believe it when I see it, sir," she said, and swept her mistress out of the room.

2

Upstairs she became the woman. She locked the door of Elsie's room, and with an arm about her led her to the bed.

"There—that's that. You sit down on the bed—and I'll undress you. So you got up again—after all?"

"Yes—Parker."

"Well—little lady—when I have put you to bed—I'll sleep on your sofa. And to-morrow——"

Her voice ceased suddenly. She had knelt down to unfasten Elsie's shoes. They were muddy and sodden, and her skirts were still wet to her knees. Parker held her breath.

"Bless us!"

But that was all she said. Her thoughts went deep, but they did not break to the surface, and she drew off the wet shoes and stockings as though no hint of a passing tragedy were attached to them. So, something had happened?

Parker had been struck by the man's worn face and his flickering and uncertain eyes, and by the yieldingness he had shown. Had it so happened that his wife had frightened him?

Suvla John

Parker dissembled her thoughts. She had won her child—her grown child, and could boast of a triumphant devotion torn from the enemy—man.

"You must be tired—my dear."

"Very tired—Parker."

"Poor dear little lady! You let old Nanna look after you."

"You must be tired too, Parker."

"Tired! Bless you—I could jump over the moon."

3

When the door closed on Parker and Elsie, Suvla moved to the open window, and stood looking in.

Richenda joined him. This billiard-room at Wynyats was to remain a cabinet of vivid memories, or a stage brilliantly lit. Its colours would live, the pale buff of the walls, the faded reds and blues of the coloured prints, the green of the table with one red ball lying on it, the tawny leather of the chairs. The figure in black and white sitting down rather wearily in one of the chairs drew the eyes of these two adventurous ones.

"Blaber."

Suvla spoke very softly, and the man in the chair did not move. He remained staring at his own feet, his face in the shadow.

"Haven't you finished yet?"

His flat eyes gave a momentary and peevish glance at the figure by the window.

"Nearly. Our caravan is at Panhurst Mound. I shall expect you to-morrow evening."

"To report progress—I suppose!"

"Yes, to report progress."

"All right."

That was all that was said, though Suvla remained there for half a minute, looking with curious steadfastness at the man in the chair. There was a faint smile at the back of his eyes. His face expressed neither mockery nor compassion; it was the calm and attentive face of a judge.

Suvla John

He felt Richenda's hand on his arm.

"Come," she said, "there is nothing big in him. He has had his chance."

And when Blaber raised his eyes the window was empty. He stared at it for a moment, and then got up and closed the window and drew down the blind.

XXXIII

I

WHEN Richenda woke she was conscious of someone moving about the caravan. It was full of the first greyness of the dawn, though the pictures upon the walls, and the china and books on the shelves, were still dim and uncoloured. The blind was up, and she saw Suvla standing at the window, looking out. His head made her think of the head of a man upon the prow of a ship gazing across a grey sea towards some land unknown. He was restless. He wanted something: he wanted her to share it.

She sat up in bed.

"What is it, John?"

Her voice was gentle, but he did not turn his head.

"One more look at the old place. Come with me. Day's just breaking. There will not be a soul about."

She slipped out of bed and began to dress.

"You'll go," she said, "so I suppose I had better come with you."

He turned an ironical head.

"To keep me out of trouble!"

"To share it if it came."

He went quickly across to her and, taking her face between his hands, looked into her eyes.

"Richenda. Dear heart. I think I shall be better at loving you than any young pup would be. I'm better at loving than I was."

She held his wrists.

"And not so good at hating?"

"I won't promise you that! But England has made me sentimental."

"Then I had better keep my man in England."

"Ah, would you! The desert, my dear, great spaces of sand, and a great space of blue sky at night. And then—again—this greenness, and the old van on the edge of a wood. Come along."

He kissed her, and went to open the door. The dawn was very still, with a grey sky that would clear presently. Pockets of mist were lying in the hollows. The trees looked dim and vapoury, and there was no sparkle yet in the dew.

He sat on the steps while Richenda put on her clothes. He looked lovingly at the woodland, but with the love of a wanderer whose pleasure was in going and returning. He was thinking of his brother whose happiness lay in remaining in the same place.

"Queen."

"Hallo."

"Things went very quietly last night."

"What else did you expect?"

"Oh, nothing—with a tame white rat—like our villain. He ought to have shot me or himself, or the whole lot of us. He ought to have been lying down there in the heather—to get me when I opened this door."

"Don't be sensational."

She heard him laugh.

"What a queer business! I let him off. It ought to have made him savage. I should have savaged a man who had let me off."

"No, you wouldn't."

"How do you know?"

"How do I know! What a question! I'm ready."

They went out together, holding hands, and Suvla took one of the Panhurst tracks which brought them to the waste above the Feldhurst woods. The trees were still asleep in the greyness, the distances lost in vapour. There was not a sound. The earth was theirs, and no man trespassed upon it.

"Adam and Eve!"

He laughed.

"To be—where no one else is. Doesn't modern man ever grow sick of the mush of civilization?"

"He's part of it, my dear."

"Poor devil!"

"You abominable individualist! You savage!"

"Well—you are almost as bad."

"I admit it. I don't want to be part of the mush. I would rather be a tigress than a socialist. Suppose we are primitive people, John?"

Suvla John

"No," he said, "we're not. We're just natural people. A bit wild. We haven't lost the use of our teeth."

They came down into the Feldhurst valley where a path cut the old oak palings of the park fence. A beech tree overhung the kissing gate. They stood here and looked down upon Feldhurst still asleep in the greyness. They saw the house, the gardens, the grey bridge over the moat, the soft slopes, the misty and untroubled trees. It was all as peaceful as sleep.

"In a little while Elsie will be there. Poor little—dreaming Elsie."

"And you broke her dream, John."

"I know. I shall not forget it. A wild man ought not to hunt in this valley."

"Have you forgotten St. Hubert?"

"Have I forgotten the Devil? And Dick will be kind to her. Dear old Dick."

She kept silent, holding his hand, her eyes on the sleeping house.

"Things work out better than we think—sometimes—John."

"I have nothing to complain of," he said, putting a sudden arm about her.

She smiled.

"This—is the last time—you know."

"I know. I'm dead—and alive with you. God bless them—down there—anyway."

2

The Sheres were at breakfast.

At dinner the previous night a note had been brought in from Parker to tell them that her mistress had returned, and at the breakfast-table they discussed Elsie and Elsie's marriage. Dick, with a spoon deep in the blue-and-white marmalade pot, and looking brown and boyishly wise, was saying that Blaber should have been a schoolmaster, one of the bachelor kind. "The sarcastic sort—you know, a real stinker." Shere had his back to the window. Moreover, he had spilt some marmalade on Sybil's precious and much-polished Hepple-

298

Suvla John

white table, so he was busy with the point of a knife, and a corner of his table-napkin.

"Sorry—old thing!"

He saw his wife's eyes widely open. Nor was it the blemish on the table and his boyish efforts to efface it that had shocked her. She was looking out of the window.

"Elsie—— !"

Elsie it was. She had Parker with her, a seraphic Parker austerely pleasant in black. She came to the open window. Sybil stood up.

"Oh, you are at breakfast. I haven't had any."

"My dear—— !"

"We had our early tea. You see, Robert and I have agreed to separate, and Parker and I came away early."

Shere had risen and was leaning on the back of his chair. He looked at Elsie, and then he looked more attentively at Parker.

"Well—come in and have breakfast. You'll stop here."

"May I? Just for to-day? Parker says that I must cash a cheque. And Robert is going up to see his lawyers."

"Come in."

"Parker will want some breakfast, too. Ring the bell, Dick."

"I wonder if you could send up for our luggage. It is all ready. Of course—we might have had the car, but we thought that we would come away quietly."

"I'll arrange that," said Shere.

Elsie came through one of the long windows into the white panelled room with its cornice and fluted pilasters, its old rose carpet, and its Georgian furniture. Parker followed her mistress, but remained standing by the window. She felt it to be a happy room, with its paint none too white and its colours all mellowed. It had a perfume. Several generations had lived in it, and looked out of its windows, or sat by its fire, and on the whole they had been happy, pleasant people.

"Sit down, dear. And you, Parker. I'll go and arrange things."

Sybil went out. She was astonished. There had been times when she had said to Elsie, "Be free," but she had never believed in the human chances of such a revolt. And yet it had happened. Moreover, Elsie had walked

299

into the room with a new self-consciousness; she was
different, wideawake, and though leaning upon Parker,
she had suggested a naïve self-importance. The sex dream
had dropped from her.

Sybil visited the kitchen. When she returned to the
"white" room she found Elsie alone.

"Dick wanted to speak to Parker. They have gone
to his den."

Sybil missed that emotional mistiness in Elsie's eyes.
She looked sun-washed, like a nice child who feels secure
in the presence of an affectionate nurse. A disillusionment may produce curious surprises.

"I am to have thirty thousand pounds, Sybil. What
a lot one can do with thirty thousand pounds. Parker
thinks we ought to travel."

Sybil sat down in a chair by the near window. She
had an open mind, but Elsie amazed her.

"My dear, how did it happen?"

She fancied that she detected a secret look in the
other woman's eyes.

"Oh, it just happened. But I'm free, Sybil. I don't
think I quite realized what freedom is like until I walked
out of the house with Parker this morning."

This was a new Elsie, an Elsie who avoided a direct
question, and who—in order to preserve a nice reticence—
disarmed you with an air of frankness. It suggested
to Sybil that Elsie had learnt to draw a curtain, and
that she had ceased to be ready to weep on the world's
bosom. And Sybil accepted the situation. Her one concern was that it should be stabilized and given
permanency.

"I suppose your husband——"

Elsie nodded.

"I have it in writing—signed, and a cheque for my
immediate needs. I shall want Dick to advise me about
lawyers."

"It's mutual—then?"

"Yes. He is to promise not to come near me—unless
I wish him to——"

"I see. And what——? You can stay here—for a
time—if you like."

"Thank you so much, dear. But I think I will go
right away with Parker. She is devoted to me. I feel
like a child going to play on the sands with my nurse."

Meanwhile, in Shere's den, where guns and golf-clubs

and books and fishing tackle and account books and
letter files lived together in happy confusion, Parker made
her explanation. She had Blaber's cheque and the
promises he had put on paper to substantiate her statements, but she was no sentimentalist. The victory should
be pushed home.

"I think everything ought to be done, sir, quickly,
while he is still frightened."

"Frightened?"

Parker nodded a shrewd head.

"That's how it strikes me, sir. Something funny happened last night, but I don't go squeezing a fresh bruise.
Not hers, I mean. I think Mrs. Elsie gave him a fright."

Shere's eyes were asking "How?"

"Well, as a matter of fact, sir, after Mr. Blaber had
dragged me out of bed—and the business between them
—whatever it was—was all over—I found my little lady's
shoes and stockings and dress all mud and water. She
had been in the water somewhere—up to her knees. And
twice in one day. So perhaps she gave him a scaring, and
he let her have her way."

"Is that the only inspiration you can think of?"

Parker smiled one of her wooden smiles.

"It may seem strange, sir. There's nothing soft about
Mr. Blaber, but something had scared him last night. He
looked beaten-like. I have lived at Wynyats a long time.
I suppose I know the life of it inside out. Some men are
born cruel, and they do say that a bully is a coward. Anyhow—she seems to have scared him."

Shere put a match to his pipe.

"So your point is—Parker?"

"Make him sign things, sir, before he gets over his
fit of the shakes. I'll see to it that he doesn't get a chance
to come and snivel to her—even if he wants to."

Shere looked at her gravely.

"One moment, Parker. Are you quite sure? You remember the old saying?"

"I'm quite sure, sir," and she met his glance steadily,
"she's never been happy with him. He's an uncomfortable
man. All these years she's never had a chance to be herself, snug and happy. Well, you'll excuse me saying so,
sir, but a woman can make something of her life—without
a man."

"Yes," said Shere, but without great conviction, "I
suppose she can."

Suvla John

3

Richenda sat on the steps of the caravan with her face towards the sunset. Suvla was lying down in the van, but the door was open, and he could see Richenda and the sunset, and the deep green of the Panhurst beeches under the blues and golds of the sky. It had been a day of waiting, and Suvla had spent the greater part of it inside the caravan, for the debonair young man who farmed Panhurst Great Farm had strolled up to show a superfluous interest in Richenda. Richenda had repulsed this interest, while Suvla, shut up in the green van, had laughed silently over the dialogue.

"Hubby hasn't arrived yet?"

"I beg your pardon."

"All on your lonesome still?"

"I hope so. By the way—what do I owe you?"

"Call it a washout."

Egregious male! Suvla had not been able to resist the mischievous inspiration. He had produced a very vibrant snore.

"I was asking you what I owed you for the keep of the horse. We—are leaving to-morrow—early."

There had been a distinct drop in the debonairness of the young man's voice.

"Oh, are you? Let's say five shillings. I don't want to disturb the gentleman."

And a triumphant snore had trumpeted him upon his way.

Richenda had opened the door and had scolded Suvla.

"You are incorrigible. I had nearly said——"

"Well—I was listening, intelligently. And after all, my snore was more efficacious than your frostiness, my dear."

The dusk was blue between the trees, but the light still hung in the tops of the firs. Purple and green, losing the vividness of their contrasts, began to merge towards amethyst. The woods grew dark, as dark as Richenda's eyes. She sat and watched, and presently she said : "He's coming."

Suvla came to the doorway of the caravan, and standing there behind Richenda, watched the man making his way across the heather. He walked with a jerky swiftness, head down, his hands in his pockets. From time to time

Suvla John

he gave a glance in the direction of the caravan and the canopy of the firs above it, and then dropped his head again. He had the air of doing the thing unwillingly and of wishing to be through with it.

"It's an intelligent beast," she said.

"Yes—there is no need to over-explain. He knows the lie of the land now."

Blaber came to the foot of the steps. He seemed to look both up and down, and his thin face was all shadow. He took something white from his pocket, and handed it to Richenda.

"That will explain."

She passed it to Suvla, and taking the letter from the envelope he spread the sheet and read what had been typed in the office of Dodson, Fagg & Chesterton.

"This is addressed to your wife."

"Just so. I presumed that you would require evidence. That is a duplicate."

"Right. And Elsie——?"

"I haven't seen her. She left early this morning."

"Where?"

"She is with your brother and sister-in-law."

Suvla folded up the letter and put it in his pocket.

"We hold a watching brief, Blaber. We are the gods behind the gods. I need not explain. We shall want to see all the documents. They can be sent to my wife. Let us say to 'Mrs. John Suvla, *Poste Restante*, General Post Office, Exeter.' Will Exeter do?"

Richenda nodded.

"Yes. My man can report on them. And I shall be in touch with Elsie."

There was a pause, while Blaber, motionless, stared at the hub of the off fore wheel.

"Anything else?"

Suvla smiled down upon him.

"No. Just one point. I'm dead; don't forget it. But if you should happen to forget it—with reference to my brother—I shall come to life again. That's all."

They watched him disappear across the waste in the direction of the darkening woods.

"Yes, it's an intelligent beast," said Richenda; "he won't try to bite his own tail."

XXXIV

I

IT was seven o'clock in the morning. The dew lay heavy upon the fern, and the branches of the Scotch firs saluted a cloudless sky. Richenda had been down to Panhurst Great Farm to fetch the white horse, and she was harnessing him to the caravan. Suvla, on his knees, washing his hands after greasing the wheel hubs, whistled and took note of the open sky and of the freshness of the morning. Also, he watched Richenda, looking at her with the happy, sidelong glances of a lover.

With the traces fastened and straps adjusted, Richenda stood and stroked the white horse's neck, her eyes turned towards the beech woods. Her thoughts seemed to have gone far away into the woods, and Suvla, who was drying his hands, let her thoughts wander as they pleased. He climbed into the van, and hanging the towel neatly on the rail, placed himself in front of Richenda's mirror. A length of black ribbon served him as a tie, and he threaded it under the soft collar of his shirt.

His movements within it had made the caravan sway on the undercarriage, and its faint creakings brought Richenda back from the woodlands.

"John——"

"Hallo."

He came out to her, and she saw the black tie, and the solemn mischief in his eyes.

"Have you turned undertaker?"

"I'm burying myself a second time."

"Thanks, "she said. "Thanks!"

All the gear had been packed up, and she climbed to her driving seat, and again her thoughts seemed to rise and hover over the woods. Suvla stood looking up at her, and at the serene and glowing darkness of her meditative face.

"What is the morning's wisdom, O queen?"

304

Suvla John

She smiled suddenly down at him.

"I was thinking that a devoted handmaid is better than an indifferent husband."

"Which leads one to ask——!"

"Yes—what the world will say about the man."

Suvla threw up his head, laughing.

"Why—that's obvious. People will say that Blaber has behaved with remarkable generosity."

Made and Printed in Great Britain by
The Greycaine Book Manufacturing Company Limited, Watford.
75.827

V6